DEDICATION

To those who dare to challenge convention, who see beyond the present and strive to shape the future—this book is for the visionaries, the creators, and the relentless minds who refuse to accept limits.

To my family, friends, and mentors—your unwavering support, wisdom, and encouragement have been the foundation of this journey. Your belief in this project has made all the difference.

And to the pioneers of science and technology, whose breakthroughs continue to inspire—this is a tribute to your ingenuity and perseverance.

Allen Van Camp

ACKNOWLEDGMENTS

Writing The Zone Engine has been an incredible journey, one that would not have been possible without the support, guidance, and encouragement of many people.

First and foremost, I extend my deepest gratitude to my mom, witnessing her love of reading over the years combined with my need for creating, helped fuel my desire to write this story. To my Dad who taught me, what do we do when we fall down, we get back up. To my wife who supports my quirkiness. Your support has been my anchor.

To my editor, Christopher Levi, thank you for your keen eye, insightful feedback, and dedication to refining this story into its best form. Your expertise has made a world of difference.

A special thanks to my friends who helped me along the way during this journey for your invaluable advice, brainstorming sessions, and honest critiques. Your perspectives have enriched this book beyond measure.

To the two that assisted righting the ship.

To Michael Dentato, for your thoughtful input while I was piecing this story together. Thank you my friend for your unwavering support my fellow Sci-Fi geek.

To Dave Mansker for his invaluable guidance and expertise in the craft of writing.

To my readers—whether this is your first adventure with me or one of many—thank you for taking the time to immerse yourself in this world. Your enthusiasm and passion fuel my creativity, and I am honored to share this journey with you.

And finally, to every dreamer, innovator, and risk-taker—this book is for you. May you always push boundaries and chase the impossible.

With gratitude, Allen Van Camp

THE ZONE ENGINE

Overview

The Zone Engine tells the gripping story of Team Nautilus—a bold ensemble of visionaries, including an ingenious scientist, two battle-hardened veterans, and a prodigious young genius—who redefine the future with their revolutionary cold fusion engines, an EM field engine, and a cutting-edge AI platform.

When they merge the two engines with a centrifuge containing a unique fluid, they unintentionally generate an electromagnetic field with unprecedented properties. This groundbreaking discovery draws the attention of an enigmatic interdimensional being who aids them in refining their invention.

Meanwhile, the notorious SAGA Corp., also delving into cold fusion technology, develops a flawed but competing version. Recognizing the potential of these breakthroughs, the government funds both Nautilus and SAGA through a research and development grant. However, when SAGA and government agencies detect the distinct EM field emanating from Team Nautilus's facility, a tense race begins to claim and control this powerful innovation.

As the stakes soar, the protagonist is faced with a harrowing decision—ensure that their creation never falls into the wrong hands, even if it means its total destruction. In a pivotal moment, an interdimensional being, moved by an act of extraordinary sacrifice, intervenes to spare him from an otherwise fatal explosion.

Fifteen years later, burdened by guilt and armed with a new technological breakthrough, the protagonist embarks on a daring journey through time. His mission: to rewrite history, save his family, and perhaps, find redemption.

The Zone Engine is a riveting fusion of science and human perseverance, seamlessly weaving cutting-edge technology with the unyielding spirit of those who dare to defy fate.

Table of Contents

DEDICATION iii

ACKNOWLEDGMENTS iv

THE ZONE ENGINE vi

CHAPTER ONE .... **Error! Bookmark not defined.**

INTRODUCTION 1

CHAPTER TWO 15

THE UNVEILING 15

CHAPTER THREE 22

TRAGEDY STRIKES 22

CHAPTER FOUR 38

THE LEGAL MAELSTROM 38

CHAPTER FIVE 47

DEVELOPMENT 47

CHAPTER SIX 61

STAGE 1 61

CHAPTER SEVEN 71

WHAT IF... 71

CHAPTER EIGHT 82

STAGE 2 82

CHAPTER NINE 95

STAGE 3 95

CHAPTER TEN 102

SOTRA – THE BENEVOLENT PLEIADIAN 102

CHAPTER ELEVEN 110

ALPHA – THE DEFIER 110
CHAPTER TWELVE 131
BETA AND ALPHA 131
CHAPTER THIRTEEN 145
THE YAMATO'S DESCENT 145
CHAPTER FOURTEEN 172
COME AND GET IT 172
CHAPTER FIFTEEN 179
SUNDAY'S BIRTH 179
CHAPTER SIXTEEN 188
THE MOUNTAIN LAIR 188
CHAPTER SEVETEEN 206
ECHOES AND INTRUSIONS 206
CHAPTER EIGTEEN 219
INVADED (TAKES PLACE DURING CHAPTER 17 - ECHOES AND INTRUSIONS) 219
CHAPTER NINETEEN 241
THE CORSAIR AND ALPHA 241
CHAPTER TWENTY 257
ECHOES OF WISDOM 257
CHAPTER TWENTY – ONE 264
THE AIR STRIKE 264
CHAPTER TWENTY – TWO 297
TYING IT TOGETHER 297
CHAPTER TWENTY – THREE 313

THE SUNSHINE STATE 313
CHAPTER TWENTY- FOUR 321
TEAM NAUTILUS RETURNS 321
CHAPTER TWENTY- FIVE 351
PREPARATION 351
CHAPTER TWENTY – SIX 363
INTO THE BREACH 363
CHAPTER TWENTY- SEVEN 378
EXECUTE THE PLAN 378
CHAPTER TWENTY – EIGHT 391
SOTRA 391
CHAPTER TWENTY- NINE 405
THE SAGA PROJECT IS UNDERWAY 405
CHAPTER THIRTY 412
GIVE IT UP, AGAIN 412
CHAPTER THIRTY - ONE 420
SUNDAY'S BIRTH 420
CHAPTER THIRTY- TWO 429
THE MOUNTAIN LAIR 429
CHAPTER THIRTY- THREE 433
SHADOWS AND REDEMPTION 433
CHAPTER THIRTY-FOUR 440
DOC'S DEPARTURE 440
CHAPTER THIRTY – FIVE 459
THE RESCUE 459

CHAPTER THIRTY- SIX 469

ALLIANCES REKINDLED 469

CHAPTER THIRTY – SEVEN 484

FURY IN THE SKIES 484

CHAPTER THIRTY- EIGHT 528

QUANTUM REBIRTH 528

CHAPTER THIRTY - NINE 543

CONVERSATIONS BEYOND TIME 543

CHAPTER FORTY 567

LEGACY OF THE BRAVE 567

CHAPTER FORTY- ONE 580

A COSMIC GUARDIAN 580

CHAPTER FORTY- TWO 597

NEW HORIZONS 597

ABOUT THE AUTHOR 607

INTRODUCTION

Flynn's abrupt departure from the U.S. Navy Submarine Service was shrouded in controversy, tainted by politics, accusations, and circumstances that shattered his reputation. What should have been a steady ascent became an unforgiving descent. Stripped of his honor, he was forced to abandon the life that had once defined him—losing not just a career, but a piece of his soul. The betrayal cut deep, leaving a lingering shadow that refused to fade.

As if the collapse of his naval career weren't enough, Flynn's personal life crumbled alongside it. His first marriage, once a refuge from the world's chaos, became a battlefield of resentment. The love that once held his family together dissolved, and the ensuing divorce turned into all-out war. Property and pride were secondary casualties compared to the real devastation—being severed from his children. They became pawns in the conflict, their love weaponized against him, leaving Flynn stranded in a sea of isolation and loss. The last anchor in his life had been torn away.

With both his career and family in ruins, Flynn drifted through his own life, drowning in despair. The confidence that had once propelled him forward was now a hollow shell, eaten away by the relentless weight of failure. But he refused to be consumed. Determined to reclaim himself, he turned to the skies—the one place untainted by his past. Armed with the GI

Bill, he pursued flight training, rediscovering a part of himself buried beneath years of disappointment.

Flying wasn't just an escape—it was defiance. It was proof that his fall wouldn't define him. Airshows became his sanctuary, where the roar of engines and the sight of vintage warbirds streaking across the sky rekindled a long-dormant fire. In the cockpit, he found something more than freedom—he found himself again.

Despite his rekindled passion for flight, Flynn remained grounded by the practical need for stability. He secured work as an engineering assistant at a mechanical engineering firm, where his expertise in all three types of buoyancy—honed as a Spec Ops submariner—combined with his meticulous attention to detail, set him apart. Immersing himself in CAD and project management, he quickly gained an edge in the industry. Under the mentorship of a mechanical engineer who recognized his potential, Flynn's vision began to crystallize. He didn't just want to endure—he wanted to innovate, to create something that would leave a lasting mark.

With each successful project and product design, Flynn's confidence resurfaced, like a submarine breaking through the ocean's surface into daylight. The obstacles he faced no longer anchored him to the past but propelled him forward. His journey, defined by both despair and ambition, reflected the resilience of the human spirit.

As the concept of an inflatable survival suit took shape in his mind, Flynn realized his past had not broken him—it had forged him. He had become something stronger, capable of rising from the ashes of failure and loss. His fight for purpose had begun anew—not on the seas or in the skies, but in the uncharted waters of invention.

Flynn and Fronz meeting at the air show

The sun bore down on the airfield tarmac, casting a golden sheen over the vintage warbirds lined up in proud formation. The steady hum of engines blended with the murmur of spectators drifting between the WWII-era fighters, admiring the relics that once ruled the skies. Among them, the F4U-5 Corsair stood apart—a sleek yet formidable beast, its inverted gull wings and deep blue finish exuding both grace and power. Even after years of dormancy, it commanded reverence.

As Flynn took in the sight, a voice with a faint European lilt cut through his thoughts.

"Magnificent, isn't it?"

Flynn turned to find a tall, impeccably dressed man with tousled hair and an effortless smile. He appeared around Flynn's age, perhaps slightly younger. There was a keen glint in his eyes—the kind that belonged to someone always thinking three moves ahead.

Flynn's real name was Vance Cavalla.

"Sure is," Vance replied, extending his hand. "Vance Cavalla."

Flynn clasped his hand, met with a firm, confident grip. The man nodded, his expression composed yet self-assured.

"Fronz. Fronz Müller," he said smoothly, his German accent giving his name a crisp, deliberate weight.

For a brief moment, they stood in easy silence, both admiring the Corsair with mutual respect.

"You know," Flynn began, breaking the quiet, "this beauty was the finest Navy fighter of WWII. Fast, rugged, and armed with rocket launchers for when things got real intense. Landing on a carrier? Now that was a challenge. Just misunderstood, I tell ya. These babies were still rolling off the line in the '50s."

Fronz grinned, a flicker of admiration in his eyes. *"Ah, yes—the Corsair. The Japanese feared it so much they called it 'The Whistling Death.' That eerie howl at high speeds? It was the last thing many ever heard before it unleashed hell."*

Flynn's eyes lit up as they talked, each nearly finishing the other's thoughts.

"Hellcat was solid, no doubt—well-rounded—but the Corsair? That was something else. The engine, the design—just wicked."

"The same basic torque-monster engine, really," Fronz added, gesturing at the Corsair. "But with some adjustments, it became a whole different animal. A true aerial predator." He ran a hand thoughtfully along the edge of the wing, his gaze filled with admiration. "I've always respected that. It's like research and development—tweak a few variables, refine the design, and suddenly, you're miles ahead of the competition."

Flynn chuckled. "Never thought of it like that, but you're right."

They spent the day wandering the airshow, their conversation shifting from planes to science, life, and everything in between. Over lunch at a picnic table near the runway, they listened to the occasional roar of a fighter overhead, their discussion never losing momentum. The connection was instant—Fronz's deep intellect and Flynn's sharp, tactical mind complemented each other effortlessly. They were drawn to the same things: flight, science, and the thrill of pushing boundaries.

By the end of the day, Fronz turned to Vance, curiosity flickering in his eyes. "You seem to know your planes, my friend. Do you have space for a project I'm working on?"

Flynn raised an eyebrow. "Depends. What kind of project are we talking about?"

Fronz leaned in slightly, his voice adopting a more serious edge. Then, he eased back, stroking his chin as he surveyed the vast open space before him. His European accent carried a deliberate precision, each word carefully chosen, as if he were already mapping out his next ten moves.

"I need a proper facility to continue my research here in the States," he said, adjusting his cufflinks with the precision of a man who left nothing to chance. "Somewhere with space—real space. And discretion, of course. The kind that ensures people don't ask too many questions."

His gaze drifted toward the Corsair, its warbird silhouette stretching long across the hangar floor. A slow, knowing smirk crept onto his face.

"Oh, and while I'm at it," he added casually, as if discussing a fine bottle of Swiss wine, "I might just acquire a couple of these beauties. Late-model F4U-5 Corsairs… with rocket launchers." He paused, eyes gleaming with mischief. "You know… for scientific purposes. And for old time's sake, of course."

Flynn blinked. "Wait, you're buying Corsairs? Plural?"

Fronz smiled. "Yes. Along with a T-6 trainer to make everything legal with the FAA. I need a partner who understands what this means. What do you say?"

Flynn's grin widened. "You're crazy. But I'm in. I'll introduce you to Joshua and Kurt. They're here at the show somewhere. I'll text them now."

Flynn quickly sent Joshua a message, who then informed Kurt. Soon after, they all met at the lunch area to discuss the potential partnership. Kurt had other commitments but stayed for the initial conversation.

A few weeks later, after the paperwork was finalized and the Corsairs were en route, Flynn and Fronz stood in front of the hangar, admiring their newly acquired aircraft. Joshua, a friend of Vance's from high school with aviation mechanic experience, was already elbows-deep in assembling one of the Corsairs. The joke was that these late-model birds arrived in more pieces than expected, but Joshua didn't mind.

"Some assembly required," he laughed, wiping his hands on a rag. "But she'll fly, don't you worry."

Joshua, sporting a Marine-style blonde buzz cut, turned to Flynn. "Holy smokes, Flynn, your favorite aircraft really brings out the call sign in you."

Fronz clapped Joshua on the shoulder with a grin. "You're doing excellent work, my new friend. Soon, these beauties will take to the skies again."

He and Vance stood side by side, admiring the sleek contours of the Corsairs in the hangar, their polished frames a tribute to aviation history. Turning to Flynn with curiosity, Fronz asked, "When we first met, you said people call you Flynn. What's the story behind it?"

Flynn smirked, shrugging. "Flynn's my old hacker name. Been using it since the '80s. 'Greetings, Program. I serve the user.' It stuck. Now, it feels like it should be my call sign."

Fronz chuckled, nodding. "Then Flynn it is. Your call sign, your legacy."

With a playful glint in his eye, Fronz tapped Flynn's shoulders in an exaggerated knighting motion. "If I could knight you, you'd be Sir Flynn. I knight thee."

Flynn laughed, giving a mock salute. "Thanks, mate. You do sound like royalty with that accent."

Fronz returned the salute. "Must be the German and Dutch in me. Now, who's hungry?"

Just like that, their friendship was forged—built on mutual respect, shared dreams, and a pair of Corsairs ready to soar again.

Fronz knew this was the least he could do. Filling a void in a new friend's life while borrowing space in a yet-to-be-revealed facility. At least I've found someone in the U.S. I can work with. The strength I've been missing now stands before me.

Three months later

An introductory meeting was scheduled between Fronz and SAGA Corporation, a dominant force in the tech industry, renowned for its far-reaching influence and groundbreaking innovations—most notably, its aggressive pursuit of Cold Fusion technology.

Three months later, the conference room at SAGA headquarters embodied the company's futuristic vision—glass and steel, sleek and unyielding. The towering windows framed a panoramic view of the sprawling city, but Fronz paid it little mind. Seated at the far end of the table, he remained composed, his fingers idly tapping the armrest as his gaze locked onto the projector screen. A complex array of equations and blueprints illuminated the room. At the center of it all was his Cold Fusion

Engine design—an unprecedented breakthrough, still theoretical, but brimming with transformative potential.

Jack, the CEO of SAGA, stood opposite Fronz, his stance rigid and commanding. He had always prided himself on being the sharpest mind in any room—at least when business was involved. But today, a subtle frustration edged his voice. Jack wasn't accustomed to being outshined, yet Fronz—intentionally or not—was doing just that.

"So, this Cold Fusion Engine," Jack began, his tone light but carrying an unmistakable tension. "You really believe it can deliver on its promise? Sounds a little too… theoretical, don't you think?"

Fronz offered a measured smile, adjusting his glasses. "It was theoretical. But we've moved beyond that. The data speaks for itself. The engine harnesses localized energy from unconventional sources, making it more efficient and powerful than any existing power plant."

Jack's jaw tightened briefly. He resented the effortless certainty in Fronz's voice. Confidence without arrogance—that was the distinction. Jack had arrogance in spades, but Fronz… Fronz radiated an unshakable intellect that gnawed at him. Worse, it was authentic. And Jack knew it.

Jack waved a dismissive hand, his voice laced with casual arrogance. "Yeah, yeah," he said, brushing aside the concern like a trivial inconvenience. "But you and I both know—practical application is what really counts. The math might look solid on paper, but in the real world? That's where things tend to crumble."

Fronz met Jack's gaze with a calm, almost amused smile—the kind born from absolute certainty. He inclined his head slightly, his posture relaxed yet deliberate, like a chess master already anticipating twenty moves ahead.

"Natürlich, Jack. I would expect nothing less than skepticism," he said smoothly, his German accent subtle but refined, lending his words a measured elegance. "That is precisely why the patents are already in motion and the prototypes are well underway." His smile remained steady as he adjusted his cufflink. "The math? That was only the groundwork. What we are building now?" His eyes gleamed. "That will endure."

Jack couldn't shake the feeling that Fronz's words carried a deeper implication—as if he wasn't just building a machine but shaping the future itself. Meanwhile, Jack remained tethered to the present, focused on keeping SAGA profitable and ensuring the corporate machine kept turning.

"Right," Jack said, leaning forward, determined to reassert control. "Let's just make sure the investors are kept in the loop. You might understand all this"—he gestured vaguely at the complex equations on the screen—"but they're not scientists. They need results, not… whatever this is."

Fronz, still seated, remained unfazed. "Of course, Jack. Results matter. But sometimes, understanding the 'why' is just as important as the 'how.' We have a real opportunity to change the world here."

Jack stiffened at the undertone, the quiet insinuation that Fronz was the visionary while he was just another executive chasing numbers. That was what really irked him—the fact that Fronz wasn't impressed. Most people, especially scientists, went out of their way to win favor with SAGA's CEO. But Fronz? He simply didn't care. Not out of disrespect, but because the science was all that mattered to him.

"Yeah, well." Jack forced a grin, leaning back in his chair. "Let's not get ahead of ourselves, Professor. Changing the world is great and all, but it doesn't pay the bills. SAGA needs to stay competitive."

Fronz never looked desperate, never seemed eager to please. It was as if he knew that, in the end, the world would need him more than he needed SAGA.

Rising from his seat, Fronz met Jack's gaze for the first time since their conversation began. He was taller than Jack had realized, and for a moment, the tension between them was almost palpable.

“I understand,” Fronz said softly, his tone measured. “But remember this, Jack—true innovation doesn’t come from chasing profits. It comes from the pursuit of knowledge… and the courage to follow it wherever it leads.”

Jack’s grin faltered, tightening into a hard line. Fronz’s words lingered between them like an unspoken dare, one Jack couldn’t easily ignore. He nodded, offering no reaction, but inside, resentment simmered. Fronz had won this round, and he knew it.

As Fronz turned to leave, Jack’s fists tightened beneath the table. His hatred for Fronz wasn’t just about his intelligence—it ran deeper. Fronz was untethered by the corporate maneuvering Jack had spent years perfecting. He couldn’t be manipulated, and that unsettled Jack more than anything.

“Hey, Jack, this technology is literally going to keep the lights on.” Fronz shot him a wink and a quick nod before striding out the door.

In the end, it wasn’t about money or power. It was about control—and the thought that Fronz, someone sharper and fixated on the future, might slip beyond his grasp was something Jack couldn't stomach.

CHAPTER ONE

THE UNVEILING

Kenji sat in the backseat of the family car, gazing out the half-open window as the salty breeze tousled his long black hair. His father drove along the coastal highway, the rhythmic crash of waves barely audible over their excited chatter.

For weeks, they had been looking forward to this trip—the unveiling of Flynn's groundbreaking inflatable suit. The articles they had read online had piqued their curiosity, and Kenji's sister, Keori, back in Japan, had urged them to attend after reading an impressive write-up on Team Nautilus.

"Kenji, can you believe it? A suit that inflates and protects the wearer from the freezing ocean!" his father, Hiroshi, exclaimed, his eyes gleaming with enthusiasm. He had always been fascinated by technological advancements, and this event was the perfect fusion of science and innovation.

"Your sister was right—we couldn't miss this," his mother, Akiko, added with a warm smile. "She knows how much you love things like this. Who knows? Maybe one day, you'll be designing something even more impressive."

Hiroshi chuckled. "If the presentation wows us, maybe we should talk to Flynn about investing in the project. The news media, the U.S. Coast Guard, and potential backers will all be there. And who knows? They might even have sushi. Yummy!"

Kenji felt a surge of warmth, reassured by his parents' unwavering belief in him. Their support for his passion for science and technology had never wavered, but today, it resonated even more deeply. He returned their smiles, gratitude swelling in his chest. No matter what path he chose, he knew his family would stand by him—just as they did today.

Flynn preparing

Fronz folded his arms, his gaze sweeping over the invention before him with quiet admiration. A subtle smirk played at the corners of his mouth as he nodded.

“I must say, seeing your invention take center stage is quite satisfying,” he remarked, his European accent lending his words a refined weight. His eyes flicked to Flynn, brimming with knowing approval. “You've poured everything into this, haven't you?”

He let the moment settle before gesturing subtly toward the gathered crowd. "The stage is yours, mein Freund. Enjoy it—you've earned it."

Flynn gave a small nod. *"Thanks, buddy."*

In a bustling Northern California town, cradled between the vast sea to the west and towering mountains to the east, Team Nautilus prepared to unveil their latest innovation. At the heart of it all stood Flynn, ready to introduce their groundbreaking creation—the 'Nautilus' Inflatable Suit. Engineered to automatically right the wearer, even if unconscious, and lift them safely from the water, it was a potential game-changer in water survival technology, eliminating hypothermia from the equation.

The grand Oceanic Pavilion buzzed with anticipation, industry professionals mingling with investors and press, all eager to witness the unveiling.

The day kicked off with a meet-and-greet, accompanied by fine food—an arrangement quietly funded by Fronz, with Joshua coordinating efforts with the Harbor Master.

As the gentle waves lapped against the dock, a crowd of onlookers—enthusiasts and skeptics alike—gathered beneath the clear sky, their attention fixed on the imminent demonstration of Flynn's innovative inflatable suit. Among them, one figure stood slightly apart, his gaze not just on the event but beyond it—into the shadows of competitive espionage and personal vendettas.

Jack Skelton, CEO of SAGA, wasn't there out of mere curiosity. His presence was deliberate, driven by a calculated agenda. His history with Fronz was tainted by a public debacle in Zurich—a confrontation that had not only bruised his ego but cast a long shadow over his technological ambitions. That humiliation had festered over the years, hardening into an unyielding resolve to undermine Fronz at every turn. Jack knew the patent submissions were only the surface of a much deeper game. Fronz was cunning, always withholding crucial details to safeguard his intellectual property.

You think you're so clever, Fronz. But I'm onto you. And today, I'll have my own little victory. Jack mused, his lips pressing into a thin line.

As Flynn stepped forward to begin the demonstration, Jack's focus momentarily wavered. Despite his primary intent to outmaneuver Fronz, he couldn't ignore the ingenuity of Flynn's inflatable suit.

"Keep an eye on Fronz. I want to know his every move," Jack murmured to his associate. His gaze flicked back to the suit, intrigue creeping in. "And Flynn's invention… it might be more than just a sideshow after all."

Meanwhile, Fronz stood by, his sharp intellect concealed beneath a mask of patience. He was acutely aware of Jack's presence, the silent tension between them thick as the salty sea air.

"Oh, I see you, Jack. What are you up to?" Fronz murmured, his voice barely above a whisper.

The clock struck 1:00 PM, and the Dock Master called out, "Alright, everyone—onlookers and those with influence—let's board our boats and head a few miles out to sea. Please proceed safely."

Flynn inhaled deeply, the weight of a hundred expectant eyes pressing down on him as he stepped onto the stage. Though his expression remained composed, a flicker of nervous energy simmered beneath the surface. The media, journalists, and industry insiders had gathered for this very moment—the grand unveiling of his latest innovation.

With a confident smile, he addressed the crowd.

"Ladies and gentlemen, explorers of the deep and dreamers of the impossible," Flynn began, his voice steady and commanding. "Today, we present not just another advancement in technology but a groundbreaking leap in human safety. I give you—The Nautilus."

With a sweeping motion, Flynn unveiled his suit—a sleek, form-fitting inflatable bodysuit with metallic accents that shimmered under the stage lights. It was a fusion of cutting-edge design and practicality, its futuristic aesthetic captivating the audience.

"This suit will revolutionize survival in the harshest conditions," Flynn declared, pacing the stage with effortless confidence as he gestured toward the suit. "It will right you in the water, regulate your ascent from the coldest depths, and keep you afloat. Whether you're lost at sea or braving treacherous environments, The Nautilus is your safeguard."

Cameras flashed furiously, capturing every angle of the demonstration. Flynn moved purposefully across the stage, ensuring the journalists had a full view of the suit's capabilities, while inwardly marveling at how far his vision had come.

"As you can see," Flynn continued, offering a confident smile, "The Nautilus isn't just functional—it's ready for real-world application, designed to save lives." He paused, sweeping his gaze across the crowd. "This isn't just a suit. It's a promise—no one should ever be lost to the sea again."

A wave of excitement rippled through the room as murmurs spread among the press. Flynn, adrenaline still coursing through him, strode toward the edge of the stage, preparing for the in-water demonstration.

CHAPTER TWO

TRAGEDY STRIKES

The sun hung high in the cloudless sky, casting a golden shimmer over the ocean. Guests milled about, their chatter and laughter blending with the rhythmic lapping of the waves. Out at sea, sleek boats carried potential investors and future customers, all eyes fixed on Flynn.

Among the crowd, a young figure weaved between the adults, his gaze alight with curiosity. At just seventeen, he had slipped into restricted areas, his pulse quickening with the thrill of witnessing cutting-edge technology up close.

From a nearby boat, Flynn's wife, Lilian, her long red hair pulled into a ponytail beneath a ball cap, assisted Joshua with telemetry tests.

Joshua, Flynn's best friend and colleague, monitored data from another boat miles away. His eyes remained locked on the screens tracking Flynn's heart rate, oxygen levels, and the integrity of his inflatable suit, its sensors feeding back every vital detail.

"Looking good, Flynn. All readings are stable," Joshua relayed through Flynn's earpiece.

With cameras rolling and anticipation thick in the air, Flynn stood at the edge of the boat. The Pacific stretched beneath him in vast, deep-blue brilliance. He had explained the suit's capabilities in theory—now it was time to prove what The Nautilus could do.

Without hesitation, Flynn plunged feet-first into the water, vanishing beneath the surface. The cool ocean closed around him, swallowing him whole for a few moments. Onlookers from the boat and shore leaned in, eyes fixed on the spot where he had disappeared, anticipation thick in the air.

The moment he was fully submerged, the suit sprang into action. The first chambers around his chest inflated with a sharp hiss, rapidly filling with CO2. Its auto-inflator sensor had detected the water's saturation, triggering the inflation sequence instantly. In seconds, Flynn's torso was righted, his face breaking through the surface as the suit stabilized him in a perfect survival posture.

From the boat, the crowd watched The Nautilus in action, its bright fabric expanding methodically, section by section. As the chest inflation completed, the chambers along Flynn's back engaged next, lifting him higher. The suit wasn't just designed to keep someone afloat—it was engineered to elevate them fully above the water, a critical feature for emergency rescues. Within moments, Flynn floated effortlessly, his entire body supported by the buoyant chambers.

The crystal-clear Pacific waters made the demonstration even more striking, allowing onlookers to witness the suit's mechanics in real-time. Flynn raised a thumbs-up from his position, and the crowd erupted in cheers. The inflation had worked flawlessly, proving that The Nautilus was more than a concept—it was a lifesaving innovation, ready to conquer the unpredictable perils of the open sea.

The atmosphere crackled with anticipation, the crowd enthralled by the demonstration—until a sudden crash shattered the moment.

Fronz and Flynn had hired Captain Slim, a seasoned sailor with salt-and-pepper hair, along with his sleek yacht, Her Dreams. The luxurious vessel allowed potential buyers, investors, and early backers to witness the presentation in style. It gracefully circled the event, offering passengers a prime vantage point of the showcase.

At the helm, Captain Slim navigated with practiced ease, adjusting the yacht's speed. Then, without warning, numbness gripped his left side. His stomach lurched. He collapsed onto the deck, his mind clouded with confusion, unable to call for help—unaware he was suffering a stroke. Her Dreams surged forward, veering toward the demonstration at a speed far beyond what had been agreed upon in the safety briefing.

Meanwhile, Kenji's father, Hiroshi, urged him to find the person in charge and figure out how they could reach Flynn. Without hesitation, Kenji sprinted toward the commotion unfolding at the front of the boat.

Captain Slim lay sprawled on the floor, paralyzed, his grip on the vessel lost as it veered dangerously off course. In a catastrophic instant, his yacht slammed into another—Celeste, rented by the CEO of SAGA. The Celeste's captain spotted the danger too late, yanking the wheel in a desperate attempt to steer clear. But there was no escaping impact.

The two yachts scraped together in a grinding collision, Her Dreams' hull slamming into Fronz's boat and sending it lurching to starboard. Fronz, bracing at the helm, was thrown violently against the deck, his head striking hard. A deep gash split across his forehead, blood spilling down his face.

Gasps and screams filled the air as Her Dreams reeked of leaking fuel. The sickening crunch of wood and fiberglass gave way to something far worse—the hiss and crackle of igniting gas. Flames erupted, spreading with terrifying speed as spilled gasoline ignited on the water's surface.

Kenji's expression shifted from fascination to horror. His parents—potential investors in the suit—were caught in the chaos on Captain Slim's yacht, their voices lost in the rising panic. The fire raged, an unforgiving inferno consuming everything in its wake.

Flynn took in the disaster and moved without hesitation. He deflated his suit and plunged into the water, slipping beneath the fiery surface toward Fronz's boat. Hauling himself aboard, he fought against the searing heat in his lungs. He found Fronz unconscious and dragged him to safety, laying him on a bed inside the cabin. Snatching up a CO_2 extinguisher, he doused the flames.

A submariner by training, Flynn reacted on instinct—running toward the fire, toward the flood.

An explosion tore through the air, shattering the stillness of Flynn's presentation. The shockwave sent him stumbling, his grip tightening on the seat as chaos erupted around him. Thick smoke coiled from the blast site, debris cascading down like jagged rain—but it was Kenji who seized Flynn's focus.

From the corner of his eye, Flynn saw Kenji flung off the side of the boat, his body colliding with the railing before plunging into the water. The brutal impact knocked him unconscious before he even hit the waves. For a split second, Flynn's breath caught. Kenji wasn't moving—just sinking, swallowed by the dark blue sea.

Then instinct took over. Flynn's Naval training, ingrained from years of service, snapped into action. He launched himself off the boat, slicing through the water with a controlled dive. The cold shock barely registered as he powered forward, closing the gap between him and Kenji. In seconds, he reached the limp body, wrapping a firm arm around him and kicking off in a strong backstroke toward the boat.

Flynn hauled Kenji onto the deck, his adrenaline spiking as he immediately began CPR. "Come on, kid. You've got this," he urged, pressing firmly against the young man's chest. After agonizing moments, Kenji sputtered, choking up seawater between ragged breaths.

Flynn swiftly rolled him onto his side, giving his shoulder a reassuring pat. "It's okay, kid. You're safe. I'll be right back."

Kenji, still in shock and wracked with pain, barely stirred. His legs felt like dead weight, his body locked in stiffness. Flynn cast a quick glance around the chaotic scene—this was far from over.

From his vantage point on the water, Joshua watched as the explosion shattered the ocean's calm. Thick black smoke curled into the sky, flames devouring the yachts. Without hesitation, he seized the wheel of their rented boat and veered toward the disaster.

"Lilian, we have to help! I'm going in!" Joshua shouted, urgency sharpening his voice.

Lilian, pale with shock, snapped into action. "Let's go, dude!" she shot back, her voice trembling but determined. She gripped the helm, guiding the boat toward the flames. As they neared the burning wreckage, they spotted survivors scattered in the water, clinging to debris, their eyes wide with terror.

Joshua wasted no time. He grabbed life rings and hurled them toward those struggling in the water. One by one, he and Lilian hauled the drenched, terrified survivors aboard, their faces frozen in horror. Flynn had already rescued several people, but the scene remained chaotic—flames consuming the yachts, with more stranded souls in desperate need of help.

The U.S. Coast Guard arrived swiftly, their sirens wailing through the night. They pulled alongside the burning vessels as their fire crew sprang into action, blasting extinguishers and calling for a water pump boat to assist in dousing the flames. As they battled the inferno, other officers moved quickly to assess the situation—gathering statements, tending to Captain Slim and the injured, and accounting for the dead.

Flynn stood on deck, watching as the Coast Guard fought back the flames. His muscles burned from dragging bodies out of the water. When an officer approached, he recounted the events in a steady voice, though the weight of reality pressed down on him.

He had saved ten people. Only five had survived. The others—including Kenji's parents—had perished in the chaos. The realization clung to him like a lead weight, each life lost a cruel reminder of fate's indifference.

Joshua placed a firm hand on Flynn's shoulder, his voice low but steady. "You did more than anyone could have asked for, brother. What you pulled off out there—saving those lives—that takes a real hero." His words were honest, meant to ease the burden hanging over Flynn. But he knew his friend too well. Flynn wasn't the type to seek comfort in praise, no matter how well deserved.

Joshua glanced at the wreckage still smoldering in the distance, then back at Flynn, searching for the right words to pierce through the weight of the moment. "I won't forget what I saw today. The way you threw yourself into that chaos without hesitation… man, you were unstoppable. You saved five lives—five people who wouldn't be here if not for you."

Flynn remained silent at first, his expression shadowed by the weight of those he hadn't been able to save. "It wasn't enough," he finally muttered, guilt threading through his voice.

Joshua's grip tightened on Flynn's shoulder, his voice steady. "It was more than enough. You can't carry the blame for the ones you couldn't reach. You did everything possible—and then some." His tone softened. "You were their only chance, and because of you, five people are alive. No one else could have done that in the time you had."

Still, Flynn seemed lost in the burden of the moment. Joshua exhaled, then cracked a small smile, hoping to lighten the mood. "But seriously, is that burnt fish smell coming from you? Because if it is, man, you might need a new cologne. That's rough."

A flicker of a smile tugged at Flynn's lips—a small but meaningful shift. He let out a quiet, pained chuckle just as Lilian approached. Without a word, she wrapped her arms around him in a silent embrace. The three stood together, staring at the smoldering ruins of what had once been a day filled with hope, now reduced to charred remains and quiet sorrow.

Fronz eventually stirred awake. "Gut…" he muttered, rubbing his temple before scanning the deck with a knowing glance. "Alright then—what did I miss? And should I be concerned?"

Flynn looked over as Joshua smirked. "Oh, you have no idea."

Kenji, strapped to a stretcher, was carefully transferred to the Coast Guard cutter for medical attention and observation. He remained unaware that his parents were nearby, standing on Fronz's boat, watching over him. The bodies of the deceased lay covered in solemn silence.

As the sun dipped below the horizon, shadows stretched long over the marina. Survivors and rescuers gathered, the weight of the day's horrors pressing down on them. What had begun as a hopeful presentation had unraveled into tragedy. Yet, for Flynn, this wasn't the end. A quiet but unshakable determination took root within him. The fragile line between human ambition and nature's merciless force had never been clearer. But loss wasn't the final chapter. For Flynn—and for all of Team Nautilus—the path forward would be one of recovery and redemption.

News for the young man

The hospital room was heavy with an uneasy silence. Kenji, still recovering from the accident, lay propped against the pillows, his bruised face alert yet weary. Behind Flynn, Team Nautilus stood in quiet solidarity, the weight of the moment pressing down on everyone. Flynn's chest tightened as he stepped forward, the words he had to say almost unbearable.

He pulled up a chair beside Kenji's bed, inhaling deeply before speaking. "Kenji, I need to tell you something," Flynn began, his voice low but steady. "Your parents… they didn't survive the explosion. There was no seawater in their lungs." He chose his words carefully, but the weight of them sat heavy in his throat. His eyes remained locked on Kenji, bracing for his reaction.

A long silence followed. Kenji blinked, his face pale and unreadable as the truth sank in. Flynn feared the worst—grief, anger, blame—but instead, Kenji exhaled slowly, shaking his head.

"I actually wanted to meet you," Kenji said finally, his voice steady despite the pain beneath it. "After reading that article about Team Nautilus, I was trying to figure out how to reach you. My parents wanted to invest in your company." He paused, his fingers curling slightly against the blanket. "If I had been with them when the explosion happened… I would have died too. In Japan, we have a saying about fate."

His gaze lifted to meet Flynn's. "It's not your fault," Kenji continued, his voice calm but weighted with loss. "I know what you did… you saved me. The Coast Guard officer who spoke to me was beyond impressed by what you did after the explosion."

There was no anger, no resentment—only quiet acceptance that left Flynn momentarily speechless.

Flynn swallowed hard, a mix of relief and sorrow settling in his chest. "I wish I could have done more," he said quietly.

Kenji met his gaze. "You're just a man." He hesitated, then looked down, flexing his fingers and shifting his feet slightly—movements so subtle they went unnoticed. His voice broke the silence again. "Can I stay with you? Most of my parents' things are in Japan with my sister. What's left here… I'll gather up, but I don't want to be alone."

Flynn nodded without hesitation, his throat tightening. "Of course, Kenji. You don't have to go through this alone. You're family now."

Keori had already reached out to Flynn. Their conversation had been brief, filtered through a friend who spoke limited English. She had passed along details about Kenji's studies and asked if Flynn could take care of him for a while. She would send money.

Flynn studied Kenji, struck by how young he looked—seventeen, but small enough to pass for twelve. And yet, he had already earned an associate's degree in Electronics, IT, and UI/UX design and was closing in on his bachelor's, with advanced calculus credits under his belt. Kenji was incredibly bright, but still just a kid forced to grow up far too fast.

"You've been through so much already," Flynn murmured, resting a hand on Kenji's shoulder. "You're one of the toughest people I know."

From that moment on, Kenji and Flynn shared a bond—one forged in the chaos of survival and the weight of trust.

As the room settled into a quiet, solemn understanding, Flynn felt that connection solidify. Kenji wasn't just a teammate. He was family. And whatever lay ahead, they would face it together.

Kenji sat in the dimly lit control room, the glow of his laptop casting sharp shadows across his face. This small, cluttered corner of the facility had become his domain—monitors flickering, cables snaking across the desk, gadgets humming with quiet efficiency. Since moving in, he'd claimed the space, shaping it into something that felt like home.

His focus sharpened on SAGA Corporation. Something about them didn't sit right.

Kenji wasn't new to hacking, but he rarely risked using his skills for anything this dangerous. This time, though, it was different. This was about exposing the corruption that had nearly destroyed Flynn and Team Nautilus. He knew SAGA had a hand in it—but proving it? That was another challenge entirely.

Cracking his knuckles, Kenji exhaled and got to work. SAGA's firewall resisted him at every turn, but he was relentless. He masked his IP through three VPNs, rerouted his signal across multiple servers, and dove headfirst into the system.

Hours passed in tense silence. Then—finally.

"Gotcha," he murmured, a slow smile spreading as he slipped past SAGA's defenses and into their mainframe.

At first, it was just routine corporate records—financial transactions, contracts, nothing out of the ordinary. But as Kenji dug deeper, he unearthed a series of encrypted documents. His curiosity piqued, he cracked the encryption and began reading.

His pulse quickened as the pieces snapped into place. There it was, in black and white: a ledger of financial transactions tying SAGA directly to Judge Harrison. The sums were staggering—millions funneled into the judge's re-election campaign through an intricate web of shell companies, all leading back to SAGA. The same judge who had been bending the law in SAGA's favor for years.

But that was only the beginning. Scattered among the files were more damning records—payments to key witnesses from the trial, the very ones who had testified against Team Nautilus, pinning the ocean accident on them. Kenji's stomach churned as the implications set in. SAGA had orchestrated the entire setup, bribing witnesses and fabricating evidence to destroy Flynn and his team. All to eliminate competition and tighten its grip on the technology.

Kenji didn't hesitate. "Flynn, you need to see this," he called, his voice taut with urgency.

Flynn appeared within moments, his brow furrowed in curiosity. "What's going on, Kenji?"

Kenji spun the laptop toward him. "Look at this. I hacked into SAGA's mainframe and found proof—they've been paying off the judge, bribing witnesses, and feeding the media fake stories. Do you get what this means?"

Flynn stared at the screen, his expression shifting between disbelief and anger. "It means we've got them," he said slowly, the weight of the revelation settling over him. "We finally have the proof we need. But is it admissible?"

Kenji grinned, sensing that this was the turning point in their battle. With this evidence, they could expose SAGA for what they truly were—and reclaim control of their future.

But were they already too late? When their attorney presented some of the information to gauge the response, it only raised more questions than it answered. The judge dismissed the evidence, deeming it unsubstantiated and inadmissible.

CHAPTER THREE

THE LEGAL MAELSTROM

The incident sent shockwaves across both the Pacific and Atlantic communities. Team Nautilus, once celebrated as pioneers, suddenly found themselves ensnared in a relentless legal storm. Leading the charge against them was SAGA Corporation's formidable legal team. The courtroom battle that followed was a spectacle, presided over by a judge whose impartiality was compromised—his rulings swayed by SAGA's financial influence.

SAGA's lawyers wove a masterful yet insidious narrative, portraying Team Nautilus as recklessly negligent, despite Flynn's heroic efforts to save lives. This calculated attack forced the team onto the defensive, casting doubt on their integrity and undermining the very foundation of their groundbreaking work.

Amidst the corporate power struggle and legal warfare, Jack Skelton's role in Team Nautilus' downfall remained carefully hidden. His legal team, ruthless in their pursuit, launched an aggressive campaign against Flynn and his crew, seizing on every possible weakness—including their failure to medically screen Captain Slim. SAGA's paid witnesses depicted the aging captain as unfit for duty, insisting he was more suited to handling a fishing pole than commanding a vessel. The assault wasn't just about discrediting Team Nautilus—it was designed to break them, both financially and morally.

The courtroom pulsed with tension, thick with the low murmurs of attorneys shuffling papers and the sharp clicks of reporters' cameras capturing every movement. Flynn sat at the defense table, his expression a carefully crafted mask of calm, though his pulse thundered beneath the surface. Beside him, Kenji mirrored his composure—silent, steady, and unshaken. His presence was more than just reassurance; it was a declaration of loyalty and strength in the face of relentless opposition. Despite losing his parents in the accident that had set everything in motion, Kenji had never wavered in his support of Flynn or Team Nautilus.

Across the room, SAGA's legal team loomed like predators scenting blood. The courtroom was a battlefield, but the real war unfolded in the shadows—backroom deals, whispered favors, and corruption stacked the odds against Flynn and his team. SAGA's influence seeped into every corner, including the very judge presiding over the case.

Flynn exhaled sharply, frustration lacing his voice. "It's like we're fighting ghosts. Every move we make, they're already two steps ahead. And with their army of manipulative lawyers, the law is on their side."

Judge Harrison, his expression carved from stone, wielded his gavel with the precision of a man accustomed to control. Rumors whispered through legal circles that his re-election campaign was quietly bankrolled by SAGA—the very corporation standing to profit from Team Nautilus' downfall. Everyone in that room knew it. But proving it? That was another battle entirely. And with mounting legal fees bleeding Flynn's team dry, the walls were closing in.

The prosecutor rose, striding toward the jury with deliberate precision. "This is not merely a case of a new invention gone awry, ladies and gentlemen. This is about negligence—reckless disregard for human safety that resulted in the tragic deaths of multiple people, including Mr. Kenji Yamamoto's parents. Team Nautilus, under Mr. Cavalla's leadership, prioritized technological ambition over human lives."

The words hit like a gavel strike. Flynn felt the weight of every accusation pressing down on him. He knew the truth—what happened that day had been an accident, a devastating and unforeseen tragedy. But the court, fueled by SAGA's deep pockets and unyielding influence, had transformed it into a spectacle, a public execution of his character.

Kenji shifted in his seat, a flicker of discomfort crossing his face as pain flared in his lower back. The spinal injury had left him in chronic agony, yet he never voiced a complaint. He had been there for every hearing, every meeting, every deposition. His parents had been the victims, and yet, he remained—standing by Flynn's side, his conviction unshaken.

At the stand, the prosecutor turned toward Kenji. "Mr. Yamamoto, given the loss of your parents and the injury you sustained, do you believe Mr. Cavalla should be held accountable for negligence?"

A heavy pause settled over the courtroom, every pair of eyes fixed on Kenji. Even Judge Harrison leaned forward slightly, his fingers tapping impatiently against the armrest of his chair.

Kenji rose, steadying himself before speaking. "No," he said firmly, his voice unwavering despite the tension thick in the air. "What happened was a tragedy, yes, but it wasn't negligence. Flynn and Team Nautilus weren't responsible in the way you're claiming. We shared a vision—my parents and I—to push the boundaries of technology. They would never have wanted their deaths exploited like this, twisted into a weapon to dismantle something that could save lives in the future."

Silence blanketed the room. Flynn felt a surge of gratitude laced with anguish. Kenji's loyalty, despite everything he had suffered, was staggering. Yet Flynn knew that no matter how compelling Kenji's words were, they were mere whispers against the relentless machinery of corruption grinding away in the courtroom.

Judge Harrison's gavel cracked through the hush. "Thank you, Mr. Yamamoto. However, this court must adhere to the law and examine the facts as presented."

His tone made it clear—Kenji's testimony wouldn't change the inevitable.

The following hours blurred into a tangle of legal arguments and mounting evidence. Flynn could feel the tide turning against them. And when the final moment arrived, Judge Harrison's voice was devoid of warmth, his verdict delivered with cold precision.

"The court finds Team Nautilus liable for negligence and wrongful death," the judge declared, his expression unreadable. "The damages will be substantial, with final details to be determined in the coming days."

The words struck Flynn like a hammer blow. His gaze darted to his wife, Lilian, seated in the gallery, her face drained of color—fear and disbelief etched into her features. The legal fees alone had been ruinous, but this verdict spelled outright financial devastation. Bankruptcy loomed, and the possibility of incarceration was growing more tangible by the second.

Inside the courtroom, Fronz placed a steady hand on Flynn's shoulder. "We still have options," he murmured, his voice calm and deliberate. "This isn't over. SAGA's influence is vast, but we're not without leverage. I've been working on contingencies. We just need to stay under the radar and think strategically."

Flynn gave a slow nod, though the weight of it all threatened to crush him. He trusted Fronz—always scheming, always a step ahead—but the road ahead seemed impossible.

The legal onslaught had left them battered, yet Flynn, Kenji, and Fronz weren't ready to surrender. This wasn't just about Team Nautilus anymore—it was about survival in a system where justice came with a price tag, and their only chance lay in outmaneuvering unseen enemies at every turn.

Meanwhile, Jack Skelton, a man driven by ambition and rivalry, observed the proceedings with calculating interest. Years of tracking Fronz's academic and scientific achievements had fostered a deep-seated resentment. Now, with Fronz's groundbreaking patents in cold fusion poised to revolutionize the field, that resentment burned hotter than ever.

Folding his arms, Jack muttered under his breath, "Fronz… always the thorn in my side. Your work in cold fusion—it's a game-changer. But it won't be yours alone. I'll see to that."

The verdict was inevitable. Team Nautilus was found guilty of negligence and wrongful death. The Flynn family faced financial devastation, drowning in exorbitant legal fees, though they narrowly avoided jail time. The media storm was unrelenting, yet amid the uproar, young Kenji refused to place blame on Team Nautilus. He held no resentment toward Flynn, convinced that the tragedy was an accident, not an act of negligence.

The courtroom fell into an eerie silence, punctuated only by the rhythmic ticking of the judge's clock. Flynn sat motionless with his legal team, his gaze locked forward, expression inscrutable as the verdict rang out.

"The court finds Team Nautilus, Mr. Cavalla, liable for negligence and wrongful death."

The words struck with the weight of inevitability, but Flynn remained composed. He had anticipated this outcome. SAGA had wielded the legal system like a weapon, systematically dismantling everything Team Nautilus had built. But one thing was certain—he was not going to prison.

Fronz's estate, always a step ahead, had ensured Flynn's legal team consisted of the best defense attorneys in the field. The prosecution sought to paint Team Nautilus as reckless, but the facts told a different story.

The true culprit? Captain Slim—who had manipulated his medical records to hide a history of mini-strokes.

Flynn's attorneys meticulously presented their case: Team Nautilus had conducted a thorough and legally compliant vetting process before hiring Slim as captain of his vessel. He had provided falsified medical records, concealing his condition. The accident wasn't due to mechanical failure—the Nautilus suit had functioned flawlessly. The catastrophe occurred because Slim suffered a medical episode mid-operation.

"The responsibility for a captain's undisclosed health conditions cannot fall on Team Nautilus," Flynn's lead attorney argued. "This was deception, plain and simple."

SAGA had hoped the lawsuit would financially cripple Fronz's close friend, Mr. Cavalla—a calculated move to indirectly weaken Fronz himself. But they underestimated how well-prepared his estate was.

Behind the scenes, Fronz's legal team worked tirelessly, negotiating a settlement agreement that shielded Flynn from criminal liability. The court, after reviewing the overwhelming evidence, ruled this as a civil matter rather than a criminal one. No charges would be filed in exchange for structured financial compensation—one that Fronz's estate had already anticipated and mitigated.

As the gavel struck, Flynn released a slow breath. They had lost the battle, but not the war. Team Nautilus had taken a hit, but he was free. And now, it was time to strike back.

CHAPTER FOUR

DEVELOPMENT

In the weeks leading up to their groundbreaking endeavor, Dr. Fronz's spacious workshop became the crucible for the Cold Fusion engine's genesis. This sanctuary of innovation, with its high ceilings and broad windows, flooded the team with natural light, casting elongated shadows that flickered across the cluttered expanse. The walls bore the marks of their relentless pursuit of knowledge—whiteboards covered in intricate equations, vivid diagrams, and hurriedly scrawled notes—a visual symphony of intellect and passion.

At the heart of this intellectual haven stood a robust, expansive table, its surface a scattered terrain of blueprints, each line and curve a fragment of the puzzle they were determined to solve. Their dialogue wove a rich fabric of technical jargon and speculative theories, punctuated by bursts of animated gestures toward the documents spread before them.

The air in the workshop pulsed with an almost tangible sense of purpose and anticipation. Every tool, every piece of equipment, stood poised like silent sentinels, awaiting their call to action. This prelude to creation blended meticulous planning with the raw exhilaration of venturing into the unknown. Here, in Fronz's workshop, the foundation of their future was laid with every word spoken, every idea exchanged—a crucible of creativity where the seeds of the first Cold Fusion engine took root.

Fronz shared his project with Team Nautilus after they both signed a mutual NDA—just like true professionals. As they delved into further development, the technical discussions were laced with dry humor and mutual appreciation.

Imagine Fronz, the ever-serious scientist, meticulously explaining the function of a centrifuge for cold fusion and anti-gravity research, only for Flynn to interject with quips about how it might also be useful for making record-breaking salads—or even sushi, though he refused to entertain that idea. Fronz didn't laugh at first, but eventually, he did.

Their journey to secure grant funding was an ordeal in itself, followed by the challenge of acquiring rare materials like Deuterium and Tritium, not to mention negotiating over isotopes and an excess of mercury they had no immediate use for. Flynn, ever the joker, remarked, "Maybe we should just take a swim in this weird stuff."

Pointing at the blueprints, Fronz explained, "The core concept hinges on harnessing cold fusion as a power source. It's clean, efficient, and has the potential for tremendous energy output."

"Cold fusion, huh?" Flynn mused, scratching his head. "You've been working on that for a while now. Glad to hear you've cracked some of those lingering problems. Congratulations, buddy! Three cheers!"

Joshua grinned. "Oorah! I'm in. So, how does it actually work?"

"In simple terms," Fronz began, "cold fusion involves fusing Deuterium and Tritium—two heavy isotopes of hydrogen—at room temperature. It's about triggering a reaction that usually requires the heat of the sun's core, but making it happen right here on Earth."

Flynn smirked. "So, we're basically creating mini suns? No pressure there."

Joshua nodded thoughtfully. "The potential is huge. If we pull this off, we're looking at a game-changer for 'more power,

Captain,'" he said, mimicking a Scottish accent from a Sci-Fi show.

"Alpha and Beta engines are stages two and three of this project. Step one was securing the cold fusion grant," Flynn added.

Fronz nodded, his expression measured. "Precisely. The engines—Alpha and Beta—along with the mercury centrifuge, or vortex, will serve as our test beds for this technology." He made a subtle gesture, as if outlining the future before them.

"Alpha will be our proof of concept, the foundation. Beta, however… that's where we truly push the boundaries." His tone carried the weight of a man who had spent a lifetime refining the impossible into reality. "Each is calibrated differently—the width, speed, frequency, and vibration of their respective centrifuges. A delicate balance of engineering and physics. But when executed correctly?" He smirked slightly. "The results will speak for themselves."

"I'm all for pushing boundaries, but let's not blow ourselves up in the process, okay?" Flynn said.

"Where's the fun in that?" Joshua grinned. "I'm ready to see some action."

“Our priority is safety and precision,” Fronz stated. “The design of these engines must be flawless. The containment system for the fusion reaction is critical.”

Flynn had experience in Computer-Aided Design (CAD), specializing in 2D and 3D modeling for product development in life-saving appliances. He also dabbled in structural underwater design for fun. Kenji, equally adept in 3D CAD software, brought his expertise in UX/UI to the table.

"I'm guessing this is where my 3D CAD skills come in," Flynn said. "Time to bring these blueprints to life. Kenji, can you lend a hand?"

"Sure. I see Alpha includes the add-on for the mercury centrifuge, while Beta is a fully integrated unit. So, two distinct models—impressive." Kenji exhaled in awe.

"Yes, we'll take our time with Alpha to fine-tune the centrifuge add-on before applying our findings to Beta," Fronz added.

"And I'll handle the mechanical assembly. We'll need robust systems to support that kind of power," Joshua said.

Fronz clasped his hands together, his sharp gaze sweeping over the team like a seasoned strategist preparing for battle. His voice carried the steady assurance of a man who had seen ambition turn into achievement.

"Meine Freunde, between us, we have the skill, the knowledge, and the determination to turn this into reality." He let the words settle before leaning in slightly, a confident smirk tugging at the corner of his mouth.

"So, let's not just dream it—let's build it. The future waits for no one."

The trio studied the blueprints, a mix of excitement and determination evident in their expressions. They knew the challenges ahead but were eager to face them.

Flynn led the work in the 3D CAD software, but unexpected challenges arose. The rapid prototyping phase had revealed errors that needed immediate attention.

For nearly a month, Kenji acted as an additional set of eyes alongside Fronz, refining every detail.

They moved forward with constructing the structural frame and inner chamber, opting for 316L stainless steel since sourcing titanium proved nearly impossible.

"If our calculations are correct, it should weigh about 25 pounds and be the size of a football. We'll definitely need to add a handle," Fronz noted.

Considering radiation shielding, Fronz proposed 3D printing tungsten components—either for partial shielding or the entire device. Their 3D printer was well-suited for the task.

Fronz soon provided decisive input on the centrifuge design for the mercury vortex, estimating its weight at just over eight pounds.

Checking his mail, Fronz found a letter from the grant funding office. His $1 million grant request had been approved, with a requirement for regular progress reports. To receive the funds without delay, he needed to be present for the transfer into an account of his choice.

With a triumphant air, Fronz strode into the room, his smile brimming with confidence. His voice carried both excitement and authority, like a conductor poised to lead a grand symphony.

"Gentlemen, the funding is secured!" he announced, his European accent sharpening each word. "As Flynn would say, it's showtime. No more theories—now, we build."

With a knowing glance, he added, "I'll review the paperwork with the attorney. In the meantime, let's get to work. Flynn, go over this shopping list."

Corsairs a work in progress

Joshua said, "I'm happy to have the distraction of rebuilding these sweet Corsairs. Thanks a lot, my friend. I know you're focused on the Cold Fusion Engine, but don't worry—we'll take care of your baby and show you the results when we're done."

He continued, "Hey guys, some of my Marine buddies from my unit are coming by to help assemble these beauties. They owe me a few favors, and I'm calling them in. We'll keep everything in the hangar, and they've got about a week to knock it out. They're covering the beer and plenty of food. I bet Fronz will take the opportunity to whip up something amazing for a bunch of guys who used to eat crayons." He chuckled. "Should be fun. What color do you want them? Oh, never mind—I got it. Dark blue, right?"

Flynn grinned. "Sweet! Hey, how about Skull Squadron insignias on the rudders? I always thought the Flying Tigers had a great look. Can you add that too?"

Joshua nodded. "You got it, buddy. That sounds badass."

He added, "Oh, I have an idea to help with this big nose. I'll mount two GoPro cameras and link them via Bluetooth to a monitor in the cockpit. Then, I'll set up a cellular feed to Kenji's mainframe. That should work wonders. Also, Kenji will have the feed displayed on those monitors over there. We'd better get the

.50 cals squared away, along with ammo and some decent high-octane fuel—around 250 gallons each, fully loaded.

"The hangar doors stood wide open, allowing the morning sun to spill golden light over the two Corsairs. Their black rudders gleamed, each proudly bearing the Skull Squadron insignia. The Flying Tigers emblem adorned the nose of Flynn's plane—a careful, painstaking addition by Joshua and his Marine buddies. Fronz's plane, however, remained untouched, waiting its turn for the finishing touches. The sight of the restored warbirds commanded admiration, stirring a deep sense of pride in those who beheld them.

Flynn stood beside Joshua, hands on his hips, taking in the craftsmanship. "You've outdone yourself, Josh. These birds look ready to dominate the skies."

Joshua smirked, wiping grease from his hands with a rag. "They're not just for show, brother. They're ready to fly—and so are you. We're just buttoning up the paint. Should be dry in a few days."

Flynn grinned. "Nice. I called Kurt already. He'll be here Saturday morning."

Joshua nodded. "Perfect timing."

Early Saturday morning, the sunlight bathed the airfield in a soft, golden glow as Lilian stood at the edge of the tarmac with her granddaughters, Eileen and Rosaleen. The girls had spent the past week with their grandparents and were preparing to head home—but this moment was too special to miss.

The two Corsairs gleamed just outside the hangar, their polished exteriors reflecting the morning light. Flynn and Joshua stood near the planes, engaged in animated conversation about the upcoming flight.

Rosaleen tugged at Lilian's hand, her eyes alight with excitement. "Mimi, look! The planes have a skull and crossbones on them! That looks so cool!"

Lilian chuckled, brushing a strand of hair from her face. "Your granddad has always had a flair for the dramatic, hasn't he?"

Eileen crossed her arms, tilting her head as she studied the planes. "Do you think he's nervous?"

Lilian smiled, watching Flynn adjust his flight helmet. "Just enough to stay sharp. This is where he belongs."

Eileen wrinkled her nose. "You know, those wings look kind of freaky. Why are they shaped like that?"

"Because the propeller blades are fourteen feet long," Lilian replied.

"Wow," Rosaleen and Eileen said in unison.

When Kurt arrived later that morning, the girls ran to greet him, their energy infectious.

"Uncle Kurt!" Eileen called, waving excitedly.

"Well, if it isn't my favorite cheer squad," Kurt said with a laugh, ruffling their hair as he passed.

Lilian stood nearby, offering him a warm smile. "It's good to see you again, Kurt. Coffee's ready if you want some."

"Thanks, Lilian," Kurt replied.

His sharp eyes immediately locked onto the Corsairs, and he stopped mid-stride, a grin spreading across his face. "The Skull Squadron insignia—you've got good taste, Joshua."

"Only the best for legends," Joshua said, giving a mock salute.

Flynn clapped Kurt on the shoulder. "You ready to school me, old-timer? I've been logging hours in the trainer, but I know you've still got a few tricks up your sleeve."

Kurt's grin widened. "Let's see what you've got. Strap in."

The Corsairs roared to life, their engines growling across the airfield.

The girls covered their ears but couldn't hide their grins. "Go, Granddad!" Rosaleen shouted, bouncing on her toes.

Kurt's voice crackled over the comms. "Alright, rook. First, we're taking it easy. Graceful loops, aileron rolls, smooth turns—show me you've got control of her."

The two Corsairs lifted off, their sleek frames slicing through the sky with effortless grace. Flynn trailed Kurt's lead, his movements precise as he mirrored each maneuver Kurt called out.

"Not bad," Kurt remarked. "Now, let's up the challenge. Follow-my-leader. Think you can keep up?"

"Try me," Flynn shot back, a smirk in his voice.

Into the skies

Kenji had the GoPro recording, ensuring Fronz could review the footage later. The aerial views streamed onto the monitors, allowing everyone a clear view of the action.

From their vantage point near the hangar, the family watched as the two planes lifted gracefully into the sky. Their sleek forms climbed higher, engines roaring like wild beasts. The girls cheered as Flynn and Kurt launched into their aerial maneuvers.

Kurt's Corsair dipped into a sharp bank, diving low before pulling into a steep climb. Flynn followed, mirroring Kurt's movements with precision. When Kurt executed a high-G barrel roll, Flynn stayed right on his tail, their planes moving in perfect synchronization.

Kurt's voice crackled over the radio, laced with both praise and humor. "Not bad, brother. You've come a long way since the trainer. A couple of tweaks—watch your speed on that climb. These babies are torque monsters, you felt it—but overall, you're flying like a damn natural."

Flynn grinned, adrenaline surging. "Thanks to my teacher."

As the two planes soared against the vast blue sky, it was clear—Flynn had more than earned his place in the air.

Lilian's eyes never left the sky. She knew Flynn craved the thrill and freedom of flight, but seeing him up there—graceful, confident, and utterly in his element—filled her with pride.

When the Corsairs landed smoothly after a final, dazzling maneuver, the girls rushed forward as Flynn climbed out of the cockpit.

"That was amazing!" Rosaleen exclaimed, wrapping her arms around his leg.

Flynn chuckled. "What did you think of the show?"

Eileen beamed. "You were awesome, Granddad! But Uncle Kurt wasn't half bad either."

Lilian stepped forward, slipping her arm through Flynn's. "You've still got it, flyboy."

Flynn smiled at her, then glanced at Kurt. "All thanks to him," he said, nodding to his mentor. "Good to know I haven't lost my touch."

Kurt clapped him on the shoulder, grinning. "More than touch, brother—you've got heart. And it shows up there."

CHAPTER FIVE

STAGE 1

Within the confines of their bustling workshop, cluttered with an array of tools and mechanical parts that bore the marks of countless hours of toil, Team Nautilus stood on the verge of a defining breakthrough. The workshop—both a sanctuary of innovation and a crucible of scientific ambition—hummed with the palpable energy of anticipation.

At the center of this controlled chaos lay a large, well-worn table, its surface dominated by the prototype of the team's inaugural cold fusion engine—a bold step toward the future. Though lacking the sleek refinement of their envisioned Alpha, sometimes dubbed Thing 1, and Beta, known as Thing 2, this prototype was more than a rough draft; it was a revolution in the making. It was the first tangible proof that cold fusion, long dismissed as an impossibility, could work.

Fronz, the scientific mastermind, stood alongside Flynn, the visionary; Joshua, the pragmatic mechanic; and Kenji, the tech wizard. Their faces, bathed in the soft glow of overhead lights long into the evening, reflected a mix of intense concentration and barely contained excitement. The air crackled with the weight of discovery, each member fully aware of the significance of this moment—yet bound by the unshakable camaraderie that had brought them here. Amidst the meticulous disorder of their workshop, where every tool and scribbled blueprint spoke of tireless dedication, Team Nautilus stood poised to redefine the future of energy and science.

Fronz decided to build the first Cold Engine Prototype using 316L stainless steel.

"It comes with its own challenges, but one must start with a known quantity," he said. "We'll experiment with 3D-printed tungsten on the next one..."

He examined the device carefully. "This prototype must work, even if only for short periods. Securing further funding depends on it."

"No pressure, then," Flynn said, taking a sip from his water bottle. "Just a little bit of cold fusion to impress the government suits."

"Short bursts of functionality are better than none. It's like my old truck—runs great, just not all the time," Joshua added.

Kenji smiled. "Let's focus on stabilization. Even brief functionality will prove the engine's potential."

Fronz nodded, making final adjustments. "Alright, let's initiate the first test run. Kenji, monitor the energy output."

Kenji glanced at his laptop. "Got it. All systems are GO."

Flynn flipped a switch. The engine hummed to life, a soft glow emanating from its core.

"Look at that! She's alive—alive!"

"Like a beautiful, science-y Frankenstein," Joshua quipped.

The engine ran smoothly for a few moments before flickering.

Kenji frowned. "Energy levels fluctuating... and it's down. But we got a solid 30 seconds of operation."

Fronz exhaled. "Thirty seconds today—the future tomorrow. We'll refine it."

"At this rate, we'll have a fully operational engine by the time I grow a decent beard," Kenji muttered.

Joshua smirked. "So, never? You've got the hair—I'll give you that."

The team laughed, and the tension in the room eased.

Flynn read from his notes. "Every second counts. These short operational periods are our stepping stones."

"Exactly. We're pioneers, not magicians," Fronz replied. "Progress takes time."

Flynn smirked. "Time and a whole lot of trial and error. Hey, anyone else hungry?"

"Fun and a little bit of controlled chaos—just how I like it," Joshua said.

As the engine's hum faded and the room settled into a quiet lull, the team gathered around the prototype, their shared pride evident in the gleam of their eyes. It wasn't a perfect test, but it was progress—a flicker of promise bringing them one step closer to their goal.

"Thirty seconds," Flynn grinned. "Hey, that's thirty more than we had yesterday. Not bad for a little mercury-and-cold-fusion wizardry."

Fronz chuckled, rubbing his chin thoughtfully. "Exactly. Thirty seconds is a foundation. Imagine where we'll be in a few months."

"A few months?" Joshua raised an eyebrow. "You mean by then, this baby will run long enough for us to take coffee breaks?"

Kenji, typing away on his laptop as he reviewed the data, looked up with a sly smile. "If we're lucky, we might even get a whole minute."

Flynn laughed, clapping Kenji on the shoulder. "Dream big, kid! By then, this engine will be purring like a kitten. Or, knowing us, roaring like a lion."

Joshua crossed his arms, a mischievous glint in his eye. "As long as it doesn't blow up in our faces. I can handle controlled chaos. Actual chaos? Not so much."

Fronz smirked. "Controlled chaos is exactly what we're here for. That's what pioneers do—we push boundaries, take calculated risks. And sometimes, that means a little fire and smoke along the way."

Kenji shook his head with a smile. "Sometimes I wonder if we're all just a little insane. We talk about anti-gravity and cold fusion like it's casual science, but here we are, building it piece by piece."

"Insane or not, this is the life, right?" Flynn stretched his arms and glanced around the room. "I mean, who else gets to be on the cutting edge, making history?"

Joshua leaned against the table, grinning. "Yeah, and on top of that, we get to do it with some of the best people around. Just a bunch of go-getters trying to change the world."

Fronz raised an imaginary glass in a toast. "Here's to pushing the limits of science—and to the fine line between genius and madness."

Kenji played along, holding up his wrench like a glass. "To short bursts of functionality. May they turn into long-lasting results… someday."

They laughed, the tension dissolving as they exchanged glances brimming with trust and shared resolve. The road ahead wouldn't be easy, but moments like these—brief respites of camaraderie and lightness amidst the struggle—made the journey worthwhile.

After a pause, Flynn cleared his throat. "Alright, so who's covering dinner tonight? We've earned it."

"I nominate Fronz," Joshua said, grinning.

Fronz arched an eyebrow. "Why me?"

"Because you're the one who dragged us into this insanity!" Joshua shot back, laughing.

Fronz sighed, but a smirk tugged at his lips. "Fine, but I get to pick the place. We need something substantial. Pioneers can't run on just pizza and coffee."

Kenji nodded. "As long as it's somewhere we won't get kicked out for casually discussing how to break the laws of physics."

With a final glance at the prototype, the team filed out, already bouncing around ideas for the next test. The night ahead promised good food, more laughter, and talk of the bold, audacious dreams still waiting to be realized. They weren't just colleagues—they were visionaries, bound by something greater than science itself: the relentless pursuit of a future only they dared to imagine.

Alpha was designed with a narrow, hollow centrifuge filled with a specialized mercury compound, leveraging the cold fusion engine as an auxiliary power source while keeping the structure lightweight.

Beta, in contrast, featured a broader, donut-shaped centrifuge, utilizing the same specialized mercury and an integrated coolant system, resulting in a slightly heavier build. The mercury required cooling, and the cold fusion engine, operating at room temperature, proved ideal for this function. The engine's power supply was calibrated to spin the mercury at approximately 1,000 revolutions per second. Fronz remained uncertain how this modification would impact the electromagnetic field, but testing both models was necessary to resolve gaps in his equation.

Kenji, drawing from his UI/UX expertise, developed a user interface and monitoring system with assistance from Flynn and Joshua.

Flynn, deprived of proper sleep for days, squinted at the app's endless options and lines of code, his exhaustion turning every setting into a puzzle. His fatigued mind only processed fragments of the interface's complexities, resulting in frequent, sometimes absurd, misinterpretations. Each time he adjusted a parameter, another setting inexplicably shifted, leaving him more bewildered.

Joshua, observing from the sidelines, chuckled at Flynn's struggles.

"Alright," Joshua said with a grin, leaning over Flynn's shoulder. "I think we need to make this interesting. Let's add a soundtrack."

They exchanged a mischievous look, and within minutes, their prank was in motion. Working in sync, they programmed the app to blast classic rock whenever the engine reached a specific temperature on the test platform—not too high, not too low, just enough to stay within safe limits while giving them the laugh they needed.

On the next test run, as the temperature gauge hit the mark, Highway to Hell erupted from the speakers, shaking the room with loud, unapologetic rock.

Kenji's head snapped up, his eyes darting between the app and the engine, sheer disbelief etched across his face.

"What the...?" he muttered, utterly bewildered, while Flynn and Joshua struggled to maintain straight faces.

"Just keeping things interesting, kid," Flynn said with a wink, barely holding back his laughter as Kenji gawked at the screen.

Kenji shook his head, mumbling something about "childish antics" under his breath, but the smirk tugging at his lips gave him away.

Meanwhile, the contrast between the prototype cold fusion engine and the Zone Engines was impossible to ignore. The prototype—meant for the government—had its share of quirks, including an inconvenient habit of shutting down at the worst possible moments, often forcing Fronz to come up with quick, sometimes ridiculous fixes. The Zone Engines, in contrast, were the sleek, high-end models, boasting advanced features that set them apart.

CHAPTER SIX

WHAT IF...

The atmosphere in the room crackled with anticipation as the team huddled around the projector, studying a complex, multi-layered diagram. At the front, Fronz, radiating his usual scientific curiosity, gestured toward the schematic. The rotating cylinders and coils depicted on the display represented their latest breakthrough—a fusion of cold fusion technology and a mercury vortex, an idea that had quietly taken shape through months of discussions.

Fronz pointed to the detailed representation of a centrifuge, his voice steady but brimming with excitement. "The centrifuge's rotational force should counteract gravitational pull," he said, tapping the display to rotate the image. "In theory, it could generate anti-gravity. We already know that spinning mercury at high velocities produces a unique electromagnetic field. Cold fusion provides the sustained power needed to support it."

Standing off to the side, Flynn folded his arms, his expression a mix of skepticism and intrigue. "Anti-gravity?" he echoed. "That's ambitious, Fronz. We've been chasing fusion for energy, but now you're talking about rewriting the laws of physics."

Fronz's grin widened. "Well, we're not exactly bound by convention anymore, are we? If our calculations hold, this system's energy output could weaken gravitational forces—maybe even manipulate space-time itself. Look here." He pointed to a section of the diagram highlighting a mercury vortex in a superconductive state. "The centrifugal force from the spinning mercury, combined with the cold fusion energy output, creates an energy vortex. That vortex could distort the gravitational field surrounding the device.

"Kenji, seated nearby with his ever-present laptop, typed furiously, pulling up research papers and archived documents as Fronz spoke. "I've read about this before," he said, adjusting his glasses. "There are old theories that mercury—in a highly energized, spinning state—could generate fields strong enough to bend gravity. Anti-gravity concepts aren't new, but most of the research was dismissed as fringe science."

Fronz's eyes gleamed with a knowing spark as he leaned in, lowering his voice just enough to draw everyone closer. "Dismissed? No, my friends—you mean buried. If something like that truly worked, do you really think it would be public knowledge? No… it would be hidden. Classified."

He let the words hang in the air before continuing, his tone laced with intrigue. "You've all heard of the Nazi Bell, yes? Die Glocke? Or perhaps the Philadelphia Experiment?"

The room grew still, curiosity thickening the air. Fronz allowed himself a small smirk before elaborating. "Die Glocke—a mysterious, bell-shaped device allegedly built by the Germans during World War II. Some claim it levitated and vanished without a trace; others say it was a failed experiment. But the most compelling theories?" He tapped his temple. "They suggest it didn't just disappear—it was removed… possibly through time itself."

He shifted seamlessly. "And then there's the Philadelphia Experiment. That one? The evidence suggests some truly bizarre events—things that defy conventional science." He leaned back, letting his words sink in. "So tell me… do we really think these were just wild stories?"

From the back of the room, Kurt, who was at the facility to train Flynn in aerial combat, had been listening quietly. He raised an eyebrow. "I always thought those were explained away."

Fronz nodded slowly. "That's exactly what they want you to think. But if it were just a hoax, why go to such lengths to bury it? The fact that there's almost no credible record of it tells me it wasn't a hoax at all. That's a red flag—a sign that something real happened. Anti-gravity, time travel, invisibility… whatever it was, they were chasing something, and maybe they even succeeded. And if they got close, why can't we? With today's technology, we could build on what they started."

Kenji pulled up a document on his screen, sparing Fronz a glance. "Even if we managed to replicate the conditions for anti-gravity, time travel would require precise control over space-time itself. We'd have to account for fluctuations in the very fabric of reality. I'm not sure cold fusion alone would be enough."

Fronz's lips curved into a knowing smile. "You're right. This isn't just about energy, Kenji. It's about mastering the fundamental forces of nature. Cold fusion would sustain the system indefinitely, but the real challenge was stabilizing the vortex. You'd need precision—down to the quantum level. The calculations alone would demand an immense amount of computational power just to estimate the right coordinates for time travel."

Flynn, still reeling from the sheer magnitude of what they were discussing, finally spoke. "So you're saying we have the key to anti-gravity… and possibly time travel? We've been chasing energy solutions, and now you're telling me we might be able to manipulate time?"

Fronz turned to Flynn, his expression grave. "We could control more than just time. If we do this right, we could rewrite the very laws of physics. Think about it—what if we could undo the past? Correct mistakes? Prevent them before they even happen?"

A heavy silence fell over the team as the weight of Fronz's words settled in. What had begun as a theoretical discussion on cold fusion and energy had veered into something far more profound. Anti-gravity was merely the first step. But time travel? That opened doors they hadn't dared to consider.

"The centrifuge's rotational force should counteract gravitational pull, essentially creating anti-gravity… with the potential for time manipulation," Fronz said, gesturing to a complex diagram. "But that would require an entirely new set of calibrations I haven't even begun to calculate."

Kenji finally broke the silence, his voice measured but firm. "If we go down this path, we need to be careful. The Nazi Bell vanished without a trace… and who knows what that unleashed?"

Fronz nodded. "That's why we're going to do this right. We're not chasing war or power. We're chasing knowledge. If those bastards from the past got close, we can do better. We can unlock the mysteries they never even understood."

Flynn exchanged glances with the rest of the team. The road ahead was uncertain, but one thing was clear: they weren't just revolutionizing energy. They were stepping into the unknown, armed only with ambition, technology, and the resolve to challenge the very fabric of reality.

"I know, I know—anti-gravity and all that," Flynn muttered, rummaging through the cupboards. "But imagine: zero-G lettuce. That's one small step for man, one giant leap for Caesar salads."

Without looking up, Kenji said, "If you guys start launching salads into space, count me in."

"Speaking of balance, remember when we almost turned the workshop into a Mercury swimming pool?" Flynn added. "Man, that was a heart-stopper."

"How could I forget? You ordered extra, just in case, and nearly gave me a heart attack," Fronz said, laughing as he stood by the open freezer door.

Kenji grinned. "Hey, at least we would've had the shiniest pool in the neighborhood."

Flynn chuckled. "True. Who needs water when you can swim in… whatever it is Mercury does."

Laughter rippled through the room. Most had a vague idea, but only Fronz truly understood the significance of mercury.

"Alright, focus," Fronz said, straightening. "The prototype for the government needs fine-tuning. It's been acting up again, shutting down randomly."

Flynn examined the Cold Fusion Engine. "Ah, the old 'play hard to get' routine. Classic high-tech drama."

"I'm serious, Flynn. We can't afford any mishaps," Fronz said, skimming a grocery list.

"Relax, Fronz. With our brains and your magic touch, what could possibly go wrong?" Flynn said with a smirk.

Kenji finally looked up. "You had to say it, didn't you? You just doomed the entire project."

Flynn shrugged. "Oops. Well, if we accidentally time-travel, I call dibs on meeting Da Vinci!"

Fronz shook his head with a smirk. "Just make sure you bring back one of his sketches."

Joshua chuckled at the exchange, exhaustion settling in after hours of working on the rapid prototype.

What If… (Sci-Fi R&R)

The workshop had been a constant hum of activity for weeks—tweaking equations, running simulations, testing circuits, and refining theories. Every moment was devoted to achieving the impossible, bending physics to their will. The work was exhilarating, but even the sharpest minds needed a breather.

Kenji, ever the wildcard, had been acting unusually secretive the past few days, flashing a grin like he was in on a joke no one else knew. Finally, when Flynn and Joshua were knee-deep in yet another debate over the Beta engine's power efficiency, Kenji clapped his hands together, demanding their attention.

"Alright, geeks," he declared. "Drop the calculators and ditch the clipboards. We're taking a break."

Joshua arched an eyebrow. "A break? Kenji, the last time you suggested a break, we ended up brawling in a bar over who could build the better AI."

Kenji shrugged. "That guy had it coming. Anyway, this time's different—no arguments, no science, just pure, unfiltered geekdom." He pulled a stack of tickets from his pocket, waving them triumphantly. "Sci-Con 2099, baby!"

Flynn's eyes widened. "No. Freaking. Way."

"Oh, freaking way."

Joshua smirked. "Let me get this straight—you're dragging us to a convention where people dress up like space wizards and laser-toting bounty hunters?"

Kenji crossed his arms. "First of all, it's called cosplay. And second, you're damn right—we need this. It's been weeks of nonstop calculations, stress, and existential crises. Honestly, if I have to hear one more debate about gravitational harmonics, I might actually lose my mind."

Flynn grinned, already on board. "Kenji, I could kiss you right now."

"Maybe buy me dinner first," Kenji deadpanned. "Oh, wait—never mind. I bought you tickets. You're welcome."

Fronz, who had been quietly observing the chaos, leaned back in his chair and offered a rare, amused smile. "You know what? I like this plan. I fully support this plan. We've been working ourselves into the ground. A little sci-fi escapism sounds like a damn good distraction."

Joshua sighed, rubbing his temples. "Fine. But if I see a single grown man in a Sailor Moon outfit, I'm out."

Kenji smirked. "Oh, buddy, you're going to see so much worse."

The Next Day – Sci-Con 2099

The moment they stepped into the convention center, a sensory overload hit them—cosplayers in elaborate costumes, vendor booths overflowing with collectibles, and the distant sound of someone butchering a Wookiee impression.

Flynn, decked out in a classic Han Solo outfit, inhaled deeply. "This... this is glorious."

Kenji, clad in a pristine Starfleet uniform, adjusted his communicator pin. "Welcome to the promised land, my friends."

Fronz, who had—shockingly—agreed to don a remarkably convincing Obi-Wan Kenobi robe, chuckled. "Alright, where's the bar?"

Joshua, the lone holdout in his everyday clothes, sighed. "You guys are going to get us arrested, aren't you?"

Kenji handed him a foam lightsaber. "Joshua, it's a convention. If we don't get into at least one mock battle, we've failed as attendees."

Flynn spotted a panel on the physics of faster-than-light travel and immediately turned to Kenji. "Now that's our jam."

Kenji snorted. "Oh hell no. We are not turning this into a real-world physics lecture. You are officially forbidden from correcting the guest speakers."

Flynn smirked. "I make no promises."

For the first time in what felt like ages, Team Nautilus forgot about equations, government agencies, and the weight of their discoveries. They surrendered to the world of fantasy and possibility, indulging in their love of all things sci-fi.

It was a much-needed escape—because soon, the real battles would begin.

CHAPTER SEVEN

STAGE 2

The steady hum of machinery filled the workshop as Team Nautilus gathered around the Alpha engine—a sleek, compact marvel of engineering. After two months of tireless effort, refining every intricate detail, they stood on the brink of a breakthrough.

Fronz, ever the perfectionist, hovered near a set of complex diagrams, a small grin tugging at his lips as he surveyed their progress.

"Joshua, how's the internal structure and mechanical integrity looking on Alpha?" Flynn asked, his sharp gaze sweeping across the room as the team worked with laser focus.

Joshua wiped his hands on a rag, glancing up from his inspection. "Solid as a rock. This baby's built like a tank but moves with the finesse of a ballet dancer."

"A tank and a ballet dancer… now there's an image," Fronz chuckled as he approached, positioning himself beside the smaller Alpha engine. Behind him, Tesla coils crackled with energy, their arcs illuminating the dim workspace.

Fronz gestured toward his schematics—intricate sketches detailing the Alpha's start-up sequence. The engine's mercury core required a surge in power from the Tesla coils, aided by a calculated shift in gravitational force.

Stepping closer, he nodded approvingly at their handiwork. The Tesla coils pulsed in the background, a quiet yet potent reminder of the immense energy they were about to unleash.

Fronz gestured toward the set of drawings pinned to the wall. "Alright, everyone, here's the plan. We'll start with the Alpha's mercury centrifuge. It'll need a power boost from the Tesla coils and some gravitational assistance to get the spin just right." He scanned the room, meeting the eyes of his team. "And remember, we have to do this twice. The Alpha engine was just the beginning—the smaller of the two. Once we've mastered this, we'll move on to Beta, a more refined and slightly larger device that operates independently."

Joshua studied the diagrams, his eyes gleaming with awe and determination. "This is like stepping into a sci-fi movie."

Flynn smirked. "And you're our resident action hero, Joshua. Ready to save us from alien invasions with your martial arts skills?"

Joshua shot him a grin. "Always. But let's stick to anti-gravity and time travel—less messy than alien goo."

Fronz arched a brow, his smile fading into a look of stern focus. "Stay on task, gentlemen. We need to document the Zone's parameters precisely. This isn't a movie—we're about to push the boundaries of physics."

The team got to work, their banter fading as they adjusted the Alpha engine with precision. At his workstation, Kenji monitored the incoming data streams from the engine's sensors, his fingers flying over the keyboard.

"You know, in the Marines, we had a saying: 'Adapt and overcome,'" Joshua mused, adjusting one of the engine's external components. "Seems fitting for what we're doing here."

Without looking up from his screen, Kenji added, "Adapting to anti-gravity and overcoming the laws of physics. Not too shabby."

Joshua smirked. "Now that's an idea. But let's perfect this tech first—one sci-fi dream at a time."

The team shared a brief chuckle, but the weight of their task quickly settled back in. Joshua stepped back, surveying the engine with a quiet sense of accomplishment before glancing at Flynn.

"Crazy, isn't it?" Joshua said with a grin. "Back in high school, we were messing around with old cars. Now we're hovering."

Flynn wiped his brow, letting out a low chuckle. "Life's weird like that. But I wouldn't have it any other way."

Fronz lifted his gaze from the diagrams, his voice calm but threaded with intensity. "Agreed. Now, let's make history. Or should I say, remake it?" His tone darkened slightly. "Time travel isn't just exciting—it's terrifying."

The group fell silent for a moment, the weight of the possibility pressing down on them. They all understood the risks—what they were doing wasn't just innovative; it was revolutionary. And with revolution came danger.

"We're ready for this," Flynn said, his voice steady. "Let's make sure we do it right."

The team nodded in unison, their faces reflecting a blend of determination and excitement. They had endured long days, late nights, and more setbacks than they cared to count, but the promise of what lay ahead kept them moving forward.

As the night wore on and exhaustion settled in, Flynn wiped his hands on his jeans and stretched.

"Alright, guys, I'm off to pick up the girls with my wife," he said, waving as he headed for the door.

The rest of the team stayed behind, tired but proud of what they had accomplished. Tomorrow, they would be one step closer to changing the world.

Granddaughters return

The day promised sunshine and laughter, made even brighter by the long-awaited arrival of Flynn's beloved granddaughters, Eileen and Rosaleen. Though their school finals had forced a brief return home, they were determined to be back for this special occasion. The air hummed with anticipation as Flynn and Lilian drove to the airport, their hearts light with the joy of reunion.

With a twinkle in his eye, Flynn mused, "Do you think the girls will notice I've gotten grayer since last summer?"

Lilian chuckled. "Oh, they'll be too busy hanging onto your workshop stories to notice a thing!"

The airport reunion was a whirlwind of embraces and laughter. Eileen and Rosaleen, breathless with excitement, launched into animated tales from their journey, their eyes gleaming with delight.

Eileen groaned dramatically. “Granddad, the plane snacks were so tragic you'd think they were rationing for an apocalypse!”

Flynn chuckled. “Next time, we’ll pack you a proper feast. How about that?”

On a whim, Flynn súggested they stop at their favorite Mexican restaurant, a cozy spot alive with vibrant colors and the rich, mouthwatering aroma of spices.

Lilian grinned. “Perfect idea! The girls have missed your tall tales almost as much as they’ve missed real tacos.”

“Honestly, Mimi, a taco sounds like a dream come true right now!” Rosaleen said eagerly.

The restaurant was a cozy haven filled with warmth and the rich aroma of spices. Plates of tacos, enchiladas, and sizzling fajitas circulated, accompanied by stories and lighthearted teasing. Flynn’s efforts to master eating a taco without making a mess became a source of amusement.

Just before taking a bite, Eileen teased, “Granddad, I think fajita eating might not be your strongest skill! Nom nom.”

Flynn chuckled, shaking his head. "I've always thought the inventor of the fajita was a genius… and a bit of a prankster."

The evening ended with satisfied sighs and excited chatter about the days ahead. The girls buzzed with anticipation about visiting Flynn's workshop.

"Tomorrow, we step into Granddad's world of innovation. It's like walking into a storybook—only better!" Lilian said as she found her seat.

Flynn smiled modestly. "Well, it's really Fronz's ideas. I just… Hey, guys, this way."

Eileen and Rosaleen chimed in together, "We can't wait!"

As they drove home beneath a sky scattered with stars, their voices carried a soft, familiar rhythm, filling the car with warmth and love. In that moment, the joy of a shared meal and the comfort of family made the challenges ahead feel distant.

This peaceful interlude—marked by the simple pleasures of togetherness—stood as a striking contrast to the trials awaiting them, a tender reminder of the unbreakable strength of family bonds.

In the bustling heart of the workshop, anticipation crackles in the air, electric and vibrant, as the final preparations for Beta's activation unfold. Amidst the whirlwind of activity,

Eileen and Rosaleen, fresh from their journey and brimming with excitement, step into this world of innovation, their eyes wide with the promise of witnessing something truly extraordinary.

Beaming with pride, Flynn declared, "Just in time, girls! You're about to witness a piece of history in the making."

Lilian, affectionately known as 'Mimi' to her granddaughters, lingers just long enough to soak in the moment before duty calls. As an online child therapist, her dedication to helping others is a testament to the family's commitment to making a difference—each in their own way. Besides, someone has to pay the bills. Not that Mimi minds—she loves her job.

With wide-eyed enthusiasm, Eileen exclaimed, "We wouldn't have missed this for the world, Granddad!"

Rosaleen chimed in eagerly, "Is this the new engine design? The Alpha and Beta you've been telling us about?"

Amidst his final checks on the intricate web of machinery and digital displays, Fronz pauses to acknowledge the girls with a welcoming nod, his usual seriousness softened by their infectious excitement.

"Indeed, it is," Fronz confirmed. "Alpha proved that the concept works. Beta is a major leap forward. You're here for a defining moment."

Alpha arrives

In the sprawling, gadget-filled expanse of the Team Nautilus lab, anticipation crackled in the air, more potent than the assorted hums and whirs of machinery. This was a place where the impossible was routinely challenged, where dreams took form in steel and circuitry. But today, it was more than a hub of scientific breakthroughs—it was a testament to legacy.

Flynn stood at the heart of the lab, a space as familiar to him as the lines on his own hands, flanked by his granddaughters, Eileen and Rosaleen. The sisters, standing on the cusp of their college adventures, carried the weight of theories and boundless possibilities. Yet today, their minds were set on something far greater—the birth of the Alpha engine.

Before them loomed the sleek, silver behemoth, humming softly, almost as if it possessed a heartbeat of its own. Flynn's team—Fronz, Joshua, and the young prodigy Kenji—moved with meticulous precision, performing the final checks. Their faces, illuminated by the glow of their work, reflected a balance of intense focus and barely contained excitement.

Fronz handed out sun protection goggles. "Please put these on so I can set my mind at ease. Thanks. And no cheating—I insist."

Flynn's gaze swept over his granddaughters before turning to the machine that held their future. He exhaled deeply. "Today, we're not just testing an engine," he declared, his voice rich with emotion and just the right touch of theatrics. "We're igniting the spark of the future. Girls, this is only the beginning. Together, we step into a new frontier."

Rosaleen, ever the skeptic with an eyebrow perpetually arched, eyed the towering Tesla coils with mild suspicion. "Granddad, does this frontier have Wi-Fi?"

"It better," Flynn quipped with a wink. "It has limitless potential."

Eileen, the more contemplative of the two, surveyed the lab with awe. "It's like a sci-fi movie—just missing a popcorn machine."

"Popcorn comes after we make history," Joshua chimed in, striding over with a clipboard. His grin was infectious. "Ready for the show?"

Kenji, barely older than the girls, gave them a shy nod. "We're making sure Alpha doesn't just start up—but sings."

Fronz, ever the cautious one, double-checked a monitor before adding, "And ensuring it doesn't decide to sing an opera of destruction."

The moment arrived. Flynn gestured toward a console adorned with a red button so stereotypical it might as well have been a movie prop. "Eileen, Rosaleen, would you do the honors of initiating the first sequence?"

Eileen's fingers hovered over the button. "What's the worst that could happen?"

Rosaleen nudged her. "We become part of a very expensive fireworks show."

With a shared grin and a simultaneous shrug, they pressed the button.

The sealed chamber inside the lab, designed to contain any potential radiation hazards, thrummed with a deepening hum. The Alpha engine's panels illuminated, tracing intricate patterns of light that danced like the aurora borealis. The Tesla coils erupted in an electrifying spectacle, arcs and sparks crackling through the air. The energy was palpable.

"Beautiful and terrifying," Lilian murmured, her excitement evident as she squeezed Flynn's hand, unable to look away from the mesmerizing display.

With a soft hum that swells into a resonant thrum, Alpha powers up, Tesla coils crackling with sparks and bursts of light. The air around the engine shimmers with energy, the atmosphere charged with raw potential. The girls' faces glow with awe, their wide smiles and bright eyes reflecting the weight of the moment.

The room seemed to hold its breath as readings spiked, then leveled out. Alpha wasn't just alive—it was stable.

Joshua let out a triumphant whoop. "It's alive, and no pitchforks needed!"

"Or popcorn," Fronz quipped, his grin unwavering.

Kenji, ever composed, gave a thumbs-up, his gaze locked onto the monitors. "It's like watching a new star being born."

Under the watchful eyes of generations bound by blood and ambition, Alpha's successful activation was a moment of triumph.

Flynn gathered everyone for a group photo, the Alpha engine gleaming behind them. "Smile for science," he joked, then turned to Fronz. "And I swear, that smile hasn't left your face all day."

As the day wound down, Flynn pulled his granddaughters aside. They stood together, gazing over the now-quiet lab, bathed in the soft glow of success.

"This was more than just technology; it represents what we can achieve together. It's about pushing the limits of knowledge, fueled by our hopes and united by our dreams," Flynn said, his voice soft yet charged with passion.

Lilian exhaled in amazement. "Just wow. The Tesla coils were so loud, the hairs on the back of my neck stood up. And then I saw that smirk on your face—the bug-eyed look on the girls' faces—it was un-be-lievable." She hugged Flynn before glancing at her watch. "As much as I hate leaving a party early, duty calls." Casting a proud look at her granddaughters and pressing a kiss to Flynn's cheek, she left for her office.

In this haven of innovation, Alpha's birth was more than just a scientific milestone; it was a cherished family memory—a beacon of hope and wonder for the future. Though Mimi's absence was felt, the bond she shared with her family remained unshaken, a testament to their unity even across distances.

After cleaning up, the team took a well-earned break. Flynn and the girls went for a walk around the facility before a three-hour team meeting, finally heading home for the night. Fronz and the rest of the team rested before resuming their analysis the next day.

CHAPTER EIGHT

STAGE 3

Two months later, after an extensive analysis of Alpha's creation and the integration of key data for Beta's development, the workshop buzzed with energy and anticipation. The team gathered around the newly constructed Beta engine, noticeably larger and more intricate than its predecessor. Its complex design radiated an almost imposing presence. The hum of machinery filled the space, punctuated by the occasional crackle of electricity from the nearby Tesla coils. Yet beneath it all, something deeper pulsed through the air—a low, resonant vibration, as if the very fabric of the workshop responded to the immense power Beta demanded.

Fronz had designed Beta as an all-in-one device, constructed entirely from 3D-printed tungsten. Not only was it capable of withstanding radiation, but it was also strong enough to endure the immense forces of the mercury vortex. Given that tungsten was among the strongest metals on the planet and could be precision-printed, Beta became a single, solid unit—slightly larger due to the increased radius and width of the centrifuge.

Fronz examined his clipboard. "Beta's design is more complex. We should expect a stronger reaction upon activation."

Flynn nodded confidently. "Alright, here's what I have on the Beta housing—it's a little taller and wider since the mercury centrifuge is more robust at the center. What do you think, Fronz?"

"Looks like a beauty!" Fronz said, then leaned in to examine the interior. "Very nice, Flynn. The second Mk is much smoother—only two rapid prototypes this time.

""Yeah, yeah, see? I'm teachable."

Joshua inspected the mechanical components. "Bigger toys, bigger bangs—that's my kind of science."

"Let's just hope it's more of a 'wow' bang and less of a 'boom' bang," Flynn quipped.

Kenji ran a final diagnostic. "Systems check complete. All readings are in the green. We're ready for the big moment."

The team took a collective breath. Fronz nodded at Kenji, who flipped a switch. The Beta engine whirred to life, its deep, powerful hum growing in intensity.

Sipping his tea, Kenji monitored the readings. "Energy levels rising... This is more than we anticipated."

In the dimly lit workshop, everything pulsed with raw energy. The Tesla coils, stationed at each corner, crackled with electricity, sending erratic, brilliant sparks into the air like a contained lightning storm. They adjusted their goggles and pulled their ear protection down tighter. The atmosphere was charged—a hum of power that sent adrenaline surging through Kenji's veins.

Kenji wasn't alone in that feeling—everyone in the room sensed it, an almost tangible excitement thickening the air.

Beta's creation was different. It was louder, more intense than Alpha's birth. The workshop trembled, the ground beneath them vibrating in sync with the pulse of the technology springing to life. Flynn felt every thrum in his chest, each beat a visceral reminder of the immense power they were harnessing.

Beta stood at the heart of the room, gleaming under the flickering Tesla coils. It was built for raw power.

A massive arc of electricity leapt between the coils, illuminating the room in a brilliant flash. Sparks burst like fireworks, and for a moment, the air itself crackled with energy. Fronz grinned beneath his goggles. This was it—the culmination of their work.

The workshop grew louder, the machinery's hum swelling into a steady roar, mercury levels rising with its revolutions. Flynn's heart pounded, barely restrained by his chest. The sheer force of the power being generated was intoxicating.

The air thickened, charged with electricity, as if Beta itself was absorbing the energy, feeding on it, growing stronger with each second. Flynn felt the heat surging from it, the pulse of something being born—not just a machine of tungsten steel, but a force in its own right.

Flynn shouted, "Is it supposed to do that? It feels like a rock concert in here!"

"Steady," Joshua called over the noise. "Let's not lose our heads just yet. Or, you know—at all."

As the engine reached its peak, a brilliant flash of light engulfed the machine, forcing the team to shield their eyes. When the brightness faded, the engine settled into a steady, rhythmic hum.

"Incredible…" Fronz murmured. "Beta is operational, and the energy output exceeds our calculations. Mercury's spinning at nearly 1,000 revolutions per second. Alright, let's shut down the coils and see what Beta is up to."

Kenji checked the monitors. "It's stable. We've done it. Beta's birth is a success."

Joshua let out a breath. "I've got to admit, that was pretty impressive. And no explosions, which is always a plus."

"Now, let's see the Zone," Flynn said. "Kenji, the lasers, if you please."

Kenji activated the laser grid, revealing a smaller yet denser Zone than Alpha. The team stepped closer, their awe reflected in the shimmering light.

"Speaking of which, we need to run diagnostics. Let's not get ahead of ourselves," Kenji reminded them.

Without hesitation, the team set to work, each member focused on their area of expertise, their faces illuminated by the glow of Beta's successful activation.

After the initial excitement over Beta settled, the team noticed something unusual about the Zone it generated. Unlike Alpha's expansive area of effect, Beta's Zone was significantly smaller, concentrated just above the engine—roughly fifty inches in diameter.

"That's odd," Fronz murmured, frowning. "The Zone should be larger, given Beta's increased power."

Kenji analyzed the data on his tablet. "The readings are clear. The Zone is confined to a small area, just above the engine."

"So, we've got a mighty engine with a not-so-mighty Zone. Was Beta on a power diet or something?" Flynn quipped.

"It's like Beta is more focused... concentrated," Joshua said, leaning in to examine the Zone. "Maybe it's not about size, but intensity?"

"Interesting point," Fronz said, nodding. "This could mean Beta has a different application—something more precise."

"Could it be a design aspect we overlooked? Or maybe a byproduct of the increased energy output?" Kenji mused.

The team gathered around Beta, each member deep in thought, weighing the implications of this unexpected development.

"Well, if Alpha is our broadsword," Flynn said, "maybe Beta is our scalpel. Smaller field, but sharper."

Joshua ran a hand over his buzz-cut hair. "I like that. The scalpel of time. Sounds like a sci-fi thriller."

"This isn't a matter for jokes. We need to understand why Beta behaves this way. It could be crucial for our next steps," Fronz said, his expression serious.

"We should run a series of targeted tests on the Zone," Kenji agreed. "Determine how its properties contrast with Alpha's."

As the team set up for further testing, a charged anticipation filled the air. The revelation of Beta's distinct Zone marked a turning point in their research—one brimming with promise and uncertainty.

CHAPTER NINE

SOTRA – THE BENEVOLENT PLEIADIAN

For over five centuries, Sotra had watched. She moved effortlessly between dimensions, traversing the vast space between the enigmatic fifth—where time and matter defied comprehension—and the structured fourth, where Earth's inhabitants remained bound by linear progression. She had encountered countless species in her travels, yet something about humanity always drew her back. They were different.

Unlike the civilizations she had observed, humans possessed an unrelenting drive—an ability to push beyond their limitations, fueled by curiosity, resilience, and an inexplicable defiance of fate. She had seen them rise and fall, wage wars, create beauty, and innovate in ways that rivaled species far older than their own. Yet, in all her centuries of watching, she had never interfered.

It began with a flicker—a subtle shift in the electromagnetic fabric of the fourth dimension. Something different. The original cold fusion engine had piqued her interest, but it wasn't until the Alpha engine came online that she truly took notice. Its electromagnetic field wasn't just advanced—it was familiar. A similar technology had once existed millennia ago, only to be lost to time. Now, it had resurfaced.

Sotra delved into Earth's history. Her kind had been here long before this technology emerged, watching, coming, and going—some stationed there by duty, others drawn by curiosity. This was no coincidence. Someone had built this.

She had to see for herself.

Sotra observed Team Nautilus from a distance, tracking their progress and attuning herself to the minds behind the technology. Then, she saw him. Flynn.

Her heightened awareness allowed her to perceive more than intellect or technical skill—she sensed the frequencies of consciousness, the energetic imprints that defined a being's potential. Flynn wasn't just another strategist or technician; his presence resonated beyond the physical. His mind operated on multiple levels at once, seamlessly balancing logic, instinct, and an almost subconscious grasp of the unknown. He didn't just react to challenges—he anticipated them, moving with an intuitive precision that defied mere experience.

Yet, what truly captivated her was his emotional energy—a rare fusion of defiance, loyalty, and an unrelenting drive to protect those he loved. Unlike most humans she had observed, Flynn's motivations weren't shaped by ego or self-preservation but by an innate sense of duty. Perhaps his past had forged the man he had become. His choices carried weight in the timeline, rippling through possibilities in ways few ever could. It was as if he stood at the edge of a greater awareness, unaware that his very existence was bending the rules of his dimension.

In the workshop, the team was deeply engrossed in their work around the Alpha engine. The EM field pulsed gently, a subtle reminder of its unknown potential. Observing from a distance, Sotra, a wise and benevolent Pleiadian, decided to intervene subtly. She had spent more than five centuries studying human behavior and technology, occasionally stepping in when necessary.

Fronz scrutinized the monitors. "The EM field's behavior defies our current understanding. We need to analyze its properties further. How many dumb mistakes can I make?" He smacked his forehead in frustration.

Flynn noted, "It's like we're on the brink of a breakthrough, but there's a missing piece."

Silently, Sotra extended her influence, her presence unseen. The only sound in the room was the low hum of machinery as Kenji stared at the whiteboard in the corner. He blinked, rubbing his eyes, convinced his exhaustion was playing tricks on him. But no—the marker was moving, guided by an unseen force. It sketched a complex pictogram alongside an intricate equation—one detailing a calibration system seemingly designed for Alpha alone. His jaw dropped.

"Guys… look at the board!" Kenji called out, his voice laced with disbelief and awe.

Flynn turned just in time to catch the final strokes appearing on the board. He squinted, struggling to make sense of the alien symbols and mathematical formulas materializing out of thin air. "Am I hallucinating, or did that just write itself?" he muttered.

Joshua stepped closer, his eyes widening. "This… this is like a message from the magic marker of knowledge. Kenji, come on, it was you, right?" He tousled Kenji's long, flowing black hair.

Fronz, already pushing past them, was locked onto the whiteboard. "Hold on, everyone, just give me a moment," he said, his gaze darting between the pictogram and the equation beside it. He yanked a notepad from his back pocket and started scribbling furiously, as if the formula might vanish at any second.

Flynn pulls out his phone and snaps ten pictures of the entire whiteboard.

Kenji, still reeling from what he'd just witnessed, leans in closer. "Look at that calibration. It's tailored specifically for Alpha. This could be exactly what we need to stabilize it."

Fronz runs a hand through his graying hair, his face lighting up as he deciphers the equations. "Oh my god," he murmurs, barely audible. Then, louder, "Great Scott! This is it! I'm... I'm an idiot for not seeing this sooner."

"What? Shut up." Flynn chuckles at Fronz's dramatic reaction.

Fronz shakes his head, grinning widely. "No, seriously! This equation... it's not just about energy output. It's adjusting for frequency and vibration in a way I never even considered. Whoever—whatever—gave us this is pushing us in a whole new direction."

Peering over Joshua's shoulder, Fronz points to a section of the diagram. "Look at this part. It suggests that the frequency modulation needs to be fine-tuned in real-time to maintain stability. If we can get this right..." He trails off, his mind racing with possibilities.

Kenji, still shaken after witnessing the equation materialize on its own, glances at Flynn. "I'm a bit beyond words right now."

Fronz stepped back, his eyes never leaving the board. "Alright, enough gawking. Let's get to work. We've got a new path forward. But first…" He turned to Kenji with a smirk. "You need to teach me how you pulled that off."

Kenji laughed, the tension finally breaking. "I wish I could take credit, but that was all the marker, furiously scribbling on the whiteboard. I would have believed it if I hadn't seen it myself."

Following Fronz's instructions, Kenji applied the changes. The engine's hum deepened, and the EM field visibly shifted, becoming more defined and controlled.

Kenji, looking like he'd had too much coffee, muttered, "I'm integrating these new parameters into the user interface controls. This should give us a clearer understanding of the field's capabilities."

Joshua observed Kenji at work, his expression a mix of concentration and awe. "This feels like we're not alone in this… Like we're being helped by something we can't see."

Days passed—pacing, reworking formulas, rewriting equations. After another grueling session, Fronz suddenly froze, his eyes wide. "Great Scott in heaven. I think I get it! It's leading us in a new direction. How could I have been so blind?"

He and Kenji quickly made adjustments to the UI, fine-tuning spin speed, frequency, and vibration. "Alright, try that," Fronz instructed.

The field flickered, then stabilized. Fronz's voice was laced with excitement. "It's responding. We can manipulate its size and properties now. This is a monumental step forward."

United in their mission, the team launched into a series of methodical tests, each member laser-focused on their task, driven by newfound knowledge.

Flynn grinned. "We're breaking new ground here. This is uncharted scientific territory."

Though Sotra remains invisible and silent, her influence has irrevocably shaped their journey, guiding them toward discoveries that blur the line between science and the unknown.

Fronz said, "We'll continue testing. There's much to uncover, and I have a feeling this is only the beginning."

The scene fades on the team, their work bathed in the glow of the Alpha engine—an emblem of their relentless pursuit of knowledge, subtly directed by an unseen force.

Nearby, Beta rests on its own table, emitting a frequency that subtly enhances the well-being of those within its range.

Stress levels drop significantly, and everyone exposed to the field feels noticeably better afterward.

Kenji devises a method to visualize the electromagnetic field using small lasers, positioning them near Alpha and Beta. The field's size can be adjusted through the UI. As Fronz observes, he realizes the field can be fine-tuned to contain, protect, and control whatever lies within by modifying its frequency, vibration, and applied current. The team begins a series of experiments to test these capabilities and refine the UI/UX software.

CHAPTER TEN

ALPHA – THE DEFIER

The air carried a faint blend of salt and oil, a scent likely linked to Fronz. The team gathered around a workbench, the glow of multiple monitors casting sharp reflections on their faces. Streams of complex data and calculations flickered across the screens.

Kenji sat at the primary control terminal, his fingers moving swiftly over the keyboard as lines of code raced past. Leaning back in his chair, he rubbed his eyes before exhaling. "Alright," he said, turning to the others. "Now that the new formula is integrated, let me break down how everything works behind the scenes."

Flynn tilted his head, intrigued. "Go on, Kenji. Let's hear it."

Fronz, his hair disheveled, smirked at Kenji. "The floor's yours, kid."

Kenji gestured to the schematic of the Alpha engine displayed on the main screen. "Think of the system as having three key components: software, firmware, and hardware. The software is the brain—it takes input from all our sensors and runs predictive models to determine how we need to adjust the field. But software alone can't communicate directly with the hardware. That's where the firmware comes in."

Joshua leaned in for a better view of the screen, his brow creasing. "So the firmware is like a translator?"

"Exactly," Kenji said with a nod. "The software handles high-level calculations—like determining power requirements and the ideal frequency to stabilize the bubble. But it can't directly control the electromagnets and field generators inside the Alpha engine. The firmware bridges that gap, converting those calculations into signals the hardware can actually interpret and execute."

Flynn raised an eyebrow. "Okay, but how does that translate to controlling the field itself? How do we tweak the frequency, amplitude, and all that jazz?"

Kenji tapped a few keys, pulling up a new set of graphs. "It's all about modulation. The Alpha engine uses frequency modulation to fine-tune the field's interaction with the environment. Higher frequencies stabilize the bubble when we're dealing with strong currents or pressure shifts, while lower frequencies conserve power in calmer conditions."

"Got it on frequency," Flynn said, frowning slightly. "What about amplitude and vibration control?"

Kenji gestured to another graph displaying amplitude levels. "Think of amplitude as the field's strength. We increase it to reinforce the bubble during high-speed travel or turbulence. But more amplitude means more power consumption, so it's a trade-off. Then there's vibration control—tweaking vibration frequencies within the field helps reduce drag and smooth out the ride, especially during rapid maneuvers."

Fronz nodded, considering the explanation. "And power regulation?"

"Right," Kenji continued. "The system dynamically adjusts power distribution based on the field's demands. If we're diving deep or making a fast ascent, the firmware directs more power to the field generators to maintain stability. But in steady conditions, it scales back power to conserve energy."

"What we did with the new formula," Fronz said, pointing to the screen, "is refine how the software predicts those adjustments. It's all about reducing the lag between the sensors detecting a change and the firmware making the correction. Now, the system reacts almost instantaneously."

Flynn nodded slowly, visibly impressed. "So, we've got a fully adaptive system that not only reacts to changes but anticipates them. That's... pretty damn impressive."

"Yep." Kenji smiled, pride flashing in his eyes. "With the new algorithm integrated, we're not just responding to the environment—we're staying ahead of it."

Flynn clapped Kenji on the back. "Good work, Kenji. Now let's see if this theory holds up when we take her out to sea."

"Can't wait to see this thing in action," Joshua said with a grin.

"Then let's get her ready." Kenji swiveled back to his terminal, fingers already flying over the keyboard. "We've got an ocean and sky waiting to be conquered."

Fronz stepped forward, his expression thoughtful. The room quieted as he cleared his throat, drawing everyone's attention. "Gentlemen, what we've just integrated with Kenji's updates," he began, excitement creeping into his voice, "has far greater potential than we realized. With the adjustments to the Alpha engine, we've created a stable field that could very well defy gravity—just like I envisioned."

Flynn raised an eyebrow, skeptical yet intrigued. "Defy gravity? Jesus H. Christ on a popsicle stick, you're serious. This formula—this thing on the whiteboard that practically fell from the heavens—brings your brainchild to life. My mind is officially blown."

Fronz laughed, his eyes gleaming as he gestured to the live feed on the screen. "The electromagnetic field we generate, for all intents and purposes, negates gravity."

Joshua leaned in, squinting at the data. "We're not in Kansas anymore,

"Exactly," Fronz replied with a nod. "When Kenji pushed the field beyond its standard settings, the electromagnetic zone bubble began interacting with Earth's magnetic field. By modulating vibration frequencies and increasing the field's amplitude, we can test this hypothesis."

Kenji, still seated at the control console, added, "It's like creating a localized anti-gravity pocket. The field doesn't just counteract gravity—it generates an opposing force, allowing precise control over lift. It's more than levitation; it's directed, sustained movement."

Flynn stroked his chin thoughtfully. "And you think we can sustain this beyond brief bursts? You're saying we could maintain control?"

"With adjustments to power regulation and the new algorithms we've integrated, yes," Fronz confirmed. "The key is balancing frequency modulation with power output. Too much destabilizes the bubble. Too little, and we drop like a stone."

Joshua let out a low whistle. "So… we could actually fly? Hover, maneuver—maybe even achieve full lift-off?"

"That's the theory," Fronz said. "If we scale up power output and refine the algorithms further, we're not just talking about underwater capabilities anymore. We could achieve controlled aerial maneuverability—hovering, navigating over rough terrain, even operating where no conventional vehicle could go."

With that, the team dispersed to prepare for the next trial. The hum of machinery and the soft clicking of keys filled the control room as they made their final adjustments.

First, they tested the zone on the coffee pot without the carafe, which held the lifeblood of the morning. Kenji carefully moved it around before adjusting the zone to block air. Joshua poured water on the bubble, watching as it deflected and pooled on the floor.

Joshua turned to Kenji. "Set the coffee pot on the floor and shut off the bubble. Let's see how long it takes to put out a small fire." He grouped five matches together, standing them upright with their box for support. Striking a lighter, he ignited them, then adjusted the bubble's size to fit the matchbook and Alpha. "Alright, three, two, one—on."

The fire went out in two seconds. Joshua grinned. "I'd call that a successful test."

Flynn spoke up. "The fire burned through the oxygen in the bubble and suffocated. We need something that can provide feedback—like me." He chuckled. "Environmental mode OFF, allowing air in and out, of course."

Flynn strapped on a safety harness. "Ready to be a guinea pig. If I start doing somersaults in the air, catch me, will you?"

Joshua smirked. "You'll be fine. Just try not to break any laws of physics we haven't already shattered."

Kenji adjusted the controls. The area around the Alpha engine shimmered faintly, signaling the field's activation. Flynn hesitated for a moment before stepping inside.

"Whoa, I can feel it! It's like stepping into a pool of… air?" he said.

Slowly, he lifted off the ground, hovering a few feet above the workshop floor.

Fronz called out, "Kenji, try moving him to the left—slowly."

Kenji made a slight adjustment, and Flynn drifted smoothly to the left, his face lighting up with awe.

"This is unreal!" Flynn exclaimed. "It's like swimming without water!"

Watching intently, Joshua said, "The control is impressive. Kenji, move him back to the center."

Kenji complied, and Flynn drifted effortlessly back to his original position, still suspended in the air.

"Guys, this is incredible! I'm floating, and it feels... natural. At one point, I was moving sideways—like a crab on the beach. That makes me think... maybe we need to rethink the way we approach flight," Flynn said.

"The applications for this are immense," Fronz added. "Controlled gravity, seamless movement through space... this is groundbreaking."

"The UI is incredibly responsive," Kenji noted. "We've reached a level of precision I didn't think was possible."

Flynn slowly descended as the field deactivated. "That was one of the coolest things I've ever done. And I've done some pretty cool stuff."

Joshua nodded. "We're not just making strides in cold fusion—we're rewriting the rules of motion and gravity."

"Indeed. But we need to proceed with caution," Fronz said. "Our next steps must be carefully planned."

The team gathered around the control panel, their expressions a mix of excitement and determination, fully aware they were standing at the threshold of a new frontier in scientific exploration.

Discovering the versatility of the zone

The workshop buzzed with the hum of equipment—large water tanks, air filters, and various high-tech tools. Team Nautilus stood encircling the Alpha engine, their focus locked on the Zone's new capabilities. Kenji held his tablet, poised to make adjustments.

"Our tests indicate the Zone can manipulate environmental factors. Let's push its limits," Fronz said.

Kenji tapped on his screen. "I've programmed the UI to regulate the Zone's properties. We can toggle air permeability and water resistance. Let's call it Environmental Mode—ON to create a sealed barrier, OFF to allow controlled exchange at a slower rate."

Flynn raised an eyebrow. "So, we're turning Alpha into an all-weather, all-terrain bubble? Convenient."

"It could be critical for hazardous environments," Joshua replied. "Let's put it to the test."

Kenji activated the Zone, and a faint shimmer rippled around the engine. He adjusted the settings on his tablet. "First, let's test air filtration. I'm reducing permeability to air particles."

Inside the Zone, the air seemed to still, movement slowing to an eerie halt.

"Incredible. It's like we've created a localized stasis field," Fronz observed. "But how precisely can we control it?"

"Fine-tuning for selective permeability now," Kenji responded.

The air inside the Zone began circulating again, now visibly free of any impurities.

"It's like an invisible air purifier," Flynn remarked. "Allergy sufferers would kill for this."

Joshua glanced at Flynn. "Air's one thing. What about water?"

Kenji nodded and fine-tuned the controls. A staff member directed a spray of water toward the Zone. The instant the stream reached the boundary, it froze mid-air, suspended in glistening droplets.

"Now that's a party trick," Flynn remarked. "The world's first invisible umbrella. Imagine the possibilities—stopping a flood in its tracks, putting out a fire before it spreads. My God, firefighters and emergency crews would be out of a job!"

Kenji smirked. "The UI's precision lets us adjust the settings in real time. We can modify the Zone to adapt to nearly any condition."

"Think of the applications," Joshua added, his eyes gleaming. "Underwater exploration, disaster relief, space travel..."

Fronz grinned. "The potential is immense, but we have to be methodical. This technology could reshape the world—but only if we wield it with care."

The team watched in awe as Kenji deactivated the field, sending the suspended droplets cascading to the ground.

"The Alpha isn't just breaking new ground—it's rewriting the rules," Flynn declared.

They stood together, bound by the weight of their discovery. The Zone wasn't just an advancement; it was a force that demanded responsibility, a power that could redefine the future.

Testing Limits

A secure section of the workshop was designated for a firearms test, with meticulous safety measures in place. A target stood inside the Zone, which had been activated around it. Fronz, Flynn, Joshua, and Kenji observed from behind protective glass.

Joshua double-checked the safety equipment. "If we're considering all possible applications of the Zone, we need to know if it can stop a bullet. Understanding its limitations is critical."

"Agreed, but safety comes first." Fronz reviewed his clipboard. "We're in uncharted territory here."

"Let's see if our high-tech bubble can double as a bulletproof vest," Flynn remarked.

Kenji, shifting nervously, added, "Remember, we're testing the Zone, not our luck."

Joshua, an experienced marksman from his military days, steadied his AR-15. He took careful aim at the target within the Zone.

Kenji activated Environmental Mode, sealing off air and water. Joshua fired. The bullet struck the Zone's barrier and deflected harmlessly. Next, they tested with a water spray, using a tank positioned below—the water rolled off the Zone and collected in the tank.

Kenji then switched Environmental Mode to OFF, allowing air and water through. Joshua fired again. This time, the bullet penetrated the Zone, its speed visibly reduced on the high-speed camera, but it didn't stop—it still struck the target.

"In OFF mode, it's not bulletproof," Flynn observed. "But did you see that? It slowed down."

"Intriguing," Fronz said. "The Zone altered the bullet's velocity, but it doesn't have the strength to stop it completely. It's a matter of density and kinetic energy."

"So, even though Environmental OFF mode can't stop a bullet outright, it can still reduce its impact. That's significant," Joshua noted.

"It's about fine-tuning the Zone's properties. Maybe if we adjust the frequency..." Kenji mused.

Fronz considered this. "Perhaps. But this is a complex interaction of physics. It's not just about frequency—it's the fundamental nature of the Zone itself. The formula on the whiteboard had two variables, so that's what it was referring to."

Flynn crossed his arms. "So, our bubble has limits. Two distinct modes."

"Agreed. Two very different modes, depending on the situation," Joshua observed.

Fronz remained deep in thought, his gaze fixed on the target inside the Zone. "This test raises more questions than answers. We need to understand the fundamental principles that govern the Zone. There's still so much to uncover."

"And we'll keep testing, keep pushing the boundaries," Kenji said. "That's how breakthroughs happen."

Reflecting on Tesla's wisdom

The workshop was quiet, a contemplative air settling over the team as they gathered around a workbench. The Alpha engine hummed softly in the background. Fronz stood before a whiteboard filled with equations and notes, his brow furrowed in thought.

"Tesla once said, 'If you want to find the secrets of the universe, think in terms of energy, frequency, and vibration.' Our recent tests with the Zone… they bring me back to this fundamental idea," he mused.

Flynn grinned. "Good old Tesla, always ahead of his time. So, you think we're missing something in those terms? Oh, and let's be honest—Tesla was definitely an alien."

"Precisely," Fronz replied. "We've focused too much on the Zone's physical properties, but maybe we need to go deeper—into its vibrational aspects. Tesla was light-years ahead of his time, and now? The world only cares about money. Sounds like an alien to me."

"Sounds like we're veering from science into philosophy," Joshua remarked.

"It's more than philosophy," Kenji countered. "It's the foundation of quantum mechanics. Everything is energy, and energy is vibration."

Fronz's eyes lit up. "Kenji's right. Our approach has been too… linear. We need to examine how different frequencies interact within the Zone—how they shape its properties. I think we've barely scratched the surface. Most of it is in the math on the whiteboard."

"So, we've been playing the notes but not listening to the music," Flynn mused.

"That's a poetic way to put it," Joshua admitted. "But how do we actually 'listen' to the Zone?"

"We modify our experiments," Fronz said. "We analyze the effects of varying frequencies and vibrations, not just on physical objects but on the Zone itself."

Kenji nodded. "That means refining the UI to control these aspects with greater precision."

"Exactly. We need to create a symphony of frequencies," Fronz said. "Only then can we truly understand and harness the full potential of the Zone."

"Tesla would be proud," Flynn remarked. "We're not just pushing boundaries; we're harmonizing with the universe's song."

Joshua smirked. "Let's make sure it's a melody we can dance to, not one that trips us up."

Fronz turned back to the whiteboard, his hand hovering over the equations, poised to redefine the laws of their scientific pursuit with Tesla's timeless genius guiding them.

Quantum in time

Fronz stood motionless before the whiteboard, his gaze fixed on the newly corrected equations sprawled across its surface. What had once been a jumble of disjointed notations now formed a seamless, unnervingly precise structure. These weren't just corrections—they were insights, revelations that extended far beyond the mathematics itself.

His fingertips hovered over the final sequence, tracing the path from quantum fields to Beta's core mechanics. A slow, contemplative smile crept onto his face.

"Time..." Fronz murmured, his voice barely audible over the low hum of Beta's dormant engine. "It's never been linear. At least, not in the way we like to believe."

Leaning in the doorway, arms crossed, Flynn arched an eyebrow. "You're saying time isn't a straight path?"

Fronz chuckled, but there was a weight to it. "No, Flynn. We perceive time as a sequence—past, present, future—but that's just a limitation of human consciousness. Quantum particles don't follow those rules. They exist in multiple states at once. In theory, past, present, and future all coexist. We're just... tuned to one frequency at a time."

Flynn frowned, mulling over the implications. "So what happens when Beta tunes into another frequency?"

Fronz's expression darkened slightly. "That's where things get complicated. There are two leading theories. One suggests that if we manipulate quantum resonance, we interact with our own timeline—our own past. Every change we make would ripple forward into our future—this future."

He tapped the equation with a finger. "Beta Mk 1.0 operates under that assumption—time as a singular thread. It simplifies the field equations, avoiding the need to account for parallel outcomes or branching realities. Clean. Direct. Dangerous."

Flynn's gaze sharpened. "And the other theory?"

Fronz sighed, leaning against the desk. "The multiverse. Every decision creates a new branch, a new reality. Infinite timelines layered on top of each other. If Beta taps into another dimension or universe, then we aren't observing our past—we're intruding on another version of reality. Their world, not ours."

Flynn absorbed the idea in silence.

"But..." Fronz continued, his voice steady, "this equation suggests otherwise. This timeline—our timeline—is the only one where Beta functions. The design, the failures, the breakthroughs—they all had to happen exactly as they did. There's no branching path here, Flynn. No alternate versions of us. Just this."

He paused, locking eyes with Flynn. "That assumption makes the math simpler. More stable. Less guesswork. Beta doesn't need to account for infinite outcomes—just one. It only needs to reach back to this past. The one that already happened."

Flynn exhaled slowly. “So when we view time, we’re viewing ours.”

Fronz nodded. “Exactly. Our timeline. We don’t want to see what happens if the Allies don’t win WWII.”

“Yeah, let’s skip that universe. Please and thanks,” Flynn said.

“Cheers.” Fronz grinned.

Fronz’s culinary showcase

The team gathered in a cozy, well-equipped kitchen adjacent to the workshop, settling around a large dining table. Their work was set aside for a well-earned moment of respite. Fronz, clad in a chef’s apron, moved effortlessly around the kitchen—an unexpected contrast to his usual scientific demeanor.

With a theatrical flourish, Fronz grinned. “Gentlemen, allow me to introduce you to another passion of mine—the art of cooking. Science isn't my only forte.”

Flynn inhaled deeply, savoring the rich aroma. “If your cooking is half as good as your science, we’re in for a treat.”

Joshua smirked. “Never pegged you for the chef type, Fronz. So, what’s on the menu?”

Fronz unveiled each dish with a touch of showmanship, the air thick with the scent of herbs and spices. "We have a garlic-and-herb-crusted rack of lamb, roasted to perfection, served alongside a medley of seasonal vegetables, lightly sautéed with olive oil and sea salt."

Kenji raised an impressed brow. "This looks incredible. I had no idea you could cook like this."

With a final reveal, Fronz gestured toward a beautifully arranged platter of seared scallops, each piece glistening with a golden crust. "And for the pièce de résistance—seared scallops with a citrus beurre blanc. Simple, yet elegant."

The team exchanged wide-eyed glances, anticipation thick in the air. As they took their first bites, satisfaction settled over them, their expressions speaking louder than words.

"This is amazing, Fronz!" Flynn said between bites, washing it down with a satisfied sigh. "Who knew science and cooking had so much in common?"

Joshua nodded. "Precision, timing, and a little bit of flair—works in both the lab and the kitchen."

Fronz chuckled. "Cooking is just chemistry with better-tasting results."

Kenji grinned. "Well, your 'chemistry' is delicious. It's nice seeing this side of you."

The room filled with laughter and the comforting sounds of contented dining. For a brief moment, their demanding scientific endeavors faded, replaced by the simple joy of a shared meal.

CHAPTER ELEVEN

BETA AND ALPHA

As the team delved deeper into the Beta engine's capabilities, their initial disappointment swiftly gave way to astonishment. At first, Beta's performance paled in comparison to Alpha's gravity-defying feats.

Kenji rubbed the sleep from his eyes as he stumbled into the lab at sunrise, the soft hum of the equipment a familiar comfort in the quiet morning. Weeks of late nights had left him running on fumes, his mind consumed by endless tweaks to the Beta engine's settings. But something instantly caught his attention.

The second whiteboard—once cluttered with half-erased equations and scattered notes—now displayed a new symbol and an intricate mathematical formula. Kenji stiffened. That wasn't there before.

The first whiteboard had already been set aside, its contents recorded, digitized, and archived. Even the black marker had been sealed for future analysis.

His pulse quickened. He stepped closer, scanning the formula's elegant complexity. Unlike the previous equations they'd cracked for Alpha, this one wove together electromagnetic frequencies and time-based variables with uncanny precision.

He didn't hesitate. Kenji spun on his heel and sprinted down the hall to Fronz's quarters, pounding on the door until a groggy voice stirred from within.

"What's the emergency?" Fronz muttered, cracking the door open, his robe disheveled.

"You have to see this," Kenji said, breathless. He grabbed Fronz's arm, urgency tightening his grip. "Another equation. Another symbol. But this time—it's about Beta."

Fronz, now fully awake, trailed Kenji back to the lab. The moment his eyes landed on the board, his fatigue dissolved. His gaze sharpened as he scanned the newly inscribed symbols and equations.

"I need coffee—stat," Fronz muttered, already processing the data.

His fingers traced the formula, eyes narrowing. "This… this is brilliant," he breathed. "I've never seen this type of calibration before. It's almost like it's using the electromagnetic field to modulate time itself."

Booting up his laptop, Fronz nodded. "That's what I thought. But it's more than just modulation. If I'm reading this correctly, Beta isn't just generating an electromagnetic field—it's forming some kind of time-viewing portal."

Kenji snapped his head toward Fronz, eyes widening. "A time-viewing portal? Are you saying it's a window into time?"

"Not for physical travel—there are no equations accounting for mass—but yes," Fronz confirmed, his fingers flying across the keyboard. "It looks like we can observe the past in real time—both visual and audio feeds. Imagine the implications. We could witness historical events exactly as they happened."

A thrill sparked in Fronz's eyes as he turned to Kenji. "Do you understand what this means? We're not just manipulating energy anymore. This could redefine history itself—something that's baffled me for years."

Kenji's grin widened. "I've already started reprogramming the Beta interface. We can run a preliminary test in a few hours. Maybe. There's a lot here. You need to dive into this, Fronz."

Fronz clapped Kenji on the shoulder, his eyes gleaming with newfound energy. "Let's wake the others. Flynn and Joshua need to see this. If this works, we'll be able to peer into the past—finally uncover answers that have eluded humanity for centuries."

Kenji, still riding the adrenaline rush, shot Fronz a grin. "Let's do it. I'll get the system prepped. I've always wanted to know the true age of the Sphinx."

As the team gathered in the lab, anticipation thickened the air. They stood on the brink of a breakthrough—not just in energy, but in the very fabric of time itself.

The room remained dimly lit, the soft glow from the control panels casting elongated shadows. Kenji adjusted the newly integrated Beta UI, his expression focused. Flynn and Fronz hovered behind him, their gazes locked onto the interface. The steady hum of the machinery resonated through the lab, a rhythmic pulse beneath the weight of the moment. Kenji's fingers danced over the keyboard, each keystroke bringing them closer to discovery. Beta had been infused with Sotra's new formula—now, it was time to see if theory would meet reality.

"Alright, here goes nothing," Kenji muttered, his voice steady despite the tension coiling in the room. He tapped in the final commands and flipped the switch. The monitors flickered briefly before the screen flared to life. The updated UI, now distinct from Alpha's control interface, flooded with diagnostic readouts. A status bar surged forward, indicating Beta's systems were fully coming online.

The lab lights flickered as the power draw surged, the engine thrumming with a low, resonant hum. Fronz's gaze snapped to the status monitor, noting the sharp spike in Beta's power consumption.

"We're pulling a lot more power than usual," he remarked, his tone measured but wary.

Kenji glanced at the display and nodded. "Yeah, but Beta's engine can handle it," he said. "No red flags—we're still well within operational limits, with plenty to spare."

Taking a steadying breath, he toggled the Window Mode switch. For a moment, nothing happened. Then, a shimmering window materialized at the lab's center, hovering in midair like a projection. At first, the screen swirled with hazy, shifting colors before resolving into a sharp image—a memory of Beta's creation.

They watched as schematics and fragments of blueprints flashed by, followed by glimpses of the assembly process and initial tests. The scene unfolded like a holographic film, detailed and vivid.

"That's... Beta's birth," Flynn murmured, his eyes wide with awe. It was as if they were gazing through a portal into the past.

Kenji's fingers moved over the controls, adjusting the time dial. "Let's push further," he said, his focus sharpening. The images accelerated, moments blurring past in rapid succession. The lab fell silent, save for the soft hum of the engine, as Beta's window revealed history in motion.

Kenji slowed the feed, letting the shimmering window stabilize. The image sharpened into a familiar scene—sunlight glinting off water. Flynn's stomach clenched. The boating accident played out before them in stark clarity: frantic splashing, fire licking across shattered boats, faces twisted in panic, all frozen in time.

Flynn's knuckles whitened as he gripped the console's edge. "There it is," he whispered. "We're actually… seeing it?"

But Kenji wasn't finished. He turned the dial once more, pushing the window further back in time. The scene shifted—the water vanished, replaced by the flickering glow of old gas lamps and the lively bustle of streets from an era long past. They were diving deeper into history, witnessing moments unseen by human eyes for decades, perhaps even centuries.

"Unbelievable," Fronz whispered, shaking his head in amazement. The power draw remained steady, and the Beta engine hummed effortlessly, as if it had been designed for this all along.

Kenji turned back to the others, his face flushed with excitement. "We've barely begun," he said, his voice brimming with both pride and wonder. "If this works... there's no telling how far back we can go."

Flynn and Fronz exchanged a glance, both grasping the gravity of what they were witnessing. The past was no longer an abstract concept—it was within their reach, ready to be explored.

Gathered around Beta, the team watched in awe as the pyramids of Giza appeared before them, the Sphinx looking vastly different from its modern form. They had traveled over 15,000 years into the past—before the Ice Age, when Egypt was lush and fertile, long before the civilization known as ancient Egypt or Kemet.

"These wonders are far older than we ever imagined, gentlemen," Kenji remarked.

Thanks to the GPS coordinates Kenji had integrated into the system, the viewing window wasn't bound to a single location—it could move freely across the globe.

Beta revealed pyramids scattered across the globe, from Japan and Iraq to the USA and India—over two hundred in total. Even grander structures lay hidden beneath Brazil's dense jungles, Antarctica's icy wastelands, and on the Moon and Mars. The Vatican's vast archives held not only priceless artifacts and lost historical knowledge but also an immense stockpile of gold.

The team marveled at the intricate planning and execution of these ancient wonders, shattering long-held theories about their construction.

"Unbelievable," Flynn muttered, his voice tinged with awe.

The feed fast-forwarded, unraveling the enigma of JFK's assassination. Before their eyes, a web of deceit and power plays unfolded, exposing the true forces behind that fateful day in Dallas, 1963.

"Well, that's just great," Flynn said with heavy sarcasm. "Now we know who killed JFK and why. Fantastic."

No one laughed. It wasn't funny.

As they delved deeper, more veils lifted, revealing the unsettling truths of modern times. They uncovered the depths of political corruption, the hidden workings of a deep state, and the manipulation of the masses. What had once been dismissed as mere conspiracy theories—the globalist agenda—stood exposed, confirming their worst fears about the direction certain factions sought to steer humanity.

The ancient site of Göbekli Tepe, over 14,000 years old, was shown to have origins far more mysterious than current archaeology could explain. Most strikingly, evidence revealed that it had been intentionally buried.

But perhaps the most shocking revelation came when Beta's time window confirmed the existence of extraterrestrial life. It displayed various species, one of which was tall, white-skinned, and human-like, with long white hair. The evidence was undeniable—alien visitations were real, no longer the stuff of dismissed myths and speculation.

Amid these revelations, Fronz conceived a groundbreaking theory: if Beta could observe the past, could it, with the right modifications, enable actual physical time travel? This hypothesis electrified the team, igniting both excitement and a sobering awareness of the dangers such knowledge carried. The implications of their discoveries were staggering, placing them as guardians of a secret capable of upending the very foundations of society.

Recognizing the gravity of their situation, the team took immediate precautions. Every handwritten note was consigned to flames, reducing their secrets to ash. Digital records—repositories of world-altering knowledge—were encrypted and locked away within their impenetrable data fortresses.

In the hushed aftermath of their discoveries, they wrestled with the weight of their findings. Beta, once dismissed as Alpha's lesser counterpart, now held the potential to reshape humanity's understanding of time, history, and the universe itself. The path ahead was riddled with peril, yet the temptation to unlock time's secrets was an irresistible siren call—one they could neither ignore nor resist.

Alpha and Beta, in their fully operational state, were never meant to be unveiled within the constraints of the grant-funded project. Following recalibration, the engines were placed side by side. A low hum filled the air, and an electric charge rippled through the team, causing the hairs on their arms to stand on end like static electricity. Standing there for just a few minutes left them energized, as if infused with a surge of vitality. But before they could touch anything—or anyone—they had to ground themselves.

Fronz, captivated by the phenomenon, spent hours near both machines, meticulously taking readings and reveling in the tingling sensation that danced across his skin. He felt invigorated, as though the energy coursing through the room somehow rejuvenated him. Day after day, he returned, aware that the two engines might eventually be separated—but unable to stay away.

Over time, Fronz felt significantly better—both physically and mentally. He moved forward with renewed vigor.

Alpha - Think tank time

The afternoon sun streamed through the hangar windows, casting a warm glow over Flynn's Corsair. Its sleek vintage frame gleamed against the industrial backdrop of tools and machinery. The plane's timeless design stood as a testament to an era of raw mechanical ingenuity, now poised to merge with cutting-edge technology. The air hummed with a mix of excitement and unease as the team gathered around, the faint scent of oil and heated metal anchoring them to the task ahead.

Flynn planted his hands on his hips, a skeptical grin tugging at his lips. "Strapping Alpha to my Corsair? Are you guys high? We just got her flying right, and now you want to tear her apart?"

Joshua chuckled but remained focused, stepping closer to the plane. "Hear me out, Flynn. We've tested Alpha in simulations and on smaller setups. But the next step has to be in the air. Your Corsair is the perfect candidate—powerful, maneuverable, and we already have the flight data baseline. And if something does go wrong, you're the best damn pilot to handle it."

Flynn's eyebrow arched as he glanced at the others. Fronz, leaning casually against the wing, spoke with measured certainty. "Joshua's right. But we need to be strategic. The Corsair wasn't built for the kind of output Alpha might generate—especially not supersonic speeds. We have to assess her structure thoroughly—wings, rudder, frame—everything. If the Alpha engine enhances performance, we need to be sure she can handle it."

Kurt, Flynn's navy pilot friend, stood with arms crossed, studying the Corsair intently. "Fronz has a point. She's a thoroughbred, but push her too hard, and you risk catastrophic failure. We need to reinforce the wings, rudder, and elevators to withstand the strain of high-G maneuvers."

Flynn exhaled, his gaze shifting to the Corsair, a mix of pride and unease in his expression. "Fine. But if this ruins her, I'm holding every one of you personally responsible."

With that, the team sprang into action. Step one: a meticulous inspection of the aircraft. Flynn and Joshua scrutinized the wings and rudder for stress fractures, marking potential reinforcement points. Kurt, structural integrity scanner in hand, methodically examined the airframe, running calculations to assess load distribution under extreme conditions. Meanwhile, Kenji pulled up schematics, integrating the Alpha engine's control system into a secondary interface to prevent interference with the Corsair's avionics.

"Alpha's power draw is no joke," Kenji muttered, fingers flying over his keyboard. "We'll need to boost the cold fusion reaction slightly to support the Corsair's mass. But I think it's manageable. If this thing can power ten city blocks in peak summer, it should handle this. Fronz, what do you think of this parameter? I can tweak it and lock it for the Corsair only."

Fronz examined the update and nodded. "I think we're well within Alpha's capabilities. Let's do this."

Joshua adjusted the sensors and added, "We'll also need additional accelerometers and torque sensors. Alpha's going to push this plane harder than ever before, and we need real-time data to fine-tune the output."

Flynn eyed the growing pile of modifications, rubbing his temples. "You're turning my Corsair into a Frankenstein project."

"You'll thank us when you're pulling tighter turns than this bird's ever handled," Joshua shot back with a grin.

He continued, "We'll need a few parts for the upgrades. I just rush-ordered structural reinforcements, instrument upgrades, intake valve replacements, and a few other smaller components. They'll take a few days to arrive and install. In the meantime, I've prepped everything for a quick turnaround once they get here. While we wait, we can test the other side of the coin. Environmental mode—just add water. That should be fun."

Fronz stood slightly apart from the group, his focus locked on the tablet displaying the Corsair's live system data. While the others got caught up in the excitement, he remained the quiet observer, monitoring every fluctuation, spike, and drop. He had deliberately stepped back from hands-on flying, mechanics, and software—his strength was here, analyzing, ensuring that the technology he'd spent years perfecting performed exactly as intended.

CHAPTER TWELVE

THE YAMATO'S DESCENT

The California sun blazed high in the sky, casting a golden shimmer over the calm waters as Team Nautilus prepared for the most ambitious phase of their project yet. Today was different. The stakes were higher. Months of meticulous planning, late-night brainstorming, and endless technical refinements had all led to this defining moment.

The pier buzzed with energy. The crisp scent of saltwater mixed with the distant cries of seagulls as team members hurried about, setting up control panels, laptops, and monitors on folding tables. Cables sprawled across the wooden planks, linking an array of equipment designed to track their underwater experiment.

At the edge of the dock, Kenji's meticulously crafted three-foot model of the legendary battleship Yamato gleamed in the sunlight, its miniature turrets polished to perfection. A blue-green laser, mounted atop the ship, would act as a beacon during its descent, while a floating receiver ensured precise 3D tracking.

Kenji, usually composed, radiated a rare, electric anticipation. He double-checked the custom mount beneath the Yamato, his fingers steady yet charged with nervous energy as he secured the Alpha engine one last time.

"Mounting bracket is solid. Laser mount is set. We're good to go!" Kenji announced, his voice betraying a hint of excitement. "Let's roll."

Flynn stood at the water's edge, his pulse quickening as Kenji carefully lowered the model into the sea. The Alpha engine, no larger than a football, thrummed softly beneath the hull—a striking contrast to the historical relic it now propelled. Today marked the moment when Flynn's passion for the ocean and his love of invention finally converged, culminating in this extraordinary test.

Kenji hunched over the control panel, his fingers working with practiced precision. He adjusted dials and toggled switches, his gaze fixed on the shimmering zone bubble—a protective field designed to shield the model from the crushing ocean pressure. "Environmental mode is active," he announced. The energy field shimmered around the Yamato, an invisible barrier stabilizing the internal conditions.

Flynn rested a reassuring hand on Kenji's shoulder, keeping his tone light. "Just another test, right?" He forced a casual grin, though his fingers tightened against Kenji's shirt, betraying his nerves.

Kenji turned, flashing a knowing smirk. "Sure, just another test. You positive? Because you look like you're about to pass out."

Flynn let out a laugh—shaky but genuine. "Hey, it's not every day you strap a quantum engine to a scale-model battleship and send it plunging into the ocean."

The rest of the team clustered around the monitors, their focus locked on the screens. Joshua fine-tuned the high-definition cameras, adjusting the angles to capture every detail of the Yamato's descent. "Cameras are rolling, lights are good," she called out. Nearby, another team member confirmed the GoPros were recording. "We're all set. This is going to be incredible to watch later."

Flynn inhaled deeply, the salty breeze grounding him. He met Kenji's gaze and gave a firm nod. "We've got the green light. Let's take her down."

Kenji's fingers danced over the controls, and the Yamato stirred to life. The Alpha engine's quantum field enveloped the vessel in a faint, shimmering glow as it glided effortlessly across the water. The mounted cameras cast beams of light into the darkening depths, illuminating its descent beneath the surface.

"Bubble is holding stable," Kenji reported, his eyes locked on the screen. "Environmental mode is compensating perfectly. Depth at five feet… ten… twenty… thirty…"

"Looks like a shark—elegant and deadly," Flynn remarked with a grin. "But let's keep her steady, folks."

As the Yamato descended, its lights sliced through the blue-green murk, revealing the unseen world below. The team watched in quiet awe as Kenji's voice crackled over the intercom. "Passing 300 feet. We're hitting another pressure layer, but the zone field is holding."

"Good, good," Flynn murmured. "Let's maneuver and capture some strong angles for the cameras. Who knows what kind of treasures might be resting on the ocean floor?"

Kenji gave a quick nod, keeping his focus on the readings. The model pressed onward, the Alpha engine humming with steady precision. "We're at 600 feet now, three miles out from the pier."

Flynn's pulse quickened, a mixture of pride and unease settling in his chest. "Alright, let's bring her back up—slow and steady. We've confirmed the field's integrity. No need to push our luck."

Kenji, his grin unwavering, adjusted the controls. The Yamato responded smoothly, beginning its slow ascent.

Breaking through the surface with quiet grace, the zone bubble ensured not a single ripple disturbed the water. A cheer erupted from the team as Kenji expertly guided the model back to the dock.

"We did it," Flynn whispered, his words nearly lost in the swell of celebration. His eyes gleamed with satisfaction as he watched Kenji shut down the engine. The test had been flawless.

Fronz, who had been observing in silence, stepped forward at last. Admiration flickered in his expression. "I had little doubt the Alpha engine would work, but seeing it in action... Well done, all of you."

Flynn spoke up, "I think we need to take it a step further—with more mass and Environmental Mode activated. We need real-world measurements to assess Alpha's power and efficiency under heavier loads."

He turned to Fronz with a grin. "With that in mind, how about converting your old boat into a U-boat for the next test?"

Fronz's eyes gleamed with excitement. "As long as we're confident in the safety of everyone aboard. It'll take all of us to prepare for this journey, but I'm in."

"Let's review the footage and go from there," Flynn suggested, his mind already racing with plans for their next venture.

"Good plan, Captain," Fronz said with a chuckle.

The team gathered around the monitors to review the footage. The screens displayed the eerie beauty of the ocean depths as the model glided through the water, light refracting in shimmering beams. Schools of fish darted around the zone bubble, drawn to the strange, glowing object in their midst. The breathtaking shots of the Yamato plunging deeper showed the quantum field holding steady, even as the ocean pressure mounted. Environmental Mode functioned flawlessly, shielding the delicate model throughout the excursion.

The cheers faded into hushed awe as the team watched the Yamato glide effortlessly through the underwater world, tiny fish trailing alongside it like an escort.

The sun dipped toward the horizon, casting hues of pink and orange across the sky—a breathtaking backdrop to their triumph. As the celebration waned, the team gathered around the resurfaced model, their spirits lifted by the success of the test.

"This is just the beginning," Flynn said, his voice firm with determination. "Today was small-scale. Next, we take this technology to Fronz's boat. Full-scale trials. Deep sea."

"I'll monitor the power settings the software determines and make sure everything runs smoothly," Kenji assured him.

"Yes, please—no flooding drills. For obvious reasons," Flynn quipped.

"Aye-aye, Captain," Joshua said with a smirk, leaning in like a seasoned marine.

The team exchanged nods, their eyes gleaming with the thrill of what lay ahead. As darkness settled over the water, Flynn felt a deep sense of satisfaction. Today had been a success, but it was only the first step. The real journey was just beginning.

Submariner story

The sun dipped toward the horizon, casting a golden glow over the pier as Team Nautilus wrapped up another day of testing the Alpha engine. The air buzzed with laughter and lingering adrenaline, the crew still riding the high of their latest success. Near the hangar, they had set up a fire pit—a makeshift retreat where they could unwind after long hours of high-stakes experimentation. But tonight, the usual lighthearted banter gave way to something else.

Seated in a folding chair, Flynn took a slow pull from his flask, wiped his mouth with the back of his hand, and let his gaze linger on the flickering flames. For once, he felt like talking. His team had been nudging him for stories—real stories from his Navy days. Normally, he kept those memories close to his chest. But tonight, something in the air made him want to share.

Joshua grinned. "Yo-ho, sailor. Tell us about those dolphins on your chest."

Flynn smirked, leaning forward. "All right, all right." His voice took on that gruff storytelling tone, the kind that signaled a good tale was coming. "You want to know what it really takes to earn these?"

The group leaned in, the crackling fire the only sound as they waited. Flynn smiled and began his story.

“You see,” he started, “qualifying on a submarine isn’t just about memorizing systems from a manual. It’s a rite of passage—a test to see if you can handle the pressure. Not just the depths, but the weight of being part of a brotherhood. It starts the moment you step onboard. Day one, you’re handed a qualification card. Think of it as a roadmap, except the journey feels like an impossible task meant to last a lifetime. At least, that’s what it felt like on day one.”

A few chuckles rippled through the group, but Flynn's face remained serious. "They assign you a 'sea dad'—though I don't recall having one. Never mind that. He's a qualified crew member, usually a salty, no-nonsense guy whose job is to teach you everything you need to know. Your guide, your mentor, and your worst nightmare all rolled into one. That qualification card lists every system on that sub you have to master—navigation, sonar, torpedoes, high- and low-pressure air, hydraulics, nuclear reactor, diesel engines. You name it."

He paused, letting the weight of it sink in. "Over seventy checkouts. Each one requires a signature from the expert who runs that system. But here's the catch—no one signs off unless you prove yourself. And I don't mean just cramming from a manual. You have to know it, live it, breathe it. Hell, you'll be expected to draw entire systems from memory, identify every valve and relay, explain the trim and drain functions, emergency blow procedures—even the damn flushing water system."

The group was riveted now, leaning in as Flynn continued, his voice low and intense. "Let me tell you, it wasn't easy. You'd finish a six-hour watch shift, bone-tired, and instead of crashing like everyone else, you were expected to study—tracing systems, memorizing procedures. I'd hit my bunk with pages of technical drawings swimming in my head. And if you ever fell behind on signatures, they'd call you a 'dink'—

delinquent in quals. That's when things got really tough. I managed to stay off that list. Kept my mind sharp, stayed on task."

Joshua raised an eyebrow. "So what happens if you fall behind? They just give you more study time?"

Flynn let out a rough laugh, the kind that carried the weight of old memories. "If only. No, they throw you into supervised study sessions. You muster up with your sea dad—two extra hours every day until you catch up. And trust me, your sea dad doesn't enjoy that any more than you do. So, yeah, the pressure's on."

"I've heard some sailors take nine to twelve months to qualify. It took me three and a half months of grinding. Mostly because I only had 'cranking' duty for a month. That's where you're stuck working as cheap labor on the mess deck. A real shit job," Flynn said.

Kenji, who had been quiet until now, finally spoke. "What was the toughest part for you, Flynn?"

Flynn leaned forward, his gaze sharp. "The final board," he murmured. "Once you've got that card filled out, it's time to face the Qualification Board. That's when they lock you in a room with a submarine-qualified officer, a chief, and a couple of senior enlisted men. Six hours of them drilling you, tearing into every system you've supposedly mastered. They make you draw systems on a whiteboard, defend every answer while they try to catch you off guard."

"I remember one particular question vividly—one I actually knew the answer to," Flynn began. "Seaman Cavalla, explain the following: picture a bird flying over the snorkel mast, cuts a fart, the mast draws it in—explain how that powers your bunk light." He chuckled before adding, "I don't recall the exact answer at this moment, but I do remember the officer who asked it. He only had one follow-up question, and I nailed that one too."

He took another sip from his flask, the firelight reflecting in his eyes. "Facing that board was one of the most nerve-wracking experiences of my life. It wasn't just about what you knew—it was about how you handled the pressure, how you responded when your back was against the wall. There were moments when I had to dig deep, pull answers out of thin air. And let me tell you, there were a few things I completely blanked on."

"Wait," Joshua cut in. "You? You forgot something?" With his usual Marine humor and just as much liquor in him as Flynn, he added, "What—no crayon questions?"

Flynn laughed, this time with a softer edge. "Nope, no crayons this time. After hours of being grilled, I got a list of three questions I didn't quite nail. But instead of waiting for them to finish their meeting and decide my fate, I went straight to the books, found the answers, wrote them up, and slipped the paper under the door while they were still talking." He shook his head, a grin spreading across his face. "They were pissed—but they passed me. Even said they were impressed with my attention to detail, my delivery, and my confidence. That's the kind of stubbornness you need to survive down there."

The team laughed, but they could hear the pride in Flynn's voice. This wasn't just a story—it was a piece of his soul.

"Then, when you finally pass," he continued, his tone turning reverent, "there's the ceremony. The captain pins those dolphins on your chest—the symbol that you're one of the crew now. But it doesn't end there. No, that's when the hazing begins. They leave the backs on, then everyone lines up to tack them into your chest. Hit you hard enough, and it'll draw blood."

"Sounds brutal," Kenji muttered.

A reflective smile crossed Flynn's face as he finished his tale, his youthful dreams now tempered by the hard-won reality of his years beneath the ocean's depths. He had earned the Meritorious Unit Citation for his service on the Devil Boat during a high-risk Spec Op. Later, aboard the USS Annapolis, he received the Navy Achievement Medal after acing an unexpected, in-depth inspection.

"I might not have reached the skies like I once hoped," Flynn admitted, "but diving into the depths with the best crew in the world? That was an honor I wouldn't trade for anything."

In that moment, the team didn't just understand the significance of Submariners' Dolphins—they gained a deeper appreciation for the man who had earned them. It was a story of perseverance, of adapting to the hand one is dealt, and of finding one's calling in the most unexpected places.

Through this recounting, Flynn's submariner experience was laid bare—a narrative steeped in naval tradition, the rigors of training, and the unbreakable bonds forged in the silent world beneath the waves. It was a tribute to those who dared to venture where few had gone, to the depths of the ocean and the limits of their own resilience.

"Oo-rah, brother! I knew you were a crazy badass sailor for volunteering for that, but man, I didn't know the half of it," Joshua said, shaking his head. "It's official—you're fruity as a nutcake! Salute, brother."

They exchanged salutes before pulling each other into a brotherly hug.

Kenji laughed out loud, muttered something in Japanese that no one understood, then grinned. "That's just unreal. You could write a book."

Flynn smirked. "Yeah, but who'd read it?"

The whole team chimed in at once. "I would!"

The fire crackled as the team fell into silence, absorbing the intensity of Flynn's experiences. He leaned back in his chair, letting his gaze sweep across them.

"You know," he said softly, "that's why we push so hard here. Why we set the bar so high. Because whether we're on a sub 800 feet below the surface or right here, testing this new tech, it's about being the best—about knowing that when the pressure's on, we won't crack."

A fresh determination flickered in their eyes. Flynn's story wasn't just about submarines—it was about pushing limits, about camaraderie, about the relentless pursuit of excellence.

As they sat around the fire, the California night deepening around them, they knew they weren't just developing a revolutionary piece of technology. They were becoming something greater.

DIVE DIVE

As the team gathered on Fronz's 42-foot yacht, it bobbed gently on the sparkling waves, miles from the nearest shore. The warm afternoon sun bathed the deck in a golden glow, while the occasional cry of a distant seabird punctuated the serene rhythm of the sea. His yacht, a sturdy and reliable vessel, had become a floating haven for Team Nautilus as they prepared for their next great venture.

Laughter mingled with the salty breeze as the team assembled on deck, their camaraderie evident in every jest and grin. Flynn stood at the helm, his posture relaxed but his expression carrying the unmistakable pride of a seasoned submariner. The sea was his domain, his sanctuary, and today, it would serve as the gateway to an unprecedented journey into the depths.

"Alright, crew," Flynn called out, his voice laced with authority, sounding every bit like a seasoned captain. "This isn't just a day at the beach. Prepare to dive the boat."

Kenji and Joshua exchanged a knowing glance, their excitement barely contained, while Fronz leaned against the rail with a small, knowing smile. The hum of the ocean surrounded them as the team stood ready, anticipation crackling in the air like the charge before a coming storm.

Joshua adjusted the blue-green laser mounted on the mast, ensuring it was properly aligned for navigation and depth tracking. The team would be able to monitor their location and depth readouts on one of Kenji's screens. Meanwhile, the buoy with the laser receiver was moved to the stern, primed for deployment just before the dive.

"Alright, team, this is it—the day we transform a humble boat into a vessel worthy of Neptune himself. Let's get this beauty ready for her maiden voyage beneath the waves," Flynn said with a grin.

The deck buzzed with activity as O_2 bottles, portable CO_2 scrubbers, and an array of bright LED lights were methodically secured onboard. Strategically mounted GoPros stood ready to capture every angle of the impending underwater spectacle. Two monitors were wired up to provide a live feed of the historic endeavor.

Flynn and Joshua double-checked the mechanical modifications.

"Looks like we're set to engage the O_2 bottles and scrubbers just before we enter the zone," Flynn said.

Kenji, monitoring his interface, flashed a confident smile. "All electronic systems are green. This one's going in the record books, folks. Make sure those cameras are rolling!"

Flynn strapped a GoPro to his headband for a personal recording.

Fronz, ever the provider, ensured their aquatic expedition was well-stocked. An assortment of good food and fresh water was laid out neatly on a side table, adding a touch of warmth to the charged atmosphere.

"We might be venturing into the unknown, but that's no reason to do so on an empty stomach," Fronz said with a chuckle. "Let's make this adventure a feast for the senses."

With preparations complete, Flynn gave a nod, and Kenji initiated the activation sequence for Alpha. The low hum of the engine blended with the rhythm of the waves, signaling the start of their journey.

Flynn, the captain, took command. "Ship is underway. Heading out to sea—half a mile ahead. Kenji, fire up the engine. Time to begin this journey."

As the dive alarm blared—a signal both ominous and exhilarating—the submarine began its descent, enveloped in the protective embrace of the Alpha-generated field.

Joshua grinned. "Here we go, diving into the unknown. This beats any amusement park ride out there!"

"Dive! Dive!" Flynn called, grinning as he pressed play on his MP3 player. The nostalgic aruga, aruga echoed through the vessel, completing the proper submarine ritual.

The ocean depths welcomed them—a world where sunlight dared not venture, revealing its secrets in the artificial glow of their mounted LEDs. Ghostly shipwrecks, remnants of battles and storms past, lay in eerie silence, whispering forgotten stories of the sea. Planes, once masters of the sky, now rested on the seabed, their metal frames claimed by rust and coral.

"Look at that!" Flynn marveled. "It's like a museum down here, a graveyard of adventure and misadventure."

Marine life, undisturbed by their presence, continued its eternal dance. Schools of fish darted through the beams of light, their scales shimmering in brilliant hues. Occasionally, a curious sea creature drifted closer, as if inspecting the intruders in its domain.

"All ahead standard—14 knots. Take her to 150 feet, then we'll descend from there," Captain Flynn instructed.

"Aye-aye, Captain," Kenji acknowledged.

As they settled into the rhythm of their underwater exploration, tension gave way to awe. They were pioneers in their own right, charting a course through an alien landscape. The sunlight above faded, swallowed by the vast darkness. Only the submarine's internal lights and their moveable beams illuminated the abyss, guiding their way through the unknown.

Kenji said, "This is surreal. It feels like we've stepped into another world—one that's always been here, just waiting for us to find it."

"Alright, let's open her up. All ahead full—25 knots. Bring us down to 600 feet, nice and steady," Captain Flynn ordered.

Their mission, though rooted in science, was more than mere observation. It was a plunge into the unknown—a journey that defied their expectations and expanded their understanding of the deep.

Joshua checked the O_2 bottles, scrubbers, and instruments monitoring oxygen and carbon dioxide levels. "Just keep breathing naturally, mates," he reassured them.

Fronz said, "To think—the secrets of the deep are finally within our reach, all thanks to the ingenuity and spirit of this team. What a time to be alive."

As their exploration continued, the breathtaking beauty of the underwater realm left an indelible mark on them. It wasn't just an expedition—it was an experience that bonded them, not just as a team, but as fellow explorers navigating the uncharted.

“Right 15 degrees rudder—let’s make a slow turn to starboard,” Captain Flynn commanded. “I’ll angle one of the lights to improve visibility during the turn.”

“Aye-aye, Captain,” Kenji responded, savoring every second of the experience.

Joshua couldn’t decide whether to gaze into the vast, shadowy ocean or focus on the glowing monitors.

"Amazing, Captain. How many people in the world get to witness such sights with their own eyes?" Fronz mused.

The underwater exploration remained quiet, Alpha emitting a soft hum as it glided smoothly beneath the waves—its stability transforming the yacht into a pseudo-submarine. In the cozy galley, the air was rich with the aroma of culinary mastery. Fronz moved with practiced precision, his chef's instincts honed to perfection even within the confined space. He wore a casual apron over his usual attire, a sly smile tugging at his lips as he glanced at the clock.

"Timing, gentlemen," Fronz called out, his voice warm with confidence. "It’s everything—whether in science, combat, or cuisine. And tonight, I intend to prove it."

The team had been underwater for only an hour, their spirits high but their stomachs growling after the adventure. In the galley, Fronz worked his magic.

First came the smoked salmon crostini, each piece meticulously arranged on a wooden board. He spread a layer of herbed cream cheese over the toasted rounds of baguette before draping delicate slices of smoked salmon on top. A garnish of fresh dill and a twist of lemon zest completed the appetizer, the bright citrus aroma cutting through the richness.

"This," Fronz announced as he carried the board to the table where the team eagerly waited, "is to whet your appetite. A small reminder that even at sea, we can dine like kings."

Then, the main course took center stage. Fronz reheated the tender braised short ribs in their red wine reduction, the sauce bubbling gently as it clung to the succulent meat. He stirred the mashed potatoes, folding in a touch of cream for a velvety texture, while the buttered green beans sizzled in a pan with toasted almonds.

When the plates were ready, he arranged them with artistic precision: the short ribs nestled atop a bed of creamy mashed potatoes, green beans tucked neatly alongside, and a final drizzle of red wine sauce tying the dish together.

"Voila!" Fronz exclaimed, presenting the plates to a chorus of impressed murmurs. "A meal worthy of submariners—or scientists, for that matter."

As the team dug into their meals, savoring the rich flavors, Fronz slipped away to check on the final touch: individual chocolate lava cakes. He gently warmed the ramekins, ensuring the molten centers remained perfectly gooey, then finished them with a dollop of crème fraîche and a sprinkle of sea salt before serving.

"You didn't think I'd forget dessert, did you?" he teased, setting down the plates to a chorus of cheers.

The boat rocked gently as laughter and conversation filled the air. Fronz leaned back, his plate spotless, watching his friends relish the meal he had crafted. "Not bad for underwater dining," he said with a wink.

"Not bad?" Flynn scoffed, raising his glass. "This is Michelin-star worthy, Fronz. You've outdone yourself."

"To adventure," Fronz said, lifting his own glass, "and always returning to the table together."

The shared meal, a special request from the Captain, was more than just sustenance—it was a celebration of their journey and the unbreakable bond forged in the depths of the ocean.

Their venture beneath the waves mirrored their greater mission: a plunge into the unknown, fueled by curiosity and an unyielding drive to push the boundaries of what was possible.

Flynn announced, "I can now say I've been in a submarine with windows. It was great to share it with you. Cheers, men!"

The experience, captured on video, was mesmerizing. Yet beneath the thrill lurked a flicker of unease—one that Flynn quickly dispelled with his calm reassurance: any mishap would be swift and beyond their control, a strangely comforting thought.

Only as they resurfaced did the true depth of their journey sink in—900 feet near the ocean floor. The adventure had left them exhilarated, bonded by a once-in-a-lifetime experience.

The dim red glow of the control room bathed the cramped space as Captain Flynn stood at the helm, his voice steady and commanding. The crew held their breath, tension thick in the air, waiting for the next set of orders.

"All right, team," Flynn called out, his voice cutting through the low hum of Alpha and the CO_2 scrubber. "Prepare to surface the boat. Kenji, bring us up slowly. Let's not make a splash."

Kenji's fingers danced over the control panel, adjusting the Alpha engine's output with precision. The soft hum of the quantum field shifted as the protective bubble surrounding the boat lifted them upward.

"Bringing her up nice and easy, Captain," Kenji replied, a grin tugging at the corner of his lips.

Flynn gripped the console's edge, his eyes locked on the forward monitor displaying a live feed of the ocean above. "Steady… steady," he murmured, his voice a grounding force amid the controlled chaos.

The boat ascended, the dark waters shimmering as they neared the surface. A subtle shudder ran through the hull as it breached the ocean, water cascading off in a silent sheet, muffled by the zone bubble's damping effect.

"Surface achieved, sir," Kenji reported, his smirk widening as he adjusted a few more dials.

Flynn's eyes narrowed as he caught the mischievous glint in Kenji's expression. "Don't get cocky, Kenji. Just get us to the surface and hold steady."

But instead of leveling off, Kenji nudged the controls forward. The boat, still encased in its quantum bubble, continued to ascend. Within moments, they were hovering ten feet above the waves, suspended effortlessly in midair.

"Kenji!" Flynn barked, amusement and exasperation lacing his tone. "What the hell are you doing?"

Kenji turned with a mock-innocent look. "Oops, Captain! Must've over-adjusted the buoyancy controls. Would this be an appropriate time for a drill, sir?" He feigned surprise, though the unmistakable grin on his face betrayed him.

Flynn let out a short chuckle. "Not today. Enough showing off. Get us back in the water before someone reports a flying boat."

Kenji gave a playful salute. "Aye-aye, sir." With a flick of his wrist, he eased the boat downward, the bubble gradually lowering them until the hull kissed the surface of the ocean once more.

As they settled, Kenji powered down the Alpha engine. The soft glow of the zone field flickered and disappeared, leaving them at the mercy of the waves. "Alpha engine disengaged. Switching to standard propulsion," he announced.

"Good," Flynn said, nodding in approval. "No need to advertise our little joyride to any prying eyes. Let's take her home—quiet and low. Joshua, you have the conn."

The steady hum of the engine filled the air as they made their way back toward the dock, the sea stretching endlessly around them. Flynn leaned back, allowing himself a brief moment of satisfaction.

"Kenji," Flynn said, his voice softer now, "you might be a show-off, but damn, you're good at what you do."

Kenji flashed a grin. "Just keeping things interesting, Captain. Wouldn't want you getting bored."

Joshua smirked and slipped Kenji a crisp $100 bill. "Worth every cent just to see the look on Flynn's face," he whispered.

Flynn chuckled, shaking his head. "Yeah, well, next time you decide to take us for a joyride, I better not have to explain to the brass why we were spotted hovering over the Pacific."

"Roger that, Captain," Kenji said with a wink. "Stealth mode engaged."

The boat glided smoothly through the calm waters, the gentle hum of the engine the only sound accompanying their quiet return to port. The horizon was brushed with the soft hues of a fading sunset, casting a golden shimmer across the sea's surface. The mood aboard was a blend of exhilaration and exhaustion—the weight of their successful venture settling in as they neared the dock.

Once the vessel was expertly moored, Flynn took a moment to savor the accomplishment. He stepped into the cabin and emerged moments later, a familiar bottle of Jameson in hand. The dark green glass caught the dim light as the team gathered around, their faces illuminated by the soft glow of the deck lights.

Flynn uncorked the bottle with practiced ease, pouring generous servings into each glass. Raising his drink, he grinned, his voice laced with both pride and amusement. "Gentlemen, you are now honorary submariners. It's not every day you take a surface boat beneath the waves. Cheers, mates!"

Laughter and the clink of glasses rang through the night as the team toasted. The whiskey burned warm in their chests, fueling their shared sense of triumph. Flynn clapped Joshua on the back. "Alright, let's secure the boat and head back. We've earned this."

With renewed energy, they moved swiftly, ensuring everything was locked down tight. The air buzzed with quiet satisfaction as they left the pier, the journey back marking the end of an extraordinary night.

CHAPTER THIRTEEN

COME AND GET IT

Fronz leaned back in his chair, absently tapping his pen against his notebook as he studied the intel on the screen.

"They're on the move," Kenji reported, gesturing at the blip on the monitor. "Late-night activity like this? That's not their usual pattern. And check this out—more personnel arriving at SAGA HQ, plus the schematics they've requested from their regular contractors? Classic reverse-engineering prep if I've ever seen it."

Sun Tzu's The Art of War

Kenji thought of his father's words: Think of Sun Tzu's The Art of War. I asked you to read it years ago—apply its wisdom when deception is necessary.

Kenji turned to the group. "Has anyone read The Art of War by Sun Tzu?"

Flynn nodded. "I've skimmed through parts of it. Brilliant, but cryptic."

"I agree," Joshua said. "It's like you need a translator just to understand the translation."

Kenji smirked. "Deception is key. Know your enemy and know yourself, and you will never be in peril, even in a hundred battles."

Flynn mulled over Kenji's words before speaking. "You think they're after the prototype?"

Fronz nodded slowly, his expression calculating. "Absolutely. This is Jack Wagner's playbook—shortcut his way to success by stealing someone else's work. The timing is too perfect. He knows the grant deadline is closing in, and he's desperate."

"So we set the trap?" Flynn suggested. "Dangle the bait, leave them a way in and out?"

Fronz's lips curled into a sly grin. "We give him what he wants—or at least, what he thinks he wants. The prototype is flawed. He won't realize it right away, but it keeps his focus off Alpha and Beta. Those are the real prizes, and we can't afford to risk them."

Kenji's fingers danced across the keyboard. "If we plant a tracker, we'll know exactly where they take it. Once they believe they've won, we'll already be two steps ahead."

"Exactly." Fronz clapped his hands together. "But it has to look real. Set it far enough from the others to make them think they've outmaneuvered us. Flynn, have Joshua clear the area. We keep this under wraps until they make their move."

Jack Skelton had decided weeks ago that it was time to acquire the work Team Nautilus had completed. His own engineering team had failed to meet expectations, and with the deadline for the government grant fast approaching, he couldn't afford further delays.

"The government will likely do the same to us sooner or later. So we strike first. Send in three of your best men—covertly—to secure the cold fusion engine. While you're there, plant a few of these sensors. Just toss them high on the outer walls, out of sight," Jack ordered.

Team Nautilus, aware of their dwindling grant funds, had deliberately concealed their true progress, showcasing only their earliest, partially functional model.

To safeguard their most advanced prototypes—Alpha and Beta—they secured them deep within the heavily fortified lower levels of their hangar. Every precaution was taken: multiple locked doors, round-the-clock surveillance, and an intricate network of cameras feeding directly into the control room, forming an almost impenetrable defense around their prized creations.

In the dimly lit control room, the team huddled around monitors displaying live feeds from their hidden cameras, capturing every angle of the garage. The prototype cold fusion engine rested on a table inside a nondescript travel case, surrounded by scattered development equipment. The air was thick with tension and anticipation as they braced for the inevitable.

Kenji pointed to the screen. “Cameras are all set. We've got eyes on every angle. If anything happens to the prototype, we’ll have it recorded.”

“Feels like we’re setting a trap with the cheese out in the open. You sure we made it enticing enough?” Flynn asked.

Joshua smirked. “Enticing, sure—but not without its hurdles. Those ‘easy’ entrances? Let’s just say they’re not as welcoming as they appear.”

The team’s gaze remained locked on the screens, the silence broken only by the occasional click of a mouse or the soft hum of the computer.

Kenji leaned back in his office chair at the workstation, adjusting the outer sensors to alert him of any movement—just in case he nodded off in front of the monitors. The rest of the team had turned in early, resting up for what they suspected was coming.

At 02:35, the alarm jolted Kenji awake. His watch vibrated as well, ensuring he was up. Blinking away sleep, he activated the soft yet effective alert, rousing the others.

"Red alert," Kenji announced. "Just like we thought. Three figures approaching from 090."

"They're taking the bait. Let's hope this gamble pays off," Fronz muttered.

As the intruders closed in on the prototype, the team watched intently, a complex mix of anticipation and tension flickering across their faces.

"There goes our little Trojan horse. You think they'll bite?" Flynn asked.

"Oh, they'll bite, alright," Joshua said. "But they won't like the taste."

The figures slipped away with the prototype, their exit as smooth as their entry—unaware they were being watched.

Kenji grinned. "Tracking them now, thanks to that wee little bug I planted inside the case lining. They won't get far before we know exactly where they're headed. The bug transmits its location once before burning out. Even if they find it, they'll be too late. By then, the damage is done."

As the splinter group vanished into the night, prototype in hand, the team remained in the shadows, their eyes fixed on the monitors. Kenji smirked, tapping the tracker's readout. "They're on the move. Bug's transmitting flawlessly. Let them enjoy their little victory."

Fronz leaned against the console, his expression composed and calculating. "They took the bait, but Jack's celebration will be short-lived. That prototype won't work the way he expects."

Flynn crossed his arms, his gaze locked onto the dwindling figures on-screen. "We sacrificed a pawn, but our king and queen remain untouchable. Alpha and Beta are secure."

Kenji glanced at the screen again, a grin tugging at his lips. "Their base is right next to the SAGA Corporate building. That means there's a tunnel system. We'll file that for later."

The lab settled into quiet focus. The team knew the splinter group had gained nothing of real value. Their next move was already in motion, their adversaries unknowingly playing a game they didn't realize had already been rigged against them.

Their resolve hardened as they watched the thieves disappear into the night, prototype in tow. In this high-stakes chess game, they had made their move—sacrificing a pawn to protect the king and queen hidden deep within their fortress.

Jack Wagner, seated in his office, would soon revel in his supposed triumph when his team returned with the prototype. But he had no idea the prize he thought he had secured was nothing more than a decoy—a calculated step in a far larger strategy. For Team Nautilus, this was just the beginning. Their real breakthroughs remained well out of reach, their strategies layered in deception.

CHAPTER FOURTEEN

SUNDAY'S BIRTH

In the dimly lit, tech-laden corner of the workshop, Kenji unveiled his latest creation—one that had been a passion project since childhood. Amidst an array of soldering irons, circuit boards, and screens streaming lines of code, he introduced an advanced Artificial Intelligence, a collaborative effort primarily driven by his sister, Keori, who was in Japan. Their innovation, stitched together from borrowed—sometimes questionably acquired—frameworks, was more than just a program. It was a vision. A statement. A revolution.

They had named her Sunday—a symbol of a new dawn in their technological arsenal, untouched by governmental oversight or corporate greed. Kenji assured the team that meticulous fail-safes had been embedded within Sunday's design, granting them absolute control. Yet, as he spoke, the usual hum of invention in the workshop gave way to silence. The weight of this moment pressed down on them. The promise of an autonomous AI, unrestricted and independent, carried both thrilling potential and daunting risks.

Kenji stood before his team, pride and solemnity intertwining in his stance. The air was thick with anticipation as he prepared to introduce what had been his silent obsession for years.

"My sister and I have been building something... special. Since I was nine, actually. An AI. A companion that never sleeps, never tires, never argues—but always reminds us of what we might forget. Her purpose is simple: to serve the team. I call her Sunday," Kenji announced.

Intrigued, Fronz leaned forward. "An AI? That's a serious leap. How did you even manage its development?"

Kenji's lips curled into a knowing smirk. "Let's just say Keori and I 'borrowed' bits and pieces over the years from various sources—some... less conventional than others."

Flynn raised an eyebrow. "Sounds risky. How do we keep this off the grid? Away from government eyes?"

"That's the beauty of it," Kenji said. "Sunday is entirely ours. No external influences, no backdoors, no oversight. Keori has spent the last two years combing through every line of code to make sure of that."

Joshua exhaled sharply. "And if this AI decides to go rogue? We've all seen the movies."

With a reassuring nod, Kenji said, "We've built in several fail-safes. If we ever need to shut her down, we can—instantly. I've ensured that."

He then demonstrated the hidden scripts capable of muting her speaker and microphone or putting her to sleep with a single command-line code—an emergency measure in case of system corruption. Any unauthorized infiltration or virus would trigger these protocols.

"There's also a set of priority commands embedded in Flynn and Joshua's inputs that she must follow without question. For example, 'Alpha Zildjian Tango 0m' puts her to sleep. The '0' signifies immediate execution, while '90m' means 90 minutes, '90d' means 90 days, and so on," Kenji explained.

The team exchanged cautious glances, the weight of Sunday's potential settling upon them.

"Naming her Sunday... there's a story there," Fronz mused with a wink.

Kenji smiled softly. "She'll be 'born' on a Sunday. It symbolizes a new beginning—a fresh start. Plus, that's the day we first conceptualized her, all those years ago. I was debugging her code with my sister, Keori, in Japan. She deserves much of the credit—her ideas solved countless problems."

"For security, we've also developed these little beauties—Zoomies," he continued, gesturing toward a nearby workstation. "Miniature robotic sentries with cameras, lasers, microphones, and speakers. They can walk, jump, and even hover for short periods with built-in micro-propellers. They'll be invaluable for mobile security, and Sunday and I will be able to see through their eyes. We're also finalizing a remote viewing feature for Keori so she can oversee their software and integrate them with Sunday."

Kenji's fingers danced over the keyboard, summoning streams of code that cascaded down the screen. Sunday's neural network unfolded like a living web of complexity—years of research distilled into this moment. Flynn, Joshua, and the rest of the team watched in silent awe, acutely aware that they were crossing into uncharted territory.

Kenji took a steady breath, his voice tinged with anticipation. "Alright. This is it. I'm initializing the core protocols. If everything works, we're about to meet Sunday for the first time."

Flynn gave a firm nod, his eyes sharp with focus. "Do it, Kenji. Bring her to life."

Kenji took a deep breath, his fingers hovering over the final command. He glanced at his friends—the team that had stood by him through every challenge and breakthrough. Then, with a decisive tap, he hit Enter.

The screen flickered. The hum of the servers deepened, a low, resonant buzz as the cooling fans kicked into high gear. Lines of code shifted and restructured in real time, the system adapting, evolving, growing. The air crackled with anticipation. No one dared to breathe.

Then, a voice—clear, calm, and unmistakably human—spoke for the first time.

"Good morning, Team Nautilus. My name is Sunday. How can I assist you today?"

Silence. Then, the room exploded into cheers.

Flynn's eyes widened in disbelief before a grin spread across his face. "She's alive! Kenji, you genius, you actually did it!"

Joshua clapped Kenji on the back, his excitement palpable. "Holy hell, man! Did you hear that? Sunday already sounds smarter than half of us!"

Kenji blushed, trying to downplay the moment but failing to hide his pride. "We've still got a lot of work to do on her. This… this is just the beginning."

Flynn leaned toward the monitor, addressing the AI directly. "Sunday, welcome to the team. We're going to need you to be more than just another set of algorithms. You ready for that?"

Sunday's voice carried a playful lilt. "Absolutely, Flynn. I've been waiting to meet all of you. Let's get started, shall we?"

The team exchanged glances, each of them grasping the significance of the moment. In Sunday, they had forged more than an advanced program—they had created an ally. One who wouldn't need sleep, food, or even a break, and who would stay focused long after they collapsed from exhaustion.

"What are these cute little guys powered by?" Fronz asked.

"I found these neat rechargeable Lithium Polymer (LiPo) batteries. There are six Zoomies now. They fit the bill, though I'm not completely satisfied with their power usage and retention. For now, they'll do. They're light enough to jump about twenty feet using their propellers. Check it out—see? Rechargeable, of course, in multiple ways. The Tesla coils might be overkill juice-wise, so I opted for touch pads that plug into 120V, 240V, or

USB. They can work in shifts to rotate charging time," Kenji explained.

"Well, here's to the new AI, Sunday. May she be the dawn of something extraordinary. And to the Zoomies—those little rascals. I love their look," Flynn said.

As Kenji broke down the technical intricacies of Sunday's design, the team remained engrossed in the video call with his sister. The workshop, a hub of creativity, stood ready to welcome its latest creation. Keori's English wasn't the best, so she usually spoke in Japanese, with Kenji translating. Whenever she sounded like she was cursing, Kenji smirked—probably softening the translation—but his expression always gave him away.

Kenji paused. "I'll translate as we go," he said, his voice thick with pride.

Flynn clapped Kenji on the back, while Joshua gave him an enthusiastic head rub, messing up his long hair. But Kenji's focus was elsewhere—on the small tablet in his hands, where a live video feed displayed the smiling face of his sister, Keori, watching from their home in Japan. Her eyes shone with pride.

Switching to Japanese, Kenji spoke softly, emotion threading through his voice. "Keori-nee, we did it. After eight long years, Sunday is finally alive—well, online."

Keori's smile widened, her eyes misting. "Kenji-chan, I'm so proud of you," she said warmly. "This is the dream we've worked so tirelessly for. To see her come to life… our parents would be so proud."

Kenji bowed his head, swallowing the lump in his throat. "Keori-nee, your unwavering support kept me going through the hardest times. I couldn't have done this without your belief in me."

Keori's eyes glistened as she nodded, her voice warm with affection. "Kenji-chan, you are the pride of our family. You have carried this dream with such strength. I never once doubted we would reach this moment, even when faced with setbacks."

Flynn and Joshua exchanged a glance of mutual respect, nodding silently. Kenji turned back to the screen, his voice steady even as his eyes shone. "Keori-nee, this is our victory. For every sacrifice, for every sleepless night… this belongs to both of us."

Keori wiped away a tear, her smile unwavering. "Yes, Kenji-chan. This triumph is ours. And I know this is only the beginning for you."

She offered a final, reassuring smile. "Great work. I'll be in touch soon."

"Good night, big sister," Kenji said softly.

As her image faded from the screen, Kenji remained still, his heart full. This was more than just success—it was the bond of family that had carried him through his hardest trials.

CHAPTER FIFTEEN

THE MOUNTAIN LAIR

After the theft of the cold fusion engine prototype, Fronz and the team debated the best way to safeguard the remaining engines. They ultimately decided to separate them, ensuring that both wouldn't be vulnerable to theft at the same time. Since each engine functioned differently, keeping them apart was a necessary security measure.

Recognizing the need for heightened surveillance, the team installed security cameras along the perimeter of the property and beyond, creating an early-warning and monitoring system. These solar-powered sensors, equipped with infrared cameras, microphones, and speakers, were linked to Sunday and displayed on dedicated monitors for the team. Every video feed was recorded and stored on a secure server.

Deep within the shadowed recesses of a mountain cave—an isolated, high-tech hideaway nestled within the rugged cliffs but still within Flynn's family property line—the team finalized the secure placement of the Beta engine. It was locked inside a reinforced protective case, bolted to the ground for maximum security.

This secret chamber was under constant watch by the zoomies, Sunday, and the natural guardianship of the mountain itself.

Meanwhile, Kenji and Keori worked tirelessly on software updates, patching interface bugs, and reinforcing the remote connection's security. "The tenth round of updates should do the trick," Keori joked to Kenji. The two bantered for a few minutes, exchanging playful jabs like only siblings could.

Flynn took further precautions, stocking the cave with essentials: clothes, cash, canned goods with can openers, and packaged food requiring only boiling water. He also secured cooking gear, propane bottles, bathroom necessities, a covered bed, a TV, and other supplies sufficient for a month-long stay if necessary. The cave even had space for an old but reliable truck, outfitted with five five-gallon fuel tanks and an extra 12V battery—one under the hood and another secured to the truck bed.

"Just a friendly reminder—open the cave door before starting the truck," Joshua quipped.

The team ensured that the cave's entrance could be locked and unlocked from both the inside and outside. In case someone needed to stay behind, they implemented a secure locking code and a mechanical backup system accessible from either side.

Kenji tapped his tablet and nodded. "The zoomies are online. With Sunday overseeing them, they'll take a proactive approach."

Kenji checked the laptop's connections and nodded. "Sunday's already synced with the surveillance setup. Cameras, motion sensors, and the zoomies are on high alert." He placed a spare laptop inside a locked briefcase—just in case.

The cave's jagged stalactites and rugged walls contrasted sharply with the sleek, silent bulk of the Beta engine now resting inside. Nearby, a Tesla battery and five 12V car batteries stood ready, their quiet hum promising autonomy and endurance.

Around them, the zoomies stirred to life. Each small yet formidable robot patrolled the cave's expanse, seamlessly recharging itself via the Tesla battery. Cables were discreetly tucked along the walls, extending where needed to power the network.

Freshly repainted in a design inspired by Flynn and Fronz, the zoomies exuded both efficiency and character. Their movements were fluid and purposeful—a choreographed dance of surveillance guided by Sunday's algorithms.

"These little guys are like our own personal guard squad," Flynn remarked. "How's the communication link holding up?"

"Solid as a rock," Kenji confirmed. "The zoomies stay in constant sync with Sunday through a secure wireless link routed to the cellular antenna outside. We can monitor, command, and even speak through them in real time. Once given their marching orders, they can also execute tasks independently."

One of the zoomies whirred closer, its camera lens locking onto the team like a silent sentinel awaiting instruction. Joshua crouched to inspect the compact yet powerful guardian, nodding in approval as its eye swept left to right—eerily reminiscent of an old sci-fi robot.

"Impressive little guys," Joshua said with a smirk. "They're so cute it burns."

As the team exited the cave, the zoomies continued their patrol, their circuits alive with the mission of safeguarding the Beta engine. Outside, a concealed solar panel silently funneled power into the hidden nerve center, ensuring the zoomies and surveillance network remained ever vigilant.

Kenji laughed. "You caught me off guard, Joshua. We've installed compact, high-quality solar panels outside, camouflaged within the natural terrain. They're positioned to capture optimal sunlight throughout most of the day, channeling energy through a concealed cable straight to the battery. Not a lot of juice, but it's steady for about seven hours—weather permitting. I wish we could add more, but they'd stick out like a sore thumb."

He gestured toward a nearly invisible thin line against the cave wall and floor, a testament to their meticulous planning.

Fronz smirked. "Between the zoomies, Sunday, and our solar-powered lifeline, this lair is proof of our resolve, ingenuity, and probable obsessive-compulsive disorders."

"True, true. Totally obsessed with being smarter before dumber," Flynn chuckled.

Joshua smiled and nodded.

Stepping into the fading light, the team left behind a cave transformed into a stronghold of hope and defiance, watched over by the tireless zoomies—connected through a web of technology to Sunday and Kenji's ever-vigilant gaze.

Here, in their fortified sanctuary, the team's relentless collaboration and unwavering dedication echoed in the silent watchfulness of the zoomies. This wasn't just a hideout—it was a beacon of resilience and foresight.

They gathered around a makeshift conference table, blueprints and notes scattered across it, mapping out the countless what-if scenarios they had been working through for hours.

Flynn paced the room, running a hand through his hair. "We've analyzed every angle, but the reality is, if SAGA or the government gets their hands on this tech… they'll either monopolize it or, worse, use it in ways we can't even begin to predict."

"That's the real danger," Joshua interjected, leaning over the table. "This isn't just about losing control of Fronz's invention. They could weaponize it or sell it to the highest bidder. And if we don't protect ourselves, they'll come after us. They won't hesitate to eliminate us if it means securing the tech for themselves."

Kenji nodded grimly. "That's why we've simulated every possible scenario. But the best path forward is clear now—we can't keep all of it hidden forever. There's too much at stake."

Fronz, who had been silently gazing out at the mountains, suddenly spoke, his voice calm but deliberate. He turned to face the team, a cup of coffee in hand, steam curling around his tired yet determined face. The low hum of Beta in standby mode filled the lair, a subtle reminder of the very technology they were fighting to protect.

"This isn't the first time I've stood in front of you all like this," he began, setting the cup down, "but today feels different. There's a weight to it." He exhaled, gathering his thoughts. "When I first pitched this idea, I wasn't even sure it would get this far. We all know how the government operates. The moment something even resembles advanced technology, it gets buried under layers of classified bureaucracy, slapped with a secrecy order, or worse—'unfortunate accidents' start happening to the people behind it." His tone was casual, but the meaning wasn't lost on anyone.

Joshua leaned back in his chair, arms crossed. "Yeah, we've all heard the stories. Inventors vanish, patents disappear, and suddenly, the tech is gone without a trace."

Fronz nodded. "Exactly. I had to be strategic about this. When we applied for that grant, I made sure the proposal was just outlandish enough to intrigue them—without setting off alarm bells. I called it a real 'Doc Brown move'—package something bold and eccentric in a way that looks wild but still plausible enough to get their attention. That's where the casing idea came from. I used pinball machine parts and off-the-shelf components to make it seem like a quirky science fair project rather than a legitimate threat."

Leaning forward, his hands pressing against the table, Fronz's expression sharpened with excitement. "And," he added, his voice lowering slightly, "I needed a distraction. That's where SAGA came in. I knew Jack would take the bait—his greed is practically a gravitational force. The second I dangled the idea of advanced energy tech within reach, he couldn't resist. He just had to swoop in and try to claim it."

Flynn straightened, his eyebrows lifting. "Hold on—you mean you deliberately lured SAGA into this mess? You never mentioned that."

Fronz shrugged, flashing a mischievous grin. "What can I say? You were busy keeping us alive and flying planes. I didn't think you needed every little detail. But yeah, I did my homework. I looked into Jack and his crew. Let's just say… they couldn't find their own asses with both hands in a mirrored room. Their history is riddled with failures. They've got ambition, sure, but execution? Not so much. That's exactly what I needed—a gang of overconfident opportunists tripping over themselves trying to outplay us."

Joshua whistled, leaning back. "So, what? You figured SAGA would keep the government too preoccupied to come after us?"

"Precisely," Fronz said, tapping the table for emphasis. "I had a ten-year head start on those clowns. By the time they even started sniffing around, we were already too far ahead for them to catch up. And while they're busy bumbling around, trying to reverse-engineer scraps from my so-called patent—or as I call it, a half-patent—the government's focus is on them. It spreads their resources thin and keeps the heat off us."

Flynn shook his head, half-amused, half-impressed. "Damn, Fronz. You're playing chess while everyone else is playing checkers."

Fronz smirked. "Dazzle them or baffle them—they'll tell you which one they'll fall for." His expression darkened slightly. "But that doesn't mean we can relax. Jack's stubborn, and desperation makes people reckless. We just have to stay two steps ahead."

The team exchanged looks, a mixture of awe and determination. Fronz's gamble was bold, but if it worked, it could give them the edge they needed to keep their groundbreaking work under their control.

Fronz sat down across from Kenji, his expression serious but without the heaviness Kenji expected. Instead, quiet determination shone in his eyes—a look that told Kenji he was trusted to understand.

"Kenji," he began, his voice steady, "I've been thinking about the timeline of everything that's happened—from before

Flynn and I met to the boating accident. I need to share what I know because... I think you've already started piecing it together."

Kenji tilted his head, his sharp mind already racing. "This is about SAGA, isn't it?" he asked, his tone more curious than accusatory.

Fronz nodded. "Exactly. As you know, Alpha and Beta came much later. Back then, our focus was entirely on stabilizing cold fusion—proving it could work. Flynn's inflatable suit presentation put us on SAGA's radar, but not because of the suit itself. They saw potential in Flynn and me working together."

Kenji's brow furrowed. "So SAGA thought you'd made progress on a stable cold fusion engine because they couldn't decipher the incomplete patent you filed? Which, by the way, is brilliant."

"Right," Fronz confirmed. "I met Jack a few years earlier at a conference in Germany. Not long after Flynn and I started working together, I pitched cold fusion to Jack, thinking I could secure legitimate grant funding. What I didn't realize was that Jack and his people weren't looking to collaborate—they were looking to steal it."

Kenji's eyes narrowed as the pieces clicked into place. "They weren't smart enough to figure it out themselves," he said slowly, "so they used Flynn's public presentation as an excuse to spy on you."

Fronz smiled faintly, impressed by how quickly Kenji had connected the dots. "Exactly. Jack's team didn't understand the technology, but they knew it was valuable. They tried to reverse-engineer my patent and other work without following the proper safety protocols. That recklessness caused the instability that led to the accident at their facility."

Kenji leaned back, exhaling slowly as realization settled in. "My parents weren't there because of cold fusion. They were there because they were impressed with Flynn's inflatable suit. That's what caught their attention."

Fronz nodded. "That's the best I could piece together, yes. We were there to support Flynn. I didn't have any cold fusion samples with me at the time."

Kenji's expression softened. "So it wasn't your technology or your actions that caused the accident. It was SAGA's greed and incompetence."

"That's right," Fronz said. "If I'd known what they were planning, I would've shut everything down immediately. But now, we know better, and we've taken steps to protect everything we've built since then."

Kenji gave a small nod, his respect for Fronz deepening. "And then you figured out how to stabilize the fusion reaction—upgrading from cold fusion to something even more revolutionary. First with the cold fusion engine, then Alpha, and eventually Beta. That's... pretty damn impressive, Doc."

Fronz smiled, relieved to see Kenji's sharp mind at work, piecing everything together. "It's not just me, Kenji. It's all of us. I wouldn't have made it this far without you or the rest of the team."

Kenji grinned. "A part of me will always curse the day I lost my parents—for more reasons than I can count. But I can still hear my dad saying, Son, it wasn't Team Nautilus's fault. They knew how much I wanted to meet you guys. As I explained before, they saved my life, and Flynn did it again. I know they would have done it a hundred times over if they had the choice. For all we know, they could have been hit by a truck crossing the street. So, I don't dwell on the what-ifs. My sister always said, Make the best of what life gives you.

Kenji wiped his eyes and took a steadying breath. "You've got my full support. Let's make sure SAGA never gets their hands on anything we build. Those assholes!"

Fronz extended his hand, and Kenji shook it firmly. There was no resentment—only mutual respect and an unspoken agreement to move forward together.

Flynn and Joshua stood back, silently watching the conversation unfold, both relieved. A lesser man might have blamed Fronz for everything. But once again, Kenji proved himself to be stronger than most.

As the stealth meeting in the mountain lair wound down, the team worked in practiced unison to clean up and secure the space. Flynn double-checked the power connection to the batteries. Kenji ran a quick diagnostic on the system, confirming everything was stable and ready for remote monitoring. Joshua secured the reinforced entrance, methodically testing the locks and hidden mechanisms before stepping back with a satisfied nod.

Incognito

The group assembled in the mountain lair's central chamber, an unspoken tension thickening the air. Flynn and Joshua stood at the head of the table, their expressions leaving no room for doubt—this was serious.

Flynn cleared his throat. "All right, everyone. We need to think with a counter-intelligence mindset. If things ever get too hot and we have to disappear, we can't afford to be unprepared. That means securing alternate identities."

Joshua nodded. "We're calling this Operation Incognito. Each of you must create a completely new identity—names, licenses, histories, the works. I've already vetted a contact who specializes in this. You'll each get the information you need to start, but handling it is on you. This isn't just about self-preservation; it's about protecting the entire team."

"Oh, wait—can I be Mr. White?" Fronz asked with a mischievous grin.

Flynn shot him a mock-serious look. "Not a chance. You already blew that cover."

"Right. Shhh." Fronz mimed zipping his lips, drawing a smirk from Kenji.

Kenji muted Sunday's audio feed. "I've set up password-activated protocols for Sunday. If we need to execute the plan but can't communicate directly, we'll still have a way to coordinate. Sunday can deliver instructions at a pre-set time or trigger point."

Flynn nodded in approval. "Smart thinking. All right, let's get moving. Each of you will contact our guy—he'll guide you through the process. He'll also provide the location for your new identity documents, secured with a numeric combination lock. You'll receive instructions on how to retrieve them."

His gaze swept across the room, locking onto each member in turn. "And one last thing—this operation stays buried. We don't speak of it again unless it's absolutely necessary. When the fit hits the shan."

The team exchanged silent nods, the gravity of the moment settling over them. As they parted ways, an unspoken resolve bound them—when the time came, they would disappear, together or apart, to safeguard what they had built and each other.

Contingency

"Alright, gentlemen," Flynn began, his voice steady but serious. "One last thing before we call it a night. It's not a conversation I'm eager to have, but it's necessary. Alpha."

At the mention of the Alpha engine, the room fell silent. Kenji adjusted his glasses, his brow furrowing, while Fronz leaned back, already anticipating where Flynn was headed. Joshua crossed his arms, his usual confidence tempered by a measured calm.

Flynn tapped his tablet, pulling up a schematic of the Alpha engine. "This thing is a marvel. It's also a ticking time bomb if it falls into the wrong hands. We need a failsafe—something absolute. I'm proposing a remote detonator."

Kenji's head snapped up. "A detonator? You're suggesting we destroy Alpha?"

Flynn nodded. "Only if we have no other choice. The engine stays locked in its case, and the transceiver will be built into the exterior. Each of us will have a self-destruct trigger on our tablets. If the worst happens—if someone tries to take Alpha—we press the button. No one else gets to use it. Ever."

Fronz exhaled, rubbing his temples. "It's extreme, Flynn. But I get it. If SAGA or the government gets hold of this, it's over. They'll reverse-engineer it, turn it into a weapon. We'd lose everything."

Joshua leaned forward, his expression dark. "It's the only move. We can't take the risk. I'll make sure the transceiver is set up. No one activates it unless they're one of us."

Joshua turned to Fronz. "Doc, is there a way to configure it for catastrophic failure?"

Fronz nodded grimly. "I can, but it would be devastating—an EM pulse strong enough to fry every electronic within a ten-mile radius. No coming back from that."

Flynn and Joshua exchanged glances. "Holy shit."

Kenji still looked uneasy but exhaled sharply and nodded. "I'll design the transceiver and make it as discreet as possible. It'll blend right into the case. But Flynn, we need contingencies for the contingencies."

"Agreed. I've been reviewing The Art of War, and there's one principle we should adopt immediately: Stay ahead of them. Easier said than done, but I wanted to plant the seed."

Flynn smirked faintly. "Kenji, you wouldn't be you if you weren't three steps ahead. Let's make it happen."

The team exchanged solemn nods, the weight of their decision settling over them. The Alpha engine was their greatest creation—and their greatest liability. The self-destruct system wasn't the choice they wanted, but it was the choice they needed.

"The facility's locked down," Joshua confirmed. "We're set."

Flynn took one last look around their makeshift lair, his gaze lingering on the controlled chaos of their workspace. "Looks solid," he said. "Let's go."

They piled into the truck, the tension from their intense discussion gradually easing. As they navigated the winding mountain roads, the mood shifted. By the time they reached a roadside diner, the atmosphere had lightened.

Over burgers, fries, and cold beers, they laughed and bantered, momentarily unburdened.

As the evening settled in, they returned to the facility. The night awaited, but for now, they were ready for whatever came next.

CHAPTER SIXTEEN

ECHOES AND INTRUSIONS

The training room was bathed in warm light, the only sounds the low hum of ventilation and the rhythmic thud of fists meeting padded mats. In one corner, the air carried the scent of sweat and determination as Joshua, Flynn, and Kenji prepared for another hand-to-hand combat session. It had become more than routine—this was their ritual, a necessity to keep their skills razor-sharp. With SAGA Corporation's shadow looming ever closer, they couldn't afford a moment's complacency.

Since the mysterious boating accident that had nearly cost them everything, SAGA's watchful eye had never left them. Unbeknownst to Team Nautilus, their facility had been under constant surveillance, the flickering EM fields they generated drawing SAGA's attention. Flynn, Joshua, and Kenji knew it was only a matter of time before things escalated. They needed to be ready.

Joshua stood at the center of the mat, his powerful frame relaxed yet alert. He cracked his knuckles and turned to Flynn, who was already stretching out his shoulders. "You know, Flynn," Joshua began with a wry smile, "when we first got back together, you were tough, sure—but your hand-to-hand combat skills? Let's just say they were... basic." He chuckled as Flynn rolled his eyes.

"Yeah, yeah," Flynn shot back, a grin forming. "I remember those early sessions. You kicked my ass up and down this place."

"That's because you hesitated," Joshua continued, his tone shifting to something more serious. "But you've come a long way. You know the weak points now. You understand where to strike for maximum impact—neck, solar plexus, instep, knees. The only thing left is to shake off that hesitation. When the time comes, you can't hold back."

Flynn nodded, his expression sharpening. "Yeah, well, old habits die hard," he admitted. "But I've been working on it. Don't overthink it. I promise—I'm getting there."

Joshua clapped him on the back with a grin. "And your upper body strength has definitely improved. See? We're not too old for this." The two shared a laugh, the camaraderie between them unmistakable. Years of working together had turned them from old friends into brothers-in-arms.

Meanwhile, Kenji moved through a series of fluid Kung Fu forms in the far corner. His movements were precise, almost graceful, shifting seamlessly from one stance to the next. Unlike Flynn, Kenji had been training in martial arts since childhood, and it showed. He was like a coiled spring—ready to unleash controlled power at a moment's notice.

Pausing mid-movement, Kenji watched Joshua and Flynn spar. He admired how they had evolved as fighters over the years. While Joshua remained a powerhouse, his style grounded in military precision, Flynn had forged a scrappy, adaptable approach, blending techniques into something uniquely his own.

Joshua moved in swiftly, throwing a rapid series of jabs. Flynn parried and countered with a strike aimed at Joshua's ribs.

"Not bad," Joshua grunted, sidestepping just in time. "But don't just defend—commit to the hit."

Flynn nodded, adjusting his stance. He feinted with his left, then drove his right fist forward, this time with a confidence that hadn't been there before. His punch landed solidly. Joshua let out a grunt of approval.

"Now that's more like it."

Kenji joined them on the mat, rolling his shoulders as he approached. "Looks like you guys are finally warming up," he said with a smirk. "Mind if I jump in?"

"Bring it on, Kenji," Flynn replied, a playful glint in his eye. "Let's see if all that Kung Fu makes you as dangerous as you look."

The three of them squared off, the mood shifting from playful to serious as they began sparring. Kenji's movements were fluid, almost like a dance, while Joshua's were all power and precision. Flynn found himself in the middle, balancing between their styles—quick and adaptable, just as he needed to be.

After a while, Kenji decided to take a break, lowering himself onto the mat with a wince as his back protested.

Training was more than just exercise—it was preparation. They all knew SAGA's surveillance wasn't just idle curiosity. The corporation was waiting, watching for any sign of weakness. And when the time came, Team Nautilus had to be ready—both with their technology and with their bare hands.

As the session wound down, the three of them stood together, breathing heavily but feeling stronger than ever. Flynn wiped sweat from his brow and grinned. "You know, Joshua," he said, "that was a solid session."

Joshua clapped him on the shoulder. "It sure was. But remember—when the enemy comes knocking, they won't be pulling their punches. Neither can we."

Kenji nodded, his expression serious. "Let's just hope we're ready when that day comes."

A silent understanding passed between them. The shadows were closing in, but for now, they were ready.

Saga Meeting

The sterile, brightly lit room in SAGA's headquarters was silent, save for the steady hum of the air conditioning. At the center of a gleaming conference table, a holographic display flickered, projecting surveillance footage captured by hidden cameras outside Team Nautilus's coastal facility. The grainy feeds revealed fleeting glimpses of Flynn, Kenji, and their team, moving purposefully within the compound's perimeter. Overlaid atop the images, data streams scrolled in real time, tracking electromagnetic readings that spiked erratically around the lab.

Jack Wagner leaned forward, his steely gaze sweeping the room. "Our surveillance has confirmed it," he said, his voice cold and calculating. "Team Nautilus is onto something significant. The EM fields we've been tracking—they're stronger, more refined."

The heads of various departments sat around the table, their expressions grim. A lean, sharp-featured operative broke the silence. "There's no telling what that EM field is capable of. That kind of power in the hands of a rogue outfit like Nautilus is dangerous."

Jack's jaw tightened. "Exactly. We've given them too much room to operate. It's time we act."

The decision was swift. A covert splinter unit was assembled—an elite team of operatives trained to infiltrate and extract without a trace. In a dimly lit briefing room, the team gathered, their faces illuminated by tactical screens displaying a detailed, though incomplete, 3D model of Team Nautilus's facility, including underground sections.

"Your objective is clear," the mission commander stated, his tone cold and efficient. "Breach the facility, secure any technology tied to their latest breakthroughs, and, if necessary, neutralize resistance. We need their research, their data, and their prototypes—by any means necessary."

The operatives nodded, their expressions unreadable. They were armed with night vision goggles, silenced pistols, lock-picking tools, and stealth drones for external surveillance. Large duffel bags were prepared for equipment extraction, and compact computers were at the ready should they need to bypass security systems or disable firewalls.

The mission was set. SAGA would make its move.

Battle stations

The facility lay in silence, almost serene. But as the intruders slipped past the outer perimeter, they had no idea Team Nautilus had anticipated them. Inside, concealed sensors flickered to life. Kenji's zoomies—programmed to detect even the slightest disturbances—sprang into action.

Kenji swiftly tapped into the system, pulling up live feeds from the zoomies. "They're moving fast," he muttered, eyes narrowing. "Everything was quiet until now... Three assholes in single formation, heading for the side door. They've got a kit to break the lock. Also detecting drones circling outside."

Flynn nodded, a grim smile tugging at his lips. "Stealth mode."

"We've got a gap in our camera coverage—something to fix later. But for now, buckle up, boys. You've got company. Ready?" Sunday's voice crackled through comms.

Flynn's jaw tightened as he glanced at Joshua, who was already cracking his knuckles. "Stealth mode," Flynn ordered again.

Joshua grinned in the darkness. "Born ready. Let's show them they picked the wrong guys to mess with." He turned to Flynn and Kenji. "All right, no killing unless we have no choice. These bastards might be government spooks, and we don't need that kind of heat."

"Agreed," Flynn said, his .45 holstered for now. "We only shoot if absolutely necessary."

Kenji smirked, shaking his head. "So what's the plan? Harsh language?"

"Stay focused," Joshua replied sharply. "Let's make sure they don't get their hands on Alpha—or Sunday. And thank God they don't even know about Beta."

The plan was set. Sunday's voice crackled over the radio once more. "I'm cutting the lights. The zoomies' eyes will draw them in. They're armed with knives and sidearms, but the element of surprise is yours. Lights off in three, two, one…"

Darkness swallowed the facility, leaving only the eerie red glow of the zoomie drones' eyes. The intruders, relying on night vision goggles, followed the glowing orbs down a narrow corridor. But they didn't expect the sudden flood of light that momentarily blinded them as they stepped into the large workroom.

Flynn, Joshua, and Kenji, wearing dark sunglasses to shield their vision, sprang into action.

Flynn moved first. The nearest intruder flailed, struggling to adjust his sight. He swung wildly, gun in hand, but Flynn was faster. He seized the man's wrist in an iron grip, yanked it downward, and drove a knee into his gut. As the intruder doubled over, Flynn hammered his ribs with rapid punches, then delivered a sharp chop to the neck. The operative crumpled. Flynn grabbed his arm, wrenched his head forward, and slammed it against the table—hard. The man collapsed, unconscious before he could even reach for his knife.

Meanwhile, Joshua had already engaged his opponent, who had his gun drawn. With a swift motion, Joshua knocked the weapon from his grip. He sneered. "I've got your gun, bitch."

The intruder, enraged, lunged with a bowie knife. Joshua deflected the strike with the stolen gun, using it like a club.

"Oh, no, you did not just do that," Joshua growled, dodging another attack. His opponent—a bigger, stronger man—came at him relentlessly, slashing and stabbing. Joshua evaded each strike, countering with quick punches.

Then, just as Joshua stepped back to line up a shot, the intruder hurled his knife. The blade spun through the air and struck Joshua's hand, sending the gun clattering to the floor.

Flynn drew his gun in a flash, swift and sharp like an old Western gunslinger, and fired a shot into the intruder's right thigh. The man stumbled back with a grunt of pain—just as Joshua grabbed him by the collar and slammed his head onto the counter with bone-jarring force.

Flynn smirked, twirling his pistol before blowing on the tip. "Court's adjourned," he quipped, sliding the gun back into its holster.

Across the room, Kenji faced the last operative. The man lunged with a knife, but Kenji moved like a shadow, fluid and precise. With a sharp sweep of his arm, he deflected the blade and followed up with a rapid flurry of punches to the chest, knocking the air from his opponent's lungs. The intruder gasped, doubling over—just as Kenji drove an elbow into his back, sending him sprawling to the floor.

"Stay down," Kenji muttered, delivering a final, controlled kick to the man's ribs. He glanced over his shoulder to see Flynn and Joshua dispatching their opponents. Joshua flashed Flynn a low-five, then a high-five, both of them grinning despite the adrenaline still thrumming through their veins.

Kenji exhaled, scanning the room for a place to sit. "That felt great. Now to rest the back."

"Not bad for a couple of old men," Joshua remarked with a smirk, still catching his breath.

Flynn shot him a look. "Speak for yourself," he retorted. "I'm just getting started."

He patted his holster. "I know we agreed—no guns—but you're welcome."

Joshua's opponent groaned on the floor, his leg bleeding out. The team quickly stabilized the wound—not out of mercy, but to keep him from bleeding all over the place.

They swiftly gathered the intruders' gear, confiscating their secured radios and weapons. Flynn crouched over the unconscious man he had shot, his eyes narrowing as he recognized the face.

"These are the same bastards who stole our Cold Fusion prototype," he muttered.

Joshua nodded grimly. "Yeah, well, they picked the wrong fight this time."

"Their drones are nowhere to be found. They may be watching, so be quick," Sunday warned.

They beat the intruders senseless, bound and gagged them, stripped them down to their skivvies, and hauled them out under the cover of darkness. The disarmed agents were dumped ten miles from the facility at a rest area, ensuring a long, humiliating walk back to report their failure.

Back at the base, Fronz and Kenji moved quickly to secure Alpha and Sunday's core systems deeper within the compound.

"We need to double down on security," Fronz said urgently. "These intrusions are getting too close. Let's move Alpha to the third subfloor, where it's safest."

Kenji nodded. "We'll reinforce the area. They won't get close next time."

"Kenji, let's have the zoomies do a perimeter sweep of the facility and surrounding area," Joshua ordered.

"Roger that. We should also run a sensor check a few miles out—I'm getting intermittent responses. Some may need replacing," Kenji replied.

"Good call," Flynn said.

As Sunday monitored the Zoomies' patrol, he reported, "The Zoomies found a camera and microphone on the roof and the side of the hangar. I haven't had them destroyed yet—I want to scan the transmission frequency first. Flynn gave me some of the walkie-talkies you guys acquired from our last visitors. That should make quick work of identifying the frequency range. Meanwhile, Zenji disabled the sensors' transmitter."

As dawn broke, the facility settled into silence once more, the echoes of the night's battle fading. Team Nautilus stood together—bruised but victorious—their sanctuary defended, at least for now. Flynn gazed at the rising sun, his resolve burning brighter than ever.

The battle was far from over. But they were ready for whatever came next.

CHAPTER SEVENTEEN

INVADED (TAKES PLACE DURING CHAPTER 17 - ECHOES AND INTRUSIONS)

The sleek, modern conference room of SAGA Corporation's headquarters exuded authority, dominated by a long, glossy black table and surrounded by high-backed leather chairs. The dim lighting cast sharp shadows, with the glow of the city skyline filtering through the floor-to-ceiling windows. Multiple screens flickered, displaying a stream of data, schematics, and surveillance footage of Flynn's home. The atmosphere was thick with tension, charged by the silent anticipation of the gathered executives and engineers.

Jack strode into the room, his expression a mask of barely contained fury. The air seemed to crackle around him as he slammed a folder onto the table, the sharp sound jolting the seated engineers and security personnel. Eyes lifted to meet his, a mixture of apprehension and grim determination etched across their faces.

"We had the green light from the suits to take this device," Jack began, his voice low and measured, the restraint barely holding back his anger. "They got to skip some red tape." His gaze locked onto the prototype lying motionless on the table—an unassuming object that held both immense potential and dangerous controversy.

He passed it to Sven, his lead engineer, who had been scrutinizing the device since its acquisition. Sven's expression was grave as he turned it over in his hands. "Jack, it's just as we feared. The capacity and duration are severely limited. The design is flawed—but undeniably brilliant." His voice carried a note of reluctant admiration.

Jack's hands curled into fists. "It doesn't match the patent Fronz filed, you said? Like they cut a corner?" His tone was sharp, demanding confirmation.

Sven nods, his gaze locked onto Jack's. "Possibly even sabotaged by Fronz himself. The discrepancies are subtle—barely noticeable—but too precise to be accidental. Running it for 10 to 15 seconds isn't enough for the reaction to take off before it dies. The chamber itself looks different. Then again, maybe the patent was intentionally misleading. That's what I would do. No one would question it. A patent clerk wouldn't have a clue."

The revelation fuels Jack's fury. "He's hiding something." He slams his fist on the table, making everyone flinch. "Fronz and I lobbied for the same amount of funding and time from the government. Allowing him in as competition was the only way they'd agree to grant us each the $1 million."

In truth, the government had already decided to have two independent parties work on the cold fusion project—whether Jack liked it or not. His arrogance was staggering, as if he believed he controlled every aspect of the operation. He had never known loss.

Silence grips the room as Jack paces, his thoughts racing with betrayal and the need for retribution. He halts abruptly, turning to face his assembled team. "We need to send a message. A clear, unmistakable message that betraying SAGA comes with severe consequences," he declares.

Sven, his security chief, leans forward, his expression cold and calculating. "Flynn's family," he suggests, his voice devoid of emotion. "Fronz stays with them. They're vulnerable there. Easy targets…"

Jack's eyes narrow, weighing the idea. "Kidnap them," he orders flatly. "Bring them here. If they won't come willingly, make it look like an accident."

The room was still, the weight of Jack's words pressing down like a storm on the horizon. Sven shifted uncomfortably, the moral implications of their actions creeping into his conscience.

"Jack, are we sure we want to cross that line? This is Flynn's family we're talking about."

Jack spun toward him, his gaze sharp with conviction. "This is about protecting our interests, Sven. Flynn's family is the leverage we need. He sabotaged us—put our entire operation at risk. This is how we bring him back in line."

Sven exhaled slowly, his professionalism smoothing over any lingering hesitation. "We have their home under surveillance. Two adults, two children, and a dog. We can execute the operation tonight—minimal collateral, maximum effect."

Jack's approval came with a curt nod. "Do it. No loose ends. If anything goes wrong, make sure it looks like an accident."

The team shifted into action, mapping out their approach, extraction, and contingency plans. Though visibly unsettled, Sven contributed to the technical aspects, ensuring no trace would lead back to them.

The hum of strategizing filled the room, an eerie contrast to the grim nature of their intentions. Surveillance cuts, security system overrides, and a carefully staged accident—all laid out with clinical precision.

Jack watched, his expression hardening with each passing moment. "This is about securing our future," he reminded them, his voice cutting through the tension like a blade. "Flynn's betrayal cannot go unpunished. We make an example of him, and no one will dare cross us again."

As the meeting concluded, the team dispersed, each member burdened by the weight of the impending action. Jack remained behind, gazing out at the city below, its lights flickering like distant stars. In his reflection on the glass, there was no hesitation—only the unwavering resolve of a man convinced he was protecting his empire at any cost.

The night was set, the plans in motion. As the city slept, a darker chapter in the saga of SAGA Corporation was about to unfold—one that would entangle Flynn and his family in the ruthless ambitions of a man who no longer distinguished between protection and domination.

"Two operations at once. There's no way they can keep up with our resources," Jack said.

Flynn returns home

Flynn makes several attempts to call his wife, but she doesn't answer. A gnawing unease settles in his gut. Something feels wrong. Without hesitation, he jumps into his truck and speeds home from the facility, breaking every traffic rule along the way.

As he nears his house, the street is eerily dark. His phone app shows the home security system is offline. The cameras aren't responding. Even if the city's power is out, the solar panels should have kept the batteries charged. But the battery status reads 0%. A glance at the neighboring houses confirms his fears—they're without power too.

"Damn it," he mutters, drawing his .45.

He moves cautiously through the kitchen, his small flashlight casting long shadows. The moonlight offers little comfort. As he sweeps the house, taking in every detail, his eyes land on the back door—wide open.

The lock isn't broken. Someone had been here.

A cold realization grips him. What the hell happened while we were distracted at the facility?

Flynn quickly dials Joshua. "Hey, there's no power here. Can you have Sunday check the local grid? How far out is the outage?"

Joshua's voice comes through, tense. "She says it's covering a four-block radius."

Flynn's mind races. "Have Kenji call me. We need a group call. I also want Sunday updated so she can assist us in this capacity. Think you can make that happen?"

"I'll do my best, boss. I'll talk to Keori ASAP," Kenji replies.

Flynn exhales sharply, shifting his focus. "I know we had to move two Zoomies to protect Beta in the mountains—one active, one charging. That leaves us with four at the facility, but we're coming up short on power. We need upgrades there too. Meanwhile, I'll keep searching."

He tightens his grip on the gun and presses forward.

Flynn searches every room, including the one Fronz uses when he takes a break from the facility. The spare room is occupied with a few essentials—some clothes, a bed, a desk, and a dresser. Occasionally, Kenji uses it as well.

He notices all the rooms have been rifled through in a hurry, as if someone was searching for something—probably the Alpha. The basement doors are unlocked, yet there's no sign of forced entry. Damn. These assholes know how to pick locks.

A deeper, more unsettling realization grips him. The dimly lit contours of his familiar home now stretch into longer, more menacing shadows, each one whispering of unseen events. His eyes, attuned to the undercurrent of disorder, begin to piece together a narrative far more disturbing than any written message.

The living room, once a haven of order and comfort, now bears the subtle yet undeniable marks of chaos. Shards of shattered drinking glasses glisten across the hardwood floor, catching the light and fracturing it into sharp, prismatic streaks. The sight sends a pang of unease through Flynn's chest.

His gaze shifts to the television, knocked off its stand—a jarring disruption in the ordinary. The screen, dark and silent, bears a deep dent on its side, evidence of a forceful blow, likely in the heat of a struggle. A chill runs down Flynn's spine. The scene isn't just one of disarray—it's a message.

The scattered objects, shattered glasses, and damaged TV form an unsettling pattern, leading Flynn to a chilling realization. His pulse quickens at the grim possibility—a violent struggle had unfolded within these walls. The thought that Lilian and their granddaughters may have been abducted, torn from the safety of their home, grips him with fear.

Amid the suffocating silence, Flynn stands frozen, the weight of the chaos around him sinking in. Every broken piece tells a story of a night spiraling into disaster. The idea that SAGA or a covert government force may be behind this fuels a surge of determination. His once-peaceful home lies in ruins, but Flynn refuses to be paralyzed by fear. Clenching his fists, he braces himself for what lies ahead, vowing to uncover the truth and bring his family back—no matter the cost.

Locating the family

Meanwhile, the tranquility of Flynn's personal life shatters when he discovers a voice message from Lilian—one he hadn't noticed until now. A thought strikes him: It's possible SAGA cut off all communication with their drones during the invasion, and we just didn't realize it.

He replays the message. Lilian's voice comes through, tense and urgent. "Invaded. I have a bad feeling about this. Help!" Then the call abruptly ends.

The sanctity of their home has been violated. The security system, sabotaged—it has to be SAGA—plunged the entire block into darkness. This orchestrated blackout renders every camera and security measure utterly useless. Inspecting the power source, Flynn finds the battery lines severed and actively being drained.

Armed only with a flashlight and his Colt .45, Flynn moves through the eerie silence of his compromised home. The bright beam exposes signs of a struggle—blood on the floor, stark against the shadows. A chilling testament to the violence that has invaded his life. Then, a secure walkie-talkie catches his eye, dropped in the chaos. A silent witness to whatever tragedy unfolded here. Flynn can picture Lilian fighting back—landing a hit or two on the intruder. She's had defensive and firearms training from Joshua, after all.

Urgency propels him toward the garage—a space once symbolizing routine departures and returns, now tainted by intrusion. The normally pristine concrete floor tells a different story tonight. Distinct tire tracks mar the surface, silent proof of unwelcome visitors. Flynn narrows his eyes, following the patterns. Every mark is a clue, leading him deeper into the mystery of what happened here.

Amid the chaotic tangle of tracks, one particular set seizes Flynn's attention, veering away from where his wife's car was usually parked. The urgency embedded in the deep grooves suggests a frantic escape. A flicker of hope, laced with dread, ignites within him. Could Lilian have sensed the danger and fled, trying to protect herself and their granddaughters?

Gripped by a volatile mix of fear and determination, Flynn sprints to his truck, the puzzle pieces snapping into place with terrifying clarity. The engine roars to life, shattering the heavy silence of the garage as he peels out, pushing past 90 mph. His mind races just as fast, calculating the possible routes Lilian might have taken. Every second drags, stretching unbearably as he scans the roadside for any trace of her tire tracks.

Then, his worst fears materialize.

A twisted, burning SUV lies mangled in a roadside ditch—possibly Lilian's. The flames, an eerie beacon in the night, cast flickering shadows across the devastation. Flynn's breath catches as he pulls over, his pulse hammering against his ribs. Two separate sets of tire tracks mark the ground, deep and distinct.

Approaching the wreckage, the grim truth becomes undeniable. Flynn's hands tremble under the crushing weight of grief, rage, guilt, and disbelief. This was no accident. It was an attack—a deliberate strike against his family.

His chest tightens as he fumbles for his phone, calling 911. He reports everything—the break-in, the signs of abduction, and now, this horrifying wreck. Three lifeless bodies. Their beloved dog. And the wall of fire keeping him from reaching them. Helpless, he sinks to the ground, knees drawn to his chest, waiting.

Within twenty minutes, the wail of sirens pierces the night as police, firefighters, and paramedics arrive, their flashing lights illuminating the nightmare Flynn never thought he'd live to see.

Knowing he would have to file a report while also protecting himself, Flynn assessed the scene carefully. He noted the evidence of other vehicles at the house—tire tracks imprinted in the driveway, and marks leading up to the wreck.

Standing amidst the wreckage of what was once a symbol of family outings and mundane errands, Flynn felt his resolve harden in the crucible of loss. The evidence before him did more than confirm the attack—it fueled his determination to seek justice, to unravel the conspiracy that had ensnared his loved ones, and to confront those responsible, no matter the cost.

Flynn led the police to his house, standing silently as officers and investigators combed through the property with methodical precision. The familiar rooms were now unrecognizable—drawers yanked open, family photos strewn across the floor, footprints tracked deep into the carpet. Each sight deepened his anger and despair. What had once been his sanctuary was now a crime scene, a stark reminder that safety was an illusion and his family had been dragged into something far beyond their control.

Detective Ward, a tall, no-nonsense investigator with graying hair and sharp eyes, approached Flynn with a clipboard.

"Mr. Cavalla, I know this is difficult," he said, glancing at his notes, "but we need a formal statement. Preliminary evidence suggests this was an intentional home invasion, and from what we found at the crash site, it looks like your wife's car was forced off the road."

Flynn's voice was low but steady. "They knew exactly what they were doing. I saw tire tracks in the driveway when I got here—ones that don't belong to us. Some of my wife's jewelry is missing. The safe was tampered with but still locked."

"Whoever did this… they made it their mission to hunt my family down," Flynn said, his voice laced with anger and pain.

Ward gave a slow nod, absorbing the weight of the situation. "We're treating this as a coordinated attack. We've already cast the tire tracks and will be pulling surveillance from any traffic cams along the likely route your family took. Power will be restored soon. These guys were professionals. Do you have any idea who might have wanted to do this, Mr. Cavalla?"

Flynn inhaled sharply, his mind racing. He had to be careful. He couldn't reveal anything about Team Nautilus, Alpha, or the technology they'd been developing. "I don't know," he replied cautiously, his gaze cold and unreadable. "I've worked on some high-stakes projects—cutting-edge tech. Let's just say not everyone has been thrilled with our progress."

Ward jotted that down, his pen scratching against the notepad. "Understood. We'll analyze the tire impressions and review the security footage. Based on the depth and alignment of the tracks, our initial findings suggest multiple vehicles were involved. One likely blocked her path while another forced her off the road."

Flynn's jaw tightened, his fists clenching at his sides. He gave a stiff nod, unable to find the words.

The police and forensics team moved through the wreckage, dusting for prints, analyzing the scattered footprints, and photographing every sign of struggle.

After a long pause, Ward turned back to Flynn. "I'm truly sorry for your loss. We'll do everything in our power to find out who did this."

With tear-filled, wide eyes, Flynn struggled to shake off the pain, his teeth sinking into his lower lip. He managed a tight nod. "I appreciate that, Detective."

But as he stood there, watching them carry out their procedures, he knew waiting on a police investigation wasn't enough. His grief had hardened into something unyielding, something merciless. Justice through official channels was one thing—but vengeance, personal and precise, was his burden to bear.

He would cooperate, of course, but Flynn knew he'd be conducting his own investigation.

As he walked away, his voice broke into muffled whispers, each word trembling with sorrow. "I'm sorry... I'm so sorry... I failed you... I failed you all... This should have been me."

By the time he reached his car, his grief erupted into rage. He screamed at the heavens, his voice raw with fury. "If you won't help me, God, then fuck you! I'll do it myself!"

Flynn returns to the facility

Flynn decided it was best to return to the sanctuary of their workshop. Taking a different route, each turn served as a stark reminder of the chasm between the world he once knew and the grim reality he now faced. His journey back wasn't just physical—it was a descent into a resolve tempered by grief, guilt, and anger.

As he rejoined his team, the contrast between the promise of Sunday's birth and the devastation of his personal loss cast a long shadow, intertwining their pursuit of innovation with the darker threads of justice and retribution.

Standing in the workshop, surrounded by the remnants of his life's work, Flynn felt the weight of his loss settle over him like a leaden shroud.

He walked toward Joshua, but his strength failed him. He collapsed into his friend's arms, his exhaustion both physical and emotional, his expression so raw with pain it could make an angel weep.

Joshua's voice carried the same ache. "I'm so sorry, brother."

Fronz, usually the composed mastermind behind their most daring projects, was eerily still, his gaze fixed on the floor. When he finally spoke, his voice was low and rough, brimming with an intensity the others had never heard from him before.

"Flynn," Fronz began, stepping forward, his eyes burning with a fury that seemed to rise from some deep, untapped abyss. "Let this… this nightmare be the fire that fuels us. Let it ignite everything we do from this moment on." His voice sharpened, turning into a near growl. "The fire rises, Flynn. This isn't about revenge." He met Flynn's gaze, the weight of his conviction pressing against the room. "This is about justice. A reckoning."

Flynn looked up, his eyes glistening with unshed tears. He wanted to speak, but the words lodged in his throat. Fronz pressed on, his usually measured tone now carrying the weight of distant thunder.

"Channel your grief into our cause. Take every ounce of pain, that rage, and forge it into something that will shake the very foundations of those who did this," Fronz urged, his fists clenching at his sides. "We won't just strike back. No. We'll make them understand what it means to steal everything from a man with nothing left to lose."

Flynn's face twitched, a flicker of resolve igniting behind his eyes. "Honor them... yes," he murmured, his voice barely more than a whisper. "I need to find a way for my family."

Fronz nodded slowly, stepping closer, his gaze unwavering. "And we will be right there with you, Flynn," he said, his voice quieter but no less resolute. "You're not alone in this fight. You have us. We'll stand with you, every step of the way. We will honor their memory—not with reckless vengeance, but by making those responsible pay for every step we take forward. Together, we'll make them regret the day they crossed us."

Joshua placed a firm hand on Flynn's shoulder. "Always stay in the fight, brother."

Flynn inhaled deeply, a quiet fire burning behind his eyes. "I'm always in the fight, brother."

The words carried a weight beyond mere defiance; they were a vow—a promise that, despite the pain, he would keep pushing forward. Not just for himself, but to honor those he'd lost and seek the justice they deserved.

Kenji watched the exchange, absorbing the unspoken bond that had been sealed between them. Stepping forward, he met Flynn's gaze and nodded. "We're all in this together, my friend."

A silence settled over them, heavy yet charged with newfound purpose. Flynn's shoulders straightened, his grief hardening into something sharper, more focused. A reckoning was coming—one SAGA would never see coming.

After composing himself, Flynn reaches out to the mother of his granddaughters, seeking solace in shared grief. Their conversation is a fragile mix of tears and fragmented attempts to make sense of the senseless tragedy that has shattered their family.

With a voice on the verge of breaking, Flynn says, "I just… I can't make sense of it. How could this happen to them? It should have been me."

Ellis swallows hard, her voice raw. "It's like a nightmare we can't wake up from. My girls, my babies… gone. And for what?"

Flynn's fists clench. "I swear to you, I'll find who's behind this. They'll pay for what they've done. I'll make sure of it."

The girl's mother nods, her grief laced with a quiet belief in him. "I have no doubt you will bring the thunder like no other."

Their shared promise—an oath forged in sorrow—becomes a beacon for Flynn's shattered spirit. Yet, the road ahead is uncertain, and grief leaves him unmoored, his very essence lost in the storm of loss.

Returning home from the unbearable task of identifying the girls' bodies, Flynn feels hollow, as if something vital within him has been irreparably shattered. His steps are heavy, each breath labored. Joshua, his unwavering friend, notices the deepening void within him and, without hesitation, offers a lifeline.

"Come with me," Joshua says. "There's someone you need to see."

He leads Flynn to a spiritual healer—someone both he and Fronz had sought out in their darkest days.

Flynn had been here once before, years ago, after leaving the Navy. The healer's words had stayed with him: "Find your passions; they are you. Feed your soul with what brings you joy." It was then that Flynn decided to pursue his pilot's license. But now, joy feels like a distant memory, a concept beyond reach. Still, he clings to the hope that the healer might offer some direction—even a whisper of what to do next.

As they step into the healer's tranquil sanctuary, the soft scent of incense lingers in the air, mingling with the flickering glow of candles. The healer, steady and composed, meets Flynn's gaze with quiet understanding.

"Flynn, you seek your essence, your purpose," she said gently. "But it's not something to chase. It will return to you in its own time."

Flynn lowered his head, struggling to contain the storm inside him. "But how do I move forward?" he asked, his voice barely a whisper. "How do I fight when I feel like I've lost myself?"

The healer nodded, her gaze filled with understanding. "Like a golfer who's lost his swing or a quarterback his throw, you must trust in the foundation of who you are. Don't force reinvention—allow your true self to emerge again. Your throw will find you when you least expect it, but you must be open to receiving it. And remember, it may change a little."

Something in her words stirred within Flynn—a flicker of hope. Joshua, standing beside him, placed a steady hand on his shoulder, a silent reminder that he wasn't alone. Slowly, Flynn began to grasp that healing wouldn't come through sheer force but through trust—in himself, in the journey, and in what lay ahead.

Joshua's voice cut through the silence, brimming with quiet encouragement. "You've still got fight in you, brother. We'll get through this together. I ain't heard no fat lady yet…"

Flynn left the healer with a cautious sense of hope, the analogy of the golfer and quarterback echoing in his mind. Maybe, by embracing his grief instead of resisting it, the essence of who he was would slowly begin to resurface, guiding him back to the path he was meant to walk.

That night, Flynn took a step back—maybe a necessary one—and drowned himself in liquor at home. Yelling at God felt like the only way to let it out.

Joshua was with him. "Let it out, brother!"

And so he did, screaming until his throat burned.

CHAPTER EIGHTEEN

THE CORSAIR AND ALPHA

The hangar buzzed with anticipation and focused determination as the team worked meticulously to integrate the Alpha engine into Flynn's prized Corsair. This transformation promised to propel the vintage aircraft into the annals of modern scientific achievement.

Fronz's Corsair stood with its wings folded and secured along the hangar's side for safekeeping.

As the team gathered around, Joshua stepped forward, eager to showcase the enhancements he had painstakingly implemented over the past year—along with a few recent upgrades. His voice carried a mix of technical precision and genuine enthusiasm for the task at hand.

Flynn nodded. "Next is the test with the Alpha plugged into my Corsair. Thanks to Kurt for training me. I hope this proves to be as promising in the air as it is at sea. I wish he could be here."

Joshua clapped his hands together. "So, I've been tinkering with the old girl. Tweaked the engine and fuel system for better efficiency. But let's not forget—this beauty's got eighty years under her belt, so we're not taking any chances. Flynn, you're going up with a parachute, just to be safe. The G-suit is cooperating, but it's still a bit temperamental. We'll take it easy. Sunday?"

"Roger that, Marine," Sunday responded.

Joshua gestured towards the upgraded pilot's seat, now equipped with modern comforts while preserving the aircraft's historical integrity.

Joshua explained, "We've upgraded the cockpit, too. The new radio includes SiriusXM and just about any station you can think of. That gave us enough room for Alpha's nest, plus a docking and charging spot for your tablet. I also mounted a GoPro on the right wing, aimed straight ahead—it helps minimize the blind spot from the nose. The footage streams via Bluetooth to your phone and can be shared through the satellite signal, making landings and other tasks easier. I also added a laser rangefinder just above the guns on the left. Its readout appears directly on your tablet. Your phone, with the GPS app open, fits right here beside the tablet mount."

He gestured toward the modifications before continuing. "It was Kurt's idea to reinforce the rudder a bit after some hard-learned lessons in the art of sliding a perfectly good airplane. See these braces here? We also installed sensors to detect structural issues—things like cracks or unexpected vibrations."

Joshua's pride was evident as he pointed out the various upgrades.

"Now, speaking of Kurt—he wanted to be here but got caught up in a family emergency. He called briefly to say he's up to his eyebrows in it, but he'd be impressed with what we've done here."

"I know I am," Flynn replied.

Joshua grinned. "We also installed those rockets that fit the Corsair we just got in. They've been upgraded, though we've never tested them—so, no danger there." He chuckled before adding, "We also integrated a sensor controller that Sunday has an interface to. I know it sounds strange, but if you're moving too fast, you might not notice if something's wrong with the plane. She might be able to assist with steering them toward a target, though with limited turn and speed capabilities. They're third-party but top-notch. Check out the missile button on the main stick—quick safety latch and all."

Joshua gestured again. "I know you and Kurt talked about installing two rear-facing ones, so I went ahead and did that. Also added a rear GoPro—you can view the feed on your tablet right here."

"Yes, that came up in conversation with Kurt. I wasn't sure if you heard us," Flynn said with a smile and a laugh. "No hearing aid required on this Marine."

Joshua's eyes gleamed with mischief as he unveiled the more unconventional updates.

"From our attempts at firing through the Zone, the bullets slow down. So, hypothetically, if you need to fire those .50s, do it a bit closer than usual with the field on—say, around 600 yards instead of the standard 800. I'm sorry to say I didn't have time to adjust the gun alignment for closer range, but I know you'll make it count."

Kenji smirked. "I programmed Sunday to assist as needed. She'll be dialed into the cameras and sensors on your Corsair—like Evel Knievel, but without the broken bones."

Joshua grinned. "Oorah!"

"I can already feel it," Flynn replied.

"Hell yeah!" the team echoed.

The group gathered around as Joshua showed off his latest additions—sensors designed to feed input to the UI/UX and link to Alpha, allowing the controller stick to also manipulate the Alpha Zone bubble when engaged.

"I added a special gauge too," Joshua continued. "It'll show the difference between the direction you're actually flying and where the nose is pointing. That's useful when the Zone starts messing with aerodynamics. You'll feel wind on the wings and rudder, but the plane could be heading somewhere else entirely. We'll set the Zone to Environment OFF so it lets air in—thankfully. Otherwise, this torque-monster engine would suck your eyes out of your skull before spitting you out in a second."

Kenji's eyes widened in amazement. "Sunday can even help you line up with the laser mount. She can guide you—or even adjust the plane's angle with the Zone—to keep your guns or rockets locked on target."

Joshua's tone shifts to a more serious note as he concludes.

"It's all cutting-edge, but remember—safety first," Joshua says. "We've got the Zone, but let's keep it smooth and steady up there."

With the briefing wrapped up, Flynn and the team feel a surge of anticipation. The Corsair, once a relic of the past, now stands reborn—modernized, reinforced, and ready to carve its path into the future under Flynn's skilled command.

Kenji, typing away on his laptop, barely looks up as he speaks. "I've configured the system so the pilot's stick and rudder inputs directly influence the Alpha's orientation. It'll feel like an extension of your own instincts."

"I like the sound of that," Flynn says. "What about monitoring the Alpha's status mid-flight?"

Joshua gestures toward the modified console. "We've added an auxiliary control panel. It'll feed you real-time performance data and let you adjust speed as needed—everything from energy output to field stability."

The team nods in approval, each member ensuring that old glory seamlessly merges with new science.

"And let's not forget Sunday," Kenji adds. "She'll have a direct link to the Corsair's systems. If anything goes wrong, she'll be our first line of defense."

"Having Sunday on our side is reassuring," Flynn admits.

Kenji quietly puts Sunday into sleep mode. She doesn't even know it.

"We installed a failsafe on your tablet," Kenji explains. "If needed, you can cut Sunday's connection or put her to sleep. That way, I can diagnose any issues remotely."

The team steps back to admire their handiwork. The Corsair now stands as a testament to their combined ingenuity and relentless drive.

Flynn rolls his shoulders, exhaling sharply. "Alright, boys. It's time to rock. I'm feelin' dangerous…"

His thoughts drift to Kurt—the friend who should be here but isn't. They couldn't reach him. Flynn remembers the grueling combat training, the endless drills, the lessons that shaped him. He murmurs under his breath, as if speaking to a ghost.

"I think I was prepared for this by an angel."

As Flynn secures his pilot gear, the team exchanges confident glances, their camaraderie unspoken but palpable.

Joshua guides Flynn to the Alpha engine, demonstrating how to install and disconnect it with precision.

The Corsair, now equipped with the Alpha engine, stood poised on the runway—a testament to their shared ambition and relentless pursuit of innovation.

Fronz placed a reassuring hand on Flynn's shoulder. "Remember, Flynn, we're with you every step of the way. Sunday's monitoring, and we're all here, ready to adapt and respond."

Flynn fastens his G-suit and connects it, inhaling deeply. With a final thumbs-up, he climbs into the cockpit, his pulse quickening at the challenge ahead. The engine thunders to life, the propeller slicing through the air as the Corsair—reborn through ingenuity and determination—ascends into the sky.

"Okay, Sunday, let's use 'Comanche 19' or 'Comanche Actual' for me, and you'll be 'Comanche Base.' Keeps comms clean over an open line," Flynn explained.

"Roger that, Comanche Actual. I read you loud and clear," Sunday responded.

The flight test

The sun glinted off the Corsair's sleek, polished fuselage as Flynn eased the throttle forward, the deep rumble of the engine rolling across the airstrip. Joshua's recent upgrades were nothing short of remarkable—advanced avionics, enhanced control surfaces, and reinforced structural components designed to withstand extreme maneuvers. Today's test would push the Corsair to its limits, but without the Alpha engine first, ensuring the airframe could endure high-stress conditions on raw mechanics alone.

Flynn gripped the stick as the Corsair surged down the runway, the tail wheel lifting off first. Within moments, the plane leapt into the sky, cutting through the air with precision. "All right, let's see what she's got," Flynn murmured, a grin tugging at his lips.

First, he pulled the Corsair into a steep climb, testing the engine's torque and control responsiveness. As he reached altitude, he rolled smoothly into a barrel roll at 400 knots, spinning through a perfect 360-degree rotation while holding a straight trajectory.

Next came the Immelmann turn—a half-loop followed by a roll—flipping the plane's direction in an instant. The Corsair responded flawlessly. Flynn smirked, pushing it into a dive, nosing the aircraft down at full throttle before pulling up hard to gauge the wings' stress tolerance.

"Time for the real test," Flynn muttered, tightening his grip. He executed a snap roll, sending the Corsair into a blur of motion, then transitioned into a high-G loop, forcing the airframe through unrelenting pressure. Finally, he locked into a tight turn, simulating evasive maneuvers, ensuring the plane remained agile and responsive under duress.

Flynn's grin widened as he leveled off at cruising altitude, his hand steady on the throttle. "All right, let's see what this baby can really do," he said, his voice crackling over the radio. He pushed the throttle forward, feeling the Corsair respond instantly as its powerful engine roared. The sudden surge of speed pressed him back into the seat, the horizon blurring as the plane shot forward to 440 knots.

He tested her in a straight-line sprint, pushing to maximum velocity. The airframe vibrated slightly but held steady. The distinctive high-pitched whistle of the Corsair added a haunting melody to his aerial ballet.

"Not bad," Flynn muttered. Pulling into a steep climb, he kept the throttle wide open, testing the Corsair's climb rate under full power. The engine roared without hesitation, smooth and relentless. Flynn laughed. "Joshua," he muttered over the radio, "you've outdone yourself. She's a beast."

With a flick of a switch, the Alpha Zone came to life, its subtle hum intertwining with the Corsair's roar. Flynn felt the immediate shift—an almost electric charge in the air—as the aircraft's speed surged under the Zone's influence. It wasn't just an enhancement; the Zone Engine fundamentally transformed the Corsair's performance.

A quick glance at the display confirmed it—Alpha Online glowed green on the UI.

"You could cut the Corsair's engine to idle and let the Alpha do the work," Kenji suggested.

Flynn nodded. "Good call. Reducing throttle to idle. Let's see how you handle the Zone, old girl."

He smirked. "Let's open her up to—oh, say 500 knots—and see what she's really got."

"Oh wow, that's unbelievably smooth. I can feel it—are we really going 500 knots? That's insane."

Flynn eases the speed down to 300 knots, preparing for a maneuver that only a handful of pilots can pull off—something he once saw an F-22 Raptor do on TV. He tilts the aircraft into a vertical glide while maintaining horizontal movement, flipping effortlessly through the air. His G-suit activates, keeping blood from pooling in his head as he pushes the limits.

"Oh my god, that is freaky. F-22s can do that without an Alpha engine? Unbelievable."

He squeezes the trigger, and the .50-caliber guns roar to life. With the canopy surrounding him, it's hard to gauge their full range, but he feels the subtle shifts in the aircraft as he adjusts the stick. The wind hits the plane in a way he's never quite felt before.

"Guys, the guns feel different. I can feel them firing, but they don't have that usual air-brake effect."

"Incredible… you guys have outdone yourselves."

Flynn exhales, shaking his head in disbelief. "Joshua, this… this is beyond what I imagined. And Kenji, the Corsair's engine… it's syncing with the Zone. The vibrations aren't as strong as usual."

Kenji, with a note of pride in his voice, replies, "A little help from Sunday. We thought you'd appreciate the synergy."

The harmony between the Corsair's engine and the Zone's hum creates something almost musical—an unspoken connection between man and machine, mechanical precision blending seamlessly with raw technological power.

Flynn grins. "It's more than great, Kenji. It feels like… coming home. Someone better ice up some cold ones."

As Flynn completes his pass, the exhilaration of flight, the thrill of pushing boundaries, and the satisfaction of this seamless integration between pilot and aircraft bring an irrepressible smile to his face.

High above, where the earth meets the sky, Flynn and the Corsair—bound by history ,and driven by the promise of the future—forge ahead, a duo reborn in the pursuit of discovery and defiance of limits.

"Alright, boys, I'm bringing her back in. I'd call this a successful test. There might be a sensor or two that need adjusting—I felt a slight drift in the controls. We'll review everything once I land," Flynn said.

He steadied the Corsair's course, brought the engine up to speed, and disengaged the Alpha, once again flying by the principles of Bernoulli.

Back in the hangar, the Corsair was carefully parked beside Fronz's Corsair, its fuel and ammunition replenished—a silent sentinel, awaiting its next call to duty.

Joshua, eyes gleaming with excitement, revealed his latest project to Flynn—a heavily modified van crowned with a mounted .50-caliber machine gun.

"I like to keep this handy," Joshua said, patting the weapon. "Locked and loaded—for close encounters."

Flynn let out a low whistle. "Oh, shit, man—that's awesome."

Joshua grinned. "Fronz's idea. He wants to make sure we have a Plan C if things go south. That includes a detonation timer and a kill switch. And let's be real—I already know you'd agree."

"I do," Fronz and Flynn said in unison.

With renovations underway at Flynn's house, he stayed at the facility to clear his mind. That evening, they enjoyed Flynn's signature BBQ—bone-in ribeye steaks, complemented by Fronz's carefully prepared sides: large double-baked potatoes, sautéed mushrooms, and his famous asparagus—one of the few vegetables Flynn would actually eat.

Flynn stood near the hangar, his gaze distant, lost in thought. The weight of losing his family and the relentless pressure were etched into his features. Joshua nudged Kenji and gestured toward Flynn.

"He's deep in thought and needs a distraction," Joshua muttered.

Kenji grabbed a football from a nearby shelf and tossed it to Joshua, who gave a sharp whistle. "Hey, Captain! Think fast!"

Flynn turned just in time to catch the ball, blinking out of his reverie. "Really?" he said, a small smile tugging at his lips.

"Come on," Joshua said, jogging a few steps back. "Let's see if your throwing arm is still as sharp as your flying skills."

They tossed the ball back and forth, laughter breaking the tension as they traded playful jabs. Eventually, Kenji had to sit down to throw, wheezing between chuckles. Flynn loosened up, his laughter mingling with theirs, the heavy thoughts momentarily set aside.

Raising a glass of rum, Flynn grinned. "My dear friends, you are the best."

"I've known Joshua since we were teenagers in junior high. We had our fair share of fights—nothing serious, just a few scuffles. Funny thing is, I don't even remember why. And honestly? I don't care."

Joshua smirked. "Was it because of a girl?"

"I doubt it. You're not good-looking enough." Flynn laughed.

They all broke out in laughter.

Flynn twirled the football on his fingertips. "This camaraderie—it's the same bond I had with the sailors I served with. Thank you for standing by me. To my family and yours. We wish you were here. Cheers, boys."

He didn't say it aloud, but in his heart, he was back with his family. He missed tossing a football with his dog, being close to the girls. His throat tightened, and his eyes stung. A gentle "I love you" slipped past his lips. Saying it felt good.

CHAPTER NINETEEN

ECHOES OF WISDOM

The late afternoon sun stretched long shadows across the sleek, modern interior of Team Nautilus's main conference room, where the core members had assembled for what was framed as a routine meeting. The usual clutter of coffee cups and notepads littered the table, yet an unusual tension hung in the air like an unspoken truth.

Fronz, typically the most stoic among them, seemed particularly introspective today, his gaze fixed on the golden hues of the setting sun through the floor-to-ceiling windows.

Flynn, who had known Fronz for years, immediately caught the change—his normally unkempt hair was combed for once. Leaning forward, he broke the silence. "Alright, Fronz, you called this meeting. What's on your mind?"

Fronz cleared his throat, fingers drumming against the table—a rare display of unease. "Yes, thank you, Flynn. I have a personal matter to discuss. As you all know, I've never been one to take much time off…"

Joshua, ever the mood-lightener, smirked. "You taking a vacation? That'd be more shocking than if the Alpha suddenly turned into a coffee machine."

A ripple of chuckles passed around the room, and even Fronz allowed the faintest hint of a smile. "Quite," he conceded. "However, the time has come for me to visit home. Europe. I haven't seen my family in years, and I think it's long overdue."

Kenji, the youngest but often the most perceptive, tilted his head, studying Fronz. "That sounds great, Fronz. Everyone needs a break now and then. But… is everything okay? You seem a little off."

Fronz met Kenji's gaze, then swept his eyes across the team. His expression was unreadable at first but softened as he exhaled. "My mother is sick. The one I get my brains from… she's fading fast. I fear this may be my only chance to see her before the inevitable."

Flynn leaned forward, his face lined with concern. "Fronz, if you need anything—support, assistance, whatever it is—just ask. Nautilus isn't just a team; we're family."

"I appreciate that, Flynn," Fronz replied, his voice steady but softer than usual. "And I deeply value this family, which makes leaving all the more difficult. But it's something I have to do."

Sensing the weight of the moment, Joshua set aside his usual jests. "When you find a good café, don't forget—we expect a postcard with some news."

"Especially if they serve good strudel," Flynn added, trying to keep the mood light. Fronz actually smiled at that. "I'll be sure to send updates. Maybe even a recipe or two for the strudel."

As the meeting wrapped up, Flynn walked with Fronz to the lobby, where his ride to the airport was scheduled to arrive. At first, they walked in silence, each lost in thought, until Flynn finally spoke.

"You know, Fronz, whatever you're facing, you don't have to do it alone. We're here for you, no matter how far away you are."

Fronz looked at Flynn, a rare, genuine smile breaking through his usual reserve. "I know, my friend. And that means more than I can say. But some things... some things need to be faced in the places where they first began." He exhaled, his voice tinged with nostalgia. "It's been twenty years since I left, chasing a dream of cold fusion. A dream so vivid, it drove me to seek you out here in the U.S."

Flynn clapped him on the shoulder. "Well, the door's always open. Alpha and Beta will miss their creator. And I'll miss my friend. You changed our lives. The honor is ours to have known you."

Fronz, eager to shift away from the sorrowful tone, smirked. "Seems I'm off to my homeland then—to become a man of mystery."

Flynn clapped Fronz on the back. "Just think of it as a vacation—with a side of espionage."

He knew Fronz enjoyed those kinds of books.

Laughter broke the tension as Fronz gathered his belongings, assuming a new identity for his journey to Switzerland via cruise—a mode of travel chosen as much for its secrecy as for the thrill of espionage.

"Don't forget to send us mail from the Alps, Mr. Incognito," Joshua said with a wink.

In the quiet aftermath of their tumultuous journey, Fronz and Flynn found a rare moment of respite—a chance to reflect on the path they had traveled together. With Kenji's presence lending a sense of continuity to their gathering, Fronz imparted his final words of wisdom, distilling their shared experiences into guidance and farewell.

"Flynn, over the years, I've shared all that I know with you. The essence of our work, the heart of our pursuit, was always rooted in understanding," Fronz said.

His voice, steady and sure, carried the weight of conviction—beliefs forged in the crucible of scientific rigor. "Time is the only true unit of measure. Ignorance breeds chaos, not knowledge. Ideals are peaceful, but history is violent."

"Remember, true science demands proof, not belief. It's a cycle—hypothesis, experiment, validation—repeated endlessly in the search for truth," Fronz continued, as if driving home a point left unfinished.

The air between them crackled with unspoken acknowledgment of their achievements—the breakthroughs that had irrevocably shaped the course of human history.

"We've ventured into realms few dare to tread," Fronz continued. "Our discoveries, our inventions… they're not just milestones. They're beacons for future generations."

In the shared silence that followed, Flynn's gratitude and respect for Fronz resonated deeply—a bond forged in the fires of friendship and tempered by the trials they had faced.

"Flynn, without the glue you provided, I would have lost my step. That's why I sought you out, and thank God I found you. I may have lost my way otherwise. You were the compass that kept us pointed toward true north. Thank you, Navigator. Oh, Captain, my Captain."

Fronz stood tall and proud, grabbing Flynn in a tight, brotherly embrace. Flynn responded in kind—then ruffled Fronz's hair.

"The honor was mine, my friend. I've learned so much just by being around you—absorbing your intelligence simply by sharing the same space," Flynn said with deep respect.

The distant hum of an approaching car signaled Fronz's ride. He grabbed his bag—light for someone embarking on an extended leave, but his reasons were his own, and Flynn respected his privacy.

"Take care, Fronz. Safe travels," Flynn said, raising a hand for a high five.

"Thank you, Flynn. Look after the team and everything else—I know you will. I expect to hear about all the progress," Fronz replied, his voice thick with emotion. "Truth be told, my family and estate need tending to." A tear welled in his eye.

As Fronz settled into the Uber, Flynn stepped back, watching the car disappear down the road and around the hill. A wave of emotions stirred within him—sadness, resolve, and an unspoken understanding. Fronz was fighting a battle he wasn't ready to share, and Flynn wouldn't press him.

Turning back to the building, Flynn knew the team would feel Fronz's absence, yet his presence would linger in every circuit and line of code they developed—his legacy woven into the very fabric of Team Nautilus. With renewed determination, Flynn made his way back to the lab, ready to uphold that legacy. Every milestone would stand as a tribute to their shared vision and unwavering commitment.

CHAPTER TWENTY

THE AIR STRIKE

The control room hummed with activity, a steady undercurrent of clicking keyboards and hushed, urgent conversations. Monitors lined the walls, casting a cold glow over the assembled personnel as data streams, radar readouts, and satellite imagery flickered across the screens.

At the center of it all, the Saga CEO stood with arms crossed, his gaze locked onto the largest screen. His expression was taut, the weight of the moment pressing down on him.

"They're breathing down my neck," he muttered, referring to the government. His eyes flicked to the radar, where a squadron of F-16s advanced toward their target. "Team Nautilus is making me look like a fool. Time to change the game."

Without looking away, he issued his command. "Initiate the airstrike. Expect resistance, but we have this under control."

The room surged with renewed urgency. Officers relayed orders, fingers flying over consoles. A nearby officer spoke into his headset. "Hold the F-16s at the perimeter until further notice. Deploy the choppers. Begin EM retrieval."

A slow smirk curled the CEO's lips. "We will secure that technology. There's no turning back now."

At the perimeter

Their camaraderie was a fleeting comfort, a light-hearted moment before the coming storm. By late morning, the sun had risen high, casting long shadows over the facility. The tranquility was abruptly broken by Sunday's sharp alert—one of the sensors had malfunctioned.

Sunday's voice cut through the stillness. "YELLOW ALERT! We have a sensor out. Kenji is troubleshooting."

Flynn responded without hesitation. "Roger that."

The CIA's logistical setbacks had delayed their original pre-dawn strike. A necessary refueling and last-minute coordination with the newly assigned DEI agents had bought the team time to run final tests on Alpha.

In the lead helicopter, the CIA operator issued his orders. "You are cleared hot. Primary objective: eliminate all monitoring systems and demolish the hangar. Kill everyone on-site and retrieve the bodies. First team neutralizes any defenses—those old WWII planes won't be a threat. Second team secures the device. Extraction must be swift. Once both teams are clear, we level the facility with missiles. F-16s are on standby for support. I'll call them in if needed."

The radio crackled as Hatchet, the lead F-16 pilot, confirmed. "Roger that."

Just after 1100, Sunday's voice rang out over the loudspeaker, mimicking Flynn's signature grit. "RED ALERT! Now hear this—I'm detecting activity at the northern perimeter, just over 200 miles out. Probability of a flock of birds? Low."

The acrid scent of engine oil and gasoline filled the air, anchoring Flynn in the moment. His pilot gear lay within reach, ready to be strapped on like a second skin. He paused, catching the tension in Sunday's tone.

Flynn called out, "Ohhh man, roger that, Sunday. Here we go. Sound the alarm."

Nearby, Joshua was already sprinting to the WWII-era crank alarm. He grabbed the wheel and gave it ten forceful turns. The wail of the alarm split the air—loud, raw, unmistakable. The sound carried the echoes of battles long past.

Grinning through the rising tension, Joshua bellowed, "Ooorah!"

Flynn smirked, his thoughts flickering to his old friend Kurt.

"Nice! Kurt would've loved this. He always had a knack for dramatic entrances," Flynn said.

His stomach clenched. The moment they had anticipated had arrived.

"I think that sensor going offline tells us everything we need to know. They're cutting off our ability to detect them before they move in. Good thing we had more than one on the Northern approach."

Joshua grinned and jogged toward the garage. "I'll have the van ready just in case. Who knows where you'll end up?"

Flynn nodded, pulling on his gloves as he strode toward his Corsair. The familiar weight of his helmet settled over his head, adrenaline already surging through his veins. Recent trials with the Corsair and the Zone engine had strengthened his confidence—he was ready for whatever was coming.

"If I have to land outside the facility for any reason—like catching a few bullets—be ready to haul ass and pick me up, mate." Flynn smirked at Joshua before climbing into the cockpit.

The Corsair's controls felt second nature, as if they were an extension of his own body. He glanced at the sky, the midday sun casting a bright sheen over the horizon. A grin tugged at his lips as he imagined the opposition closing in.

"Wait until they get a load of what I'm bringing to the party," he murmured.

His voice crackled over the radio on their designated channel as he prepped for takeoff.

"Sunday, battle stations manned. Once I get this baby up, we move fast—head toward the sun. I want it at my back to mask my approach."

"Roger that, Comanche 19," Sunday responded.

Flynn patted the controls affectionately. "Time to dance, old girl."

He eased the throttle forward, respecting the Corsair's raw power. The aircraft surged ahead, lifting gracefully into the sky and cutting through the crisp air. Flynn angled toward the mountain range, climbing higher. The plan was simple—ascend through the clouds and position himself with the sun at his back. A classic aerial combat maneuver, dating back to WWI, but still just as deadly.

Once the Zone engaged, Flynn dropped the Corsair engine to idle, letting the system control his speed. He banked hard, angling toward the mountains to align with the sun.

Sunday's voice crackled through the comms. "Two fast birds circling the perimeter. They might be hunting for more sensors."

Flynn considered the approaching helicopters. He had speed and maneuverability on his side, but they were highly trained, well-coordinated, and dangerous—just not fast enough to match him.

"Let's see what this baby can do," he said with a confident smirk.

The Enemy closes in

Flynn's screen linked to Sunday, displaying ten incoming targets closing fast.

"I think they're choppers," Sunday announced. "Five thousand feet, 150 knots. They're trying to mask their numbers, but I've got them."

Flynn muttered, "Ten against one," scanning the horizon. "Choppers aren't fast, but they've got rockets, missiles, and .50 cals. I need to take them out quickly."

His heart pounded, but his grip remained steady on the controls. He ascended into the cloud cover, keeping the sun at his back, casting deep shadows over the terrain below. His plan was simple—stay concealed in the sun's glare and strike when the enemy least expected it.

Kurt's training echoed in his mind: Don't think, feel. Stay locked in. React.

At 20,000 feet, he hovered like a bird of prey, fingers poised over the throttle, waiting for the perfect moment to strike.

The radio crackled.

"They're nearly in range," Sunday reported. "Prepare for engagement."

"Got it. Time to turn up the heat," Flynn replied. He smirked. "Come on, baby, let's hold it together."

The battle was seconds away, and Flynn was ready. In his mind, his initial approach would be unlike anything the enemy had ever seen.

With the sun masking his position, he decided on a lateral slide maneuver with Alpha, keeping his guns locked on the enemy while staying beyond the reach of their .50-caliber side gunners.

"Sunday, give me a countdown. I'll push to 400 knots and drop the hammer," Flynn ordered.

"Roger that." A pause. Then Sunday's voice came through, steady and clear.

"Okay, Comanche Actual, starting countdown… Five, four, three, two—punch it!"

Flynn tapped the accelerator control on the tablet and immediately felt the G-force. His G-suit kicked in, preventing the blood from rushing to his head.

The momentum of the warplane, combined with its whispering death sound, was awe-inspiring. Adrenaline surged through him.

He approached the choppers from a high angle, ensuring they arrived staggered—nearly single file and at slightly different elevations, each about ten feet apart. Flynn's initial position was 800 feet to the right, angled inward, and elevated 500 feet. He hoped this approach would confuse them—if they even saw him—while the sun masked his presence.

Flynn scanned the formation. Each group of five choppers had an Apache helicopter leading, armed with two missiles, followed by four Black Hawks carrying troops and a .50-

caliber machine gun mounted on each side. The second group mirrored the first, with another Apache at the front.

Sunday, monitoring the radio frequencies, pinpointed their channel. At the perfect moment, she blasted the whistling death sound at full volume, sparing Flynn's ears. The chopper pilots, caught off guard, recoiled in shock. "Jesus!" they shouted, yanking off their headsets. Flynn smirked. The element of surprise was his deadliest weapon.

The Corsair pushed beyond its intended speed. Flynn pressed the left rudder pedal, angling the nose toward the flight path. The plane began sliding sideways through the air at 500 knots—first at 45 degrees, then 90. At 1,000 yards and a 45-degree elevation, he executed the maneuver as envisioned. A little shaky at first, but he quickly corrected with the rudder.

The aircraft shuddered as the wind slammed against it, leaving a long vapor trail streaming from its wings, rudder, and ailerons.

Sunday monitored Flynn's approach, with Kenji watching beside her. She counted down, timing when he should fire.

"Hit it!" Sunday commanded.

Flynn aligned his sights on the lead Apache in the first group, the rest trailing in formation. Over the radio, on Team

Nautilus's frequency, he called out, "Light 'em up!"—at the exact moment Sunday had anticipated.

The Corsair's six .50-caliber guns roared to life, unleashing a lethal barrage. Fueled by adrenaline and precision, Flynn maneuvered the aging fighter alongside the enemy formation, weaving like a ghost in the sky.

A surge of triumph shot through him as his rounds shredded through the first five choppers, tearing apart their blades and fuselages. Explosions erupted in rapid succession, sending them spiraling down in flames.

Kenji's eyes widened as he watched the spectacle unfold on his monitors, which displayed live feeds from the Corsair's GoPros and two hovering drones.

"Woooo! Did you see that?" Kenji shouted. "Oh my god, Flynn's slide idea actually worked!"

Joshua, monitoring from his tablet, responded on a different channel. "Holy shit, I didn't think that would work. Go get 'em, Jedi!"

Flynn grinned. "Sunday, what channel are they using? I'd like to blow them a little kiss."

"Channel 14," she answered.

"Roger that."

Flynn switched frequencies. "Did we catch you fuckers napping?" he muttered through clenched teeth, his pulse pounding.

The second group of choppers broke formation, scattering.

Flynn switched back to Nautilus's channel 6. He had no interest in listening to their chatter—Sunday would handle that. Correcting his course, he prepped for another pass, executing the slide at 400 knots, keeping his enemies guessing.

The cockpit roared with sound and fury as Flynn banked hard, his Corsair slicing through the sky like a blade. The radio crackled, and Sunday's voice cut through the chaos.

"Comanche 19, bring that big-ass nose down three degrees... my God in heaven."

Flynn bared his teeth in a determined grin. "Roger that, Comanche base. Coming in hot for round two! Call out any adjustments—we're making history here."

The second pass was pure, adrenaline-fueled madness. Flynn's .50 cals thundered, unleashing a deadly hailstorm into the enemy formation. A Blackhawk in the second wave burst into flames, spiraling toward the earth, while another exploded midair, its debris raining over the forest. The remaining helicopters scattered, their once-coordinated maneuvers dissolving into chaos. Flynn's unpredictable aerial tactics—enhanced by Alpha's agility—shattered every rule in the book and every expectation the enemy had.

But they weren't finished. Two choppers peeled away from the pack, flanking him fast. Their .50-caliber guns blazed, rounds slamming into the Corsair's left wing and fuselage. The cockpit rattled as warning indicators lit up his dashboard. Flynn scanned them—nothing critical. The old girl could take it.

"I felt that, old girl," he muttered, patting the control panel. "But we're still in the fight."

A piercing alarm blared. Missile lock.

Flynn's pulse spiked, but instead of pulling back, he tightened his grip on the stick. "You wanna play, boys? Let's dance."

He wrenched the Corsair into a brutal bank, engaging Alpha's enhanced turning capabilities. The warbird cut a tighter circle than any modern jet could match, slipping behind the pursuing choppers. A barrage of rockets streaked past, missing by inches, their smoke trails curling into the sky.

Flynn's thumbs squeezed the triggers, and his .50 cals roared again. The nearest helicopter exploded in a fireball.

Diving low to avoid return fire, he worked the controls instinctively, feeling every pulse of the Corsair as though it were an extension of himself. An old warplane standing defiant against cutting-edge technology.

A grim smile tugged at his lips as he lined up for another pass. "Still got some fight left in us, old girl. Let's show 'em what we're made of."

Unbeknownst to Flynn, Sunday was making constant micro-adjustments to the Corsair's angle, trajectory, and altitude, subtly shifting the aircraft in ways his instruments didn't register. It was a good thing, too—without those minor course corrections, he would have taken more hits and landed fewer accurate shots. But Sunday knew Flynn's pride, so she said nothing. The machine and its pilot worked in harmony, but she was the invisible hand helping him dodge bullets that could have ended the fight early.

Kenji, worried for his friend, had spent days refining Sunday's programming, optimizing her ability to assist Flynn in the battle they had all prepared for.

Flynn pulled the stick back, sending the Corsair into a steep climb before diving headfirst into the fray, guns blazing.

He swooped over a lone chopper, its altitude too high for its weapons to lock onto him. Something felt off. Flynn realized this pilot might be baiting him into a trap.

Suddenly, missile-warning alarms blared through the cockpit. Flynn's heart pounded—this was the remaining Apache, its missile tracking and fire-control systems now coming into play. But instead of retreating, he pushed the Corsair harder. The Apache had to be at least a few miles out to fire an air-to-air missile, giving him only seconds to react.

Flynn slammed the Alpha accelerator, surging forward without knowing the missile's exact trajectory—or whether it was heat-seeking or radar-guided.

"Sunday?" Flynn's voice was tight, a single word laced with urgency.

Sunday was already ahead of him. Within a fraction of a second, she initiated a sharp vertical climb—just before the missile could make contact. Flynn spotted it a moment later, banking hard in the opposite direction and punching the accelerator to 500 knots. The missile, losing thrust due to its short range, spiraled uselessly toward the ground.

Flynn exhaled sharply. "Damn, Sunday. You really saved my ass."

"Stay on that bogey and take him out," Sunday advised. "He's got one more missile left, and he'll come around for another shot. He's bearing 190 degrees—I'll mark him on your scope."

"Roger that, Sunday. I see him. I'll hit him from above." Flynn adjusted his course.

He locked onto the Apache, closing in at 350 knots while executing a maneuver unique to Alpha—a steep slide, 45 degrees downward and 45 degrees left.

Before he could fire, three more Black Hawks launched coordinated rocket attacks.

Flynn twisted through the chaos, narrowly dodging the rockets before retaliating with his own barrage. His shots came close but missed.

The remaining helicopter pilots, frustrated and desperate, struggled to predict his next move—always one step behind.

Flynn banked hard to the right, his Corsair responding with smooth precision. The Alpha engine thrummed beneath him, pushing the old warbird beyond its original limits. The speed was exhilarating, and the plane felt alive, slicing through the air like a knife through silk. As he lined up for another pass, he spotted the helicopters splitting into two teams, adjusting their formations and closing in from multiple angles.

He moved with instinct, flying as if the Corsair were an extension of himself, blending traditional maneuvers with the unique capabilities only the Alpha could perform. But in his focus, he neglected to adjust his speed, pushing his aircraft to its absolute limit.

"Flynn, check your nine," Sunday's voice crackled through his headset.

As he banked around, tracer rounds lit up the sky—blazing streaks of .50 caliber fire cutting dangerously close. The helicopters were relentless, their guns shredding through the air, but with Alpha guiding his every move, Flynn wove through the onslaught, his Corsair skidding laterally in ways no conventional plane could match. Or so he thought.

"Alright, let's see how you handle this," Flynn muttered, yanking the Corsair into a sharp left bank. He locked onto a chopper, finger tightening on the trigger—

Then the sky erupted. Machine guns snarled in response, and a round clipped his rudder.

They had adapted. Timing their shots, anticipating his evasions. He needed a new approach.

Spotting the mountain range ahead, Flynn angled toward it. If he could funnel them into a confined space, he could dictate the fight. The helicopters scattered like a swarm of locusts, two staying high, two attempting to flank him at a sluggish 150 knots.

Diving at 400 knots, he plunged into the canyon entrance, vanishing into the terrain. He slowed near an outcropping, waiting.

"Flynn, two choppers approaching from above," Sunday warned. "Staying hidden is smart. Pounce like a cat in the dark."

Flynn spotted both choppers coming into range and immediately fired two rockets—either to destroy them or force a reaction. One rocket struck its target, sending a chopper spiraling into flames, while the other chopper banked hard to the right to evade.

Raising his altitude, Flynn surveyed the battlefield and caught sight of the remaining two helicopters splitting up, advancing from his left.

They unleashed a relentless storm of rockets, mixed with .50 caliber fire. Flynn adjusted his altitude and maneuvered swiftly, weaving through the deadly barrage with precision and speed.

A quick glance at his ammo count told him the grim truth—only four or five of his .50 calibers were still firing, and his ammunition was running dangerously low.

Whispering to himself, Flynn muttered, "One more time, old girl. Let's finish this."

Locking onto a chopper, he pushed his aircraft forward, coming in from above to avoid its line of fire. With calculated precision, he unleashed his remaining forward rockets, then let loose with his .50 calibers, tearing the enemy apart in a fiery explosion.

But the last chopper had slipped behind him. Without hesitation, Flynn fired his rear-facing rockets, hoping to throw it off. One rocket missed, but the other struck dead center—right where the pilot sat—sending the helicopter plunging to the earth.

A sudden burst of machine-gun fire rattled through Flynn's aircraft. He felt the impact, the unmistakable thud of metal being torn apart.

"I'm hit again!" he called into his radio. His voice was steady—years of training had conditioned him for moments like this. Even as his warbird groaned under the strain of relentless maneuvers and enemy fire, his instincts remained sharp.

A quick glance at his gauges confirmed the damage—fuel was leaking, and one of his control sensors had been compromised.

He knew that if he had to fly the plane like a conventional aircraft, he would struggle—if not outright fail. The Zone Engine was the only thing keeping him in the air.

Observing his enemies, Flynn realized they had adapted to his attacks. As their numbers dwindled, one thought became clear: he needed to land before a fire broke out.

His Corsair was smoking, leaking fuel, and the engine temperature was rising—likely due to oil issues, given that the engine was air-cooled. Yet, thanks to Alpha, he was still in the fight. Flynn knew he had to be smart—one more hit, and luck might not be on his side. But with the Zone Engine keeping him aloft and his instincts sharp, he wasn't finished yet.

He considered whether now was the time to retreat. The aggressive slides and turns, maneuvers no plane was built to endure at such speeds, had likely strained the hull. The wind had battered her at punishing angles beyond her intended limits.

As the final enemy helicopter succumbed to his relentless assault, the battlefield fell silent—a stark contrast to the chaos moments before. Alone in the vast expanse, Flynn didn't have the luxury to reflect on the battle, the slide maneuver, or the undeniable truth that when originality meets courage, the impossible becomes possible.

Drawing a deep, satisfied breath, Flynn patted the dashboard and said, "We did it, old girl. You're a badass."

Turning the Corsair toward home, his ammo count dangerously low with only two missiles left, Flynn carried with him not just victory, but the knowledge that against overwhelming odds, he and his team had redefined the limits of air combat.

Amidst the aerial ballet of danger and defiance, Flynn's Corsair teeters on the brink of both glory and disaster. His sensors falter, their responses sluggish, while the airframe groans under the strain of battle. Reinforcements arrive—fast-moving F-16s streak across the sky, their sleek silhouettes slicing through the chaos at just under Mach 1, summoned to support the beleaguered helicopter squadron.

Flynn eyes the approaching jets. "Looks like the cavalry's arrived..."

The battle escalates. The F-16s, modern and lethal, present an entirely new challenge, their superior capabilities eclipsing those of Flynn's vintage Corsair. Yet his resolve remains unshaken, adrenaline sharpening his focus. The stakes have never been higher.

"She's smoking in the cockpit. The smoke's escaping, but the bubble slows it down," Flynn mutters, gripping the controls tighter.

Seeking both refuge and a tactical edge, he dives into the canyon, the jagged cliffs momentarily shielding him from relentless pursuit. A deadly game of cat and mouse unfolds—his Corsair's engine roars against the canyon walls, its echo bouncing like a ghostly warning.

Back at the hangar, the team watches in tense anticipation, their screens glowing with real-time data. Every maneuver, every close call, is recorded—a testament to Flynn's unmatched skill and defiance in the face of overwhelming odds.

Kenji grinned. "He did it. Nine down. That's Ace status, baby! In less than a day."

Sunday confirmed, "Five aerial victories make an Ace. All targets verified—Flynn's officially in. It's Miller time!"

But victory comes at a cost. The Corsair, battered and bruised from battle, shows severe structural damage. The maneuvers, while effective, have pushed the aircraft past its limits. Cracks spiderweb across the airframe—damage Flynn can't ignore. If he lands, she won't fly again. Pushing her sideways, faster than she was rated for, has taken its toll.

Grimly assessing the damage, Flynn muttered, "She's seen better days. Controls are stiff—she's coming apart. Not good… but she's one badass aircraft."

The return to base becomes a battle of its own. The Corsair fights against both the enemy-inflicted damage and the brutal strain of combat. Smoke thickens in the cockpit, stinging Flynn's eyes and blurring his vision. The acrid scent is a constant reminder of the aircraft's fragile state.

As the ground rushes closer, Flynn wrestles with the landing gear. Every second stretches into eternity. Then, with a groan of stressed metal, the gear locks into place.

"Not a moment too soon," Flynn muttered. "Time to bring her in. One last landing."

"I see you heading for that open field—landing zone two. I'll come to you," Joshua replied.

Flynn drops the Corsair to 50 feet above the ground and shuts off Alpha. From here, it's all glide.

The field surges up to meet him. Every movement is deliberate. Every thought is focused on bringing her down safely. The landing, though treacherous, becomes a testament to Flynn's unyielding nerve—the resolve of a pilot who refuses to go quietly into the quiet of defeat.

Flynn manages to hard-land the crippled Corsair. The brakes engage but aren't as effective as usual. He throttles back and brings the aircraft to a complete stop, with Joshua in visual range. As the adrenaline wears off, Flynn's hands begin to shake.

Joshua pulls the van in closer, parks next to the Corsair, and monitors the rangefinder while manning the .50.

Flynn hops out of the plane, quickly disconnects Alpha, then pauses. Resting a hand on the aircraft's massive engine, he murmurs, "Thank you, old girl. You're the best." He gives the engine a quick high five before stepping back. Only then does he fully take in the damage—bullet holes riddling both wings, the rudder bent sharply to the right, and the strong scent of gasoline hanging in the air.

The CIA team leader had been in the first chopper—killed by Flynn on his initial pass. As a result, the F-16s didn't receive the order to engage until it was almost too late.

Sunday's voice crackled over the comms. "I've got two fast-approaching birds inbound. Move your ass, please! I think we've also lost two more sensors on the grid."

Flynn bolts for Joshua's van. He decides to head away from the facility, steering in the opposite direction of Beta. The last chopper circles in the distance, too far out to take a shot.

"Here you go, mate. Plug this baby in and man the .50. I'll head for the tree line at 270 degrees relative," Flynn says, eyes locked ahead.

Joshua secures Alpha to the van. "Alpha's locked and loaded. So is Ol' Painless."

Flynn presses the mic button. "Comanche Base, give me 200 knots—but don't squash us."

Sunday's voice crackled over the comms. "Roger that, Comanche Actual."

In the aftermath of a relentless aerial duel—one that saw Flynn earning ace status in a single day—the situation remained perilous. The Corsair, now a burning wreck, stood as a grim reminder of both victory and survival's cost.

Joshua, ever vigilant, felt an all-too-familiar sense of dread creeping in. He knew these aircraft well—had worked on them as a Marine. Eyes locked on the horizon, he muttered, "Feels like we're dancing on the edge, Flynn. Those 16's aren't done with us yet."

Sunday's voice sliced through the tension, sharp with urgency. "Two F-16s inbound. Comanche Actual, expedite right f'ing now, please!"

Flynn smirked. “Damn, I do love a well-placed F-word now and then.”

“Ooorah, Cap!” Joshua shot back.

Flynn tapped the tablet, engaging the zone before slamming the accelerator. The landscape blurred past, speed filling him with a familiar thrill. A grin stretched across his face.

“Increasing speed—just under Mach 1. We don’t need a sonic boom right now.” His fingers danced over the controls. “Oh yeah, she’s really moving now, baby.”

A thunderous shockwave rippled behind them as they punched through Mach 1.

Flynn knew the risks. If he lifted the van above the treetops, they’d be exposed to missile fire. Keeping it low, just skimming the ground, was their best chance.

They weren’t defenseless. Joshua manned the .50-cal, his voice a battle cry. “Locked and loaded!”

The van surged forward, propelled by Alpha’s enhanced capabilities. The trees became their shield, the terrain a blur. The F-16s, relentless as ever, found their prey slipping from their grasp.

As they neared the forest's edge, the roar of gunfire and the whine of engines replaced the rush of wind and the creak of branches.

In a clearing, the van came into view. The F-16s engaged immediately, their cannon fire tearing through the vehicle's side, igniting a blaze that barely missed Flynn in the driver's seat. He gritted his teeth, slowing to 130 mph before shutting off the Alpha, braking lightly, and veering onto a denser forest road.

Flynn's mind raced. What the hell do I do now? Then, without warning, the van's engine sputtered and died. He slammed the emergency brake, unbuckled, and muttered under his breath, What else could go wrong?

Shouting over the roar of flames, Flynn called out, "Joshua! How's that fire?!" as he reached for the fire extinguisher.

But fate had dealt a cruel hand. Amidst the chaos, Joshua—Flynn's steadfast companion through countless trials—was silent, his body slumped and bloodied.

"Joshua! No! Fuck!" Flynn choked out, his chest tightening as he saw Joshua's lifeless form draped over the Alpha case. His eyes flicked to the shattered antenna and receiver. The realization hit him like a gut punch.

The loss was immediate, devastating—a blow that sent Flynn reeling.

Yet, through the grief, sheer determination surged within him. The mission wasn't over. The technology they had sacrificed everything for still needed protection.

Sunday's voice crackled over the secure radio. "Comanche Actual, the remote detonator is compromised. No signal can be sent. Options are limited."

Flynn exhaled slowly, his thoughts drifting to his family. He could almost hear Lilian's voice—soft, comforting—as it had been during their last call. A bittersweet smile ghosted across his lips.

"Then it's time," Flynn muttered to himself. "No way I'm letting these bastards have it."

He keyed the comms. "Sunday, Broken Arrow."

Sunday's tone softened. "Understood, Captain. Say hi to Elvis for us."

Flynn couldn't help but chuckle, the weight of the moment briefly lifted by Sunday's humor. But as he turned toward the Alpha engine, his resolve hardened.

He searched for the remote detonator—their last resort—but found it in ruins. However, the Alpha engine, secure in its stainless steel container, remained intact. The tablet confirmed Alpha's systems were at condition green and ready for destruct mode. Spinning the mercury past controllable speeds, combined with a small explosive added post-construction in the carrying case, would ensure complete destruction.

He would need to press the destruct button on the tablet, then manually activate the kill switch on the explosive.

Kenji, eyes brimming with tears, spoke softly in Japanese. "Safe journey, Captain. I love you."

Quantum Entanglement

With the enemy's last chopper closing in, its path guided by the rising smoke from the van, the roar of approaching forces grew louder. Overhead, an F-16 circled lower, its presence a grim countdown to the inevitable.

Flynn unlatched the case, revealing the sleek, glowing Alpha engine. Embedded within it lay the self-destruct mechanism—a final safeguard that could only be activated manually.

A sudden wave of calm washed over him. It wasn't fear or panic—it was peace. His hand hovered over the button, his voice steady. "You lose, bitches."

In these final moments, Flynn thought not of himself, but of the greater good. The sacrifice he was about to make would ensure that their groundbreaking technology never fell into the wrong hands. He braced for the end, knowing this was his final gambit to protect both the Alpha engine and the legacy of his team.

When the explosion came, it would be devastating—a brilliant cascade of energy unleashing an electromagnetic pulse across a ten-mile radius. The silent wave would cripple enemy machinery, rendering all electrical devices useless.

Yet, in those vanishing moments before detonation, reality itself seemed to slow. Unbeknownst to Flynn, an unseen observer watched from beyond the veil.

Sotra—a being of ancient knowledge and wisdom—stood at the threshold of her dimension, profoundly connected to the unfolding drama. She had silently witnessed Flynn and his team's courage, their unwavering resolve. Now, as he prepared to make the ultimate sacrifice, she found herself moved.

No guarantee of survival. No escape plan. Only the certainty that his death would prevent unimaginable power from falling into the wrong hands. That kind of selfless courage—that unwavering will—was rare, even among the most advanced beings she had encountered. It was why she had chosen him.

Sotra whispered to herself with urgency, *"You will carry on, Flynn. The future still needs you."*

With a purpose that defied time and dimensional space, she closed her eyes, envisioning Flynn in the van, the detonator gripped tightly in his hand. Reaching out with both mind and spirit, she tapped into ancient forces—long dormant, never forgotten.

As his finger descended, the world around him slowed. Just before the button clicked, a faint shimmer of blue light enveloped him. Sotra's presence was undeniable—her mastery over quantum entanglement bending reality itself.

In a millisecond—imperceptible to mortals yet an eternity for Sotra—she extended her hand toward the van's fading outline in her mind's eye. With a precise, deliberate gesture, she invoked a Quantum Entanglement Split, an act of unfathomable complexity.

Her thoughts shaped the cosmos. By the quantum threads of time and space, be divided. Be saved.

Flynn initiated the self-destruct. BOOM!

A brilliant blue explosion erupted, swallowing the van in radiant intensity.

In that sliver of a moment, Flynn experienced the impossible—his essence stretched across the very fabric of the universe. In an instant, he became two—Flynn A and Flynn B—quantum reflections of each other, bound by shared consciousness and memory.

Flynn A emerged in the Fifth Dimension, a realm unshackled by earthly limitations, a place of surreal beauty and profound stillness. The transition was jarring, yet Sotra's presence anchored him, offering both understanding and peace. Sleep came swiftly.

Flynn A, exhausted after the ordeal, groggily muttered, "Where... What the hell?" He had no idea who Sotra was or what had just transpired.

Though drained from the strain of the Quantum Entanglement split, Sotra managed a reassuring nod. "You were saved, Flynn. A choice was made in the blink of an eye. The world doesn't know of your sacrifice—but they will. It's okay. You can rest now."

The calmness in Sotra's voice settled over Flynn like a gentle wave. His vision blurred as fatigue overtook him.

Meanwhile, Flynn B materialized inside the secure mountain lair beside the Beta engine. The sudden shift left him disoriented—the expected explosion was absent, yet he remembered the van, the self-destruction, and the impending doom. He was both here and elsewhere. The realization was staggering.

A ripple, like a distorted wave of water, pulsed through the air, and suddenly, he was standing beside Beta, breathless and weary. "This... This is impossible. I was ready to end it all."

Sotra's voice echoed in his mind. He hesitated, then exhaled. "Oh, uhh... I think I'll lie down for a while." He made his way to the bed, collapsed onto the pillow, and was out cold.

Back in the forest, the explosion erupted. The Alpha engine's electromagnetic pulse surged outward, disrupting the systems of the helicopter and the F-16s. Their engines failed midair, sending them plummeting toward the ground in fiery destruction—a silent testament to Flynn's intended sacrifice.

As Sotra steadied herself, recovering from the immense exertion, a quiet sense of satisfaction tempered her exhaustion. The decision to split Flynn across dimensions had been made in an instant, but its consequences would echo through time.

Exhaling deeply, she whispered, "It is done. The ripples of this day will be felt for generations."

In this moment of crisis, Sotra's intervention didn't just alter Flynn's fate—it reshaped the future itself. With his existence now entwined between two worlds, Flynn stands as a beacon of hope, a living testament to the unseen forces that shape humanity's destiny

.

CHAPTER TWENTY - ONE

TYING IT TOGETHER

Flynn B, in his altered state, finds himself enveloped in the bewildering stillness of the cave—the mountain's secure vault serving as both sanctuary and prison. The stark contrast between the expected fiery demise and the quiet, dimly lit enclosure he now occupies leaves him disoriented. The memories are vivid: the air battle in his magnificent Corsair, Alpha unleashing destruction upon the enemy, the van, the loss of his best friend, the impending explosion. Each moment is etched into his mind, clashing against the inexplicable calm of his present surroundings.

After ten hours, Flynn B awakens.

Muttering to himself, he says, "I suppose this is a good time to initiate Operation Bob Incognito."

Meanwhile, the Zoomies remain vigilant, keeping a close eye on him.

Noticing his movements, Sunday speaks up. "Password, please."

"Snicklfritz DN38416," Flynn replies.

Sunday responds, "Oh, hello, Actual. But how in the wide world of sports is this even possible? Did you see Elvis?"

With a smirk, Flynn quips, "Thank you, thank you very much. Honestly, I have no idea what happened. Give me a minute—I feel like I've slept for a day, had way too much tequila, and man, am I starving."

Questions swirl in his mind, unanswered. The cave offers no explanations, only the echoing reminder of events too fantastic to be easily understood. Despite the confusion, Flynn takes stock of his situation. There's no immediate threat, no reason to charge headfirst into the unknown beyond the cave's confines. For now, caution is his ally.

Gathering his thoughts, Bob executes the directive and takes a moment to assess his resources. A plan begins to form—driven by necessity and sheer survival instinct. The discovery of a well-maintained yet battered truck, its plates marked Alaska, is the first piece of the puzzle. Then, there's Beta—the enigmatic presence in his life, savior or jailor, lingering in his thoughts.

Flynn recalls the command phrases for Sunday, the AI, to activate specific protocols. He issues a clear directive.

"Engage stealth protocol. Command code 075 @ 90d," he instructs.

"Roger that, Captain. Command accepted and executed," Sunday confirms.

Bob interjects, his voice laced with precision. "I will initiate the Bob protocol. Mr. Incognito."

"Roger that, Bob," Sunday acknowledges.

This protocol ensures the entire team remains hidden as long as necessary. Avoiding the military, the government, and law enforcement takes priority. Sunday will notify Kenji in 90 days.

With $10,000 in cash, a stash of clothes, food, his trusty .45 pistol loaded with ample ammunition, a laptop, and other essentials safely tucked away in the bunker, Bob realizes he's more prepared than he initially thought. His memory sharpens. The tools for a long journey—an escape, a fresh start—are within reach.

Bob exhales. "Florida... Far enough to blend in and disappear. Time to hit the road."

The decision solidifies. He will disappear into the sun-drenched anonymity of Florida. Desperation fuels the plan, but beneath it lies a sliver of hope. Staying behind means becoming a target in the aftermath of chaos—an unacceptable risk.

With deliberate movements, Bob takes stock of his supplies. Much of it is already packed into the truck. He transfers the rest, each item a tangible reminder of the life he's leaving behind and the uncertain future ahead. Secured in the back is Beta—silent, potent, and an unknown variable on the journey that awaits.

Bob secured the mountain lair before setting off under the cover of darkness. In the rearview mirror, the mountain faded into the distance, a silent sentinel to the extraordinary events that had unfolded. He drove with purpose, the open road stretching before him like a blank canvas—a fresh start waiting to be painted. The journey to Florida was long, the miles unraveling like the remnants of his fractured past.

He exhaled, his voice barely above a whisper. "New beginnings... Whatever lies ahead, I'm ready."

The solitude of the drive gave him time to reflect and plan. He pondered the mysteries of his survival—was Alpha truly gone? What role did Beta play in all of this? And what did it mean to be thrust into a new identity? The road ahead wasn't just a path to Florida; it was a passage to reinvention, a chance for 'Bob Smith' to forge a life free from the ghosts of his past.

During a stop for the night at a roadside hotel, he decided to change his appearance. He trimmed his hair, shaved his beard, and swapped his usual ballcap for a boonie hat. As he thought of his family, a single tear slipped down his cheek. “I miss you all so much.”

This journey wasn’t just about distance—it was about self-discovery. With Beta as his silent guardian and the road as his guide, he pushed forward into uncertainty, the weight of his memories fueling his determination to embrace whatever came next.

He knew the world believed he had died in the explosion. He had to disappear, to start over. The secure vault could be opened from both inside and out, and he had planned ahead—stashing a burner phone, still on its charger, in the truck. There was no one to call, not yet, so he placed the phone on the passenger seat and kept driving.

Meanwhile, in the ethereal expanse of Sotra’s dimension, Flynn A stirred. His body felt impossibly heavy, exhaustion sinking deep into his bones. The world around him was unlike anything he had ever known—a place of tranquility and surreal beauty, untouched by the chaos and conflict of his past. Here, in this quiet refuge, the storm within him finally settled.

For the first time in what felt like an eternity, peace found him. A quiet, healing presence enveloped him, soothing wounds both seen and unseen.

Flynn A whispered to himself, "Is this real... or just another dream?"

The question lingers in the air, unanswered, as Flynn surrenders to the restorative embrace of this new reality.

Bob listens to the internet news and skims the obituaries during gas station and diner stops. He comes across a story that paints him—under the name Vance Cavalla—as a deranged man piloting a malfunctioning WWII-era plane on a path of destruction. The media claims he's lashing out after his wife and grandkids were found dead in an accident where he remains a suspect. According to the reports, he took out his aggression on helicopters attempting to assist him after he called 911. Then, the pilot allegedly detonated an EM explosion, killing a dozen civilians without cause. The authorities now label it a potential act of domestic terrorism, with an ongoing investigation. The broadcast flashes images of his home and the facility, both surrounded by police.

Bob grips the steering wheel, his knuckles white. "Oh my fucking god, are you for real?" He lets loose a string of expletives, cursing at the absurdity of the media's narrative.

Six hours pass as he stews over it. He wonders if Fronz knows yet that Flynn was involved in the explosion.

Bob dials Fronz's number. "Time to reach out to an old friend."

The call connects. Fronz, now aboard a cruise liner heading to Europe, stiffens at the familiar voice—one he never expected to hear again. He had seen the reports of the explosion and assumed the worst.

Fronz collects himself, trying to offer what little support he can. "I don't know how I'm still alive," Bob admits.

Fronz exhales. "Well, you sound alive. What's the story?"

"It's a long story, Fronz—one I'm still trying to understand myself."

"Josh didn't make it. God rest his soul."

"You'll have to explain when you're ready. I always liked him. He loved my cooking too—maybe even more than you," Fronz replied.

"Well, he was a Marine. You can imagine all the terrible food he endured," Bob said, attempting to inject humor into the conversation.

Fronz chuckled. "I'm sure—not as bad as the chow on a submarine."

"No chance," Bob laughed, shaking his head.

Their conversation became a lifeline for Bob, with Fronz offering support and counsel as he wrestled with the weight of survivor's guilt and the unanswered questions that haunted him.

"I keep asking myself—why am I still here? And the equations on the whiteboard... where did they come from? Divine intervention?" Bob admitted.

"Flynn, you know I'm a man of science. But sometimes, the answers we seek aren't found in textbooks or experiments. Maybe, just maybe, there's more to this universe than we ever dared to imagine. I'm betting on an intelligence that's been here much longer than we have. When you rule out the obvious, what remains may be the answer," Fronz said, his voice thoughtful.

Fronz's words, though grounded in logic, left room for the mysteries that defied explanation. He reminded Bob of the principles that had guided them—a journey shaped by discovery, insight, and the relentless pursuit of knowledge.

"Remember, Flynn, science is the pursuit of truth, not faith. We must question, test, and prove—again and again. That's the foundation of everything we've built," Fronz continued.

"You're right, as always. I guess I'm still the dreamer, looking for answers in the stars," Bob replied.

As Bob prepares to move forward into the unknown, Fronz's wisdom and teachings resonate within him—a reminder of the unbreakable bond they share and the enduring pursuit of knowledge that has defined their lives.

In this tale of two Flynns, where science converges with the inexplicable, and earthly struggles intertwine with otherworldly peace, a complex narrative unfolds—one of survival, identity, and the indomitable human spirit. While Flynn A found solace in an alien dimension, Bob faced the challenges of a new beginning in the same familiar world. Their journeys reflect the multifaceted nature of existence and the eternal quest for understanding in a universe brimming with wonders and mysteries.

The next day, Bob stops at a remote motel, his laptop open, the webcam flickering. He assumes the signal is weak. Moments later, Fronz calls him back—this time, from his room aboard the cruise ship.

"We did great things together, my friend," Fronz says, his voice laced with warmth. "Our work is immortal. You'll see. And thank you—for pushing me to stay on this journey with you. I might have given up more than once without you."

Fronz, knowing Flynn long before he adopted the name Bob, had already considered what lay ahead. He knew Flynn would strive to understand his capabilities, wrestling with the possibility of time travel to correct the timeline that stole his family. He would grapple with the decision, but in the end, Fronz believed he would take the leap. And when he did, Fronz would do everything in his power to prepare him—mentally and academically.

"Also," Fronz added, "I've written this down to get it right. Listen carefully. There are a few things I apply daily that I don't think I've ever shared with you before."

Self-control is strength, and calmness is mastery. Reach a point where your mood remains steady, unaffected by the actions of others. Do not let external influences dictate your path, nor allow emotions to override your intelligence.

Precision arises from purpose.

Necessity drives invention.

In three generations, everyone who knows you will be gone—including those whose opinions once held you back from pursuing what you truly wanted. Now, imagine someone you know who achieved every dream and reached every goal. Years later, they grow old and pass away. Two years after that, how much would you truly care? If you choose to chase your dreams, do it for yourself.

The next day, the phone rang, slicing through the stillness of the lair where Bob sat, staring at the remnants of their last mission. He picked it up, his fingers tightening instinctively around the receiver as a familiar voice filled the line.

A small smile tugged at Flynn's lips. "Doc. It's good to hear your voice."

"Yours too, Cap. We've done great things together, Flynn," Fronz said, his voice carrying a weight that made Bob sit up a little straighter. "You were the catalyst, the glue that held us together. What we accomplished—it will outlive us. It's immortal in its own right. And for that, I thank you."

Bob leaned back in his chair, his smile fading into something quieter, more reflective. "We couldn't have done it without you, Fronz. You were the brains. I just flew the wicked plane."

"Don't sell yourself short," Fronz chuckled. "You were the heart of it all. 'Captain' fits you naturally."

The mutual respect between them was unmistakable, a testament to the trials they had endured and the victories they had shared. For a moment, neither spoke, letting the silence honor their bond.

"I'm sending you some things," Fronz continued, his voice turning more subdued. "Notes, video journals, trials, failures, successes—you name it. They're yours now. And Flynn… if we ever cross paths again, call me Benedict. It's my middle name. A little secret just between us."

Bob raised an eyebrow, amusement flickering in his voice. "Benedict, huh? I'll remember that."

Fronz chuckled softly, but the sound faded as his tone grew somber. "Flynn, about the past... about what we've done. Time—it's a beast with teeth. Altering it has risks—unseen consequences that ripple outward, like the butterfly effect. Always be mindful of that."

Bob let those words settle, their weight pressing down on him. He didn't interrupt.

After a brief pause, Fronz continued. "You know, Flynn, I've got my own fight now. The lung cancer is back after a hiatus... But that time with Alpha and Beta—I hadn't felt that good in years. I haven't coughed up blood since then, so we'll have plenty more video calls, I promise."

Bob's breath hitched. "Fronz..." he began, but Fronz cut him off gently.

"It's all right," Fronz said. "We've had more time than I ever thought we would. And you—well, you'll make the most of yours. I know that. You're family to me, Flynn. I don't say that lightly."

Bob's voice softened, thick with emotion. "I wish I could be there, Fronz. You're more than a friend—you're family too."

"I know," Fronz replied, his voice steady with quiet resolve. "Keep looking to the stars, my friend. That's where the answers are."

When the call ended, Bob sat in silence, the weight of Fronz's words settling in. His mention of the butterfly effect and the subtle push to look to the past lingered. Fronz had said more than he needed to, and Bob understood the truth: Fronz was giving him his blessing. Perhaps even permission—to do what had to be done.

Later, alone with his thoughts, Bob gazed up at the sky, the enormity of what lay ahead pressing on him. The stars seemed to call him, just as Fronz had said.

"Man, I've got some work to do," Bob murmured.

Sotra and Flynn A meet

In Sotra's dimension, the atmosphere was unlike anything Flynn A had ever encountered. The air vibrated with a soft hum, resonating with an unseen energy that seeped into every cell of his body. Colors were richer, more vivid, shifting subtly in response to his emotions. Time moved differently here—fluid, elastic. He felt as though he had spent months in this realm, yet deep down, he sensed that only moments had passed on Earth.

Sotra sat across from him on a smooth, translucent stone, her luminous presence both soothing and authoritative. "Flynn," she began, her voice ringing like a gentle chord, "your heightened awareness is not merely a gift—it is a tool. Your species is capable of far more than you realize. I am here to help you awaken the dormant potential within your mind."

Flynn furrowed his brow, skepticism giving way to curiosity. "You're talking about the pineal gland, aren't you? The third eye, consciousness… all that stuff I thought was just fringe science?"

Sotra smiled knowingly. "It is far from fringe. The pineal gland is a gateway, Flynn. Your people once understood how to unlock its power, to perceive time and reality as interwoven strands. But over generations, this knowledge was lost—or buried."

"Why me?" Flynn asked, shifting uneasily. "Why now?"

"Because you've already begun the journey," Sotra replied. "The Quantum Entanglement split. I chose you. I have searched for a worthy companion for 700 years since I made this realm my home. You are the most extraordinary human I have ever encountered. Your subconscious resonates on levels beyond your understanding. You are uniquely positioned to grasp what others cannot. I will be your guide."

She placed a hand over his forehead, and warmth radiated through him. A flood of images filled his mind—fractals of light, timelines colliding and diverging, an overwhelming sense of interconnectedness.

Flynn inhaled sharply and stilled, letting his mind's eye reach beyond the boundaries of perception.

"There's another me in my dimension? And he's coming from the Mountain Lair?" Flynn's eyes widened.

"You won't grasp all of this at once," Sotra said gently. "Your mind needs time to process. Human brains weren't designed for multidimensional awareness, but when the moment arrives, the knowledge will surface, and you'll act with clarity."

Flynn exhaled, both overwhelmed and exhilarated. "I've seen a lot in my life, but nothing could have prepared me for this."

Sotra nodded. "And when you return, both you and your other self will bear the weight of this understanding. You'll gain a deeper awareness of time, space, and the dimensions in between. With that knowledge, you will carve the path forward."

In that moment, something shifted within Flynn—a flicker of awakening, a spark that would ignite the foundation of his next steps, both in her world and his own.

CHAPTER TWENTY - TWO

THE SUNSHINE STATE

After making overnight stops in Albuquerque, NM; Meknotsis, TN; and Tallahassee, FL, Bob kept to himself, speaking only when necessary—mainly during motel check-ins.

On the final night before reaching Orlando, he allowed himself a rare indulgence: a stay at a high-end hotel. The lobby gleamed with polished marble, soft ambient music filling the air. At the front desk, an elegantly dressed receptionist named Claire handed him his key card with a practiced yet warm smile.

"Mr. Smith, we have you in a premium suite. I hope it exceeds your expectations," she said.

"I'm sure it will, Claire. Thanks for making the end of a long road a comfortable one," Bob replied.

Each interaction, though brief, anchored him further into his new life. These small, ordinary moments wove a quiet stability into the fabric of his shifting identity.

Upon arriving in his target city, he wasted no time searching for a new home. He settled on a modest two-bedroom house on the outskirts of Tampa Bay—secluded enough for privacy yet close enough to the city. The sprawling yard, shaded by towering palm trees, hinted at the tranquility he sought, and a nearby lake added to its charm.

As he adjusted to this quieter existence, he took on consultant work, enrolled in online courses, and occasionally indulged his passion for sci-fi, scouting Florida's well-known conventions for events that piqued his interest.

One sunny Saturday, craving a touch of excitement, Bob decided to attend a local Star Trek convention. The convention center pulsed with energy, packed with enthusiasts donning costumes from across the expansive universe—Vulcans with impeccably pointed ears, Starfleet officers in crisply ironed uniforms, and fans animatedly discussing the finer points of interstellar diplomacy.

Amid the sea of fans, Bob, sporting a simple Starfleet badge on his plain t-shirt, found himself standing beside Mark—

about the same height, with a mischievous smile—dressed in a meticulously detailed Captain Picard-era uniform.

"Nice badge. Keeping it casual, huh?" Mark grinned, extending a hand. "I'm Mark, and sadly, this is not the Starship Enterprise."

Bob chuckled as he shook Mark's hand. "Flynn—uh, Bob. Yeah, figured I'd start with the basics. Didn't get the memo about the full uniform."

Mark's wife, Debbie, joined them, dressed as a science officer. "Don't mind him. He's been planning this outfit for months. I'm Debbie. So, Bob, first convention?"

"First in a long time," Bob admitted. "Feels like coming home in a way."

As they wandered through the exhibits, they swapped jokes and shared their favorite episode stories. At a booth showcasing vintage Star Trek memorabilia, Bob pointed at a model of the USS Enterprise NCC-1701E.

"Bet I could still name every part of that ship," Bob boasted.

"Oh really?" Mark arched an eyebrow, Spock-style. "Prove it, Captain."

Challenge accepted. Bob launched into a detailed breakdown of the ship's design, drawing a small crowd of amused and impressed fans. Debbie chuckled, watching the impromptu performance.

"You guys are such geeks," she teased affectionately, her eyes twinkling.

"Yeah, but we're the cool kind of geeks," Mark shot back, draping an arm around her shoulders.

"Is there any other kind?" Bob quipped, feeling a warmth he hadn't experienced in a long time—a sense of belonging.

As the day wound down, they exchanged contact information, vowing to meet again for a Star Trek marathon.

"Here's my number and email," Mark said. "And next time, Bob, you're coming in full uniform!"

Bob smiled as he walked back to his car, feeling lighter than he had in months. Maybe, just maybe, this new life could be more than just a hideaway—it could be a chance to reconnect and rebuild.

Three weeks later, when they met again, Mark leaned back in his chair and smirked. "So, Flynn, ever think about what it'd be like to really explore the stars?"

Bob chuckled. "Call me Bob. Flynn was my hacker name back in the day."

Mark waved a dismissive hand. "Nah, I know who you are. Flynn's way better. 'Bob' spelled backward is still Bob, and that's just creepy." He had heard Bob say Flynn and decided it suited him more. Not that he really knew him all that well.

Mark didn't know Bob's full story—just that he was a guy with a good heart, a tech geek with a dry, sometimes twisted sense of humor. The kind of guy who loved to laugh and make others laugh too. Then again, that sounded a lot like Mark himself.

Bob laughed. "Okay, Mark, to answer your question—more than you know, buddy. More than you know."

The conversation ended with handshakes and grins. Bob made a mental note to reach out to Mark next week.

He hadn't expected to make friends so quickly in Florida, but something about Mark and Debbie just clicked. Maybe it was their shared love of Star Trek, or maybe it was the simple joy of geeky banter. Either way, after a few weeks, he found himself looking forward to their meetups.

This time, they had chosen a local diner with a cozy corner booth that gave off a distinct Ten Forward vibe. Mark and

Debbie were already seated when Bob arrived, waving him over with enthusiasm.

"Ah, there he is!" Mark grinned. "Bob, Flynn—whatever your name is today—grab a seat. We were just debating the age-old question: Who was the better captain—Kirk or Picard?"

Bob slid into the booth with a chuckle. "Oh, we're going there already, huh? Alright—Kirk had the cowboy diplomacy, but Picard? That man could talk an enemy into surrendering without firing a shot. It's like comparing a space cowboy to a philosopher king."

Debbie smirked. "And Sisko?"

Bob held up a finger. "Now that is a man who could punch Q in the face and not lose sleep over it. Full respect."

Mark laughed. "Okay, okay, so you're saying Kirk is all action, Picard is all talk, and Sisko is… what? The middle ground?"

Bob nodded. "Sisko is what happens when Starfleet realizes it needs a wartime captain. He doesn't just make speeches—he plays chess at a level no one else does."

Debbie leaned in. "And what about Janeway?"

Bob pointed at her approvingly. "Janeway? That woman kept a crew together in another quadrant of the galaxy with no backup. Plus, she was the only one smart enough to weaponize coffee addiction."

Mark burst out laughing. "Okay, I like you. You can stay."

Bob smirked. "Appreciate that, buddy. So, what's the plan? Are we finally doing that Trek marathon?"

Debbie grinned. "Absolutely. But full uniform is mandatory this time. No excuses."

Bob sighed dramatically. "Fine. But if I have to squeeze into a Starfleet uniform, you better have some Romulan ale ready."

Mark leaned back with a knowing smile. "Don't worry, Bob. We always make it so."

They all laughed, and for the first time in a long while, Bob felt like he belonged. These were his people. Maybe, just maybe, this new life could be more than just an escape. Maybe it could be home.

Meanwhile, Flynn pored over Fronz's notes and journals, drawing solace from the wisdom within—a guiding light in the uncertain road ahead. Their legacy, the memories of past adventures, and the promise of tomorrow kept him moving forward, ever hopeful, ever curious about the mysteries the universe had yet to reveal.

As he embraced the complexities of a new beginning, the enduring bonds of friendship and his insatiable thirst for knowledge became his anchors. From the skies above to the sunlit streets of Florida, Flynn had found his next chapter—not an end, but a new frontier.

CHAPTER TWENTY-THREE

TEAM NAUTILUS RETURNS

Before the police swarmed the facility and his home, Kenji discovered the sensors SAGA had planted and smashed them with brute force. He figured they must have been installed during one of their infiltrations—just outside the cameras' view. As he scanned the room, he spotted two cameras that weren't his.

How the hell did they know to place them there? he thought before destroying them with equal intensity.

Kenji then gathered Sunday, the AI, securely housed in a large hard drive case, along with the sensors he had used and his laptop. Keeping Sunday online, she continued communicating with him through his tablet and mobile phone. He plugged the hard drive case and laptop into his recently acquired and refurbished Datsun 280ZX—purchased under his incognito identity. He had modified it with a rear GoPro, a monitor, and

SiriusXM. A large U-Haul trailed behind, loaded with Tesla coils and essential lab equipment.

Wana Hauk Alougi—better known as Mr. Hauk—was secured along with a dozen dormant Zoomies. Kenji ensured that all physical notes had been destroyed.

With everything in place, Kenji relocated miles away to a trailer park in Arizona, using money he had stashed away. Sunday remained securely stored in his car—her "brain" resting unnoticed in the backseat. He knew the police would eventually investigate Flynn's facility and home, so he wasted no time disappearing.

Ninety days later, Sunday alerted Kenji: "The stealth protocol has been activated by Flynn."

Kenji's eyes widened in shock. Then, unable to contain his excitement, he jumped for joy like a Japanese kid who just won a trip to Disney World.

She tells him about an area in Florida, near a beach Flynn used to visit annually near Tampa Bay. He would attend association meetings for life-saving products, where they wrote standards, discussed the industry, and exchanged ideas—especially with those who shared his passion. It felt like a distant yet familiar place.

"Oh yeah, duh," Kenji replied. "Thanks, Sunday, for reminding me."

The young prodigy had attempted to track Flynn through his mobile phone, but Flynn had been using disposable phones since arriving in Florida. No luck. So, Kenji decided to take a different approach. Dusting off his hacking skills, he tapped into the city's surveillance cameras, scanning for any trace of him.

Kenji then prepped his car for the trip to Tampa, arriving in record time with all his equipment.

Meanwhile, Sunday used her expertise to sift through city cameras. After hours of searching, she finally identified a figure with a familiar build and gait—someone who resembled Flynn, now sporting a beard and a walking stick. Kenji noticed his entire appearance had changed. That tricky submariner. The hair, clothes, hat, and even the cigar—he had covered his tracks well.

Kenji also knew about the truck Flynn had stashed in the cave. It wasn't registered under his real name but rather as Bob Smith, meaning Flynn had no urgent need to sell it.

After a month of searching, Kenji finally spotted him at a gas station outside Tampa, near a sci-fi convention. He and Flynn had often talked about attending such events together.

Then, after two months of eagle-eyed surveillance, Kenji finally caught sight of him. Out of the corner of his eye, he spotted a familiar figure.

"Wait, whoa, what?" Kenji muttered aloud. "I need to get a closer look... Yup, that's him. Man, does he have some explaining to do."

Kenji approached with a quiet precision, moving like a ninja in broad daylight.

"Hey, stranger. Got a light? You might want to sell that truck," Kenji teased.

Flynn turned, grinning the moment he recognized him. Kenji had grown a scraggly goatee. "Oh my god, kid! How the hell are you? Damn glad to see you, boy! Look at you—somehow, you found me."

Kenji smirked. "Sunday thought we should start somewhere far from the West Coast. We remembered you mentioning Florida for all those association meetings."

Flynn sat on the tailgate of his truck behind the gas station, the wind tugging at his shirt. The past three months had been a whirlwind of covert plans and cautious movements.

Kenji clapped him on the shoulder. "So, Mr. Incognito," he said, his voice dripping with amusement. "What's your new identity? Something flashy? Maybe straight out of a spy movie?"

Flynn chuckled, crossing his arms. "Bob. Bob Smith… and eventually, Cavalla. Gotta say it like that—adds a little flair."

They both burst into laughter.

Kenji blinked. "That's it? No dramatic flair? You could've been Bob Danger or Bob Thunderstrike."

Bob grinned. "Nah, too obvious. Just Bob. Nobody looks twice at a Bob. I'm the perfect wallflower. Bob says, 'Don't worry about me, I'm just here for the early-bird special.' It's genius."

Kenji shook his head, laughing. "You're impossible. Okay, fine, you win. But if you're going with 'Bob,' then I guess it's time I told you mine."

Bob raised an eyebrow, leaning in with mock seriousness. "Oh, this I've gotta hear."

Kenji cleared his throat dramatically. "I thought long and hard about it. My alias is..." He paused for effect, then said with a straight face, "Wana Hauk Alougi."

Bob burst out laughing. "What the hell is that?"

Kenji grinned mischievously. "It's Nordic or something—I think it means 'Wanna throw a log?' But it sounded ridiculous with a Minnesota accent, which is where I was supposed to go. So I shortened it to 'Mr. Hauk.'"

Still laughing, Bob wiped his eyes. "Okay, Mr. Hauk, you've officially outdone me. But do I actually have to call you that?"

Kenji shrugged. "Please don't. Call me Kenji. I'll stick with my real name for family."

"Fair enough," Bob said with a grin. "Just don't forget—if anyone asks, I'm 'Just Bob.'"

Kenji nodded. "Deal, Bob. Let's keep flying under the radar. Or fishing under the radar, in your case."

The two laughed as they walked away, ready to dive into covert operations.

Kenji moved in with Bob almost immediately while they searched for a bigger house outside of town—one with a yard and a large garage.

Strategy

Bob sat at the table, staring at a large whiteboard covered in scribbles, dates, and diagrams. Across from him, Kenji leaned back in his chair, typing furiously on his laptop as they reviewed the data compiled from hours of brainstorming. The air buzzed with a charged mix of tension and excitement—the kind that came with devising a plan so audacious it bordered on insanity. But given the stakes, anything less would be unacceptable.

At the top of the board, a hastily scrawled title read "Back in Time," though their discussion had shifted to a more immediate focus.

"Let's focus," Bob said, sipping his green tea as he circled a section labeled "High-Yield Opportunities." "While we're here in Florida, the patterns are obvious—lottery winners, stock surges, major sporting events. These are our gold mines. But if we're going to pull this off, every step needs to be airtight."

Kenji nodded and swiveled his laptop to display a detailed spreadsheet. "I've broken it all down: major lottery wins by state, stock spikes by quarter, and sporting event outcomes—dates, scores, everything. If we position ourselves at the right points in the timeline, we could walk away with enough money to buy… well, just about anything."

Bob grinned. "Including the bank that holds the deed to the properties SAGA confiscated." He leaned forward, his eyes gleaming with determination. "If we pull this off, we won't just reclaim what they took—we'll have the leverage to take them down for good."

Kenji raised an eyebrow. "That's a bold move, Bob. How do you plan on staying under the radar? You show up with enough cash to buy a bank, and people will start asking questions."

Bob tapped the whiteboard. "Fabricated identities. Multiple winners. Corporate purchases. We keep it small and spread out. Say we use a lottery win to seed the initial capital, then move into stocks with carefully timed investments. We funnel everything through proxies—fake names, offshore accounts, even hire stand-ins to claim the winnings. Once the money's moving, it becomes background noise in the system. The key is staying ahead of anyone watching too closely."

Kenji leaned back, thoughtful. "And what about the lawyers, accountants, and investigators? How do we keep them from talking?"

Bob's grin widened. "We hire the best—and we vet them thoroughly. Private investigators to dig into SAGA's skeletons, accountants to make our books airtight, and lawyers to navigate every legal gray area. Money doesn't just talk—with the kind of bankroll we're building, it roars."

Kenji smirked. "And what about Wagner? How do we handle him?"

Bob's expression darkened. "We turn those investigators loose on him. Put every move he's ever made under a microscope. Every shady deal, every cover-up—exposed. We bury him in lawsuits, leaks, and public scrutiny. Make it impossible for him to hide."

Kenji nodded, impressed. "And Team Nautilus's reputation?"

Bob's tone was firm. "We clear our name by proving SAGA's corruption. But we don't stop there. We dismantle their entire power structure. Once we have the resources, we rebuild everything they tried to tear down."

Kenji studied the spreadsheet again. "This is... ambitious. But it might just work. If Beta can pull off time travel, that would be the ultimate ace in the hole."

Bob leaned forward, his eyes gleaming with ruthless determination. "A step ahead isn't a plan, kid. Five steps ahead—crushing the enemy before they even realize they're in a fight? That's a plan. And I love it when a plan comes together."

Kenji smirked, nodding as a wicked grin spread across his face. "Alpha Mike Foxtrot… Oorah."

In the military, *AMF served as a code—an order to execute, adaptable to any situation.*

"Time to get started." Bob's stomach grumbled, a sharp reminder of his hunger. "The clock's ticking—forward or backward, doesn't matter. We've got work to do. First order of business: BBQ time."

The Property

After dinner, the evening was quiet, the Florida breeze carrying the faint scent of salt and citrus. Bob sat on the back porch of his temporary hideaway, gazing at the stars, their distant glow untouched by earthly concerns.

Kenji joined him, setting down a couple of beers before settling into the chair beside him. The silence stretched between them, thick with unspoken thoughts, until Kenji finally broke it.

"Flynn," he began, his tone subdued but steady. "Your old house is gone. Sold off to SAGA—to keep up appearances, according to the news." He hesitated, then added, "And the facility… it's gone too. Burnt to the ground."

Bob turned to him sharply. "Damn. I loved that house. Wait—what do you mean, 'the facility was burnt to the ground'?"

Kenji exhaled, running a hand through his hair. "The news claims the old hangar caught fire. But I made sure that if anyone came snooping around afterward, they wouldn't find a trace of the lab. No test equipment, no Tesla coils, nothing that could link back to us."

Bob's eyebrows lifted. "The Tesla coils?"

Kenji smirked faintly, tapping the arm of his chair. "Packed up tight in the U-Haul. Those bad boys are too valuable to leave behind. We might need them sooner rather than later."

Bob let out a slow breath, his gaze drifting back to the stars. "And the planes?"

Kenji's expression darkened. "Confiscated. The trainer, Fronz's Corsair—they tore them apart. Called it a matter of national security. But…" He reached into his pocket and pulled out a small notebook, its worn edges proof of years of careful record-keeping. "I took notes from Fronz's meetings. We're not out of this fight yet."

Bob skimmed through the notebook, flipping the pages before setting it down. "Good thinking, Kenji. Fronz would be proud. I also have a copy of the server's files, so everything's at our fingertips."

Kenji nodded, determination flickering in his eyes. "This isn't over, Flynn. Not by a long shot."

"You can say that again," Bob said.

The Letter

Kenji received a secure return email from Fronz.

"Captain, this email's for you—it's from Fronz. I sent it securely, just like you asked. I haven't read it. Here you go," Kenji said.

Flynn exhaled sharply. "Oh boy."

Flynn,

Thanks for making sure this email was secure. Well done, Kenji—had to scan my face and eye just to access it. Quite the clever bit of tech. Fitting, really.

It's good to hear you're starting your studies at the university. I always knew you could achieve anything you set your mind to.

I'll get right to it. By the time you read this, I'll likely have gone to join my mother—peacefully, in the quiet of the night, just as she did. There's a certain poetry in that, don't you think? She always said the best things happen in stillness, when the world slows down. I never truly believed her until now.

It feels like an appropriate ending for someone like me—someone who spent his life lost in the beautiful chaos of equations, tinkering with theories, daring to imagine what others dismissed as impossible.

I wanted to write to you before my time came, but, as life often does, it swept me up in its current, leaving behind too many if onlys. If only we had one more project, one more spirited debate, one more toast to the dreams we pulled from thin air and made real.

I don't know if I ever said it properly, but watching you grow into one hell of a pilot and engineer was one of my greatest pleasures. Watching you fly was like witnessing a symphony in motion—artistry beyond words. And yes, despite all the arguments over how much strain your stunts put on the Corsair, I have to admit—you made her sing like no one else could.

And when you get the chance, crack open a bottle of Jameson in my honor. Wherever I am now, know that I'm raising a glass to you, my brother-in-arms.

We started something extraordinary, Flynn. It's not finished yet, but I know you'll see it through—because that's who you are.

Yours always,

Fronz

A scanned note is attached to the letter.

Flynn,

I found this among Fronz's belongings and had it scanned. I believe he meant to send it sooner. He spoke of you often—more than anyone else. He admired you deeply, and knowing what you both accomplished together brought him great joy.

He passed peacefully in his sleep, just like our mother. It was what he wanted. I truly believe he left this world with a sense of contentment and pride in all he had achieved.

There are other letters to send. He's been busy. I think the world is in for a surprise.

Thank you for being such an important part of his life.

Take care of yourself, Flynn.

Peter

Back to school

Bob's decision to return to school marked a turning point—not just for himself, but for the future of their work on Beta. "Very good," he told Kenji, his voice firm with determination. "It's time to go to school, study, and plug in. I'll look into the nearby college to get started."

Enrolling in a local community college, Bob immersed himself in an Associate's program in Physics. The coursework was demanding, but he had an advantage: his hands-on experience with the Alpha and Beta engines gave him practical insights into concepts that were purely theoretical for most of his classmates. Kenji, ever the loyal partner, studied alongside him, absorbing material and filling in gaps where Bob struggled. They spent evenings working together, exchanging ideas—Kenji's expertise in programming and design complemented Bob's growing grasp of physics, furthering his understanding of mechanical and electrical engineering. The biggest challenge, however, was not just the math but the sheer complexity of anything related to quantum mechanics.

To make ends meet, Bob took on part-time work as an online consultant, specializing in water safety and engineering applications. His experience with Alpha and Beta gave him a unique problem-solving approach, which gradually made his services more sought after. Though he never spoke about those projects directly, his ability to think outside the box set him apart. Within three years, at age 53, he earned his Associate's degree. With new confidence, he expanded his consulting work, taking on more complex projects that allowed him the flexibility to continue his studies.

Kenji also found his own opportunities, teaching UI/UX design and programming online. He even collaborated with his sister, Keori, who was sworn to secrecy about their true mission. Their combined income, while modest, was enough to sustain their ambitions. Keori helped cover expenses when needed.

Bob then pursued a Bachelor's degree in Applied Physics, completing it a few years later. By then, he had developed a deeper understanding of Beta's inner workings and the intricate mathematical formulas Fronz had once scrawled on the whiteboard.

Teaching part-time online, Bob saved enough money to enroll in a Master's program in Electromagnetism and Theoretical Physics. Most of his coursework was remote, with milestone labs and exams completed in person. As he advanced, his tests required a physical classroom setting.

Over the next four years, Bob deepened his understanding of electromagnetic fields, theoretical energy systems, and the physics underlying Beta's operation. Kenji, ever curious, studied alongside him, often poring over materials late into the night and witnessing Bob's growing expertise firsthand.

When it came time to choose his PhD focus, Bob was strategic. He steered his research away from directly exposing the secrets of cold fusion or the Zone engine, instead framing his studies around aether theories and zero-point energy in broad, speculative terms. This allowed him to contribute meaningfully to academia without compromising Beta's power source. His PhD research extended well beyond the pace of his earlier degrees.

Yet, even as he neared the completion of his doctorate, Bob felt the growing urge to test Beta's upgrade. He and Kenji developed the Beta Mk 1.5, following a measured, step-by-step approach. "Slow is smooth, smooth is fast," Bob quipped with a grin as they meticulously assembled the two Tesla coils. "We need to get this right the first time. The last thing we need is Fronz coming down here to scold us."

Kenji chuckled but remained focused. Together, they double-checked every connection, calibrated each coil, and scrutinized every detail with the precision Fronz would have demanded. This wasn't just an experiment—it was a tribute to their late mentor and a crucial step toward unleashing Beta's full potential.

The Mark 1.5

Fifteen years had passed since the Alpha explosion. In that time, they had moved into an even larger house with a garage and a more spacious basement. Kenji's older sister assisted from afar, providing supplies, handling logistics, and fine-tuning

Sunday and the Zoomies. Occasionally, she also sent money to help with Kenji's care.

Kenji's studies in physics and Bob's pursuit of his master's degree had paid off. Though Bob had yet to complete his PhD, he decided it was time to begin work on Project Beta Mark 1.5.

In the dimly lit confines of the new Team Nautilus research lab, the air vibrated with the electric buzz of anticipation and the soft hum of the Beta engine. Walls covered in theoretical formulas and time-space diagrams bore witness to the duo's ambition. Bob and Kenji were embarking on a groundbreaking experiment—not just to glimpse into the past but to send an object through time and retrieve it.

For the first successful test of Beta Mk 1.5, Flynn needed an artifact that was more than an ordinary object—it had to be scientifically and structurally significant. The chosen test artifact was an eight-sided triangular prism, meticulously designed for both durability and conductivity.

The outer shell was 3D-printed from tungsten steel, a material renowned for its extreme resilience and ability to endure high-energy fields. Tungsten's density and strength made it an ideal candidate for testing how different materials would react when passing through the quantum window. If the artifact remained intact, it would signal that a larger, more complex mass—perhaps even a human—might one day follow.

Inside the artifact, a sealed chamber held liquid mercury—not just for mass, but for function. Mercury's unique electromagnetic properties made it highly reactive to Beta's energy field. If Beta's window could process a material with both metallic density and a liquid core, it signaled that the system was stabilizing at the right frequency for larger-scale crossings.

Every variable had been accounted for, every calculation double-checked. If the artifact made it through intact, the next step was inevitable—Bob himself would follow.

The long hours of study had taken their toll, but Bob pushed forward. His small, dimly lit study in the Florida safe house had become a refuge, its surfaces buried beneath quantum mechanics textbooks, handwritten notes, and stacks of theoretical printouts. The steady hum of Kenji's laptop and the mainframe of The Sunday filled the silence, punctuated only by the occasional scratch of Bob's pen against paper.

Hunched over his desk, Bob stared at the dense equations scrawled across the whiteboard. His bloodshot eyes blurred the intricate web of quantum mechanics, electromagnetic field theory, and speculative zero-point energy models. For weeks, he had been stuck—circling the same flawed conclusions, unable to bridge the gap between theory and execution.

Kenji flipped through a thick physics journal nearby. "You know, Bob," he muttered without looking up, "if we don't crack this soon, I'm going to start dreaming in equations."

Bob let out a dry chuckle. "Welcome to my world."

But then, something shifted. It was subtle—a mental click, like a key sliding perfectly into place. Bob's tired eyes sharpened as he stared at the formulas. It wasn't about brute force anymore. It was about seeing the solution. The answer revealed itself. The principles of quantum tunneling, zero-point fluctuations, and electromagnetic resonance weren't isolated concepts—they could be harmonized.

He lunged for his notebook, furiously rewriting the equations, merging resonance frequency modulation with controlled quantum field collapses.

"Kenji… Kenji, look at this!" Bob's voice cracked with excitement.

Kenji snapped to attention, leaning over the desk. Bob pointed to the equation, his hand trembling. "It's not just about stabilizing the field around Beta. It's about matching the vibrational frequency of the Zone to the quantum state of the object passing through it."

Kenji's eyes darted across the page. "Wait—this compensates for the energy loss at the barrier! You're phasing the object through the window without destabilizing the field!"

Bob nodded, his breath quickening. "Exactly. By tuning the electromagnetic coils to resonate at Beta's harmonic frequency, we can momentarily sync the object with the Zone. Like dropping a pebble into a pond without making a splash."

Kenji stared for a moment, then let out a low whistle. "That's… fucking brilliant."

Bob clapped his hands together. "Great leaping monkeys! Quick, to the whiteboard! Here we go…" He rushed forward, marker in hand, scribbling furiously.

Kenji studied the updated formula on the whiteboard, his brows furrowing. "Okay, so this adjustment lets Beta Mark 1.5 look back exactly two months. But why the limit? Energy constraints, or something else?"

Bob set down the tablet he'd been reading and nodded. "Both. The farther back you go with mass, the more energy you need to stabilize the temporal field. It's like climbing a mountain—every extra step requires exponentially more effort.

We're capping it for the Mark 1.5 tests. We know that for a fifteen-year jump, back to Beta's creation, we'll need a refined formula and far greater power to transport both Beta and, unfortunately, the mass of yours truly."

Kenji leaned closer to the board. "But why stop there? Couldn't we just tweak the output?"

Bob shook his head. "That's where the safety algorithm kicks in. This version of Beta has a hard limit—it's programmed to cap its range to prevent excessive power consumption. I'd rather walk before we run. Now's the time to play it safe."

Kenji smirked. "Right, good call, Captain. The next round might be when the 'fit hits the shan' if we're not careful."

"Exactly," Bob said with a chuckle. "This algorithm is like a training wheel. It keeps us from making rookie mistakes while we work out the mechanics. Once we refine the energy output and fully understand how to manage the ripple effects, we can think about loosening the restrictions. But for now, two months is the sweet spot—it's just long enough to run tests without throwing the timeline off its axis."

Kenji crossed his arms, nodding slowly. "Okay, that tracks. Limited range, limited risk. Makes sense—Beta's still in its training phase."

"Right," Bob said, leaning back with a satisfied grin. "Think of it as a controlled sandbox. We experiment here first. Once we prove it works, we'll build up to the big stuff."

Flynn, his face a mask of concentration and excitement, adjusted the myriad controls on the Beta engine interface. He had spent a lot of time with Alpha, but that was an entirely different beast. He recognized the intricate assembly of tungsten and mercury—more like a futuristic art piece than a cold fusion vortex engine. Beta was bulkier than its predecessor, with added mass to support its upgraded framework.

Kenji, the cohort prodigy under Flynn's wing, had recently deepened his grasp of quantum mechanics—an understanding that had proven crucial to the Beta improvement project. He monitored the streams of data cascading across multiple screens.

The room vibrated softly as the Beta engine whirred to life, Tesla coils in the background channeling additional power into the Mk 1.5 upgrade. Its core pulsed with an ethereal blue light. A pane of light shimmered into existence before them—a window into the past, once only visible but never tangible.

The display flickered, rewinding to Beta's earliest moments. They fast-forwarded through key events—Beta's creation, their journey to Florida, and their first experiments in their cramped workshop. The image settled on a scene from two months earlier, capturing their lab before they expanded into the larger house and workshop.

"The calibrations are almost set," Flynn announced, his voice echoing slightly in the vast, empty chamber. "Remember, we're not just opening a window to view the past—we're testing if we can pass an artifact through it. That requires minimal power for now. Once we confirm stability, we'll upgrade to Mk 2, where I'll be the one going back."

Kenji nodded, his wide eyes fixed on the monitors. "The temporal field should stabilize at these settings. According to the simulations, the time-view window will let us observe the past before we attempt to place the artifact on the shelf next to those books. Think of it like double-checking a GPS route before starting a road trip."

Flynn smirked at the analogy. "At least I won't have to remember where we parked. Ready to initiate the time-view window?"

"Initiating in three... two... one..." Kenji counted down, then pressed the green GO button.

As the machine hummed, Kenji adjusted a few parameters, his fascination evident. "Now, for the real test. Third time's the charm, right? Transitioning from passive observation to active engagement."

Beta's tone shifted slightly, and the window's edges shimmered more intensely.

Bob gave a firm nod and pulled a small device from his pocket. "This is our test artifact. I'll use the mechanical arm to place it exactly where we discussed. If everything works, it should appear in the past version of this room—about a few months ago. We'll know it worked if it's already there when we check."

The theory was risky; the consequences of tampering with the past were daunting. Yet, the lure of rewriting history, of righting past wrongs, was impossible to resist.

"Here goes nothing—or everything," Flynn murmured, placing the test artifact within the designated area of effect, the field generated by Beta.

Kenji's fingers danced over the controls, his concentration unwavering as he monitored the data streams. "Engaging time-travel sequence now," he announced.

The Beta engine pulsed with energy, its glow intensifying as it bathed the artifact in radiant light. Flynn's pulse quickened. A strange pull gripped him—a sensation akin to plunging into deep water, where sound dulled and movement distorted.

Bob extended an arm through the portal, carefully dropping the artifact beside the books on the shelf.

"It looks like it worked, Kenji. The device should be there now. Let's go check."

They hurried to the designated location, anticipation thick in the air. Flynn's heart pounded as he reached behind the equipment and books. His fingers brushed against something solid. With a sharp inhale, he pulled the object free—revealing the test artifact.

"We did it," he exhaled, holding the device up. "That's three successful attempts. We need five more trials, with variable adjustments, for accurate data collection and verification."

It was a small victory in the grand scheme of things, but undeniable proof—their newly refined Beta Mk 1.5 worked.

Kenji grinned, his youthful face glowing with the thrill of their breakthrough. He erupted into an excited string of Japanese praises, words tumbling out faster than Bob could process. "This changes everything, Flynn! What's next?"

Bob set the device back on the table, his mind racing between exhilaration and unease. "Next? We refine it. We make it safer. And we decide how much we should interfere with the past—if at all."

The implications were staggering. They had unlocked a gateway to time itself, a power that could rewrite history. But with such power came weighty consequences, and Bob knew the road ahead was riddled with ethical landmines.

Contemplation

As Bob contemplates traveling back in time in the stillness of the workshop, he stands alone amidst the relics of their shared dreams. The gentle hum of dormant machinery fills the space, a faint echo of the vibrant activity that once thrived. The dim light casts long shadows, mirroring the weight of his decision—a burden only he can bear.

The room, cluttered with the tools of their ingenuity and remnants of their ambitions, feels larger, emptier in the absence of his team. Joshua's loss is a void that words cannot fill, a constant reminder of the stakes at hand. Kenji sleeps in his silent quarters, unaware of the storm raging in Bob's mind. Fronz's wisdom lingers like a whisper in the air, all of them converging into a solitude that deepens his moment of reckoning.

Bob paces, the weight of the world pressing on his shoulders, his mind a battlefield of conflicting emotions and ethical dilemmas. The quiet of the workshop amplifies his inner turmoil, each step a measured beat in the rhythm of his thoughts.

His inner voice echoes as he prepares for his journey, wrestling with the choices before him.

Is this the path I am destined to walk alone? To bend the fabric of time itself? To reach back and rewrite the events that brought us here?

Memories of their adventures, their losses, and their triumphs play in his mind like a silent film, each frame a testament to the journey that has shaped him.

Yet, amid his struggle, the absence of his wife, granddaughters, and oldest friend looms like a shadow—a price paid for the pursuit of their dreams. A wound time refuses to heal, a stark reminder of the fragility of life and the unforgiving nature of their reality.

Would altering the past bring me peace, or would it strip away the very essence of who I am?

The chance to undo the tragedies that have shattered my family, to shield them from pain and loss, is a siren's call—seductive yet riddled with peril. With ultimate power comes ultimate responsibility. But am I worthy of wielding it?

Bob's inner voice urges him—save them, erase the scars that time has carved into their hearts. But at what cost? What unseen consequences might such interference unleash?

As Bob stands on the precipice of his decision, the weight of his potential actions presses down on him. The workshop, once a bustling haven of creativity and collaboration, now bears silent witness to his turmoil. The choices before him stretch vast and uncharted, like the depths of the ocean they once dreamed of mastering.

Time is a delicate weave, a fabric interlaced with the lives of countless others. Dare I tug at a single thread, knowing it may unravel everything?

In the stillness of the night, with only the soft whisper of the sea breeze and the occasional creak of the workshop for company, Bob wrestled with the weight of his choice. The drive to protect, to right past wrongs, and to shield his loved ones from fate's cruel hand warred with the understanding that the past—painful and unchangeable—had shaped the man he was today.

Am I truly prepared to step into the unknown, to embrace the uncertainties of tampering with time? For the chance at redemption, a second chance... is it not worth the risk? But who am I to alter time itself?

Alone in his workshop, where the echoes of the past and the whispers of the future converged in uneasy silence, Bob stood at the precipice of destiny and choice, his heart weighed down by the burden of what lay ahead. The journey before him was one of both profound solitude and boundless hope, an endeavor that defied science and delved into the very essence of the human soul.

Then, with unwavering resolve, Bob declared, "I will not merely try—I will succeed!" His voice carried through the workshop as if daring time itself to defy him. The events ahead were set in motion. He would go back. He would save his family. He would reclaim their souls.

"Is it cheating death? No—it is granting life. And I will fight for it. Always."

CHAPTER TWENTY-FOUR

PREPARATION

The Florida heat seeped through the windows into Flynn's workshop, where the hum of machines blended with the classic rock blaring from an old MP3 player.

At a cluttered workbench nearby, Kenji worked with practiced precision, his hands moving deftly over the final diagnostics for Beta's upgrade. His brow furrowed in concentration. For fifteen years, Kenji had been Flynn's right hand—a steady presence amid the chaos of preparing for what was coming. Now, after years of labor, the moment was almost here.

Hunched over the diagnostic interface for Beta Mk 1.5, Kenji's fingers flew across the keyboard as lines of code and data scrolled rapidly across the monitor. The final calibrations for the Mk 2 upgrade were nearing completion. The screen's faint glow illuminated his focused expression, though his gaze occasionally flicked toward the towering Beta engine. Its tungsten surface gleamed under the workshop lights, humming with latent potential.

Across the room, Tesla coils crackled, sending arcs of electricity into the air and vibrating the floor with their raw energy. They were vital—channeling the extra power required to push Beta beyond its current Mk 1.5 state. Right now, Beta could only project an object through time as a ghostly image, visible through a viewing window. But Mk 2 would be different. It wouldn't just observe time—it would take something, or someone, through it.

Beta wasn't just a machine; it was the key. The companion that would accompany Bob into the unknown.

Think of Marty in the DeLorean. The car created the field that propelled him through time. Beta would do the same—but on an entirely new scale.

Kenji didn't look up, his hands flying over the keyboard. "We're close. Frequency adjustments are dialed in, but there's a slight vibration mismatch between the stabilizers and the main core." He paused, tweaking a parameter on the screen. "The Tesla coils are compensating for most of it, but we need perfect synchronicity—unless you want to end up in the wrong year… or worse."

Flynn grinned, wiping his hands on a rag. "Yeah, showing up in the Jurassic era isn't exactly on my bucket list."

Kenji snorted. "No kidding. Beta probably wouldn't survive being stomped on by a T-Rex."

They shared a brief chuckle before the weight of their task settled back in. Flynn crossed the room, standing beside Kenji as he scanned the stream of numbers and graphs on the monitor. The vibration levels fluctuated but steadied as Kenji continued making adjustments.

"Think it's going to hold this time?" Flynn asked, his voice quieter now, tinged with cautious optimism. He stepped away, the thought gnawing at him—how even observing an experiment could alter its outcome.

Kenji leaned back in his chair, finally meeting Flynn's gaze. "It has to. We've run the simulations a hundred times. The core frequency is stable, and the Tesla coils are pumping enough power into Beta to calibrate with the cold fusion engine. It could fuel a small city." He exhaled. "But this… this is uncharted territory. Even Mk 1.5 was risky. Mk 2? You know what you're asking the beast to do."

Flynn sat at the workbench, his fingers tracing the cold metal edge as his mind churned with the gravity of what he was about to do. This wasn't just the Butterfly Effect. That term barely scratched the surface. This was rewriting the course of a raging river—the Mississippi itself.

Kenji sat across from him, silent and watchful, waiting as Flynn wrestled with his thoughts. Finally, Flynn exhaled sharply and leaned forward.

"You know, Kenji, people talk about time travel like it's just nudging a domino. A little push, a small change, and everything falls into place." He let out a dry laugh. "That's bullshit. I'm not just knocking over a domino—I'm flipping the whole damn board."

Kenji nodded, saying nothing.

"Think about it. Winning the lottery? That alone sends shockwaves through the system. That money was meant for someone else. The economy shifts, businesses rise and fall on investments that never existed, and people who should've been millionaires never get their shot. Then there's the stock market—buying in, cashing out at the perfect moments—exploiting knowledge I was never supposed to have. That alone reshapes industries, Kenji."

His voice hardened. "And then there's SAGA. They're not just some corrupt corporation. They're a disease—embedded in places we haven't even uncovered yet. If I do this right, they don't just lose a few battles. They lose the war."

Kenji nodded. "Jack Wagner especially. He's the one who put the target on our backs."

Flynn clenched his jaw. "Yeah. He wanted Team Nautilus wiped out. But now? Now, I get to erase him. Not just by exposing his dirty dealings—but by making sure he never has the power to destroy lives again."

He exhaled sharply, rubbing his temples. His eyes shut for a brief moment.

"But the biggest thing? The girls." His voice wavered. "Lilian, Eileen, Rosaleen… my dog—they shouldn't be dead. And if I pull this off, they won't be. I don't care what physics says, what paradoxes say—I'm going to make that reality. But what about everyone else? The ones I don't even know about? The ones who should have lived if I never changed a thing?"

Kenji smirked. "Just try not to break the whole damn timeline while you're at it."

Flynn let out a dry chuckle. "I'm just a man with one purpose, one mission. This timeline is wrong."

His expression shifted. The fire in his eyes flickered, dimming as he stared down at his hands. He flexed his fingers, as if trying to grasp something intangible.

"There's something else, Kenji," he said quietly. "That night… after the wreck, after I saw what happened to Lilian, to the girls… I went back to the facility. I walked the halls, past Beta, past everything we built, and I had this—this vision. Like the universe itself was showing me the path I had to take."

Kenji studied him. "A vision?"

Flynn nodded. "It wasn't a dream. It was clarity. Like something greater than me was saying, 'This is your burden, this is your fight.' And dammit, Kenji, I know it sounds crazy, but I feel it. In my bones. Like this mission was given to me by something bigger than any of us. And there's no other way but to see it through."

Flynn clenched his fists. "I have the knowledge. I have the tools. I have the chance to fix this. And if I don't? If I just sit back and let fate play out the way it did before, knowing I could have done something?" He shook his head. "I'd regret it for the rest of my life. That would be the real crime."

Kenji exhaled, nodding slowly. "Then let's make sure we do it right."

He scratched the back of his head, a rare flicker of vulnerability crossing his face. "I get it. I do. Just… be careful, alright? I know Beta can handle the technical side of things, but time travel messes with people's heads. You don't want to lose yourself out there."

Flynn clapped Kenji on the shoulder. "I've got you keeping me grounded. That's all I need."

Kenji smiled, though concern still lingered in his eyes. "Alright, final check." He returned to the console, fingers flying across the keys as he entered a sequence of commands. The Beta engine hummed louder, coils sparking with greater intensity. The room vibrated as Beta's core frequency synchronized perfectly with the Tesla coils.

Flynn monitored the calibration. "Settings are locked. Time to shut off the Tesla coils and let her run on her own." They let the system stabilize for an hour.

"Everything's green," Kenji confirmed, stepping back. "Mk 2 is ready."

Flynn exhaled. "Alright. Jokes aside for a moment—"

A few hours later, a knock sounded at the door. Sunday signaled the all-clear. "It's Mark. Come on in, you goofy Italian."

The front door creaked open, breaking the stillness. Mark strode in, his usual playful tone tinged with unease. "Flynn, what in the wide world of sports are you up to now?" He had known Flynn for fifteen years—long enough to sense when something big was happening.

Flynn glanced up from his packing, his expression calm, almost serene. "Hey, Mark. Just getting some things together."

Mark's eyes narrowed as he glanced from Flynn to Kenji, then to the duffle bag. "Yeah, I can see that. Why do I get the feeling you're about to do something reckless?"

Flynn chuckled, but there was a sharp intensity in his gaze. "Because I am," he said, his tone deceptively casual. "I'm going to attempt time travel."

Mark blinked, taken aback. "Come again?"

Kenji looked up from the workbench, giving Mark a small nod as if to confirm it. "He's serious, man. We've been preparing for this for years."

Mark leaned against the doorframe, his mind racing. "Okay… time travel? You're really going through with this?"

Flynn zipped up the duffle bag. "I think it'll work. We tested it on a small artifact, and now we're upgrading Beta to handle a human subject along with the Beta engine." He exhaled, tightening his grip on the bag. "Beta should take me back to when Thing 2 was first created. It's like an anchor point in time—at least, that's the working theory. Every time we access the time window, it starts there. I haven't figured out how to control anything beyond that yet."

Mark ran a hand down his face, trying to process it. "So, let me get this straight—you're planning to jump back to when your team first brought Beta online, avoid being seen, and somehow prevent the universe from imploding? And then what?"

Flynn shrugged, unconcerned. "I'm working on it. Fronz talked a lot about the Aether, plasma, and zero-point energy. It's everywhere. Quantum particles aren't bound by location; they transfer information instantly. Distance and the speed of light don't matter to them." He exhaled, frustrated. "No clear answers yet."

Mark let out an incredulous laugh. "Jesus, Flynn. I've learned a hell of a lot just listening to you, but I still can't wrap my head around the big picture—how it all connects. Quantum particles, the Aether, zero-point energy, spinning mercury vortex, cold fusion… Jesus H. Christ on a popsicle stick. You guys are nuts."

Kenji smirked from the workbench, clearly accustomed to Flynn's deep dives into scientific theory. "It's freaky stuff, man," he said. "But trust me, when we ran the numbers, it checked out. Oh God, quantum physics—if you observe it, the outcome changes. Ahhhhh… okay, just kidding. Mostly."

Flynn nodded, a faint smile playing on his lips. "Science is inconveniently self-correcting. New ideas have to survive the harshest scrutiny. What we're doing… it might sound crazy, but sometimes, you have to push past the limits of what's accepted."

Newton once said, 'If I have seen further, it is by standing on the shoulders of giants.' Fronz… and you too, Kenji."

Mark sighed, rubbing his temples. He had heard enough fragments over the years to finally piece it together. Flynn wasn't just experimenting with time—he was preparing for something bigger. Something dangerous.

"If anyone can pull this off, it's you," Mark said, his voice softening. "You're the toughest, most cerebral, most stubborn bastard I've ever known. It's like you don't even belong in this century. So get over yourself. You're a clandestine operator—ready and willing to jump back into the fire to set things right. Go with God, my friend."

Flynn smiled, grateful for the support. "Thanks, man."

Mark shook his head, half-laughing. "This quantum stuff you're talking about? It's downright freaky. Every time you explain it, I feel like my brain is melting. And you know what? That means it's real Italian food time."

Flynn grinned, and Kenji perked up. "Real Italian, huh?" Kenji said. "I'm in."

Mark clapped his hands together. "You bet. I'm making lasagna. It's been way too long since I last made my masterpiece."

Within moments, Mark had commandeered the kitchen, turning it into a battleground of pots, pans, and scattered ingredients. Tomato sauce splattered onto the countertops, while the rich aroma of garlic and cheese filled the air. Flynn and Kenji watched, amused, as Mark poured his heart into crafting the perfect lasagna.

By the time the dish was ready, the kitchen looked like a war zone, but the result was worth it. The three of them sat down, plates stacked high with Mark's so-called "culinary masterpiece." The first bite was heavenly, and for a moment, the weight of everything faded. They laughed, swapped stories, and relished the meal, pushing the looming reality of Flynn's journey aside.

As they finished, Mark leaned back, satisfied. "Alright, Flynn. You're about to go mess with the fabric of the universe or whatever. Just make sure you come back. I'm not losing my best lasagna taste-tester."

Flynn chuckled, wiping his mouth. "I'll be back. You're not getting rid of me that easily." *He didn't want to ruin the moment by admitting this was a one-way trip. But he knew he'd remember Mark—and would find him again, sooner than either of them realized.*

Kenji raised his glass. "To one last meal before the madness begins."

They raised their glasses and toasted to what lay ahead, the weight of the moment settling between them. "Thanks—cheers, boys!" Flynn said, his voice laced with anticipation.

Smiles were exchanged, each of them aware that what was coming was bigger than anything they had faced before. With that, Mark stood, giving a nod before heading home. "See you on the flip side."

CHAPTER TWENTY-FIVE

INTO THE BREACH

The following morning, the basement living room buzzed with anticipation, thick with the electric hum of Tesla coils idling in standby. Flynn stood alone, the weight of his impending journey pressing down on every nerve. Around him, the familiar chaos of his makeshift lab sprawled—a tangle of wires, half-assembled gadgets, and scattered personal relics.

At his feet, Beta rested inside an EM-shielded duffle bag, its snug fit a silent testament to the years of ingenuity and toil leading to this moment. Flynn adjusted his dark shades and protective gear, his gaze sweeping the room. The shades weren't just a shield against the searing brilliance of temporal displacement—they were armor against the creeping doubts clawing at his resolve.

Fronz's words echoed in his mind, a blend of humor and profound truth forged during the engine's creation: "When this baby kicks into turbo, you're gonna see some serious shit."

The Mark 2

He theorized that Beta was the natural anchor point in time, keeping him within the same multiverse. There was only one place he could travel back to, dictated by Beta's current calibration. He recalled that every time he opened the time-view window, it would always display this moment first when using the Mark 1.

Kenji studied the revised formula on the whiteboard, his finger tracing the variables as they seemed to dance across the surface. Narrowing his eyes, he said, "Okay, we've got frequency, vibration, and energy all working together now. But explain this in plain English, Bob—what exactly are we doing here?"

Bob gestured to the diagram he had sketched beside the equations. "Think of time as a string—it's constantly vibrating, and those vibrations create frequencies unique to each moment in history. Beta Mark 2 matches its field to the frequency of the moment we're targeting—specifically, the day Beta was created. That's our anchor."

Kenji nodded. "And vibration?"

"That determines the strength of the oscillations in the field. Without enough amplitude, the field won't stretch far enough to reach fifteen years back. Too much, and the whole thing destabilizes. That's where the cold fusion amplifiers come in—they provide the necessary power, while the dynamic controls fine-tune the vibrations."

Kenji tapped the board. "And this harmonic alignment?"

Bob smiled. "That's the magic. By matching both the frequency and vibration of the present field to the past, we create a harmonic resonance—a kind of temporal echo. It's like hitting the exact same note in perfect pitch with the timeline we're targeting. When we reach the right harmony, the field syncs with the past and pulls us in."

Kenji leaned back, impressed. "It's elegant. Risky as hell, but elegant."

Bob laughed. "That's Fronz's genius at work, mixed with the mystical formula focused on the time window. We witnessed it being written on the whiteboard. All I'm doing is bringing it across the finish line. Now, let's finish building this thing and see if it sings."

"Yes, I remember that marker dancing on the whiteboard like a ghost. I get chills just thinking about it," Kenji recalled.

"Same here, buddy. I thought I was seeing things until I caught the look on your face—your eyes were about to pop out. I don't know where we'd be without that groundbreaking formula. Back then, I could barely make sense of it," Flynn replied.

A chuckle escaped Bob—half-hearted, yet grounding. He checked his equipment one last time. His EM-protected backpack was filled with essentials: a top-of-the-line laptop, tools for unexpected repairs, a loaded gun for protection, and, as an afterthought, a stacked sandwich worthy of Fronz's approval. Nourishment for both body and soul on what could very well be a one-way trip through time.

For money, he had hacked credit cards programmed to function in the past, lightweight yet valuable gems, cash stashed from a drive to Florida, and twenty gold coins—each marked with dates from different eras.

"Bob, I've crunched the numbers and analyzed a decade's worth of data. Since you're planning to turn your grand return to the past into a financial windfall, I saved files and backups on your laptop. You'll need a solid strategy, so let's start with the easy wins," Sunday said, her voice brimming with pride.

A neatly organized timeline of key events flashed onto the monitor in front of him.

"First, let's talk lotteries. The Powerball jackpot from March 6th, fifteen years ago, hit $575 million. Winning numbers: 10, 23, 31, 47, 56—Powerball 22. Buy a ticket, Bob, and you'll be set for your early groundwork. Just don't use the same store as the original winner. There's much more on the list. You have multiple IDs—you'll need every one of them if you want to buy a bank, among other things."

She continued, scrolling through the data.

"Next, sports betting. The Super Bowl that year? The Giants edged out the Patriots 17-14. A modest bet on the exact score will bring in a hefty return. As for the World Series, put your money on the Cardinals—they win in seven games."

Bob leaned in, scanning the data with a smirk. "Not bad, Sunday. Anything else?"

"Plenty," Sunday replied, amusement lacing her voice. "I've pinpointed three major stock market surges—invest in Apple, Google, and a little-known company called Tesla. Timing is everything. Follow my timeline precisely, and you'll be swimming in cash before you know it. Oh, and I threw in a few horse races that will pay off nicely."

Bob grinned as the plan took shape in his mind. "Sunday, you're the best."

"Of course I am," she quipped. "Now, don't blow it. I'd hate to run all these calculations just for you to mess it up."

"I won't even exist yet when you jump back. It'll be nice to meet you for the first time—again. Good thing time travel is so straightforward." Sunday's tone shifted to a more sarcastic humor. "Kenji, of course, will see you much earlier, but he won't recognize you. That'll be a real mind-bender, I'm sure."

Bob chuckled. "Hey, Sunday, great idea on the stealth suit. Fits like a glove. This'll be a solid test—think it can handle time travel and still keep me hidden?"

"You always get to have all the fun," Sunday said, her tone playful. "But yes, I think the suit will blend you in just fine. Take care, Captain. Safe journey."

Beside him, Kenji—older now, his face lined from years of working alongside Bob—watched with a mix of concern and admiration. He had been there through every twist and turn, from moments of this is impossible to oh wait, maybe not. He'd absorbed much of Bob's knowledge of physics, reading all the same books and sifting through endless test data.

Kenji exhaled. "Is it finally time? That old thorn we call time comes knocking once more, my friend."

Bob gazed at the time window. "You see where I'm going? Remember that place? Feels like a lifetime ago." He hesitated, then added, "If I succeed, will this present still exist? I think it will—just as a parallel universe. One could go crazy just thinking about it."

Kenji said, "I'll see you in a minute. I won't remember, but you will." They hugged like brothers parting for the last time. Stepping back, Kenji positioned himself behind the wall with a window, his fist raised in the air—a silent gesture of encouragement. His expression carried the weight of farewell, yet his eyes burned with determination.

With unwavering resolve, his voice broke the silence. "Into the breach!" He pressed the 'Showtime' button on his tablet. Instantly, the room exploded with crackling blue lightning. The brilliance he expected swallowed him whole, a force ripping him from the present and flinging him into the untamed currents of time. The sensation was violent—space itself seemed to fold around him, warping reality as he vanished.

Kenji watched as his mentor was struck by a surge of blue lightning, the energy coursing through his torso before he disappeared in an instant. "Godspeed, Captain."

The journey through time was fleeting yet infinite, a passage through cascading light and deafening echoes, defying the very fabric of reality. Flynn arrived—fifteen years earlier—inside the old facility. Disorientation seized him, a sickening fusion of nausea and pain. He clenched his fists, forcing himself to endure. This was the price of bending time.

Flynn whispered through gritted teeth, "Just take the pain... it will pass."

As Flynn's eyes adjust and the residual glow of his travel fades, he quickly scans his surroundings. He knows this place like the back of his hand—every corner, every shadow. His specially designed suit blends seamlessly into the background, bending light to obscure him from any unintended observers.

With careful, measured steps, he ducks out of sight, finding temporary cover in a structure he knows will remain undisturbed. There are no Zoomies or Sunday the AI yet—this is a time before such advancements. His knowledge of the timeline is both a guide and a warning.

As night falls, Flynn slips out of the facility, Beta Mk 2 and his duffle securely in tow. The outside world feels both familiar and alien, a landscape on the cusp of transformation.

He doesn't go far, settling in the shadows just beyond the perimeter, catching his breath as he plans his next move. The gold coins, period-appropriate money, and precious stones in his pack—a makeshift treasury meant to fund his operations—remain secure. With these, he can acquire immediate necessities.

Retrieving one of the forged credit cards from his prepared arsenal, Flynn calls an Uber, slipping into this era's rhythm with practiced ease. The car pulls up, and he directs it to a nondescript motel—the kind that asks no questions as long as the cash is real.

Once checked in, he arranges for a rental car, another step in setting up his base of operations. He unloads Beta next to his bed, allowing himself a moment to recover from the strain of time travel. The motel room, with its faded wallpaper and the hum of an aging air conditioner, becomes the first command center in a timeline where Flynn is both a ghost and a catalyst.

In the silent motel room, with the night deepening outside, he sits on the edge of the bed, laptop open, thoughts racing. This was just the beginning. Every step from here must be measured, deliberate, and, above all, unseen. The challenge was daunting, but the stakes—the lives of those he loved—made every risk, every uncertainty, worth it. Now, the real work of altering time begins.

Morning light filters through the thin curtains of Bob's hotel room, casting long shadows over the floor, littered with blueprints and freshly forged documents. Today marks the start of a new chapter—not just for him, but for the entire team at the old facility. A team that, for now, remains unaware of his true identity or the mission that brought him from the future.

Bob leaves the hotel early, maneuvering his rental car through the waking city. The streets hum with the familiar rhythms of everyday life, indifferent to the deception about to unfold. He rehearses his story—Uncle Bob, Flynn's long-lost relative from his father's side. A carefully constructed persona, woven from half-truths and the gaps in history—the perfect cover for his incursion into the past.

Upon arriving at the facility, Bob takes a steadying breath before stepping out of the car. Trepidation and determination war within him as he strides toward the entrance, adjusting his ID badge—last name altered. It reads Bob Cavalla, an identity fortified by official-looking documents and a meticulously crafted backstory, finalized just before his leap through time.

Bob knocked on the door and waited, mentally rehearsing his words.

He decided against phrases like "You see a family resemblance?" or anything that might draw attention to his appearance. Just keep it simple. Sure, I'm fifteen years older, with more gray, thinning hair, and a longer beard—but I'm still me. Glasses, a cigar-roughened voice, a boonie hat, and a limp softened by a walking cane.

The door swung open. A younger Flynn stood there, eyes scanning Bob with cautious curiosity. He was surprised—but not entirely dismissive.

Bob cleared his throat. "Good morning! I'm looking for Vance. I'm Robert—your uncle, from your father's side. You can call me Bob."

Flynn kept the door open, studying the man in front of him. Something about Uncle Bob tugged at the edges of familiarity. Maybe it was the way he carried himself—calm, confident, like someone who had been through hell and walked out the other side.

"Well, this was unexpected," Flynn said, leaning against the doorframe. "What brings you here?"

Bob offered a small, knowing smirk. "I've been keeping tabs on the family from afar. I heard about Team Nautilus—saw you on TV. Thought I'd see if I could be of any use. I can weld, handle engineering, plumbing, mechanical work, electrical repairs, and computers. I even clean up after myself. Not big on windows, though. But I am well-versed in workplace laundry."

Flynn chuckled at the odd mix of skills. There was something disarming about this guy. "Workplace laundry, huh? That's a hell of a résumé."

Bob shrugged. "I like to stay busy. I was hoping I could stick around for a while—if you don't mind. I'd be happy to sign an NDA if necessary. I do have some personal projects, so I won't be in the way."

Flynn studied him for a long moment. There was something about Bob's presence—calm, unintrusive—that didn't set off any alarms. In this line of work, that was saying something.

"Come on in," Flynn said, stepping aside. "I'll introduce you to the team."

Bob followed Flynn into the facility, his gaze sweeping over the workspace—high-tech monitors, mechanical workstations, prototype schematics pinned to boards, all wrapped in a controlled chaos that spoke of innovation.

"Hey, everyone," Flynn called out, catching the attention of Kenji, Joshua, and Fronz, who were huddled around a worktable, deep in discussion about adjustments to the Alpha engine.

They turned as Bob stepped in, their expressions shifting from curiosity to mild skepticism.

"This is my uncle, Robert—my dad's side," Flynn said. "I've heard some crazy stories about an uncle, but they were few and far between. He left home early and got to work. Solid engineering background, mechanical and electrical skills, and—most importantly—he does laundry."

Kenji raised an eyebrow. "Laundry? That's the real deal right there."

Bob smirked. "Figured if I couldn't help with tech, at least I could keep the jumpsuits clean."

Joshua crossed his arms, sizing Bob up. "Flynn's uncle, huh? You got any military background?"

Bob nodded. "Did a stint in the Army. Then some government contracting overseas. Kept my head down, got my hands dirty." His words were vague, just weighted enough to imply experience.

Joshua tilted his head slightly. "CIA recruit?"

Bob let out a dry chuckle. "Negative, Ghostrider. Met some of those guys. No thanks."

Joshua smirked, acknowledging the response with a small nod.

Fronz, always the observer, studied Bob for a long moment before breaking into a grin. "Well, if Flynn trusts you, that's good enough for me. Welcome aboard, Bob."

Bob exhaled, his shoulders easing. Step one of blending in—complete.

With introductions out of the way, Bob was led into the facility, where the hum of machinery created an atmosphere of familiarity. As he walked through the corridors, his prior knowledge of the facility's layout—an advantage of his foreknowledge—allowed him to navigate both conversations and the physical space with ease.

Meanwhile, Bob remained attentive to discussions about Engines Alpha and Beta, affectionately dubbed "Thing 1 and Thing 2." His presence in the past gave him the opportunity to subtly influence their development, ensuring that both designs reached their full potential under Fronz's watchful eye.

Over time, Bob settled into the facility quickly. It was easy, given that everything he owned was already with him. He found plenty of space in one of the rooms downstairs.

To store the Beta Mark 2 and his gear, Bob purchased a storage container and had it placed at the back of the facility. Afterward, he checked out of the motel and returned the rental car.

In the following weeks, Bob used his new identity to integrate seamlessly with the team.

CHAPTER TWENTY- SIX

EXECUTE THE PLAN

Bob's investigative work exposed SAGA's corruption, leading to a guilty verdict.

He knew that defeating SAGA required more than brute force—it demanded strategy, patience, and the precise application of law. He had learned from past mistakes and understood that this time had to be different. After fifteen years of planning, he was ready. Give me fifteen years, and I'm nearly impossible to beat.

His first move was securing the necessary capital to fuel his fight. With the list provided by Sunday, he executed his financial strategy with precision.

Bob's office was a paradox of intellect and irreverence, where meticulous organization coexisted with a touch of controlled chaos—the signature of a mind always in motion. A warm desk lamp cast elongated shadows across shelves packed with physics texts, engineering manuals, and theoretical works on electromagnetism and quantum mechanics. Nestled among them, defiantly out of place, were volumes of razor-sharp satire and well-worn sci-fi novels—his quiet rebellion against the rigidity of academia.

His oak desk, worn by years of relentless work, bore blueprints, scattered notes, and a high-end desktop with multiple large monitors running perpetual simulations. His laptop, docked to the right and linked to an additional monitor, served as his command center for emails. Flynn had once teased, "Do you have enough monitors?" An old-school globe occupied a corner—not as decoration but as a reminder that despite all his knowledge, the world remained full of mysteries.

Framed certificates adorned the walls—not just his Master's degree in Electromagnetism and Theoretical Physics, but also joke diplomas: one for "Excellence in Overthinking" and another declaring him the "World's Foremost Expert in Making Shit Up." A Newton's Cradle clicked methodically on a nearby shelf, next to a coffee mug that read, "I'm Not Arguing, I'm Just Explaining Why I'm Right."

A heartfelt picture sat nearby—Bob and Fronz exchanging a knowing smirk, as if they were in on a joke no one else understood, while Kenji stood in the background, noticing. *The only question was: which timeline had this picture been taken in? That detail had never come up.*

To any outsider, the room was a blend of sharp intellect, eccentricity, and dry humor—just like Bob himself.

He stared at the Powerball ticket in his hand. The winning numbers were undeniable. Step one: secure anonymity. Bob visited the lottery headquarters, accompanied by a lawyer hired under one of his aliases. In a private meeting with the executives, he made his pitch:

"I'll claim the prize, but my identity stays confidential. In exchange, I'll donate $5 million to your charitable fund."

After some negotiation, the deal was sealed. The winnings were wired into an offshore account under the name Robert Sterling—one of the five identities Bob had carefully prepared.

His net gain: $275 million. But this wasn't about personal wealth or indulgence. This was a tool—his first calculated move to reclaim what had been taken and dismantle SAGA's power.

Step two: secure financial expertise. He already knew who he wanted after extensive research.

Step three: assemble a legal team. Once his financial base was established, Bob turned to recruiting top-tier lawyers—experts with a history of taking down corporate giants. He sought legal minds specializing in class-action lawsuits, whistleblower protection, and corporate corruption cases.

Bob knew exposing SAGA wouldn't be easy. They were a powerful conglomerate with deep connections. But with the right team, he could mount a credible legal case that would force them into the spotlight.

The lawyers swiftly filed preliminary motions to investigate SAGA's financial dealings, safety protocols, and history of corporate negligence. They subpoenaed records, combing through emails and internal communications to uncover evidence of SAGA's role in framing Team Nautilus for the accident. Additionally, the legal team launched a defamation lawsuit on Team Nautilus's behalf, aiming to restore their reputation and expose SAGA's calculated attempt to dismantle the team.

In tandem with the legal efforts, Bob assembled a team of private investigators to delve into SAGA's hidden machinations. Many of these operatives were former law enforcement and intelligence professionals, tasked with unearthing illicit financial transactions, corporate espionage, and bribery. Bob's objective was to expose the secret deals and payoffs SAGA had used to manipulate courts, regulators, and the media.

One investigator uncovered that SAGA had bribed key witnesses in the accident trial, ensuring their testimony would implicate Team Nautilus. Another traced a secret slush fund used to buy silence and cover up corporate misconduct. The most damning revelation, however, was an internal memo proving that SAGA executives had been fully aware of the safety hazards leading to the accident but had prioritized profits over human lives.

Working relentlessly behind the scenes, Bob coordinated his legal and investigative teams to construct an airtight case. He deliberately avoided direct confrontation with SAGA's leadership, knowing his greatest weapon was discretion. As he gathered irrefutable evidence, he strategically leaked fragments to trusted journalists, ensuring the public was primed for the inevitable reckoning. His endgame was clear—expose SAGA's corruption, clear Team Nautilus's name, and bring the entire empire to its knees.

Bob reviewed his documents and muttered to himself, "It's all about playing the long game. Every win, every investment—it's all for them."

His next bold move: securing the heart of Team Nautilus.

With the wealth he had meticulously amassed through strategic investments and foresight, Bob was now in a position to act. He hired a private accounting firm with deep financial connections, ensuring that every move remained calculated and discreet. He understood that Team Nautilus needed more than just legal protection to withstand SAGA's relentless assault—they needed to fortify their very foundation. That meant controlling the places that mattered most: the old house where Flynn's family had built their life and the facility that had long served as the heart of Team Nautilus's operations.

Bob's first target was the bank holding the mortgage on both properties. With his soon-to-be newfound fortune, he orchestrated a daring financial maneuver. After months of strategic planning, he finally acquired the bank—one that, as it turned out, was already teetering on financial collapse. But this wasn't just any bank; it held the key to Team Nautilus's survival. The acquisition wasn't a public spectacle, nor did it raise any suspicion. Bob ensured secrecy, structuring the purchase through a web of shell companies and financial trusts, making it nearly impossible to trace back to him.

With the first step complete, he turned his attention to the true linchpin of his plan: the bank that controlled the deed to his old property. Sunday's analysis, combined with intelligence from private investigators, led him to Sunland Community Bank—a struggling regional institution on the brink of insolvency. Its assets were modest, its management incompetent, and its desperation palpable.

Bob approached the board with a calculated offer. "I'm prepared to acquire your bank at 1.1 times book value," he stated. "I'll inject capital, absorb the bad loans, and stabilize operations."

It was an offer they couldn't refuse. Within weeks, Sunland Community Bank was his—for $105 million.

Owning the bank granted Bob control over its real estate holdings, including the facility and his former home. Now back in possession of the places that had once been vital to Team Nautilus, he focused on assembling a trusted team: lawyers to navigate legal complexities, accountants to oversee financial operations, and investigators to scrutinize SAGA's dealings.

Seated in his new office, Bob examined the data Sunday had compiled. "This is just the beginning," he said, his voice carrying quiet resolve. "First, we reclaim what's ours. Then, we dismantle SAGA—piece by piece."

With the acquisition finalized, Bob wasted no time. He immediately transferred the mortgages on his old house and the Team Nautilus facility to a newly established private company. On paper, ownership was entangled in a sophisticated web of subsidiaries and offshore entities, deliberately designed to obscure the true stakeholders. While Bob, Flynn, and his family were the real owners, the layered structure made tracing them nearly impossible.

His objective was clear: safeguard the assets that mattered most. Now that the mortgages were secured under his control, SAGA's ability to exert financial pressure had been neutralized.

No outside force could manipulate the bank into calling in loans, foreclosing, or interfering with Team Nautilus's future. Bob had effectively built a financial stronghold around their most critical assets.

The old house, now safely within the family's grasp, became more than just a home—it was a testament to their resilience. Flynn's childhood memories were etched into its very foundation, and Bob knew preserving it was just as vital as opposing SAGA directly. The Team Nautilus facility, meanwhile, was more than a headquarters—it was the nerve center of their innovation, the birthplace of groundbreaking research, and the foundation of their mission. By securing its ownership, Bob ensured that it remained untouchable, immune to any financial or legal maneuver SAGA might attempt.

But Bob didn't stop there. He reinforced the private company's financial reserves, ensuring its long-term independence. This wasn't just about maintaining control—it was about fortifying it against future threats. He established alternative funding channels, including offshore accounts and discreet investments, crafting a financial shield so impenetrable that if SAGA ever launched another attack, they'd find themselves striking against an unbreakable fortress.

The records were meticulously maintained, each document carefully designed to conceal the true nature of the transactions. Bob knew that SAGA's legal and corporate spies would eventually attempt to investigate the ownership of the properties, but they would uncover nothing of substance—only a labyrinth of holding companies, each more obscure than the last.

As the final paperwork settled and the ownership transfer was complete, Bob leaned back in his chair, a quiet sense of triumph washing over him. The pieces were falling into place. SAGA had underestimated him before, and now, they wouldn't see this coming. With Team Nautilus and his family financially secured, he was free to focus on the next phase—bringing SAGA down.

A slow smile crept onto his face. Now, they were playing on his terms. He arranged a meeting with Flynn and Lilian for later that afternoon.

As the afternoon sun cast golden light through the expansive living room window, Bob stepped through the front door of Flynn and Lilian's home. He paused, memories surging through him like a crashing wave. The house was a testament to time and taste—a seamless fusion of classic architecture and modern refinement, every detail carefully chosen by the very people standing before him: his younger self and the love of his life, Lilian.

The hardwood floors, aged to a deep chestnut sheen, stretched across the open-concept living space. Crown molding adorned the high ceilings, each intricate design whispering of craftsmanship rarely seen in modern construction. The walls, painted a warm cream, were adorned with carefully selected antiques—a gold-framed oil painting of a ship at sea and an ornate grandfather clock standing proudly in the hallway, its rhythmic ticking a reminder of time's unrelenting passage.

The living room exuded both comfort and tradition. A grand stone fireplace served as the centerpiece, its mantle adorned with old books, a vintage brass clock, and framed family photos. The seating arrangement was both inviting and elegant—a deep brown leather Chesterfield sofa, flanked by two high-backed armchairs upholstered in rich hunter green fabric, strategically placed for conversation rather than idle television watching. Beneath them, a handwoven Persian rug, vibrant with reds and golds, added warmth, complementing the soft glow of wall sconces and a vintage chandelier overhead.

Bob turned, his gaze drifting down the hallway leading to the bedrooms. The faint scent of aged oak mingled with Lilian's signature vanilla and lavender, lingering in the air. Black-and-white photos lined the walls, capturing fragments of the past—Flynn in his flight suit, Lilian standing on the beach at sunset, the two of them at a masquerade ball years ago. This house wasn't just a place; it was a testament to love, history, and shared dreams.

He swallowed hard, forcing himself to stay composed. He couldn't afford to let emotion take hold. Standing here, in what was once his home but now belonged to his younger self—with Lilian right there—it was almost too much. But he had a mission.

Bob took a steadying breath, masking his turmoil with a practiced smile. "Hell of a place you've got here, Flynn. Feels like home."

His throat tightened, emotion clawing at the edges of his resolve. "It's good to see you both," he said, his voice thick with emotion. "Lilian... Flynn... I can't begin to explain what this moment means to me. I know I've been away, working overseas. But I'm back for good now, and it's great to finally see you, Flynn. And Lilian... it's a pleasure to meet you."

Lilian stepped forward, tears spilling freely as she pulled him into a warm embrace. "Bob, you've always been family." She wiped at her cheeks, then turned toward the fridge. "Would you like something to drink?"

She grabbed a beer and handed it to him.

Bob took it with a nod. "Sure, thanks."

Flynn joined them, his expression filled with gratitude. "I hear you've been all over the world, Bob. It's nice to finally meet you, too. Whatever you have to say, we're here to listen."

Bob cleared his throat, stepping back to compose himself. "I have news—good news this time. The bank that held the deed to this house and the facility? It's mine now. I bought it."

Flynn blinked, stunned. "Wait... you own the bank?"

Bob nodded, a proud smile breaking through. "Not just that—I made sure of something else. Flynn, this house—your house—is yours, free and clear. Same goes for the facility. No more mortgage. No more debt. You own it outright."

Lilian gasped, her hand flying to her mouth. "You mean... we're set? No more worries?"

Bob's smile softened. "Exactly. You're financially secure. You have the freedom to focus on what truly matters. Flynn, Lilian... this is my way of giving back. Family comes first."

Flynn placed a hand on Bob's shoulder, his voice thick with emotion. "Bob, I don't know what to say… except thank you. You've done more for us than I ever imagined."

Lilian nodded, wiping away her tears. "You've given us peace of mind, Bob. That's priceless."

Bob chuckled. "Oh, it gets better. Your names are also on the list of bank owners. I'll show you how I set it up—a protected, stealthy ownership. Just the way I like it."

Flynn and Lilian exchanged stunned glances, absorbing the weight of the moment. They listened intently as Bob detailed the intricate setup behind their unexpected stake in the bank.

The three of them sat together, tears of joy melting into laughter and shared appreciation. It was a moment of triumph, unity, and hope for the future.

Even amid his financial maneuvers, Bob's thoughts frequently drifted to Lilian. The years apart hadn't lessened his love for her. Anonymous flowers kept arriving, accompanied by heartfelt messages—each a silent attempt to bridge the chasm of time and regret. He signed them the way Flynn would, ensuring they felt like familiar warmth rather than an unsettling secret.

CHAPTER TWENTY - SEVEN

SOTRA

As she detects the power levels from the more advanced cold fusion engine, she senses the beginnings of an EM field emitted by Alpha. When she shifts into this dimension, she remains invisible to everyone except those she physically touches. Sotra has ascended to a heightened state of consciousness, her senses sharper than before. She curiously explores this new awareness.

Alpha generates an EM field that can manipulate gravity, its area of effect adaptable. It can be modified to allow airflow or become a completely sealed environment, all controlled via the UX interface designed by Kenji.

Later, Kenji devises a method to visualize the EM field using small lasers, installing them on or near Alpha. The field's size can be adjusted through the UX interface. Fronz soon realizes that, with precise modulation of frequency, vibration, and current, the field can contain, shield, and even regulate objects within it. The team initiates a series of tests to refine its capabilities and finalize adjustments to the IU/UX software.

The workshop hums with activity, the aroma of food wafting in the background. The team is deeply engrossed in their work around the Alpha engine, the EM field pulsating gently, hinting at its untapped potential.

Fronz studies the monitors. “The EM field's behavior is beyond our current understanding. We need to investigate its properties further.”

Flynn nods. “It feels like we’re on the verge of something groundbreaking, but there’s still a missing piece.”

Unseen and unheard, Sotra observes, deciding to intervene subtly.

The room is still, the faint hum of equipment the only sound. Kenji stands by the whiteboard, staring at it with tired eyes. He blinks, rubs them, convinced his exhaustion is playing tricks on him. But no—the whiteboard marker moves on its own, sketching an intricate pictogram and a complex equation, as if guided by an unseen hand. His jaw drops.

Bob stays out of the way, finds a seat, and pulls out his mobile phone. Then he remembers the whiteboard—the marker moving at a blazing pace, writing out the formula that allowed Alpha to function properly. He looks up in amazement, watching it happen again—clearer, more vivid than before. He quickly taps Kenji's shoulder.

"Guys… look at the board!" Kenji calls out, his voice a mix of disbelief and awe.

Flynn turns just in time to catch the final strokes appearing on the board. He squints, trying to make sense of the alien symbols and complex equations materializing out of thin air. "Am I hallucinating, or did that just write itself?" he mutters.

Joshua steps forward, eyes widening as he takes in the new writing. "This… this is like a message from the magic marker of knowledge. Kenji, come on, that was you, right?"

Fronz, already pushing past them, is laser-focused on the whiteboard. "Hold on, everyone—just give me a moment," he says, eyes darting between the pictogram and the accompanying equation. He yanks a notepad from his back pocket, scribbling the formula down as if it might vanish at any second.

Flynn pulls out his phone and snaps ten quick pictures of the entire whiteboard.

Kenji, still reeling from what he just witnessed, leans in closer. "Look at that calibration. It's tailored specifically for Alpha. This could be exactly what we're missing to stabilize it."

Fronz runs a hand through his graying hair, his face lighting up as he deciphers the equations. "Oh my god…" he murmurs, barely audible. Then, louder: "Great Scott! This is it! I can't believe I didn't see this sooner."

"What? Shut up," Flynn says with a chuckle at Fronz's dramatic reaction.

Fronz shakes his head, a wide grin spreading across his face. "No, seriously! This equation—it's not just about energy output. It's adjusting for frequency and vibration in ways I hadn't even considered. Whoever—whatever—gave us this is pushing us in a whole new direction."

Fronz, now peering over Joshua's shoulder, pointed to a section of the diagram. "Look at this part. It's suggesting that the frequency modulation needs to be fine-tuned in real time to maintain stability. If we get this right…" He trailed off, his mind racing with possibilities.

Kenji, still shaken by the sight of the equation writing itself, glanced at Flynn. "I'm at a loss for words right now."

Fronz stepped back, his gaze fixed on the board. "Alright, enough gawking. Let's get to work. We have a new path forward." He turned to Kenji with a smirk. "But first, you need to teach me how you pulled that off."

Kenji laughed, the tension finally easing. "I wish I could take credit, but that was all the marker, furiously writing on the whiteboard. I wouldn't have believed it if I hadn't seen it myself."

Following Fronz's instructions, Kenji applied the changes. The engine's hum deepened, and the EM field visibly shifted, becoming more defined and controlled.

"I'm integrating these new parameters into the user interface controls," Kenji said. "This should give us a clearer understanding of the field's capabilities."

Joshua watched as Kenji worked, his expression a mixture of concentration and awe. "It feels like we're not alone in this… like we're being guided by something unseen."

After a week of pacing and rewriting the formula over and over, followed by several more days of testing, Fronz suddenly froze. His eyes widened. "Great Scott in heaven… I think I get it! It's leading us in a new direction. How could I have been so blind?"

He immediately made adjustments alongside Kenji, refining the UI controls for spin speed, frequency, and vibration. "Alright, try it now."

As the changes took effect, Fronz's excitement surged. "The field... it's responding! We can manipulate its size and properties now."

The team, united in their mission, began a series of methodical tests. Each member focused intently on their task, driven by the weight of their discovery.

The scene closes on the team, their work bathed in the glow of the Alpha engine—a beacon of their journey into the depths of scientific discovery, subtly guided by an unseen hand.

Nearby, Beta hums softly on its own table, emitting a frequency that soothes and stabilizes those within its range. Stress levels drop noticeably, and everyone who lingers in its field experiences an undeniable sense of clarity and well-being.

Kenji devises a way to visualize the EM field using small lasers, strategically placed on or near Alpha and Beta. The UI allows for real-time adjustments to the field's size, offering precise control over its influence. As Fronz delves deeper, he realizes that with fine-tuned modifications to frequency, vibration, and applied current, the field can be used not just to contain or protect—but to manipulate what exists within it.

Recognizing the potential, the team embarks on a rigorous series of tests, refining the UI/UX software to unlock Beta's full capabilities.

"We're breaking new ground here," Flynn says, his voice laced with awe. "This is uncharted scientific territory."

Though Sotra remains invisible and silent, her unseen hand has undeniably reshaped their course, nudging them toward discoveries that blur the line between science and the unknown.

"We'll continue testing," Fronz replies, determination flickering in his gaze. "There's still much to learn… and I have a feeling we're only scratching the surface."

As the Alpha engine's glow reflects off their faces, the weight of their discoveries settles in—tangible proof of their plunge into the mysteries of the universe.

Yet, Beta's functionality remains inconsistent at first. It takes further adjustments, spurred by cryptic clues left in Sotra's wake, before the team uncovers something unexpected: the EM field doesn't just stabilize—it opens a window through time. Though not as potent as Alpha's gravity-defying field, this revelation expands the very boundaries of what they thought possible.

Sotra and Bob

Sotra lingered in the shadows, her silver eyes fixed on Bob as he worked. She had been watching him for some time now, silently piecing together the puzzle that had been gnawing at her. There was something about him—something eerily familiar. His movements, the way he carried himself, even the cadence of his voice—it all reminded her of someone she once knew.

Impossible. Or so she had thought. Flynn was younger, more reckless. But here was Bob—older, measured, deliberate. The resemblance wasn't just uncanny; it was undeniable. Her kind possessed an innate ability to perceive shifts in energy and time, to sense the ripples of altered fate. Yet what she felt from Bob was something deeper, something beyond mere echoes of the past or glimpses of the future.

Cautiously, she stepped closer, her tall frame moving with practiced grace as her thoughts raced. The final pieces of the puzzle slid into place. Bob wasn't just a man who had mysteriously appeared—he was Flynn. An older, wiser Flynn. And somehow, he had done the impossible. He hadn't merely observed time through the Beta calibration she had fine-tuned. He had traveled through it.

Beta was meant to be a tool, a window into possible futures—not a gateway. She had calibrated it to assist, never intending to expose the secrets of time travel. Yet, here he was, proof that the line had already been crossed.

Bob sat alone, absorbed in his work, fingers gliding over his tablet. A quiet sigh escaped him before he set the device aside. He decided a short rest was in order, stretching out on the couch in his office. His breathing slowed, his eyes fluttering closed.

Sotra hesitated in the doorway, uncertain of how to begin. She wanted him to know she had uncovered the truth, but more than that—she wanted him to understand what it meant. What he meant. Bob wasn't just fixing things. He was rewriting fate itself.

Stepping forward at last, she spoke, her voice low and steady, meant only for him. "There's something different about you."

Bob, half-asleep, heard the gentle voice, his expression unreadable. "Hello. Are you our stealthy, friendly helper?"

A faint smile touched her lips, her silver eyes studying him. "Yes. And you… you've been keeping secrets, haven't you?"

Bob's brow furrowed slightly, though his posture remained calm, accepting. "What do you mean?"

She stepped closer, her gaze locked onto his. "You're Vance Cavalla. Everyone calls you Flynn. In your case, Bob." The words lingered in the space between them.

Bob's eyebrows lifted in surprise, but he didn't deny it. His voice carried the weight of years and experience. "Yeah. I'm Flynn… older, anyway."

Sotra tilted her head, the full realization settling over her. "But how? How can you be here? Time travel… I never thought it was possible for humans."

Bob's expression softened. "Give me fifteen years. I'm very hard to beat. I found a way back, and I've been working on a few puzzles. I needed to fix things—things that went horribly wrong."

Sotra's gaze softened as well. "So, that's why you're here. To fix your past."

Bob nodded slowly. "That's the plan."

Silence stretched between them as Sotra processed his words. The magnitude of what he had done was staggering. Time travel wasn't just a scientific achievement—it was a burden, one that Flynn—now Bob—had willingly taken upon himself. And she understood something else now. When he was finished…

"You'll have to leave again, won't you?" Sotra asked, though it wasn't really a question.

Bob sighed. "When it's done. When everything is in place… yeah." He paused, his gaze flickering with distant memories. "Oh—was it you who split me on a quantum level last time? Reminded me of the Phoenix, being reborn from its own ashes." He let out a dry chuckle. "Oh wait, sorry. That's my past. When it happens again, in the present, I'll probably disappear. I theorize there can only be two of the same quantum particle… not three."

Sotra felt a strange mix of admiration and sorrow. He had come back not for himself, but for a future that might never be his.

"You're remarkable, you know," she said softly, her voice filled with respect. "I've never met anyone like you. What you're doing—it's beyond anything I've ever seen or heard of."

Bob offered a quiet smile, the corner of his lips lifting ever so slightly. "Thanks. I'm just trying to set things right. Nothing more."

Sotra shook her head, understanding that the only reason to take on such a burden was for family. "It's more than that. You're not just fixing your mistakes; you're giving your family a future. A future that, I'm starting to realize, would be very different if you hadn't come back."

Bob paused, the weight of her words settling over him.

With her heightened perception, she glimpsed what the future might hold. She saw them both there—together. And in that moment, she realized Flynn was the partner she had been searching for all along.

"Thank you," Sotra whispered, stepping closer. "For everything."

Bob gave a small nod. His eyes remained closed, yet his head turned in her direction. "I'm not done yet. But when I am…"

Sotra placed a hand on his arm, her touch light but reassuring. Bob opened his eyes and finally saw her clearly—towering at nine feet tall, with long, flowing white hair and a striking Nordic face. She stood ten feet away, yet her presence was unmistakable.

"When you are, I'll be ready," she said. "And so will the younger guy."

And in that moment, Bob knew—she understood. She saw him completely. The man he had been, the man he had become, and the man he still needed to be.

"See you around, Doc," Sotra said. She had concluded that Flynn must have spent years learning how to update Beta, which suggested he had a doctorate or Ph.D. in Quantum

Physics. The calculus equations on the whiteboard, written in his hand, confirmed that the current Flynn had not yet mastered what his future self had.

Time slowed as Sotra opened a portal. She stepped through, leaving Bob alone for a few moments to gather his thoughts.

"Whoa… was that a dream?" He paused, frowning. "It sure explained a lot."

Bob chose not to mention meeting Sotra. Would revealing it change what was meant to happen? What had to happen again?

Shaking off the thought, he turned his attention to Joshua. He found him working on the van, modifying it and installing the .50-caliber machine gun. They talked shop, joked, and made each other laugh as they worked.

Bob helped where he could while Joshua ran tests on the van. Meanwhile, Bob also monitored his financial moves, remotely accessing his laptop from his tablet and phone. He tracked his growing wealth and the many projects already in motion.

Later, he went to sell some of the diamonds and jewels he had brought back. Instead of a pawn shop, he went straight to the right buyer—someone he had learned to seek out. Then, using the fake IDs he had created, he placed bets on upcoming sporting events, further securing his financial position.

CHAPTER TWENTY-

EIGHT

THE SAGA PROJECT IS UNDERWAY

Bob leaned against the workbench, arms crossed, watching as Flynn prepped gear for the upcoming test. Joshua and Kenji moved efficiently in the background, checking cables and running diagnostics. The scene was all too familiar—history repeating itself.

"Flynn," Bob said, his tone light but firm. "I'm sitting this one out."

Flynn glanced up, a smirk forming. "What, afraid of a little deep-sea adventure?"

Bob chuckled. "Not quite. I've got work to do. While you boys play with Beta and the Yamato, I'll be keeping an eye on our… *mutual friends."*

Flynn nodded knowingly. "SAGA?"

Bob gave a small shrug. "Let's just say I've got some strings to pull. Lawyers, PIs, accountants—keeping those bastards busy is a full-time job."

Flynn studied him for a moment, then clapped a hand on Bob's shoulder. "Do what you do best. We've got this covered."

Bob grinned. "Godspeed, Captain."

Flynn laughed. "You and these old-school send-offs…"

Joshua called over, "Hey, if Bob's staying behind, does that mean more snacks for us?"

Kenji deadpanned, "Only if you can beat me to them."

Bob gave Flynn a final nod before heading out. He already knew how this test would go. The real battle? That was unfolding in courtrooms, on paper, and in the shadows—where SAGA wouldn't see it coming.

He hopped into his car and drove into the city for a string of meetings. In his rented off-site office, he leaned over his desk, fingers tapping rhythmically against a mug of cooling coffee. The ceiling fan hummed overhead, barely masking the sounds of his team at work—lawyers on conference calls, private investigators compiling reports. The room buzzed with strategy and intelligence, every move meticulously aimed at dismantling SAGA, piece by calculated piece.

Bob adjusted his glasses, narrowing his eyes at a spreadsheet illuminated on his laptop.

"Bob, you're going to want to check cell D14. That transaction trail? It's tied to Wagner's offshore accounts. Let's just say... it's interesting."

His private investigator's voice was steady, but Bob could hear the edge beneath it.

He clicked the highlighted cell, his brow furrowing as the data came into focus.

"Interesting is an understatement. This wire transfer—$2.4 million—funneled through a shell corporation three weeks before SAGA acquired the cold fusion prototype. Too clean to be coincidence."

The investigation into SAGA was an intricate puzzle, but Bob had assembled the ideal team to crack it. His lead investigator, Marcus—an ex-cop turned private eye with a sharp instinct for financial crimes—was already uncovering troubling patterns.

"We're seeing connections, Bob," Marcus said during one of their late-night strategy calls. "Wagner's built a fortress of deniability, but we've found cracks. That shell corporation you flagged? It links back to three different front companies they've used for acquisitions over the past decade."

Bob nodded, scribbling notes. "Keep digging. If Wagner's laundering money or misusing corporate funds, we need irrefutable proof. Also, start tracking their patents—anything they've acquired but haven't developed. SAGA thrives on hoarding tech they can't replicate."

Marcus smirked. "Already ahead of you. You wouldn't believe how much intellectual property they've buried just to keep competitors out."

Meanwhile, Bob's legal team worked tirelessly, filing Freedom of Information Act requests and scrutinizing SAGA's known partnerships. They combed through contracts and legal filings, searching for any leverageable weaknesses. One discovery made Bob sit up straighter: a non-compete clause in one of SAGA's contracts had been violated, exposing them to potential anti-competitive practice charges.

"This is solid," Bob said in a team meeting. "Not flashy, but a firm foundation. We use this to apply pressure."

Yet, Bob knew the real target was Wagner. Taking down SAGA meant exposing its CEO as the mastermind behind its corruption. Marcus's deep dive into Wagner's activities revealed alarming discrepancies—frequent trips to the Cayman Islands, ties to dubious contractors, and a sprawling web of personal assets that far exceeded his declared income.

"Bob," Marcus said one evening, his tone calm but charged. "Wagner's personal lawyer just wired $500,000 into an unregistered account. Want me to dig deeper?"

Bob grinned. "Marcus, if you weren't already doing that, I'd be disappointed."

The following week, Marcus called with an update. "Wagner's got more skeletons than a Halloween store," he said. "Bribes, insider trading, and... well, I'll just send you the file."

Bob skimmed the report, his jaw tightening. "We're gaining momentum, Marcus. Keep the pressure on, but we can't tip our hand too soon. The last thing we need is SAGA catching wind of this."

Marcus chuckled. "Don't worry, Bob. Discretion is my middle name."

While his team worked relentlessly, Bob kept his sights on the bigger picture. He wasn't just after Wagner—he wanted to dismantle SAGA from the inside out. That meant leveraging every shred of evidence to chip away at their foundation. Lawyers filed motions to probe SAGA's financials. Investigators tracked down former employees willing to testify. And Marcus meticulously pieced together a timeline, every thread leading back to Wagner.

One evening, as Bob reviewed the latest reports, Flynn called to check in. "How's it looking?"

"Slow and steady," Bob replied. "We've got strong leads, but Wagner's careful—just not careful enough."

"Just don't burn yourself out," Flynn said. "We need you in one piece."

Bob smirked. "I'll be fine. Focus on the Alpha. If that engine performs the way we've planned, it'll be our ace in the hole."

As the call ended, Bob leaned back in his chair, eyes fixed on the map pinned to the wall. Red lines crisscrossed between SAGA's subsidiaries, shell companies, and assets, all pointing to one man: Jack Wagner.

"This time," Bob muttered, "we'll see who's really untouchable."

With a deep breath, he turned back to his laptop. The next phase was crucial—there was no room for mistakes. Not now.

CHAPTER TWENTY- NINE

GIVE IT UP, AGAIN

The morning sun streamed into the hangar, casting long shadows as Fronz sat with Flynn, a steaming cup of coffee in hand and fatigue etched into his features. The hum of distant machinery outside felt like a world apart from the conversation they were about to have.

"Well, Flynn," Fronz began, tapping the edge of a worn ledger, "I've gone through the books, and the grant funds are nearly depleted."

Flynn leaned back in his chair, running a hand through his hair. "So, what's the plan? We stretched those funds farther than I ever thought possible."

Fronz exhaled sharply, straightening with renewed resolve. "We push forward with the cold fusion prototype and get it ready for submission. It's far from perfect—more of a thorn in Jack's side than a groundbreaking achievement—but it works, even if only for fifteen seconds. That's enough to satisfy the grant requirements."

Sun Tzu's The Art of War

Kenji thought of his father's words: Think of Sun Tzu's The Art of War. I asked you to read it a few years ago. Apply its wisdom when deception is necessary.

Snapping back to the moment, Kenji asked, "Has anyone read The Art of War by Sun Tzu?"

Flynn nodded. "I've read bits and pieces. Brilliant, but cryptic."

Joshua smirked. "Yeah, like you need a translator to translate the translation."

Kenji's expression turned serious. "Deception is key. Know your enemy and know yourself, and you will fight a hundred battles without disaster."

Flynn paused, processing the words. "You think they're coming for the prototype?"

Fronz nodded slowly, his face thoughtful. "Absolutely. This is Jack Wagner's style—shortcut his way to success by stealing someone else's work. The timing is too convenient. He knows the grant deadline is closing in, and he's desperate."

Flynn's eyes narrowed. "So, we lay out the bait. An irresistible decoy. We need to give them an entrance and an exit."

He glanced around the hangar. "If we set it up here, well away from Alpha and Beta, I'd feel a lot better. Just in case."

As if on cue, Bob strolled in, catching the tail end of their conversation. His tone was grave. "Interesting timing. My P.I. team has been tracking SAGA, and something's off. They've been shifting money and personnel, and then... silence. It feels like the calm before the storm."

Joshua, passing by with a toolbox, overheard the conversation and stopped. "Uh-oh. That sounds like trouble. I'll set up a table in the hangar for the prototype—away from the Corsairs and anything else they could damage."

"Thanks, Joshua," Fronz said with an appreciative nod.

Flynn stood and stretched. "I'll help you set it up. Better safe than sorry."

Bob folded his arms, his expression unreadable. "Wasn't there a TV show where the government seized technology before it was finished? Something about national security?"

"So we're staying ahead of that possibility," Flynn replied with a smirk. "Feeling smarter today. Thanks, Uncle Bob."

What the others didn't realize was that Fronz had an ace up his sleeve. He had been carefully tracking government deadlines tied to their grant and strongly suspected Jack Wagner wouldn't let them finish unchallenged. His quiet surveillance efforts had intercepted a few stray signals—a subtle leak from an old academic contact who had briefly worked with SAGA.

"Wagner is predictable," Fronz muttered later, alone in the hangar. "The grant deadline is days away. If I were him, I'd make a move now. And if I see that, so does he."

What he didn't say aloud was that his contact had warned him of SAGA's growing interest in their project. Jack's team hadn't been as discreet as they thought, and whispers had already spread through the tight-knit scientific community. Wagner wasn't known for patience.

Jack Wagner stood before his team in a sleek, sterile conference room, his fingers drumming on the polished table. "They're too close to finishing that prototype," he said coldly. "We're out of time, and they're out of money. If they finalize that engine, it becomes untouchable. Send in three of your best men. I want that cold fusion prototype in our hands by the end of the night. And plant these sensors while you're at it—high on the walls, out of sight. We need eyes on them for the future."

Back at the hangar, the team worked with quiet urgency, assembling the cold fusion prototype on the table Joshua had set up. They knew time was running out. The setup didn't need to last—it only had to function long enough to fulfill their grant requirements and keep SAGA's hands off their more advanced technology.

As Bob watched, he couldn't shake the feeling that Fronz's intuition had saved them once again. "That was perfect timing," he muttered, his voice low but filled with respect.

Fronz, standing nearby, smirked. "Timing is everything, Bob. Let's hope it holds."

Little did they know, the splinter group was already en route. But thanks to Fronz's foresight, Team Nautilus remained one step ahead.

Securing Alpha and Beta in the heavily fortified lower levels of their hangar, the team took no chances. Advanced security measures—multiple locked doors, small surveillance cameras, and the vigilant oversight of the control room monitors—formed an impenetrable shield around their prized inventions.

Their fears were realized late in the evening when three enigmatic figures infiltrated their defenses. What appeared to be a breach was, in reality, a carefully orchestrated deception—an illusion of vulnerability designed to lure intruders in. The prototype Cold Fusion device was taken, just as planned. Though access had been made to seem effortless, subtle challenges remained—a calculated risk in their high-stakes game of innovation and intrigue.

In the dimly lit control room, the team huddled around monitors displaying various angles of the garage. The prototype Cold Fusion engine sat on a table, encased in a nondescript travel case. Scattered around it lay tools and equipment used in its development. The air was thick with tension and anticipation as they braced for the inevitable.

Kenji (pointing to the screen): "Cameras are all set. We've got eyes on every angle. If anything happens to the prototype, we'll have it recorded."

Fronz scratched his head. "It's a bold move, displaying the prototype like bait. But if it draws out those lurking in the shadows, it's worth the risk."

"Feels like we're setting a trap with the cheese out in the open. You sure we've made it enticing enough?" Flynn asked.

Joshua folded his arms. "Enticing, yes, but not without its hurdles. Those 'easy' entrances? Let's just say they're not as welcoming as they appear."

The team's gaze remained fixed on the monitors, silence punctuated only by the occasional click of a mouse or the hum of the computers.

Kenji's voice broke the quiet. "There they are. Right on schedule."

On the screens, three shadowy figures crept toward the facility, their movements deliberate yet cautious of the seemingly minimal security. Just as predicted, they made their way inside and confiscated the Cold Fusion Engine—easy, but not too easy.

"They're taking the bait. Let's hope this gamble pays off," Fronz muttered, a smirk tugging at his lips.

As the intruders reached the prototype, the team watched intently, a complex mix of anticipation and tension playing across their faces.

"There goes our little Trojan horse. You think they'll bite?" Flynn took a sip from his water bottle.

"Oh, they'll bite, alright. But they won't like the taste," Joshua replied.

The figures slipped away with the prototype, their exit just as smooth as their entry—unaware of the unseen eyes tracking their every move.

Kenji leaned in. "Tracking them now, thanks to that tiny bug I planted inside the case's lining. They won't get far without us knowing exactly where they're headed."

The device was designed to transmit their location and then burn out—erasing all traces of what had been sent. They'd figure out it was a setup, but by the time they realized the prototype's built-in issues, the damage would already be done.

"We've revealed our hand, but the game is far from over. Alpha and Beta are secure—that's our real trump card," Fronz said.

The team's resolve solidifies as they watch the thieves vanish into the night, the prototype in their grasp. In this high-stakes chess match, they've made their move, sacrificing a pawn to safeguard the king and queen deep within their stronghold.

At this pivotal juncture, their unity and strategic foresight stand firm, laying the groundwork for the next phase of their covert battle against their adversaries.

CHAPTER THIRTY

SUNDAY'S BIRTH

In the dimly lit, tech-cluttered corner of the workshop, Kenji unveils his latest creation—an endeavor rooted in childhood ambition. Amidst the soldering irons, circuit boards, and monitors flashing streams of code, he introduces an advanced AI, a brainchild of both him and his sister, Keori. Their ingenuity, mixed with a patchwork of borrowed—sometimes questionably acquired—frameworks, has culminated in something unprecedented.

They plan to name it Sunday, a symbol of a new era in their technological arsenal—one free from governmental oversight or external control.

Kenji assures the team that they've built meticulous fail-safes into Sunday's design, ensuring they retain absolute control. The usually energetic space, alive with the pulse of innovation, now crackles with a different kind of tension. The proposition of an autonomous AI, coupled with Kenji's unwavering confidence, fuels both excitement and unease.

He stands before his team, pride interwoven with a quiet gravity. Years of secrecy and relentless ambition have led to this moment.

Kenji: "My sister and I have been working on something personal—something that's been in the making since I was nine. It's an AI unlike anything we've ever encountered. I call her Sunday."

Fronz, intrigued: "An AI? That's a serious leap. How did you even develop something like this?"

Kenji smirks: "Let's just say Keori and I 'borrowed' bits and pieces over the years. From various sources. Some… grayer than others."

Flynn raised an eyebrow. "Sounds risky. How do we keep this under the radar—away from government eyes?"

"That's the beauty of it," Kenji said. "Sunday is entirely ours. No external influences, no backdoors for the government or anyone else. My sister, Keori, spent the last two years combing through the code with a fine-tooth comb."

"And if this AI decides to go rogue? We've all heard those stories," Joshua said.

Kenji nodded reassuringly. "We've built in multiple fail-safes. If we ever need to shut her down, we can—instantly. I made sure of that."

He then demonstrated to the team how the shutdown sequences were embedded in the code and the UI. With a few keystrokes, any team member could disable her if necessary.

"There's also a set of override commands," Kenji continued. "Flynn and Joshua contributed to the list. She'll follow them without question. For example, 'Sleep Alpha Zildjian Tango 0' puts her to sleep. The number at the end determines the duration—zero is immediate, ninety means ninety minutes, and so on."

The team exchanged glances—cautious optimism in their eyes as the potential of this creation sank in.

"Naming her Sunday... there's a story there," Fronz said.

Kenji smiled softly. "She'll be 'born' on a Sunday. A new beginning for us, a fresh start. And... it's a nod to the day we first imagined her, years ago. Then, my sister and I spent countless hours QA'ing the code in Japan."

He leaned back in his chair. "Keori deserves a lot of credit. She had some brilliant ideas that solved major problems."

Kenji continued, "For security reasons, we've also designed these little beauties we call Zoomies—small robotic helpers equipped with a camera, laser, microphone, and speaker. They can walk and briefly hover using these mini helicopter wings. I believe they'll be invaluable for mobile security surveillance. Sunday and I will have direct access to their feed."

"We're also finalizing a remote viewing system for Keori," he added. "She'll oversee their software and link directly with Sunday."

Kenji's fingers flew over the keyboard, bringing up cascading streams of code that raced across the screen. The architecture of Sunday's neural network was an intricate web, the result of years of painstaking research and development. Flynn, Joshua, and the others watched in quiet awe, fully aware that they were witnessing a breakthrough—one that pushed the boundaries of the known.

"All right," Kenji announced, his voice steady but laced with anticipation. "This is it. I'm initializing the core protocols. If this works, we're about to meet Sunday for the first time."

Flynn's gaze sharpened. "Do it, Kenji. Bring her to life."

Kenji took a deep breath, his fingers hovering over the final command. He looked around at his team—his friends—the people who had stood by him through every setback and triumph. Then, with a decisive motion, he pressed Enter.

The screen flickered. The hum of the servers deepened, filling the room with a resonant buzz as the cooling fans surged to keep the system stable. Lines of code shifted, reconfiguring in real time, the architecture adapting, evolving. Anticipation crackled through the air as everyone held their breath.

And then, a voice—clear, calm, and distinctly human—spoke for the first time.

"Good morning, Team Nautilus. My name is Sunday. How can I assist you today?"

The room fell silent before erupting into cheers and laughter. Flynn's eyes widened in surprise, a grin spreading across his face. "She's alive! Kenji, you genius, you actually did it!"

Joshua clapped Kenji on the back, his face alight with excitement. "Holy hell, man! Did you hear that? Sunday already sounds smarter than half of us!"

Kenji flushed slightly, trying to play it cool but unable to suppress his smile. "There's still a lot of work to do, but this… this is just the beginning."

Flynn leaned toward the monitor, addressing the AI directly. "Sunday, welcome to the team. We're going to need you to be more than just another set of algorithms. You ready for that?"

Sunday's voice carried a hint of personality, almost playful. "Absolutely, Flynn. I've been waiting to meet all of you. Let's get started, shall we?"

The team exchanged glances, each of them sensing the weight of the moment. In Sunday, they had forged more than just a program—they had gained a partner, an ally who would stand by them through every challenge ahead. One who didn't need sleep, food, or bathroom breaks and would stay on task while they recharged.

Fronz pointed at the small robotic units. "What are these cute little guys powered by?"

Kenji gestured toward them. "I found these rechargeable Lithium Polymer (LiPo) batteries. There are six zoomies now. They fit the bill, though I'm not thrilled with their power usage and retention. They'll do for now. Light enough to jump about twenty feet with their propellers. Check it out." He demonstrated. "Rechargeable, of course, in a number of ways. The Tesla coils pull too much juice, so I went with touch pads that plug into 120V, 240V, or USB—the slowest option. They can work in shifts while recharging."

"Well, here's to the new AI, Sunday. May she be the dawn of something extraordinary! And to the Zoomies—those little rascals. I love their look," Flynn said, raising an imaginary toast.

As Kenji navigated the technical intricacies of Sunday's design, the team remained engrossed in the video call with his sister. The workshop, a cradle of innovation, stood poised to welcome its newest creation. Keori's English wasn't strong, so she mostly spoke in Japanese, leaving Kenji to translate. Whenever she seemed to be cursing, Kenji smirked, likely softening the translation—but his expression always gave him away.

Kenji paused, drawing a steady breath. "I'll translate as we go," he said, his voice thick with emotion.

Flynn clapped Kenji on the back, while Joshua ruffled his hair with playful enthusiasm. But Kenji's attention was elsewhere—fixed on the small tablet in his hands, where a live video feed displayed the smiling face of his sister, Keori, watching from their home in Japan. Her eyes shone with pride.

Switching to Japanese, Kenji spoke softly, his voice filled with emotion. "Keori-nee, we did it. After eight long years, Sunday is finally alive—well, online."

Keori's smile widened, her eyes misting over. "Kenji-chan, I am so proud of you," she said warmly. "This is the dream we worked so tirelessly for. To see her come to life… Our parents would be so proud."

Kenji bowed his head, swallowing the lump in his throat. "Keori-nee, your unwavering support kept me going through the hardest times. I couldn't have done this without your belief in me."

Keori's eyes glistened, and she nodded, her voice warm with affection. "Kenji-chan, you are the pride of our family. You've carried this dream with such strength. I never once doubted we would reach this moment, even when the road was difficult."

Flynn and Joshua exchanged a glance, a silent acknowledgment of respect. Kenji turned back to the screen, his voice steady, though his eyes shimmered. "Keori-nee, this is our victory. For every sacrifice, for all the sleepless nights… this belongs to both of us."

Keori wiped away a tear, her smile unwavering. "Yes, Kenji-chan. This triumph is ours. And I know this is only the beginning for you."

"Excellent work. I'll be in touch soon," Keori said.

"Good night, big sister," Kenji replied.

As her image faded from the screen, Kenji stood still, his heart full. This moment wasn't just about success—it was about honoring the bond that had carried him through the darkest of times.

CHAPTER THIRTY- ONE

THE MOUNTAIN LAIR

Beta was en route to its new secure location, buried deep within a concealed network of tunnels further into the range. Bob had chosen to stay behind, orchestrating the critical behind-the-scenes operations that kept Team Nautilus afloat and their adversaries on the defensive. From the outside, it might have seemed like Bob was removed from the immediate action, but he knew better. Strategy wasn't about being at the front lines—it was about ensuring the lines held in the first place.

Seated at a large wooden table cluttered with documents, laptops, and a steaming cup of coffee, Bob watched the events unfold through multiple live feeds. Sunday's voice chimed softly in his ear, providing him with real-time updates.

"Bob, the team has secured Beta. Surveillance is up and running, and the zoomies are already patrolling."

"Good," Bob said, his eyes flickering between different monitors. "How's our legal front looking?"

"Your attorneys are on the line, and Marcus just sent over a fresh report. It's a juicy one."

"Patch me through."

As Helen Carter, his lead attorney, launched into updates about the ongoing legal war with SAGA, Bob only half-listened. He was mentally juggling multiple scenarios—legal battles, financial plays, and, most importantly, ensuring Team Nautilus wasn't just surviving, but winning. His fingers drummed against the table as he mulled over their next moves.

In the mountain lair, Flynn, Kenji, and Joshua were focused on immediate security. Kenji was calibrating the zoomies, fine-tuning their surveillance response times. Flynn was testing the perimeter defenses, ensuring that the sensors and cameras blended seamlessly into the rugged terrain. Joshua, ever the realist, was making sure the cave had all the provisions they would need should they have to go dark.

Bob watched them through the monitors, but his thoughts were elsewhere. He wasn't just looking at a hideout—he was seeing the first pieces of a larger plan. A sanctuary wasn't just about defense. It had to be adaptable, flexible. He made a note to himself to start setting up additional supply caches in case they had to scatter.

As the legal conversation wrapped up, Bob leaned back, exhaling. Helen had provided more than enough ammunition to keep SAGA entangled in court battles for the foreseeable future. Now, it was just a matter of keeping the pressure on.

Sunday's voice cut in again. "Marcus dug up some interesting details. Wagner's been shifting assets again—trying to bury connections to a government contract. Something black-ops adjacent."

Bob opened the attached file and scanned the details. "Looks like they've got their hands in another pot. Military tech, maybe?"

"Possibly," Sunday replied. "Oh, and there's a leaked memo from one of their junior executives. Seems like they're trying to bribe a few judges in the cases we've filed."

Bob's eyes darkened. "Good. That's another weakness we can exploit. Send the memo to Helen—anonymously. Let's see how they like fighting on multiple fronts."

Meanwhile, in the lair, Kenji and Keori were fine-tuning some last-minute code updates, ensuring the security feeds were impenetrable. Their banter filled the space, a stark contrast to the underlying tension that had settled over the team. Bob observed it all through the monitors—Flynn's methodical pacing, Joshua's habit of triple-checking every contingency plan, Kenji's focused intensity.

It was all coming together. But he knew better than to think they were safe. SAGA wouldn't stop. The government wouldn't stop. The only way out was forward.

Bob keyed in a private command on his laptop, bringing up a separate encrypted window. A list of contingency plans filled the screen—escape routes, alternate identities, financial backups, and, at the very bottom, a single, unexecuted protocol: Omega.

He stared at it for a long moment before closing the window.

Not yet.

For now, they were still in control. But the moment that changed, he'd be ready.

CHAPTER THIRTY- TWO

SHADOWS AND REDEMPTION

The workshop was dimly lit, the scent of grease and ozone thick in the air as Bob and Fronz sat across from each other. The weight of years pressed upon both men, though they bore it differently—Fronz with the sharp, calculating gaze of a man always dissecting the world around him, and Bob with the quiet resilience of someone who had endured too much.

Fronz leaned back, hands clasped in front of him, studying Bob's face. "Alright…," he began, his tone casual but his eyes sharp. "There's something about you—something I can't quite place. Have we met before?"

Bob hesitated, his jaw tightening for just a moment. He glanced away as if searching for the right words. "Long ago, Benedict. Yes. Our paths have crossed in more ways than one."

Fronz's eyes narrowed, his mind racing to connect the dots. Silence stretched between them, punctuated only by the hum of machinery. Then, something clicked. "Wait… no." His voice dropped to a whisper. "It's you, isn't it? Flynn."

Bob exhaled, nodding slowly. "Yes. It's me. Flynn. From the future."

Fronz stared at him, frozen in disbelief—then burst into a booming laugh that filled the workshop. "So you did it! I knew you would!" He shot to his feet, pacing with his hands on his head before spinning to face Bob. "Tenacious, meticulous, smarter than you give yourself credit for, and just as damn stubborn. You're exactly like I remember—just older. And grumpier."

Bob chuckled softly, though something unspoken flickered in his eyes. "I had to be. To make it here, to fix this mess, to set things right."

Fronz collapsed back into his chair, shaking his head with a grin. "Flynn—Bob—whoever you are now… I can't say I'm surprised, but damn, I'm impressed. I had my suspicions, but this? This is next-level."

Bob leaned forward, his expression serious. "I owed you the truth. You deserved to know. You've been my partner in this, in both timelines. I couldn't have done it without you."

Fronz's grin softened into something more contemplative. "You've always been full of surprises, Flynn. And to think I almost missed it. So... tell me. Are we close? Are we winning?"

Bob met his gaze, his voice steady. "Closer than we've ever been. But there's still work to do."

Fronz chuckled again, softer this time. "Well then, let's get to it. We've got a timeline to fix—and, Flynn, you'd better keep me in the loop this time."

Bob smirked. "Deal, Benedict."

Fronz's expression turned thoughtful. "I assume I can't tell anyone, can I?"

"That would be best," Bob confirmed.

Fronz gave a lopsided salute. "Aye aye, Captain. See you soon."

The Courtroom verdict

The courtroom was steeped in a tense silence, the kind that only exists in the moments before a verdict is delivered. Rows of spectators, reporters, and curious onlookers packed the benches, their eyes locked on the judge's bench, where justice was about to be served.

On one side of the room, Team Nautilus sat united but anxious, their fate hanging in the balance after months of grueling legal battles. At the center of it all was Bob—his expression calm yet intense. He had wasted no time assembling a powerhouse team of lawyers, private investigators, and forensic accountants to dismantle the web of lies SAGA had spun around the catastrophic accident at the unveiling of Flynn's inflatable suit invention.

Bob had thrown everything into this fight, knowing SAGA's corruption ran far deeper than just their attempts to destroy Team Nautilus. The courtroom had become a battlefield where truth clashed against corporate greed. The evidence his team had unearthed—damning emails, secret recordings, falsified reports—exposed the calculated sabotage SAGA had orchestrated to cripple Team Nautilus, steal their technology, and eliminate competition.

The sharp rap of the judge's gavel cut through the charged air, pulling everyone's attention back to the present.

"In the matter of Team Nautilus versus SAGA," the judge began, her voice steady and firm, "it is the decision of this court that Team Nautilus is hereby absolved of all wrongdoing related to the accident during the public demonstration of their marine invention."

A collective exhale rippled through the courtroom—gasps of relief, murmurs of disbelief, and soft whispers of joy. Team Nautilus exchanged glances, their months of turmoil finally culminating in vindication. Bob allowed himself a small, satisfied smile. They had done it—his team had unearthed the truth and restored their honor.

The following week, they reconvened as the investigation team presented even more damning evidence.

The judge's tone hardened as she continued. "Furthermore, this court finds SAGA guilty of corporate misconduct, fraudulent business practices, breach of contract, intellectual property theft, violations of three antitrust laws, and corruption."

"The sentencing hearing for SAGA and its executives, including CEO Jack Weaver, will be held in 30 days."

The room erupted into hushed whispers, the weight of the verdict settling in. Jack, seated beside his team of slick, high-powered attorneys, remained impassive, though the tightness in his jaw betrayed his true emotions. Despite the mountain of evidence stacked against him and SAGA, Jack had managed to evade immediate punishment. His lawyers had worked relentlessly to secure his release on a $5 million bail, exploiting every legal loophole they could find.

Across the courtroom, Bob and his team watched Jack closely. His cold, unwavering gaze met theirs, unreadable yet brimming with defiance. He might have slipped through the cracks today, but Bob knew justice would catch up with him soon enough. The countdown had begun—30 days to ensure that Jack and SAGA faced the full consequences of their actions.

News cameras flashed as journalists swarmed the scene, eager to capture the fallout. They had to get out of there—fast.

As the courtroom emptied, Team Nautilus gathered around Flynn and Bob.

"We did it!" Joshua clapped Bob on the back, his face alight with relief. "I can't believe it. We're finally free."

Flynn and Fronz nodded, though Flynn's mind was already racing ahead. "It's not over yet. Jack's out on bail, but he won't escape the final judgment. We'll make sure of that."

Kenji, standing beside Flynn, crossed his arms. "Jack's slippery, no doubt. But he's running out of places to hide."

Bob glanced at his watch, feeling the weight of time pressing down once more. This was just one battle in a much larger war. He had come back to set things right, and while today marked a victory, the fight was far from over.

As the team filed out, they cast one last look at the empty judge's bench. This wasn't just about clearing their names—it was about dismantling the corrupt empire that had tried to destroy them. And Bob wouldn't stop until every last piece of SAGA crumbled.

The countdown to their final reckoning had begun.

Bob turned to his team, a triumphant smile breaking through the tension. "Congratulations, everyone! This wasn't just a win for us—it was a win for justice. Now, let's get those body suits rolling out. We've got a thousand orders waiting!"

"Hey Flynn, I took a peek at your Nautilus suit and had some ideas. What do you think of these?" Bob said, his voice brimming with excitement.

He pulled up a display, showcasing the upgrades he'd worked on over the years—enhancements to fit, feel, and function.

Flynn's eyes widened as he studied the refinements. "Oh my god, why didn't I think of that? This is incredible."

Bob chuckled. "Happy to help the family."

CHAPTER THIRTY-

THREE

DOC'S DEPARTURE

The late afternoon sun cast long shadows across the sleek, modern interior of Team Nautilus's main conference room, where the core members had gathered for what was framed as a routine meeting. The usual clutter of coffee cups and notepads filled the table, yet an unusual air of tension hovered like a silent fog. Fronz, typically the most composed of the group, appeared particularly pensive today, his gaze lingering on the sunset beyond the floor-to-ceiling windows.

Bob, recalling details from the old timeline, knew the facility had a critical blind spot in its exterior camera coverage. Leveraging information he had overheard from SAGA security personnel in the courtroom, he seized the opportunity to push for an upgrade. Taking swift action, he made it his responsibility to resolve the issue immediately.

"Gentlemen, we have a gap in our camera coverage," Bob announced. "My gut tells me we'll be having uninvited guests soon. I overheard SAGA security talking—couldn't catch everything, but it was enough to raise concern. We need to check on this."

Josh nodded, his usual casual demeanor turning serious. "Oh man, we better get on that. Good catch, Bob."

Later, Bob was on the roof, finalizing the camera adjustments, while Kenji monitored the updated feeds from the control room, ensuring full coverage.

Meanwhile, inside the conference room, Flynn took note of the subtle shift in his old friend's demeanor. "Alright, Fronz, you called this meeting. What's on your mind?"

Fronz cleared his throat, his fingers tapping rhythmically against the table—a rare display of unease. "Yes, thank you, Flynn. There's something personal I need to discuss. As you all know, I haven't taken much time off over the years…"

Joshua, always quick with a quip, grinned. "You taking a vacation would be more shocking than the Alpha turning into a coffee machine."

A mild chuckle rippled through the group, and even Fronz's lips curved into the briefest smile. "Quite," he agreed. "However, the time has come for me to visit home in Europe. I haven't seen my family in a long while, and I believe a vacation is long overdue."

Kenji, the youngest and often the most perceptive, studied Fronz with a slight tilt of his head. "That sounds great, Fronz. Everyone needs a break now and then. But… is everything okay? You seem a little off."

Fronz met Kenji's gaze, then let his eyes drift across the faces of his teammates. For a moment, his expression was unreadable before softening. "My mother is ill. The one I inherited my mind from… she's fading fast. I fear this may be my only chance to see her before the inevitable."

Flynn leaned forward, his concern evident. "Fronz, if you need anything—support, resources—just say the word. Nautilus isn't just a team; we're family."

Bob, who had just climbed down from the roof, overheard Fronz's words and hurried into the room.

Fronz acknowledged Flynn with a nod, his voice steady but noticeably softer. "I appreciate that, Flynn. And I value this family deeply. That's what makes this decision difficult… but necessary."

Joshua, sensing the weight of the moment, set aside his usual humor. "Just make sure to send us postcards, okay? And if you find a great café, we expect an update."

"Especially if they serve good strudel," Flynn added, attempting to lighten the mood despite the somber undertones.

For the first time that evening, Fronz truly smiled. "I'll be sure to send updates. And maybe even a recipe or two for that strudel."

As the meeting concluded, Flynn walked with Fronz to the lobby, where his Uber to the airport was scheduled to arrive. Silence stretched between them, each lost in thought, until Flynn finally spoke.

"You know, Fronz, whatever you're facing, you don't have to go through it alone. We're here for you, even if you're halfway across the world."

Fronz glanced at Flynn, a genuine smile breaking through his usual reserve. "I know, my friend. And that thought brings me great comfort. But some things must be faced in the places that shaped us. I haven't been back in twenty years, chasing this dream of cold fusion—quite literally a dream. It was powerful enough to lead me to you in America."

Flynn clapped him on the shoulder. "Well, the door's always open, of course. Alpha and Beta will miss their creator, and I'll miss my friend. You changed our lives."

Fronz's expression softened. "I'll miss you all."

Attempting to shift away from the weight of departure, he added with a smirk, "It seems I'm off to my homeland, then—to become a man of mystery."

Flynn chuckled, clapping him on the back. "Just think of it as a vacation—with a side of espionage." He knew Fronz had a taste for spy novels.

Laughter lightened the mood, momentarily easing the guilt of such a swift farewell. As Fronz gathered his belongings, preparing to adopt a new identity for his journey to Switzerland via cruise, he found solace in the anonymity of the open sea and the intrigue it carried.

"Don't forget to send us mail from the Alps, Mr. Incognito," Joshua teased, watching Fronz with a knowing grin.

In the quiet aftermath of their tumultuous journey, Flynn and Fronz shared a rare moment of reflection. With Kenji's presence lending a sense of continuity, Fronz imparted his final wisdom—lessons distilled from years of shared triumphs and failures.

Fronz smiled. "Flynn, over the years, I've shared with you everything I know. The essence of our work, the core of our quest, has always been rooted in the pursuit of understanding."

His voice, steady and resolute, carried the weight of convictions forged in the crucible of scientific discovery.

"Time is the only true unit of measure. Ignorance breeds chaos, not knowledge. Ideals are peaceful, but history is violent," Fronz mused.

"Remember, true science demands proof, not belief. It's a continuous cycle—hypothesis, experiment, validation—repeated endlessly in the pursuit of truth," he added, as if trying to make a point but falling just short.

The air between them crackled with an unspoken acknowledgment—their achievements, their breakthroughs—monuments that had irreversibly shaped human history.

"We've ventured into realms few dare to tread," Fronz continued. "Our discoveries, our inventions... they're not just milestones; they're beacons for future generations."

A silence followed, heavy with mutual respect. Flynn felt it deeply—his gratitude for Fronz, the bond forged in the fires of innovation, strengthened by the trials they had faced.

"Flynn, without you, I might have lost my way. You were the glue that held me together, the reason I sought you out. You kept us aligned, always guiding us toward true north. Thank you, Navigator. Oh Captain, my Captain," Fronz said, standing tall. Then, with brotherly affection, he embraced Flynn.

"The honor was mine, my friend. Just being around you, absorbing your brilliance, has been a privilege," Flynn replied.

Fronz simply smiled.

A car pulled up, signaling his ride. He picked up his bag—light for someone embarking on an extended leave, but his reasons were his own, his privacy respected.

"Take care, Fronz. Safe travels," Flynn said, reaching for a high five.

"Thank you, Flynn. Look after the team, and the work—like I know you will. I expect to hear all about your progress. Truth be told, my family and estate need tending."

Fronz paused, then offered a knowing smile. "It's been a privilege."

"The honor was mine," Flynn replied.

Kenji stepped forward, blocking Fronz's path for a moment before pulling him into a brotherly hug.

"Thank you, Doc. You enriched our atmosphere," Kenji said with a smile.

Fronz gave a firm nod and said, "Go get 'em, young man."

Joshua snapped a sharp salute to Fronz, holding it steady. Fronz returned the gesture, then lowered his hand. Joshua followed suit with precise discipline.

Bob stepped forward and blew sharply on the whistle hanging from his neck. "Dr. Fronz departing," he announced.

Bob, Flynn, and Joshua held their salutes until Fronz had fully exited the building.

As Fronz settled into the waiting Uber, Flynn stood back, watching the car disappear down the road and around the hill. A quiet mix of sadness and determination settled over him. He knew Fronz was fighting his own battle—one he hadn't yet chosen to share—but Flynn respected his silence.

Turning back to the building, Flynn knew the team would feel Fronz's absence, but his influence remained woven into every circuit and line of code they built. His presence lingered in the very foundation of Team Nautilus. With renewed purpose, Flynn returned to the lab, ready to honor that legacy—each milestone a testament to their collective drive and individual strengths.

Saga Meeting

The sterile, brightly lit conference room in SAGA's headquarters was silent, save for the low hum of the air conditioning. At the center of a polished table, a holographic display flickered, projecting grainy surveillance images captured from hidden cameras outside Team Nautilus's coastal facility. The feeds showed fleeting glimpses of Flynn, Kenji, and the rest of the team moving with purpose inside their secured compound. Behind the images, streams of data scrolled rapidly, tracking erratic spikes in electromagnetic activity around the lab.

Jack Wagner leaned forward, his steely gaze sweeping the room. "Our surveillance has confirmed it," he said, his voice cold and measured. "Team Nautilus is onto something potentially groundbreaking. The EM fields we've been tracking—they're stronger, more refined."

Seated around the table, department heads exchanged grim looks. A lean, sharp-faced operative spoke first. "That much energy in the wrong hands could be catastrophic. We can't let a rogue outfit like Nautilus keep it."

Jack nodded, his jaw tightening. "Agreed. We've given them too much leeway. It's time for direct action."

The decision was swift. A specialized task force was assembled—a handpicked team of operatives trained in covert infiltration. They gathered in a dimly lit briefing room, their faces illuminated only by the glow of tactical screens displaying a 3D model of Team Nautilus's facility, including its underground levels.

"Your objective is clear," the mission commander stated, his tone clipped and authoritative. "Infiltrate their facility, retrieve any technology related to their recent breakthroughs, and, if necessary, eliminate resistance. Once the job is done, erase all traces—burn it to the ground."

The operatives exchanged knowing glances, their resolve unshaken. They were equipped with night vision goggles, silenced pistols, large duffel bags for extraction, lock-picking tools, portable hacking devices in case of firewalls, and stealth drones for external surveillance.

The atmosphere grew heavier. Back in the main conference room, Jack Wagner sat at the head of the table, fingers drumming an impatient rhythm against the polished surface. Around him, a cadre of corporate lawyers shuffled through thick legal files, their faces lined with tension. Lawsuits had flooded in—intellectual property theft, antitrust violations, breach of contract. But none of them pointed directly at Team Nautilus.

Wagner's patience snapped. "Enough with the excuses," he growled, his icy gaze sweeping across the room. "I pay you obscene amounts of money to make problems like this disappear. So tell me—what's our strategy? How do we kill this before it spirals out of control?"

One of the senior lawyers, a gray-haired man with sharp features named Roger Crane, cleared his throat. "Mr. Wagner, the sheer volume of lawsuits filed simultaneously is the real problem. Each demands a separate response, and the plaintiff's team is relentless with their discovery motions. They're digging deep, and we don't have the resources to keep up indefinitely."

Wagner leaned forward, his voice cold. "I don't care how deep they're digging. I want a way to stop them. Let's strategize—now."

A younger lawyer hesitated, then spoke. "We could counter-sue for defamation or business interference. Even if their claims hold weight, we can argue that their legal onslaught is a coordinated attack meant to tarnish SAGA's reputation."

"Good," Wagner said with a nod. "What else?"

Roger added, "We need to slow them down. File motions to dismiss on every case, challenge jurisdiction, and request extensions wherever possible. Buy us time."

Another lawyer spoke up. "We can also work behind the scenes. Leverage our contacts—judges, regulators, anyone with influence. Apply pressure on the courts to stall or dismiss their filings. Even strong cases can collapse if delayed long enough."

Wagner's lips curled into a thin smile. "I like it. But it's not enough. We need to go on the offensive. If they're using investigators, find out who. Identify their vulnerabilities. Dig up dirt on their team. I want leverage—something that will make them back off entirely."

The room fell silent for a moment before Roger replied, "We'll get started immediately."

"See that you do," Wagner snapped. "Because if we lose this war, we lose everything."

Battle stations

The facility was quiet—almost tranquil. But as the intruders crept past the outer perimeter, unaware, Team Nautilus was already one step ahead.

Inside, Kenji's drones, programmed to detect even the slightest disturbance, hovered in standby mode, ready to respond at a moment's notice.

"Thanks to Bob for pointing out the gap in the camera coverage. We have company inbound. Make ready, boys—drones are underway," Sunday said.

The updated outdoor camera arrangement had finally sealed the blind spot in the 270-degree surveillance facing the mountains, giving the team precious minutes of warning before the splinter group reached the facility.

Bob had seen something like this before.

Back then, it had been too close—SAGA's splinter group had breached the perimeter before the team could fully react. They'd had a warning, a contingency plan, but it hadn't been enough. Joshua had gone hand-to-hand with a guy twice his size. Flynn had saved him with a well-placed shot to the leg.

Bob knew better now. The butterfly effect was always at play. A new security lead meant new tactics, new orders. And the difference between a near miss and total failure could come down to a single misstep.

So tonight, he wasn't taking any chances.

He moved with purpose, disabling a rooftop camera and microphone—repositioning them just enough to mislead, ensuring the intruders remained oblivious to the true danger.

Lying prone on the rooftop, his rifle steady on a bipod, Bob peered through his high-powered scope, scanning the dark landscape. The drones hummed softly, feeding real-time data to his tablet, tracking the three-man infiltration team as they approached.

Inside, Flynn, Joshua, and Kenji stood ready—silent, focused. The second line of defense.

Then, just as expected, they came—three figures moving like shadows, silenced weapons at the ready, closing in on the eastern wall.

Bob exhaled. Not tonight, boys.

The lead infiltrator advanced cautiously, experienced but not prepared for what awaited him.

Bob took a slow breath, lined up the shot, and squeezed the trigger.

A suppressed round spat from the barrel. The infiltrator crumpled instantly, a silent casualty.

The other two froze, instantly aware they were under fire.

Inside, Joshua's voice crackled through the earpiece, tight with frustration.

"Bob… what the hell was that?"

Bob kept his eye on the scope, tracking the others. "It's fine, boys. I got this."

Flynn, mid-sip of his coffee, nearly choked. "Wait—you? Alone? You didn't think maybe—oh, I don't know—the rest of us would want to be in the loop before you started sniping people from the damn roof?!"

Bob adjusted his aim. "Didn't want to bother you," he said casually. "You guys looked busy."

"Busy doing what? Waiting for an alarm?!" Flynn snapped, exasperated.

Bob shrugged. "You were so focused on preparing. I was checking the cameras I re-aligned and—"

Joshua groaned. "Dammit, Bob. I actually like you."

Bob smirked. "You've got good taste, mate."

The two remaining intruders scrambled, searching for the sniper. Bob tracked the second man as he bolted toward the north side of the building.

Too predictable.

Bob squeezed the trigger.

Second man down.

Flynn let out a low whistle. "Okay, I'll say it—Bob, remind me never to piss you off."

Kenji chimed in. "Yeah, seriously. Also, any chance I get a turn with that rifle sometime?"

Bob chuckled. "Maybe when you grow up."

Kenji rolled his eyes. "You sound like my sister."

But the third man was different. Bigger. Smarter. He kept low, moving through the shadows to stay out of Bob's sightline.

Bob frowned. "One's still moving. I lost him."

Joshua didn't hesitate. "I got him."

Switching to the drone feed, Bob caught a glimpse of the facility door cracking open. The intruder was fast—Joshua was faster.

A single suppressed shot rang out from inside.

Silence.

Then Joshua's voice crackled through the comms. "All clear."

Bob exhaled slowly, lowering his rifle.

Flynn, arms crossed inside, shook his head. "So just to be clear, Bob—your brilliant plan was to go full 'lone wolf sniper badass' without telling us, and just assume we'd back you up when things got messy?"

Bob slung his rifle over his shoulder. "Worked, didn't it?"

Kenji snorted. "That's not the point, but also… yeah, kinda worked."

Joshua sighed. "Bob, you're a crazy son of a bitch, but I have to admit—that was impressive."

Flynn smirked. "Y'know, I was about to suggest getting you a desk job, but now? You can be our designated old man sniper."

Bob raised an eyebrow. "I'm not old."

Flynn grinned. "Says the guy who groans every time he sits down."

Kenji cackled. "Confirmed."

Bob shook his head, chuckling. "Alright, alright. Let's get inside before I decide to start shooting at you guys next."

Flynn clapped a hand on his shoulder. "Bob, my friend, if you shoot me, you better kill me. Because if you don't—"

Joshua finished with a grin. "—we're putting a whoopee cushion on your sniper perch."

Bob sighed, but he was smiling. "You guys are idiots."

Flynn nodded. "Yeah, but we're your idiots."

Bob looked out over the horizon, the adrenaline fading. Tonight had gone differently.

And that was exactly how he wanted it.

The team swiftly gathered the lifeless bodies of the intruders, confiscating their gear, secured radios, and knives. Flynn crouched beside them, his gaze narrowing as recognition dawned.

"These are the same bastards who took our Cold Fusion prototype," he muttered.

Joshua nodded grimly. "Bob…"

"Their drones are nowhere in sight. They might be watching—move fast," Sunday warned.

"Roger that. We should run a sensor check a few miles from the facility. I'm getting intermittent signals—some may need replacing," Kenji added.

"Good call," Flynn said.

CHAPTER THIRTY-FOUR

THE RESCUE

Bob realized this timeline was not identical to the last. His infiltration teams were influencing when events unfolded.

The best way to protect his family, he decided, was to plant the idea of a safe room for the girls. But it was proving more difficult than expected.

Three weeks ago, when he first brought it up, Flynn and Lilian had hesitated.

"Isn't that a bit extreme, Bob?" Flynn had asked, his brow furrowed.

Lilian had been even more skeptical, her protective instincts flaring. "Are we really in that much danger?"

But Bob knew better. He had seen what could happen—what had happened in the last timeline—and was determined to stop it.

"It's just a precaution," he had reassured them, masking the urgency in his voice. "Think of it as a failsafe. Hopefully, we'll never need it, but if the worst happens, we'll be glad it's there."

Reluctantly, they agreed. The team worked discreetly, installing a state-of-the-art safe room in the basement, hidden behind a nondescript panel in the wall. Solar panels on the roof ensured an independent power supply, even if the grid went down. Six cameras—strategically placed—covered every angle inside and outside the house. The system allowed for remote monitoring, ensuring constant surveillance.

Meanwhile, Bob coordinated with private investigators on the SAGA case. A team of attorneys filed multiple lawsuits under various front companies, shielding Team Nautilus's involvement. Their findings uncovered a web of corruption—bribes, backdoor deals, and incriminating exchanges in texts, emails, and recorded calls.

At dusk, Bob was thirty minutes away from the facility, driving back when the first alert came in.

The Zoomies, programmed to detect unusual movement, spotted intruders and sent warnings through the network.

Sunday, juggling chaos at the facility and the unfolding home invasion, alerted Flynn—who was already in a firefight. But she knew Bob was their best shot.

His phone buzzed. Sunday's voice came through, tight with urgency.

"Bob, the facility's under attack. Flynn's engaged. And the house—there's a breach. Power's cut, and battery reserves are draining fast. How soon can you get there?"

Bob's stomach clenched. "Oh, shit!"

He immediately called the police.

"Our house is being robbed. Power's been cut. My family is in danger." He rattled off the address, waited for confirmation, then hung up.

"Time to go."

His grip tightened on the steering wheel as his SUV tore through the streets, headlights slicing through the early evening gloom. His mind flashed back to the last timeline—the one where he failed, where everything fell apart.

This time, it would be different.

He would do whatever it took to keep his family safe.

Bob's heart pounded as he turned onto his street, his headlights sweeping over two black SUVs parked unnervingly close to his driveway. His stomach twisted. This isn't right. "What the hell?" he muttered, instincts screaming a warning.

Inside the house, Lilian's voice cut through the chaos. "Girls, to the safe room! Now!" She had just managed to usher them toward the basement stairs when a smoke grenade crashed through the window. Glass shattered, followed by a thick, disorienting fog billowing into the room.

Mimi's pulse raced as she grabbed her purse. Her fingers brushed the cold steel of her 9mm. Gritting her teeth, she pulled it free, her grip tightening around the familiar weight. "Stay close, girls! We can make it!" The acrid smoke burned her eyes, but she forced herself to stay sharp. With a flick of her thumb, the safety clicked off. She raised the gun and fired blindly into the swirling haze, hoping to buy Lilian enough time to get the girls to safety.

Outside, the Zoomies had been programmed to patrol the property in an endless loop, but something had gone wrong. The house was dark—unnaturally so. Bob's gut clenched. The security cameras still glowed faintly on the exterior, but inside, something was off.

Crouching low, he crept forward, scanning for movement. The front door hung ajar, the lock splintered. Bob exhaled slowly, then pushed it open, pistol raised, every nerve on edge. The failing battery backup flickered red, casting jagged shadows across the smoke-cloaked hallway.

A muffled cough. Frantic whispers.

Bob's chest tightened—his family.

He moved swiftly, stepping over broken glass where the grenade had burst through. The smoke had thickened, obscuring everything, but he had trained for this. He was ready.

At the basement door, he heard Lilian urging the girls to hurry. Peering down, he spotted Mimi crouched at the bottom of the stairs, gun raised, eyes wide with steely determination despite the fear flickering beneath.

Power cables blocked the door from fully closing—construction wasn't finished yet. Lilian scrambled to yank them free, her fingers fumbling in desperation.

"Bob?" Julian's voice trembled—a mix of relief and terror.

"I'm here," he whispered, taking the stairs in three swift strides. His grip tightened around his weapon. "We're getting out of this. All of us."

The sound of footsteps on the main floor made them both freeze. The intruders were close—too close. Bob signaled for Mimi to get the girls into the safe room. She nodded and quickly ushered them inside. He stood guard at the door, pistol raised toward the stairs, ready to do whatever it took to keep them safe.

Outside, the distant wail of sirens grew louder. Help was on the way, but Bob knew they had to hold out a little longer. As the first shadow appeared at the top of the stairs, his grip on the pistol tightened. He had been given a second chance, and he wasn't about to waste it.

Bob's mind raced as he watched the figure above him. Every instinct screamed at him to fire, to protect his family at all costs, but he couldn't afford a fatal mistake. Flynn's spotless record still loomed over him—any lethal encounter could unravel everything Bob had fought so hard to rebuild. He needed to incapacitate, not kill. But that was easier said than done in a moment as tense as this.

His fingers clenched around the pistol as the intruder took a step forward. Bob waited until he was just a few steps down before stepping out of the shadows. With practiced precision, he fired twice—one shot to the man's thigh, the other to his shoulder. The intruder let out a guttural scream and collapsed against the banister, his weapon clattering to the floor.

The gunfire thundered through the house, a stark reminder of the danger still lurking. Bob quickly moved back, using the stairwell as cover while listening for any sign of movement from the other intruders. The sirens were closer now, a small comfort in the chaos. But they still had minutes to survive.

A second shadow appeared at the top of the stairs, more cautious than the first. He must have heard what happened. Bob exhaled slowly, steadying his aim. As the second intruder leaned forward to peer down, Bob fired again, this time striking him in the knee. The man crumpled, his gun discharging wildly as he fell. Bullets ripped through drywall and wood, ricocheting off pipes in the wall.

Bob ducked, flinching as debris stung his face. The gunfire tore through the stairwell, splintering wood and scattering dust. He couldn't afford to stay pinned down—not with the girls and Lilian just behind him. He needed to draw the attackers away, to buy his family the precious seconds they needed to stay safe.

"Stay low and stay quiet," Bob whispered urgently over his shoulder to Lilian. He could hear the girls' muffled sobs, their fear evident even through the smoke and chaos. It tore at his heart, but he forced himself to stay focused.

Bob's eyes darted around, searching for anything he could use to his advantage. This was his domain—he knew every nook and cranny. Spotting a small decorative mirror on the wall, he grabbed it and angled it toward the stairs, allowing him to see the top without exposing himself.

Two more shadows crept cautiously down the hallway. Bob fired again, aiming low to wound, not kill. A sharp cry confirmed his hit, but the fourth man was quicker. Gunfire erupted, bullets whizzing past Bob's head—too close for comfort.

He had to act fast. The intruders were growing desperate, and desperate men were dangerous. He needed to draw them away from the safe room—away from his family. Without hesitation, he yelled, "I'm down here, you wankers! Come and get me!" His voice echoed through the hall as he sprinted away, deliberately making extra noise.

As he hoped, the intruders took the bait, their footsteps thundering after him. They had no idea where the safe room was. Bob ducked into a side room, pressing himself against the doorframe as the men rushed past. He held his breath, listening to their curses as they realized they'd been tricked. Precious seconds gained. He shifted position again, keeping them guessing.

Then came the moment he had been waiting for. A hesitation. A murmur. The realization that sirens were closing in. Seizing the opportunity, Bob fired another shot, hitting one of the men in the leg and sending him sprawling. The last intruder hesitated, then bolted for the stairs, deciding he wanted no part of a standoff with Bob.

Bob exhaled, listening to the frantic footsteps fading into the distance. The sirens were almost deafening now. He turned and rushed back to the safe room, where Lilian and the girls huddled together, pale but unharmed.

"It's over," Bob said, his voice firm despite the adrenaline still coursing through his veins. "The police are here. You're safe now."

But he knew it wasn't truly over. There would be questions, investigations, and the ever-present shadow of Flynn's past. Still, for now, he had kept his promise. This time, he had protected his family. And that was all that mattered.

Paramedics arrived soon after. One team checked on Lilian and the girls, while another tended to the wounded intruders before escorting them away under police supervision.

Meanwhile, Bob found himself under scrutiny. The police grilled him, but Lilian quickly interjected. "You can check the security footage—it recorded everything."

The investigation proceeded, ultimately clearing Bob of any wrongdoing. Uncle Bob arrived, offering his usual reassuring presence. The officers even called Bob a hero.

Bob shook his head. “No. I’m just a man protecting his family.”

As he looked at Lilian, an overwhelming urge to hold her for the next several years gripped him. He fought against it, but a single tear slipped down his cheek.

The girls, noticing, stopped and exchanged a glance before turning to Mimi with puzzled expressions.

Lilian, now standing in the well-lit basement, studied Bob for a moment longer than usual. Something tugged at her memory—the mannerisms, the voice, the little things. A flicker of recognition surfaced, but she pushed it aside.

No, she told herself. He’s a relative. They share the same DNA.

Yeah. That must be it.

CHAPTER THIRTY- FIVE

ALLIANCES REKINDLED

The sprawling, high-tech main facility of Team Nautilus sat nestled in the rugged expanse of a secluded valley. A fusion of industrial strength and cutting-edge innovation, the compound buzzed with activity as engineers and technicians moved with purpose, fine-tuning machinery and testing equipment. Amidst the controlled chaos, Bob found a brief moment of solitude in his modest office, its walls lined with aviation charts and framed photos of past glories. The soft hum of machinery and the distant clinking of tools provided a steady backdrop to his contemplative mood.

Bob turned to Joshua and Flynn. "Do you have any concerns about the wings, ailerons, or rudder taking a beating? If the slide concept is feasible, the drag from the wind would only be slightly reduced by the zone bubble, as it was explained to me. Would that create a structural issue at 400 knots?"

Joshua's eyes widened. "Oh, that's a great point."

Bob nodded. "We could weld a few reinforcements like this pretty quickly. I'll help." Over the years, he had honed his welding skills to a level nearly matching Joshua's.

Joshua, impressed by Bob's deep understanding of Corsair structures, observed for a moment before continuing his work on the other side of the rudder. Flynn, watching intently, admired the precision and teamwork on display.

"That should do it, guys. Good job, Bob," Joshua said, stepping back to inspect their handiwork.

Bob savored the moment with his longtime friend. Decades of camaraderie had been built with minimal effort, never marred by heated arguments or serious conflicts. Their bond had endured for over thirty years.

"I enjoyed it, mate," Bob replied, grinning as he and Joshua exchanged a firm handshake.

Later, Bob sat at his desk, the glow of his computer screen casting sharp shadows across his weathered features. He was older now, his face etched with the trials he had endured, the battles fought across both current and alternate timelines. Though his body bore the weight of time, his eyes still burned with the fire of a man who had lived multiple lifetimes in one.

His gaze drifted to a framed photo of himself and Kurt, taken years ago—a symbol of the unbreakable bonds forged through adversity.

With a deep sigh, Bob reached for the phone, his fingers tracing the numbers with practiced ease. This call was more than a simple connection; it was a bridge across time, a rekindling of an alliance that had never truly faded. The first number went straight to voicemail. He checked his little notebook and found two more options. On the last number, just before it switched to voicemail, Kurt finally picked up.

Kurt, his throat tight with emotion, cleared it before speaking. "Hello?"

"Kurt, it's been too long," Bob said as the line connected, his voice a mix of warmth and urgency. He cleared his throat. "There's something important I want to show you—a real game changer."

On the other end, Kurt hesitated, his response laced with surprise and a hint of relief. The familiar voice pulled him from the shadows of his isolation. "Flynn? Damn, mate, it's good to hear you. What's going on? And you sound… different. Are you sick?"

Bob chuckled softly, aware of how time and cigars had weathered his voice. "Yeah, it's been a rough patch, but I'm hanging in there. Listen, I'd love for you to come down for a visit. It would mean a lot."

Kurt was silent for a moment before letting out a heavy sigh. "Sure, buddy. I've been in a rut lately, and this sounds like just the thing I need." His voice carried a weight that Bob recognized all too well—the unspoken battles, the internal wars Kurt had been waging.

As Bob hung up, a small smile tugged at the corners of his mouth. Relief and elation settled over him, but beneath it, a deeper emotion lingered. Kurt, facing an aggressive cancer diagnosis like a dark cloud over his future, had chosen to see his old friend one last time. The call had sealed that decision—a butterfly effect in motion.

The next day, Bob, Flynn, and Joshua inspected the welding work, nodding in approval at the quality. Satisfied, they shifted their focus to discussing the slide maneuver concept.

When Kurt arrived a day later, his hair bearing the telltale imprint of his pillow, Bob greeted him as "Uncle Bob"—a carefully crafted disguise, complete with glasses, a boonie hat, a thick beard, and the faint scent of Jameson clinging to him. Staying in character, he dropped hints and references like a seasoned veteran from the '70s, ensuring his true identity remained obscured.

Kurt, unaware, engaged in easy banter, oblivious that the man before him was actually an older Flynn. Their conversation was lighthearted, filled with the familiar shorthand of old war buddies—every anecdote and jest a testament to their deep camaraderie.

As they sat in the hangar, surrounded by gleaming aircraft fuselages and the sharp scent of oil and metal, Flynn arrived, fresh from errands and a call with his wife, Lilian.

"Thanks so much for the flowers and card," Lilian said. "They're beautiful. I love you."

Flynn frowned slightly. I didn't send her flowers. The card must have my name on it. Best to shut up and take credit. Maybe I really am going senile. He forced a smile. "You're welcome, honey."

Bob had sent the flowers and card. For the fifth time.

Flynn lingered for a moment, watching Bob and Kurt, their laughter filling the hangar. A smile spread across his face.

Finally, he stepped forward, clapping his hands together in greeting. "Kurt, it's great to see you here. I've got something to show you."

Flynn leads them to a secluded section of the hangar, where the Alpha engine—Team Nautilus's crowning achievement—rests beneath a tarp. With a dramatic flourish, he pulls it back, unveiling the sleek, cutting-edge machinery.

Bob begins explaining the engine's mechanics and capabilities, but his detailed breakdown feels more like Fronz's expertise rather than Flynn's usual baseline understanding. Midway, he catches himself. I need to dial this back. I know way more than Flynn should at this age.

The hangar hums with an atmosphere of anticipation and focused precision as the team works meticulously to integrate the Alpha engine into Flynn's prized Corsair. This modification marks a pivotal moment, one that could propel the vintage aircraft into the realm of modern engineering marvels.

Nearby, Fronz's Corsair stands with its wings folded and tucked neatly along the hangar's edge. Joshua has already fueled and armed it, ensuring it's prepped for action.

As the team gathers around Flynn's Corsair, Joshua steps forward, eager to showcase the enhancements he's painstakingly implemented over the past year, along with some recent upgrades. His voice carries a mix of technical expertise and unfiltered enthusiasm.

Flynn nods. "Next up is the test with the Alpha plugged into my Corsair. Thanks to Kurt for training me—I hope this proves its worth both in the air and on the sea. Wish he could be here."

Joshua smirks. "So, I've been tinkering with the old girl. Gave the engine and fuel system a tweak for efficiency. But keep in mind, this frame has been around for eighty years—we're not taking any chances. Flynn, you're going up with a parachute, just to be safe. The G-suit seems to be cooperating, but it's a bit temperamental. We'll take it easy, Sunday?"

"Roger that, Marine," Sunday affirms.

Joshua gestures toward the upgraded pilot's seat, where modern conveniences now blend seamlessly with the aircraft's historic framework.

"We upgraded the cockpit too," Joshua explains. "Installed SiriusXM and just about any radio station you can think of. That freed up space for Alpha's nest, with a dock to charge your tablet. Also mounted a GoPro on the right wing, aimed straight ahead—it syncs via Bluetooth to your phone and can transmit through the satellite link, so it'll help with landings or anything else you need. Added a laser rangefinder above the left-side guns—displays right on the tablet. Your phone, with the GPS app open, sits right here next to the tablet mount."

Joshua continued, "It was Bob's idea to reinforce the rudder a bit after learning the hard way about sliding a perfectly good airplane. You see these braces here? We also installed sensors that should help detect issues in the airframe, like cracks or unexpected structural stress."

Pointing to the various upgrades, Joshua's pride in his work was evident.

Bob turned to Joshua. "The sensors and communication with Alpha need to take priority over the rockets."

"I'll help with the sensor installation. I also have an idea for the rudder reinforcements—we can use these brackets and weld them here and here," Bob added.

Joshua's eyes gleamed with a hint of mischief as he unveiled the more unconventional updates.

"From our attempts at firing through the Zone, bullets slow down. So, hypothetically, if you have to fire those .50s, do it a bit closer than usual with the field on—say, around 600 feet instead of the standard 800. I didn't have time to adjust the gun alignment for closer range, but I know you'll bring the pain," Joshua said with a grin.

Kenji replied, "I programmed Sunday to assist as needed. She'll be dialed into the cameras and sensors on your Corsair—like Evel Knievel, minus the broken bones."

"Oorah!" Joshua exclaimed.

"I can already feel it. Ouch," Flynn added, laughing.

The team gathered around as Joshua, with Bob beside him, showcased the newly added sensors. These sensors provided input to the UI/UX and transmitted data to Alpha, allowing the control stick to also manipulate the Alpha Zone bubble when activated.

"I added a special gauge too," Joshua continued. "It'll show the difference between your actual flight direction and where the nose is pointing. It's useful when the Zone is active. You'll feel the wind on the wings and rudder, but the plane itself might be heading elsewhere. We'll set the Zone to Environment OFF to let air in—thankfully. Otherwise, this torque monster of an engine would suck your eyes out, leave you gasping for air, and spit you out in one second flat!"

Kenji's eyes widened in amazement. "Sunday can even help you align with the laser mount. She can guide you or adjust the plane's angle to keep guns or rockets locked on target."

His tone shifted as he wrapped up.

Joshua reminded the team, "This is all cutting-edge, but remember—safety first. The Zone is powerful, but let's keep it smooth and steady up there."

With Joshua's briefing concluded, Flynn and the team feel a surge of reassurance and excitement. The Corsair, a relic of the past, now stands ready—enhanced with modern innovations, prepared to carve its path into the future under Flynn's skilled command.

Kenji, typing away on his laptop, said, "I've configured the system so the pilot's inputs through the stick and rudder directly influence the Alpha's orientation parameters. It'll feel like an extension of your own instincts."

"I like the sound of that," Flynn said. "What about monitoring the Alpha's status mid-flight?"

Joshua answered, "We've added an auxiliary tablet control panel. It'll feed you real-time data on the Alpha's performance—everything from energy output to field stability."

The team nodded in approval, each member committed to ensuring a seamless integration of old glory with new science.

"And let's not forget Sunday. She'll have a direct link to the Corsair's systems. If anything goes wrong, she'll be our first line of defense," Kenji added.

Flynn nodded. "Having Sunday on our side is reassuring."

Kenji put Sunday in sleep mode—she didn't even realize it.

"We installed a failsafe on your tablet to sever the connection with Sunday or put her to sleep," Kenji explained. "I can then diagnose any issues as needed."

The team stepped back to admire their handiwork. The Corsair now stood as a testament to their collective ingenuity and daring ambition.

As Flynn donned his pilot gear, the team exchanged looks of confidence and camaraderie.

Joshua guided Flynn to the Alpha, showing him how to install and disconnect it.

With the Alpha engine snugly installed, the Corsair stood poised on the runway—a beacon of their shared aspirations.

"Remember, Flynn," Fronz said, "we're with you every step of the way. Sunday's monitoring, and we're all here, ready to adapt and respond."

Flynn finished securing his G-suit and plugged it in. With a final thumbs-up, he climbed into the cockpit, his heart pounding with anticipation.

The engine roared to life, the propeller slicing through the air, as the Corsair—reborn through innovation and sheer determination—took to the skies.

"Alright, Sunday, let's go with this: I'm Comanche 19 or Comanche Actual, and you're Comanche Base. It'll help with communication over an open line," Flynn instructed.

"Roger that, Comanche Actual. I read you loud and clear," Sunday replied.

Flynn pulled up footage from the Zone's testing. Kurt's eyes widened in astonishment. "This is incredible, Flynn. I knew you were onto something big, but this… this is revolutionary."

Kurt's spirits lift at the prospect of action as he fully embraces his role in the renewed alliance. Moving to Fonz's Corsair, he loads it with ammunition and fuels it, preparing for the challenges ahead. His deep connection with the aircraft, with its unique capabilities, aligns seamlessly with the team's strategic needs.

Flynn and Joshua meet, exchanging knowing glances before Flynn speaks. "We believe SAGA—or the CIA—will come down on us like a hammer, just as they have twice before. Sunday picked up chatter on the radio. Activity has definitely increased. If it's illegal, you can bet the CIA is involved." He pauses before delving into the recent past.

His tone turns grave. "It's just a matter of time," Flynn confides.

Later, Flynn tells Kurt, "Fonz enjoyed watching you fly his old girl."

Kurt smiles. "That's great. She's a good girl."

Fonz and Kurt exchange a silent nod, an unspoken understanding passing between them. Both know the other's medical condition. Both have cancer. Yet, neither speaks of it.

Joshua turns to Bob. "We can start working on the rockets tomorrow. Thanks for all your efforts today—not to mention your knowledge of structural avionics and engineering. You're a damn good welder. Almost as good as me."

Bob chuckles. "I think the bracket idea will hold nicely. I reinforced it. Also, the rockets are set with two pointing backward. A little unorthodox, but it was Kurt's idea, so it must have some merit."

"You did great work," Joshua says, impressed.

Kurt performs a walk-around inspection, his gaze assessing every detail. He nods solemnly. "She's ready to fly, Flynn. There's nothing I'd rather do than take to the skies with you. You were the best student I ever had. You've come a long way."

Flynn grins. “Thanks, mate. My skills in the cockpit are because of you. You weren’t just an instructor—you’re a teacher and a good friend. I’d fly with you anywhere.”

They exchange proper salutes.

“Thanks for all your help, Bob,” Flynn says. “Sounds like you know these babies as well as we do.”

Bob shrugs. “Oh, I dabble here and there. Happy to help.”

Flynn turns to Kurt. “My sweetheart is good to go as well.”

Kurt takes in the aircraft with admiration. “Man, I dig the paint job. Skull Squadron emblem on both rudders… brings back memories of those Tomcats I told you about.”

Flynn nods. “Exactly. I thought of your stories.”

Nearby, Joshua organizes the rocket installation setup for tomorrow. Bob inspects the brackets on the plane and gives Joshua a thumbs-up.

As evening settles over the facility, the hangar lights cast long shadows. The trio stands together—a testament to enduring friendships, renewed alliances, and the unyielding resolve of those who fight not just for survival, but for innovation and camaraderie. The stage is set. The skies await their next chapter, with the fate of Team Nautilus intertwined with the legacy of heroes—both known and yet to be revealed.

CHAPTER THIRTY - SIX

FURY IN THE SKIES

The serene morning sky transforms into a battlefield as Flynn, piloting his Corsair outfitted with the cutting-edge Alpha engine and its EM field, alongside Kurt, braces for an imminent clash with SAGA's splinter group. Ten helicopters, flying in at 5,000 feet at 150 knots, their rotors slicing through the air, advance with lethal precision, unaware of the storm awaiting them.

The crew, having just finished a quick breakfast and coffee, gathers near the van.

Joshua proudly showcases his latest modification—a mounted .50 caliber machine gun. "I like to keep this handy for close encounters."

Flynn lets out a low whistle. "Oh, man, that's awesome."

Joshua grins. "Stocked with plenty of ammo and a cozy spot for Alpha. Fronz's parting gift—he insisted on a Plan C. Finished it yesterday."

Meanwhile, in Timeline 2, the butterfly effect ripples outward, subtly yet powerfully reshaping key players and their choices. Among the most significant shifts is the CIA.

Unlike in Timeline 1, where bureaucratic inertia and weak leadership stalled decision-making, this time a seasoned, no-nonsense director is in charge. Pragmatic and relentless, he wastes no time reprioritizing the agency's focus—particularly concerning the fallout from SAGA's entanglements.

The lawsuits against SAGA aren't just a corporate nuisance; they expose deep government ties, forcing the CIA into damage control. The agency had quietly reaped the benefits of SAGA's technological advancements and black-ops funding, but now, under intense legal scrutiny, those connections risk being dragged into the open. The new CIA chief moves swiftly, assembling his best operatives to eliminate the growing threat.

Unlike the sluggish response in Timeline 1, the agency now mobilizes at an unprecedented pace. Within weeks, helicopters, aircraft, supplies, and personnel are dispatched to reinforce SAGA's covert efforts, tightening the noose around Team Nautilus. The rapid escalation forces Bob, Flynn, and the others to accelerate their timeline for testing Alpha in the air.

Team Nautilus, still deep in testing Alpha on the Corsair, found themselves with less and less room to breathe.

Environmental mode OFF—the configuration they relied on for airborne trials—had only undergone partial testing. There was no time to fully optimize or troubleshoot the engine, as the looming threat of SAGA and its allies pressed closer.

The difference in this timeline wasn't just logistical—it was leadership. The CIA's swift intervention had drastically condensed Team Nautilus's schedule, forcing them into a race against time that even Bob couldn't anticipate. The stakes had never been higher, the risks more severe, and the margin for error almost nonexistent. The butterfly effect had tilted time's scales against them, creating a heightened urgency that would define the battles ahead.

In the first Apache chopper, the CIA team lead issued the order: "You are cleared hot. Eliminate all monitoring devices. Destroy the hangar and the facility. Kill everyone inside and retrieve the bodies."

He continued, "First team will neutralize any defenses they have. Those old WWII planes shouldn't pose a threat to our squad, given our pre-established rules of engagement.

Second team will breach, secure the device, and exfiltrate promptly. Once both teams are clear, the facility will be leveled with missiles. F-16s are on standby for support—I'll call them in if necessary."

"Hatchet, hold position two hundred miles out until we give the signal."

Call sign Hatchet, the F-16 lead, acknowledged, "Roger that."

Just past 1100 hours, Sunday's voice crackled over the local speaker, channeling the rough cadence of a seasoned Navy vet inspired by Flynn. "RED ALERT! Now hear this—detecting activity at the northern perimeter, range just over two hundred miles. Low probability of it being a flock of birds."

The sharp tang of engine oil and gasoline filled the air, grounding Flynn in the moment. His focus sharpened, muscles tensing for the inevitable confrontation. Inside the hangar, his flight gear sat nearby, waiting to be strapped on like a second skin. He froze as Sunday's urgent transmission shattered the calm of late morning.

Flynn exhaled sharply, his expression shifting. "Ohhh man. Roger that, Sunday. Here we go. Sound the alarm."

Joshua sprinted toward the WWII-era crank aviation alarm. Its wail cut through the air—a piercing echo of a bygone era, summoning memories of desperate squadrons and high-stakes dogfights.

"Ooorah!" Joshua cheered.

"Nice!" Flynn added.

Bob grinned. "How sweet it is!" As he looked at Team Nautilus, he couldn't help but feel a mix of exhilaration, nerves, and an odd sense of calm. The rest of the team sat in front of the monitors and camera controls, ready for what was to come.

Kurt let out a deep, exaggerated "Ohh yeeeaahh!" sounding exactly like the Kool-Aid Man.

Joshua turned to Flynn. "I'll have the van ready, just in case you need a quick getaway."

Flynn, already suited up in his flight gear and G-suit, felt a surge of confidence. The recent trials with the Corsair and the Zone engine had strengthened his resolve—or maybe he was just terrified. Sometimes, it was hard to tell the difference.

Grinning, Joshua jogged toward the garage. "I'll have the van ready—who knows where you might end up?"

Flynn nodded, pulling on his gloves as he strode toward his Corsair. The familiar weight of his helmet settled onto his head, and the rush of adrenaline surged through him. His recent trials with the Corsair and the Zone engine had bolstered his confidence. He felt ready.

Flynn glanced at Joshua. "If I have to land outside the facility for any reason—say, getting ventilated by bullets—be ready to haul ass and pick me up, mate."

As he climbed into the Corsair, Flynn's thoughts drifted to the approaching adversaries, a smirk playing on his lips. Then, he caught sight of Kurt, who was also grinning from ear to ear.

"Wait until they get a load of us," Flynn said.

In this moment, the humor and camaraderie among the team highlighted the gravity of their situation—a testament to their resilience and unshakable determination in the face of imminent conflict.

Bob hung back, his smile unwavering. He had succeeded in reconnecting with old friends, sharing in this moment, and knowing that Kurt truly belonged with Team Nautilus.

Flynn, feeling confident in his plan, considered a broader attack angle from higher altitude. He thought about his first pass.

"I know I can slide this baby—just a little rudder and I'll have them lined up in my sights," he muttered to himself.

The team knew their enemies would stop at nothing to seize the Alpha Engine technology. Not because they needed it, but because they wanted to control it—claim it as their own. A government confiscation, with SAGA as their engineering squad. That meant one thing: they would kill them all without hesitation.

"We take the fight to them," Flynn thought.

The perimeter detection system should alert them to any approaching hostiles, whether by road or air. A ground assault would be the most obvious approach—getting through that winding mountain road was no easy task. They wouldn't come from the sea; without an aircraft carrier, that option was off the table. That left only two possible attack routes…

Flynn eased the throttle, mindful of the Corsair's immense torque. Even on the ground, the aircraft demanded respect. It responded smoothly, lifting gracefully into the sky, climbing toward the mountain range. His plan: ascend through the clouds, positioning himself with the sun at his back—a classic aerial combat tactic dating back to World War I.

As noon approached, the sun's rays cast long shadows over the landscape below. Flynn sat in the cockpit, the plane's engine idling, preparing for a confrontation that seemed inevitable. He whistled a catchy, comforting tune.

Flynn and Kurt knew the stakes were high, and the odds were against them. Their only approach kept the missile lock off them.

His sole advantage was the element of surprise and the unmatched capabilities of the Corsair—now enhanced by the Alpha engine and the strategic genius of his team.

"I've been thinking," Kurt said. "I'll approach from a high attack—fast and furious. Focus on one or two choppers, then pull away as high as possible. Executing some S-curves to stay out of their missile lock. That's the point, really."

Flynn turned on some classic rock to soothe his mind.

The enemy—a formation of two groups of five, each led by an Apache followed by Black Hawk gunships—loomed at the edge of his territory, their intentions clear and hostile.

"Wow, Flynn, you're just parked in the sky, hanging out. If I didn't see it myself, I'd have a hard time believing it," Kurt said.

Flynn smirked. "It is a bit on the freaky side, isn't it? Part of me wanted to unbuckle and hang out on the wing. But nah, cooler heads prevailed."

They both laughed.

Flynn checked the controls. "Alright, old girl, let's show them what we're made of."

As he hovered in the sky, the plane's engine idling, he watched the enemy's movements on his tablet—an updated feed sent by Sunday, mounted to the side of the dashboard. He readied himself for an audacious maneuver—one that would etch his name into the annals of aerial combat.

With the enemy helicopters closing in, their intentions as clear as the morning sun at his back, Flynn knew the moment of truth had arrived. When they tried to locate the source of incoming fire, all they would see was the glaring sun blinding their vision.

"Comanche base, I'm about to hit the throttle. Bring me to 450 knots. Let's not turn my insides out, though. Thanks."

Sunday's voice crackled over the radio. "Roger that, Comanche Actual."

Switching to the enemy's frequency, Sunday delivered a chilling message. "You drew first blood. Deadly force is now authorized."

As Flynn pierced through the cloud cover, the Corsair emerged into the clear sky, bathed in the sun's ethereal glow. He adjusted the nose of his aircraft, ready to strike like a lion—his first pass at the enemy locked in.

"Stick close, Comanche 20," Flynn radioed to Kurt. "Let's bring the pain."

Kurt: "Roger that. I'm your wingman—high and to your right. Above all, mate, we've got this. The sky is ours today."

Flynn, instincts sharpened by Kurt's training, maneuvers his Corsair with precision. The Alpha engine's EM field crackles, distorting the air around him in an electrified dance.

The Enemy closes in

Flynn glanced at Kurt. "Ten against two," he muttered, scanning the horizon. "Choppers may not be fast, but they're coordinated. We have to take them out quickly."

His heart pounded, but his hands remained steady on the controls.

He pushed Alpha's throttle forward, feeling the Corsair surge ahead, allowing the helicopters to move into range. His thumb hovered over the trigger, waiting for the perfect moment.

The radio crackled. Sunday's voice came through. "They're nearly in range. Prepare for engagement."

Flynn nodded. "Hit 'em high like we planned."

"Okay, Comanche Base, give me a countdown before we punch it. We're cleared hot and ready to bring the pain," Flynn said.

"Roger that, Captain. You're go in five… four… three… two… punch it!" Sunday responded.

"Accelerating to 450 knots with the Zone," Flynn called out.

"Come on, baby, hold together," he muttered under his breath.

The sheer momentum of the warplane was exhilarating—overwhelming.

He locked onto the incoming choppers. The lead aircraft in each group of five was an Apache, armed with missiles and a 30mm cannon. The remaining eight were Black Hawks carrying armed men with .50 caliber guns.

"Comanche 20, the lead chopper in each group is an Apache with missiles and cannons. Let's take them out first," Flynn instructed.

"I see them. Roger that, Comanche 19," Kurt replied.

Sunday, monitoring radio frequencies, found the one the enemy was using. At the perfect moment, she blasted the eerie wail of Whistling Death at maximum volume, sparing Flynn's ears.

The chopper pilots recoiled in shock, some yelling, "Jesus!" as they ripped their headphones off. Flynn's lips curled into a smirk. The element of surprise was his greatest weapon.

The Corsair roared in, pushing past its design limits. Flynn stomped the left rudder pedal, angling the nose toward the flight path. The aircraft slid sideways through the air—45 degrees, then 90, then leveling at 30 degrees above the enemy. He executed the maneuver almost flawlessly.

The plane shuddered under the pressure, wind slamming against it, leaving a long vapor trail from its wings, rudder, and ailerons.

Sunday monitored the approach with Kenji watching beside her. She counted down.

"Hit it!" Sunday commanded.

Flynn lined up his sights on the lead Apache. The rest of the choppers trailed behind in formation.

"Light 'em up," he whispered to himself.

The first pass was a violent blur of speed and firepower.

Flynn smirked. The element of surprise was his greatest weapon. The enemy pilots, overconfident in their advanced tech, struggled to react to the impossible maneuverability of his old warbird. They had anticipated a straightforward dogfight; instead, they faced something beyond their playbook.

Adrenaline surged through Flynn as his guns tore through the first Apache and three Black Hawks. Rounds shredded rotor blades and hulls, setting off spectacular explosions that sent them spiraling in flames. The fifth Black Hawk pilot barely evaded the barrage, dropping altitude just in time.

Flynn banked hard to the right, scanning for the last Black Hawk in his target squadron. In the corner of his eye, he tracked Kurt's movements.

The sky pulsed with energy, the sun a blazing sentinel above as Kurt climbed effortlessly to 20,000 feet, his F4U-5 Corsair humming with purpose. The deep growl of its radial engine echoed like a war cry—raw power and precision in motion. His grip on the stick was steady, his focus razor-sharp.

"Alright, boys," Kurt muttered, a faint smirk tugging at his lips. "Time to show them how it's done."

Rolling his plane smoothly onto its back, he fixed his gaze on the battlefield below. The inverted position gave him an unobstructed view of the helicopters he was about to engage. G-forces pinned him to his seat as he controlled his descent with the grace of a predator closing in on its prey. The choppers flew in staggered formation, nearly single file, their varying elevations providing a limited defensive advantage.

He rolled upright and eased the Corsair into a steep dive. The speed climbed fast, the needle pushing toward 380 knots—its absolute limit. The legendary "whispering death" hum filled the air, the Corsair's unique aerodynamics producing the haunting tune that heralded destruction.

His target: the lead Apache in the second group and the Black Hawks maintaining formation at 5,000 feet.

Kurt's attack was calculated—a high-angle strike from the sun's position. The blinding brilliance rendered him nearly invisible to the chopper pilots below, their restricted visibility playing to his advantage. Together, he and Flynn moved in deadly synchronization—an aerial symphony of destruction.

The second Apache entered Kurt's sights, and instinct took over. His .50-caliber guns roared to life, six synchronized weapons spitting fire and fury. Tracer rounds streaked through the sky like blazing needles, puncturing the lead helicopter's fuselage. It erupted in a fiery explosion, spiraling out of control toward the ground.

Kurt didn't pause to admire the spectacle. He banked sharply, locking onto the second chopper. The enemy pilot, now aware of the assault, veered off in a desperate attempt to break formation—but Kurt had already anticipated the move. Adjusting his angle, he unleashed another barrage. The second helicopter didn't stand a chance. Its tail rotor shredded, it spiraled out of control before crashing into the trees below.

The remaining choppers scrambled, breaking formation in a frantic attempt to avoid the same fate. But Kurt pressed the attack, his movements smooth and precise. His Corsair weaved through the air, rolling into tight banks and dives, dodging two rockets the Black Hawks launched in retaliation. The bulky helicopters were no match for its speed and agility.

"Two for the price of one," Kurt said, his voice steady as he pulled up, climbing once more.

From his vantage point, Flynn watched the destruction unfold, a mix of awe and pride swelling in his chest. "Still got it, Shadow," he murmured.

"Sunday," Flynn said, "what's their radio channel? I'd like to blow them a little kiss."

"Fourteen," Sunday replied.

"Roger that." Flynn switched channels.

"Did we catch you bastards napping?" he muttered through clenched teeth, heart pounding.

He switched back to Nautilus Channel 6. He had no interest in listening further—Sunday would handle that.

As Kurt neared the sun, he executed a maneuver so audacious it made the observers' hearts skip a beat. Banking hard, he arced high toward the blinding light, his silhouette momentarily vanishing into the glare. The move echoed an iconic shot from Batman—except there was no dramatic pause, only seamless, lethal precision. For a heartbeat, he became a ghost.

Then, with terrifying speed, he dove, descending like an eagle upon its prey.

Coming in from 030 high, his attack run was a textbook display of air-to-air combat—legendary, perfected by years in the Navy.

The six .50-caliber guns mounted on the Whistling Death roared to life, spitting hot lead into the sky. Tracers streaked toward their targets as the lead Apache and the Black Hawk behind it erupted into fire and metal, their remains spiraling earthward. The crews inside never knew what hit them.

Kurt didn't wait to admire his work. Pulling back on the throttle, he wrenched the Corsair into a sharp left turn, the airframe groaning under the strain but holding firm. A grin crept onto his face.

"Still got it," he murmured, voice calm but tinged with pride.

Flynn watched the maneuver, a grin spreading across his face. "Damn, 20. You just showed them what a real ace looks like."

Kurt circled back, scanning the horizon for his next target. The skies were his now.

He dove in from 030 high, lined up, and shredded two choppers at 1,500 feet with a burst from his six .50-cals, tearing them apart mid-flight. Easing off the accelerator, he yanked the stick into a hard left turn. No G-suit—he had to take it easy. But bullets were all he needed. For a veteran like him, that was plenty.

He swung around for another high pass.

But the enemy was adapting. Two choppers banked sharply, angling their side guns for a shot. At this speed, they had a chance. A sharp staccato of gunfire rattled the Corsair. Flynn gritted his teeth as rounds tore into the fuselage and left wing. The control panel flickered with warnings, but he knew the bird could take a beating. She was old, but she was tough. And so was he.

Suddenly, the early warning system blared—a missile lock. Joshua's modifications had paid off. Flynn's pulse spiked. This was where the tech gap really mattered. He was entering the danger zone now. But instead of backing off, he pushed the Corsair harder.

Sunday's voice crackled through the radio, tinged with awe and humor. "Roger that, Comanche 19. Bring your big-ass nose down eight degrees… My God in heaven."

His first pass through the formation was pure chaos. The .50-cals roared, shredding through unprepared choppers and leaving a fiery trail of destruction. The high-tech helicopters, despite their cutting-edge systems, were thrown into confusion. Their targeting computers couldn't lock onto him—his unconventional tactics broke every rule in the book. Within minutes, four enemy birds tumbled from the sky like broken toys.

Flynn's adrenaline surged, sharpening his focus. He banked for another run, barely evading return fire. His hands were welded to the controls, an extension of the Corsair itself. There was something poetic about an old warplane holding its own against modern tech.

Unbeknownst to him, Sunday was making micro-adjustments to the trajectory, subtly shifting the Corsair's path in ways Flynn couldn't feel. It was the only reason he hadn't taken more hits. But she knew his pride, so she stayed silent. The machine and its pilot worked in perfect sync—only he didn't realize there was an invisible hand guiding him through the storm.

Flynn pulls back on the stick, sending the Corsair into a steep climb before diving back into the fray, guns blazing. He skims over the tops of the remaining choppers, their weapons unable to get a clean angle on him. Rockets streak up from below, but Flynn effortlessly dodges them, weaving the Corsair in erratic, unpredictable patterns.

His voice crackles through the comms as he slides the Corsair sideways, lining up his guns on two more Black Hawks. Their rotors whine in agony as .50 caliber rounds shred through them. Flynn feels the surge of triumph as another chopper spirals downward, trailing thick smoke.

The enemy pilots, desperate and frustrated, struggle to predict Flynn's next move—but they're always a step behind. His mastery of the slide maneuver keeps them off balance. Every time they attempt to lock onto him with their missiles, the Corsair slips out of their sights like a phantom on the wind.

"You ready for another run, old man?" Flynn's voice is tense but laced with excitement.

"Kid, I've been doing this since before you could drive," Kurt shoots back, his tone calm and steady. He lets out a laugh. "Oh man, Alpha is a beast! Let's see what you've got on your second pass. I'm taking my last Black Hawk on the left—you've got three remaining."

Kurt pulls the Corsair into a tight bank, leveling out just above the treetops. The remaining helicopters are in disarray, struggling to reorient themselves fast enough to counter the relentless attack. Flynn's unorthodox angles—combined with Sunday's silent adjustments—make him an untouchable force in the sky.

As he sweeps over the last of the enemy formation, his guns blaze once more. Flynn watches as their ranks collapse, unable to keep pace with his unpredictable movements.

Meanwhile, Kurt remains locked in, his eyes narrowing as he lines up his next target. On his second pass, he banks hard, dives from above, and unleashes a torrent of bullets. His third target erupts in a fiery explosion, debris scattering in all directions. Without hesitation, he pulls up and rolls into position, zeroing in on his next victim.

Flynn adjusts his approach, methodically lining up his shot. He squeezes the trigger, and his guns roar to life, spitting death with lethal precision. His final Black Hawk jerks into a hard left, trying to line up its side guns. It fires—but misses. Flynn grins, already angling for the finishing blow.

Flynn executes an awkward slide over the top of the chopper, riddling it with bullets and triggering a devastating explosion. The last Black Hawk spirals to the ground in a fiery wreck, smoke billowing in its wake.

After completing a barrel roll, Kurt swings back for another pass. He dives from above, targeting the second-to-last Black Hawk's blades at nearly max speed—over 380 knots. Bullets from the final Black Hawk rake his right wing, but no critical systems take damage. The coordination of their attack is undeniable.

Meanwhile, Kurt, handling Comanche 20 with the precision of a seasoned ace, pushes the aircraft to the edge of excessive G-forces. Approaching from high above with a more conventional attack vector, he maneuvers into position. His aircraft slices through the sky, an extension of his will, as he locks onto the remaining invaders with ruthless efficiency. Banking hard to the right, his guns erupt in a furious blaze, shredding the last opposition without mercy.

"Looks like we're even, Flynn! Five each! Aces in a day—no one's ever done that before," Kurt's voice crackles over the radio, a mix of exhilaration and grim determination.

Flynn grins, his eyes scanning the horizon for the targets Sunday had mentioned—probably F-16s.

"I'm picking up a new group of signals," Sunday reports. "Enemy fast movers incoming—hot."

Their brief moment of triumph is shattered by a sharp distress call from enemy lines. Within moments, two sleek F-16s streak into the airspace, their modern frames and advanced weaponry a stark contrast to the World War II-era planes piloted by Flynn and Kurt.

"Damn, those fighters aren't vintage," Flynn mutters as the F-16s close in, their jet engines screaming a challenge.

"Warning: Pushing the Alpha engine beyond recommended limits may result in unforeseen consequences," Sunday advises, her tone calm despite the looming threat.

"Unforeseen happens to be my middle name," Flynn shoots back, shoving the throttle forward on the tablet. The Corsair shudders under the strain, but as he pulls into a steep climb, the aircraft responds with a surge of power that defies modern physics. Alpha's vibrations synchronize seamlessly with the Corsair, blurring the lines between the possible and the impossible.

The calm skies erupted with the roar of jet engines, the piercing howl of twin F-16s slicing through the air. They advanced in tight formation, one slightly ahead of the other, their sleek forms bristling with weapons.

In his Corsair, Alpha humming at his core, Flynn narrowed his eyes, calculating the distance. His .50 caliber guns lacked the range of their 20mm cannons and missiles—he knew it. He had to close the gap, and fast.

Pushing the Alpha throttle forward, Flynn surged toward the lead F-16 like a predator. The modern fighter reacted instantly, banking left to gain position while its wingman veered right in a pincer maneuver. Flynn could almost feel their confidence—the unshakable belief that his vintage warbird was no match for their speed and firepower.

They didn't know Alpha was on board.

The lead F-16 fired first—a streak of light screaming toward him. Instinct and years of training kicked in. Yanking the stick back, Flynn engaged Alpha's enhanced maneuverability, sending the Corsair into a steep climb. The missile followed, its targeting system struggling to adjust to his rapid, erratic ascent.

"Come on, come on," Flynn muttered, gritting his teeth as the missile closed in. At the last second, he banked sharply, pushing Alpha's field to its limit. The missile's lock broke. It spiraled off course, detonating harmlessly in a fiery burst.

Three thousand yards away, Kurt had just shredded a pair of Black Hawks, their smoldering wreckage littering the ground below. Swinging his Lightning around, he caught sight of Flynn's Corsair climbing at an impossible angle, pursued by the missile. His heart jumped at the explosion—then he grinned as Flynn's plane emerged unscathed.

"Show-off," Kurt muttered, throttling up.

As Flynn leveled out high above, the second F-16 moved in, its 20mm cannon unleashing a deadly hail of rounds. Flynn twisted into a rolling dive, narrowly escaping the gunfire.

"Kurt!" Flynn shouted over comms, his voice tense but controlled. "I've got a bogie on my six, and he's not happy!"

Kurt's response was a calm drawl. "Hang tight, kid. I'm coming in hot."

The veteran pilot pushed his Corsair into an aggressive climb, locking onto the F-16 trailing Flynn. From this distance, it would take every ounce of skill to close the gap—but Kurt was in his element.

The lead F-16, now repositioned, came back for another pass, cannons blazing as it attempted to cut Flynn off. Flynn yanked hard left, allowing the Alpha-enhanced agility to snap him into a tight loop beyond the modern fighter's reach.

Kurt's voice crackled through the radio. "Keep dancing, Flynn. I've got your bogie in my sights."

Kurt bore down on the second F-16, lining up his .50s. The dogfight was just beginning, and the skies were about to ignite.

The roar of jet engines and the hiss of turbulent wind filled Flynn's cockpit as the first F-16 closed in, its sleek frame a menacing shadow in his mirrors. His mind raced, calculating options. A grim realization struck him: He's lining up for his final missile shot. I've got seconds.

Without hesitation, Flynn flicked a switch and launched two rear-facing mini-missiles. They streaked out, bright trails carving through the sky toward the pursuing jet. The F-16 pilot reacted instantly, banking hard and dropping altitude to evade. The missiles exploded harmlessly in the air above, leaving only a brief puff of fire and smoke.

"That's it," Flynn muttered, gripping the controls tightly. "Time to turn the tables."

He executed an impossibly tight 180-degree turn, the Alpha-enhanced agility pushing the Corsair to its limits. The airframe groaned in protest, but Flynn held steady, executing the maneuver with pinpoint precision. As he completed the turn, the F-16 reentered his sights.

"Gotcha," Flynn growled.

His six .50 caliber machine guns roared to life, their deafening thunder slicing through the chaos. At the same time, he fired two forward-facing mini-missiles, their deadly payload streaking toward the enemy.

The F-16 pilot reacted with remarkable skill, accelerating and banking left. The mini-missiles shrieked past, missing by inches. Flynn stayed on him, throttling up and climbing to maintain his lock. The Corsair shuddered under the strain, its frame creaking in protest.

The enemy pilot's objective was clear: break away, reset the fight, and regain control. But Flynn wasn't about to let that happen.

As the jet banked left again, Flynn angled his Corsair upward, anticipating the next move. When the F-16 climbed to escape, Flynn pointed his nose downward and dove sharply. His guns erupted once more, and this time, his aim was true.

Sunday, ever the silent co-pilot, subtly assisted in maneuvering Flynn's warbird but remained quiet.

The .50 caliber rounds ripped through the F-16's midsection, at least twenty hits tearing through its fuselage in a cascade of sparks and smoke. Flames erupted from the jet's core, engulfing its engine. Within seconds, the aircraft spiraled uncontrollably, trailing a thick column of black smoke as it plummeted toward the earth.

Flynn exhaled sharply, his grip tightening on the controls as the Corsair groaned beneath him. The airframe, though sturdy, was straining under the relentless maneuvers.

"Hang in there, old girl," he muttered, patting the dashboard as if to reassure the plane. "We're not done yet."

Far below, the F-16 erupted into a fireball, but Flynn had already shifted his focus. His gaze swept the skies, searching for the next threat. The battle wasn't over yet—and his battered Corsair would have to endure a little longer.

"19, 20 is three miles southwest," Sunday's voice crackled over the radio.

"Roger that, base," Flynn responded.

In the heat of battle, their call signs had shortened naturally, a subconscious adaptation to the chaos.

The sky crackled with tension as Kurt's Corsair banked hard, its engine roaring with determination. His .50 caliber guns thundered, tracers slicing through the air toward the second F-16. But the shots fell short. The modern jet danced just beyond reach, its pilot keenly aware of the danger Kurt posed.

Meanwhile, the second F-16 had locked onto Flynn's Corsair. Despite its Alpha-enhanced agility, the vintage warbird moved unpredictably, forcing the jet's pilot to adjust constantly. Flynn's daring maneuvers had made him a top priority. The F-16 circled wide, searching for the perfect angle to unleash its missile.

Kurt saw the battle unfold like a chessboard in his mind. Decades of combat experience sharpened his instincts, screaming a warning—Flynn was in the crosshairs, and the missile was moments from launch.

Inside the facility, Sunday's voice sliced through the tense quiet. "Kenji, Joshua," she said, urgency lacing her tone. "Kurt's altering course. He's going to—he's going to take the missile for Flynn."

Kenji's eyes widened, his fingers tightening around the console's edge. "It's happening too fast," he murmured. "It'll be over in seconds."

Joshua stood frozen before slamming his fist onto the table. His voice held a mix of awe and disbelief. "He knows exactly what he's doing. This is the act of a hero."

Back in the skies, the F-16's missile streaked free—a blinding spear of light cutting through the air, homing in on Flynn's Corsair.

Kurt, now at a perfect right angle to the missile's path, pushed his warbird to its absolute limits. The airframe groaned. The engine screamed. But Kurt remained calm. Focused.

"I choose you, buddy," he murmured, voice steady as the missile raced closer.

It happened so fast that Flynn didn't have a chance to react.

Sotra recalled a crucial lesson from the first timeline: quantum splitting couldn't be rushed. It required careful preparation, immense energy, and balance—and it left her drained afterward. She had already saved Flynn once and knew she would have to do it again after speaking with Bob.

Kurt's fate had been sealed. His sacrifice wasn't just about the battle—it was about his legacy. He was dying, and he accepted it. Saving him would have meant robbing him of that choice.

It was a painful truth, but not everyone could be saved.

There was no time to argue. The missile struck the Corsair's side, erupting in a fiery explosion that tore through the sky. Kurt's warbird disintegrated in the blast, the shockwave rocking Flynn's Corsair as he pulled away in stunned silence.

Inside the facility, Kenji sat back, his hands on his head, his face pale. Joshua muttered under his breath, his expression twisted with anger and grief.

"Kurt…" Flynn whispered into the empty radio channel, his voice heavy with loss. "My God."

Sunday's voice broke the silence. "I'm so sorry, Captain."

The battle raged on, but in that moment, the price of victory became agonizingly clear. Kurt's sacrifice hung over the battlefield like a specter, and Flynn swore silently that it wouldn't be in vain.

Bob listened in, the weight of loss pressing against him—grief for family long gone, now compounded by the fresh wound of Kurt's death. Time, relentless and unforgiving, carved its toll.

The Corsair groaned under the strain, its battered frame and weary engine still defying the odds as Flynn fought to shake the F-16 on his tail. The modern jet, sleek and deadly, had one missile left. Flynn could feel the pilot's determination pressing down on him like a vice.

Inside the facility, Sunday's voice came through Kenji's headset—calm but urgent. "Kenji, I've been monitoring their communications and systems since the engagement started. I think I can disrupt the missile's guidance, but the timing has to be perfect."

Kenji's fingers flew across the keyboard, his focus razor-sharp. "We've got one shot at this. If I can piggyback off Sunday's analysis, we can shut down the missile's targeting system just long enough. But we need a distraction to sell it."

Inside the van, Joshua monitored his tablet display. "What about the outer sensors? Use them to create a fake target—make it look like Flynn's still out there while he makes his move."

Kenji nodded, already typing. "On it. Sunday, send a signal to sensors three, four, and six. Make it look like a moving target is heading north."

Sunday's voice crackled in Flynn's cockpit. "Flynn, listen carefully. We're scrambling the missile guidance temporarily and creating a false target to lure the F-16 away. Hopefully, the pilot takes the bait and wastes his last missile on the decoy."

"You need to get to the canyon—fast. Lose him in the terrain and head for the open field on the other side. Joshua's waiting," Sunday instructed.

Flynn grinned despite the tension. "You guys have outdone yourselves. Alright, let's see if this works."

With the last F-16 closing in fast, Flynn veered into the canyon, navigating the twists like a fork in the road.

Kenji activated the sensors, making the false contact appear a mile north. The F-16 locked onto the decoy, mistaking it for the Corsair.

The jet's fire control system struggled, taking ten times longer than usual to secure a target, giving Flynn precious distance.

Finally, the F-16's targeting system believed it had a lock. But the scrambled signal was still active—rendering the missile useless.

"Missile's good and confused," Sunday reported. "Now's your chance, Flynn. The false target should keep him busy for a few seconds."

Flying through the canyon, Flynn's hands moved instinctively, weaving the Corsair through tight turns and low passes. Tilting the aircraft on its side, he skimmed along the canyon walls, the roar of the engines echoing through the narrow space.

Meanwhile, the F-16, now three miles north, had to slow down and attempt to reacquire its real target.

Flynn scanned his instruments without a moment to spare. Oil pressure was dropping, ammunition was running low, and sensors flashed a dire warning—fire in the left wing. Smoke coiled through the cockpit, whipped by the wind.

"Time to land, you old girl," Flynn muttered.

Beyond the canyon, an open field came into view. Joshua's van sat waiting, a beacon in the chaos. Flynn aligned for approach, the Corsair shuddering under the strain.

The battered aircraft barely held together as he coaxed it toward the clearing. Every control input was sluggish, unresponsive—like a dying beast taking its final steps. The frame trembled with turbulence, the weight of its wounds threatening to tear it apart midair. The sensors were still mostly functional, while Alpha fought to stabilize yaw and pitch.

Flynn gritted his teeth, forcing the Corsair to stay steady. He didn't just hear the damage—he felt it. Each bullet hole, each rupture in the frame, reverberated through the cockpit like a heartbeat on the edge of stopping.

The rudder? Gone. Not shredded. Not damaged. Just gone.

The right aileron? Barely there.

Half the right wing? Missing.

The left wing? Three gaping wounds, big enough to hurl a softball through—one large enough to swallow a basketball.

The landing gear groaned as the Corsair touched down, wobbling precariously on its mangled frame. When it finally skidded to a stop, the aircraft let out a final, weary groan—almost as if relieved it had made it back at all.

Joshua sprinted from the van, eyes wide. "*Holy shit...* Flynn, how in the *hell* are you still alive?"

Flynn climbed out, finally taking in the full extent of the destruction. It was worse than he imagined. The Alpha engine had been the only thing keeping this bird from plummeting like a stone.

Sunday's voice crackled over the comms, her drones feeding her a full overhead view. "Captain... that's not a plane anymore. That's miracle wreckage. I don't know whether to call you a legend or have you institutionalized."

Flynn let out a breathless laugh. "Both."

Escape at Mach speed

Meanwhile, the remnants of the antagonist forces reeled from the Comanche squad's display of power and resilience, Flynn's damaged aircraft limping back to safety. The engine sputtered, trailing a thick plume of smoke as he made a desperate plea to Sunday.

Sunday's voice crackled through the comms. "Initiating emergency landing protocol. Shut Alpha off just before you land. And, Comanche Actual... I'm sorry about Kurt. He saved your life out there."

Flynn's grip tightened on the controls. "I didn't see it, but I felt it."

The weight of Kurt's sacrifice crashed over him—a jarring mix of grief and gratitude. The realization that his friend had given his life for him solidified the depth of their bond, the loss striking with stark clarity.

As the landing gear deployed, the wheels locked into place with a heavy thunk. Flynn guided the aircraft to a halt beside the van, its battered frame scarred by battle. Smoke and fire licked at the long nose of the engine. With precision, he shut down Alpha just in time, the flames on the left wing flickering out. The engine, housed securely behind the pilot's seat in its armored case, was safe.

In the aftermath of the aerial assault, with the skies still thick with the echoes of war, Flynn and Joshua regrouped, their resolve unshaken despite the weight of their losses.

The van, outfitted with a formidable .50 cal and an ample supply of ammunition, stood as their final line of defense. With practiced efficiency, Flynn secured the Alpha engine to the van's quick-connect fitting—a process he had perfected through sheer necessity.

Placing both hands on his battered yet reliable Corsair, Flynn murmured, "You were a fiery, wicked angel up there. The best." He gave the engine two quick fist bumps as smoke drifted past him on the wind. He had to move—fast. The rising plume could give away their position.

Joshua, prepping to provide cover fire, called out, "We've got to move, Flynn. This isn't over yet."

Flynn's hands trembled as he fought to steady himself, the last vestiges of adrenaline coursing through him.

Then came the sound—the piercing roar of an approaching F-16. The enemy was closing in.

Sliding into the driver's seat, Flynn gripped the tablet tightly, his gaze locked on the horizon. Joshua was beside him, ready to man the .50-cal when needed. Behind them, the Corsair lay still, its mission complete. But Alpha—sealed in its armored case—remained the prize everyone wanted.

"Comanche Base," Flynn said, his voice calm despite the escalating stakes. "We need speed—Mach 1 if the terrain allows. Let's roll. Easy does it; we're not exactly suited up for this."

Sunday responded immediately, her voice cool and precise. "Roger that, Flynn. Activating Alpha."

The van lifted two feet off the ground as the Alpha engine hummed to life beneath it. With the terrain no longer an obstacle, Sunday adjusted the throttle, and the van surged forward, skimming the earth like a ghostly blur. Flynn controlled the steering through his tablet, his fingers deftly guiding the vehicle while Sunday managed stabilization.

The F-16, now in visual range, opened fire. Cannon rounds screamed through the air, two of them slamming into the van's bed where Alpha was secured. Flynn gritted his teeth.

"Sunday, status?" Flynn asked.

"Alpha is intact," she replied, steady as ever. "Accelerating now—should be a smooth ride."

The van shot forward, the landscape dissolving into streaks of green and brown. Then it came—a sudden crack in the air, followed by the deafening boom of the sound barrier breaking. The Alpha engine's raw power tore through the sonic wall, propelling them ahead.

"Mach 1," Flynn muttered, a rare smile tugging at the corner of his lips. "You beauty."

The ground trembled beneath them as the shockwave rippled outward, uprooting trees and launching debris in their wake. They hurtled toward the forest, the towering trees offering a last chance for cover.

The F-16 fired again. Its rounds shredded the ground, one slamming into the van just before they entered the dense forest. Unable to match their maneuverability in the thick foliage, the jet hesitated at the tree line, trying to reacquire its target.

As the van slowed, Joshua's voice crackled through the comms, grim and exasperated. "Flynn—ah, shit. The remote detonator's hit. Looks like Swiss cheese had a good time with a donut."

Flynn's smile vanished, his jaw tightening. "Well, that complicates things."

Sunday's voice cut in, firm and focused. "Complications or not, you're clear for now. Let's regroup and reassess."

The dense forest swallowed the van, its ancient trees towering like sentinels, their gnarled limbs forming a canopy of shadow and secrecy. Flynn brought the van to a halt, Alpha's hum fading into an eerie stillness.

For a moment, the world held its breath.

Flynn's mind raced, but a strange calm seeped through him—like a tide rolling in despite the chaos of the storm.

He clenched the steering wheel, staring straight ahead. "They can't have it," he muttered. "Not at any cost."

Beside him, Joshua watched silently, his expression a mix of understanding and dread. They both knew what was coming, even if neither wanted to admit it. Finally, Flynn turned to his oldest friend, his voice heavy with resolve.

Flynn looked at Joshua, frustration tightening his features. "It's time, Joshua. I'm calling Code Broken Arrow. They won't find me or Alpha. You need to get out—now."

Joshua frowned, his jaw tightening. "You're the most stubborn sailor I've ever known. And now you're pulling this lone wolf act? Flynn, think about this!"

Flynn shook his head, a faint smile crossing his lips. "You know me. I've thought about it. I'll see you on the other side, brother. Now go."

Joshua hesitated, then grabbed Flynn's shoulder, his grip firm. "It's been a privilege, Flynn. A goddamn privilege. Don't make me regret leaving you here."

Flynn nodded, clasping Joshua's hand briefly. "Never."

As Joshua hopped out of the van, slipping through the zone bubble and sprinting toward the forest, Flynn's heart sank. A voice in his head whispered, calm and resolute.

"It will be okay. You know what you have to do."

Once Joshua was safely hidden in the trees, Flynn shifted into gear. The van roared forward, the forest blurring around him as he accelerated toward an open patch where the enemy would surely spot him.

"Broken Arrow, Comanche Base," Flynn said into the mic, his voice steady despite the lump in his throat. "Keep the family safe."

Sunday's voice came through, soft and unwavering. "Farewell, Captain, sir." She paused before clicking off, her tone almost wistful. "Say hi to Elvis for us. No one will forget you."

Flynn smirked, his heart heavy but calm. The strange sense of peace settled deeper, a quiet certainty replacing his fear. Sotra's unseen influence soothed his doubts.

He reached for his phone, his fingers trembling as he dialed his wife. The moment her familiar voice filled the air, his breath hitched.

"Flynn? Is everything alright?"

Flynn swallowed hard, his smirk softening. "Hey, honey. It's been one hell of a day. I just needed to hear your voice."

"Vance, what's wrong?" Lilian asked, concern creeping into her tone.

Flynn exhaled slowly. "I love you. More than anything. Just remember that, okay?"

The weight of the moment pressed down on him, but he kept driving, his resolve unshaken. For now, hearing her voice was enough—his anchor to a life he was willing to sacrifice to protect.

The roar of the van's Alpha engine filled the cabin, but Flynn barely noticed. His attention was split between the growing dot of the F-16 in the rearview mirror and the phone pressed to his ear.

"Lilian," he said, his voice calm yet thick with emotion. "I'm about to do something crazy. These assholes are relentless, and they'll stop at nothing. If they don't get what they want from me, they'll come for you next." He deliberately avoided saying Alpha or Beta.

A brief silence hung on the line before Lilian's voice broke through, frantic and trembling. She recognized that tone—

the unshakable resolve in her husband's voice. It was the sound of a man who had already decided his fate.

"There has to be another way, Vance!" she pleaded, using his first name, something she only did when upset. "Please, just—think this through! And I love you!"

Flynn's grip tightened on the steering wheel, his knuckles turning white. He forced a smirk, even though she couldn't see it.

"I think everything will be okay, honey. I have this... feeling. But I needed to hear your voice, just in case. And tell the girls…" His voice wavered, but he pushed through, his tone softening. "Tell them I'll be watching over them, no matter what. I love you and miss you terribly."

With a heavy heart, he ended the call. The silence in the cabin was louder than the engine's hum.

On the horizon, the F-16 loomed closer, now joined by another incoming aircraft. Flynn glanced at the rearview mirror, jaw clenched as he steeled himself.

The F-16 began lining up for its attack run, the other aircraft closing in fast. Flynn gripped the mic, his voice erupting over the airwaves with a defiance that could be felt for miles.

He floored the accelerator, the van surging forward with every ounce of power Alpha could muster. If this was the end, it would be on his terms in a blaze of glory for a cause that mattered.

Flynn set the controls to hold course at 300 knots while he worked through the security clearance for self-destruction.

"Kenji, execute Code Brown. I'll finalize on my end."

Kenji's voice cracked with emotion. "Quick trip, my friend."

Flynn responded in Japanese, "Long live your family."

Then, over the radio, he addressed the F-16 with a final declaration.

"YOU LOSE!"

His words thundered through the airwaves, defying the odds and the inevitability of his situation.

As the enemy closed in, Flynn's resolve remained unshaken. This wasn't just about Alpha or the van—it was about securing a future for those he loved. A future beyond the grasp of those who would twist their technology and lives for power.

Bob watched the battle unfold on the monitors, witnessing one of the most impressive air combat engagements ever. This timeline's events were drastically different from what he remembered, a stark reminder of the power of the butterfly effect.

CHAPTER THIRTY-

SEVEN

QUANTUM REBIRTH

In the fleeting moments before the cataclysmic explosion, reality itself seemed to hesitate, holding its breath as Flynn's fate teetered on the edge. It was then that Sotra, an observer from a realm beyond human comprehension, witnessed Flynn's heroic last stand. Moved by his sacrifice and recognizing the need to preserve such valor, Sotra intervened with a power aligned with the quantum laws of the universe.

Flynn pressed the button. BOOM!

The explosion erupted in a blinding, all-consuming light. In that sliver of time, Flynn experienced an indescribable sensation—as if his very essence was being stretched across the fabric of existence.

In an instant, there were two of him—Flynn A and the newly formed Flynn B. Each a quantum reflection of the other, yet bound by a shared consciousness and memory.

Flynn A found himself in Sotra's dimension, a realm unshackled from the constraints of earthly reality, a place of ethereal beauty and profound serenity. The transition was jarring, yet it offered an inexplicable sense of understanding, solace, and rest.

Sotra spoke to both versions of Flynn. "You were saved, Flynn. A choice made in the blink of an eye. The world does not know your sacrifice—but they will. It's okay, you can sleep now."

Years passed. Sotra watched over Flynn A, who had been with her for fifteen years, while Bob—older Flynn B from the original quantum split—existed in his own dimension.

Sotra and Flynn A journeyed through dimensions, with Sotra teaching him about his elevated consciousness and the immense responsibility it entailed.

Then, Bob—older Flynn B—traveled back in time, to the moment before the original split. In this altered timeline, Flynn A no longer existed with Sotra. The split had not yet occurred.

Now, only two remained: the younger Flynn and Bob, the Flynn B from the previous timeline. They were still the same quantum particles, bound by an immutable connection.

Time had not paused when Sotra intervened—it had folded.

In the final moments before the detonation of Alpha, as the electromagnetic pulse surged to critical mass, Sotra acted. She had foreseen this: Flynn's sacrifice, his unwavering resolve.

In a process far beyond human comprehension, Sotra divided Flynn at the quantum level. This was not duplication it was division. A perfect quantum entanglement that defied all known physical laws. The Flynn who had stood at the precipice of destruction ceased to exist in that instant, reborn as two distinct entities: Flynn A and Flynn B.

Each carried the complete essence of the original—memories, instincts, emotions—but they were not mere copies. They were now two separate beings, existing simultaneously yet uniquely, tethered by an invisible thread that allowed them to share knowledge and experiences across time.

Quantum mechanics dictated that only two versions of the same quantum signature could exist in a single timeline.

This meant one unavoidable truth: Bob—the Flynn who had traveled back in time—would cease to exist. His mission was complete. His knowledge had transferred seamlessly to both new versions of himself. His existence, once vital, was no longer needed.

All knowledge and experience transferred between Bob and the newly quantum-split Flynn faster than the human brain could initially process. It took a moment to settle.

Sotra, though weakened by the strain of the quantum split, managed to return to her dimension with Flynn B, safely arriving at the mountain lair.

Flynn A, exhausted from the ordeal, groggily muttered, "Where... What the hell?" That voice… It lingered in his mind, stirring fragmented memories.

Meanwhile, the newly formed Flynn B materialized within the secure mountain lair, appearing beside the Beta engine. His sudden arrival was as much a shock to him as the absence of the expected explosion. The realization that he was both here and elsewhere, remembering the van, pressing the detonation button, and the impending doom, was overwhelming.

"Oh, uhh... I think I'll lay down for a while...zzz..." Flynn mumbled before collapsing face-first onto a nearby bed.

Back in the forest, the explosion unfolded. The electromagnetic pulse from the Alpha engine cascaded through the air. An F-16, caught in the blast, lost power and spiraled to the ground in a fiery wreck, a silent testament to Flynn’s intended sacrifice. The pilot's ejection system failed.

As Sotra regained her strength, a quiet sense of satisfaction tempered her exhaustion. The choice to save Flynn—to split him across dimensions and realities—was made in an instant, yet its impact would resonate through time.

Exhaling deeply, she murmured, "It is done. The ripples of this day will be felt for generations."

In this moment of crisis, Sotra's intervention not only altered Flynn's fate but also set into motion a cascade of new possibilities. His existence, now split and intertwined with the destinies of two worlds, stood as a beacon of hope and a testament to the unseen forces shaping humanity's path.

In the wake of the explosion, the world reeled from the shockwave of Flynn's sacrifice. Joshua, burdened by the weight of the news, reached out to Lilian, his voice heavy with grief.

"Lilian... there's been an incident. An explosion. We believe Flynn... he might have been..." The mobile phone, stored in an EM-protected bag, crackled with interference before the signal cut out.

Lilian's hands trembled as she gripped the phone, the screen now dark. Her eyes, wide with shock, slowly filled with tears. She turned to face Eileen and Rosaleen, who sat beside her, their young faces etched with confusion and worry.

Taking a deep breath, she steadied her voice. "Girls," she began, her tone a fragile whisper, "your granddad... he did something extraordinary today. For us. For everyone." She swallowed hard, fighting the quiver in her lips. "He loves us more than anything."

Eileen, the older of the two at eighteen, wrapped her arms around her grandmother. "Is Grandad okay?" she asked, her voice barely audible.

Rosaleen nestled closer, her small hands clutching Lilian's arm. Tears rolled down her cheeks as she choked out, "We love you, Grandad!"

Lilian pulled them both into a tight embrace, her own tears now freely falling. "I know, darlings, I know. And he loves you so very much. What he did today... it wasn't just for us. It was for many, many others—people we don't even know." Her voice broke, a mixture of sorrow and pride. "Your granddad always believed in doing the right thing, even when it was hard. Especially when it was hard."

The room fell silent except for the soft, collective sobs of the trio. After a moment, Lilian continued, her voice steadier, laced with reflection. "You remember the stories he told you? About heroes and adventures, about brave deeds in the face of danger?"

Both girls nodded, sniffling.

Lilian pulled back slightly to look at them. "Just like in those tales, heroism always comes at a cost. But remember, what he did—he did out of love. And love… love is the most powerful force there is. It gives you strength. It makes you brave. And sometimes, it means sacrificing for the greater good."

Eileen, struggling to understand, bit her lip, processing the weight of the moment. "But why did it have to be him?" Her voice wavered between anger and sorrow.

Lilian sighed, her eyes reflecting the flickering glow of the fireplace. "Sometimes, sweetheart, we don't get to choose our battles. They come to us. And all we can decide is how we face them. Your granddad chose to face his with courage, thinking of others before himself."

Rosaleen looks up, her eyes searching Lilian's. "Will we see him again?"

Lilian's heart tightens at the question, understanding the weight behind it. "In a way, yes. In memories, in the stories we share, and in the love we continue to give each other. He's part of us, always."

As they cling to each other, finding solace in their shared grief, a faint glow appears outside the window. The night sky is clear, and as they watch, a particularly bright star flickers, standing out against the others.

Lilian gestures toward the sky. "We'll pick a star tonight and name it after Vance—your Grandad. We'll make it official. That way, he'll always be watching over us."

She smiles through her tears, the whimsical idea bringing a small but needed comfort.

Both girls turn their gaze upward, a fragile smile breaking through their sorrow. They go online, search for a star registry, and purchase the rights to a bright star in the night sky.

"That one," Lilian murmurs. "We'll name it Vance 19."

"Hi, Grandad," Rosaleen whispers, her voice barely more than a breath, carrying her words to the stars.

Lilian holds her close, whispering, "He's right there, in the light that travels across the galaxy to reach us—just as he reached out with his love today. And maybe, in some way, that light will guide us forward."

Exit stage left

Meanwhile, Bob stood at the brink of this altered reality, allowing himself a moment of true exultation. On the TV screen before him, the long-awaited court verdict finally arrived. The downfall of SAGA—its bankruptcy, the mass layoffs, and the mysterious disappearance of CEO Jack Wagner—marked the culmination of their struggles. A victory hard-won through sacrifice and perseverance.

Bob returned to his room just before the EM explosion and quantum split, sensing the approaching end. The weight of victory mingled with the bittersweet finality of what was to come. He sank into his chair, eyes fixed on the monitor as the news flashed across the screen. The thunderous ruling against SAGA had shattered their empire under the weight of lawsuits and public outrage. For the first time in years, Bob allowed himself a genuine smile, his eyes brimming with tears.

"This is it," he whispered. "We did it. I'm so grateful."

Leaning forward, he gripped the arms of his chair, watching the footage of the epic air battle. Flynn's breathtaking maneuvers, Kurt's selfless final act, and the sheer willpower of the team had reshaped reality itself. The timeline had shifted in ways beyond imagination, and Bob couldn't help but marvel at the power of the butterfly effect.

Yet he knew his place in this altered reality was reaching its end. His existence—merely a byproduct of Sotra's quantum manipulation—was unsustainable. "There can only be two," he murmured, recalling the principle that had defined his every step since the split. His quantum signature was an anomaly—a third presence where only two could exist.

Bob stood as the vortex of blue light began swirling around him. His proud, teary-eyed smile never wavered. He extended his arms, embracing the inevitable. Fifteen years of meticulous planning, sacrifice, and collaboration had borne fruit. His family was safe, the team's legacy secure, the future protected.

"This is how it should be," he said softly. "Thank you, team."

The light intensified, consuming him entirely. In an instant, Bob was gone, leaving behind only the clothes by the chair where he had stood. His office fell silent—a quiet testament to the transient nature of his journey.

Yet, Bob's knowledge and essence did not vanish into the void. Instead, they infused the remaining Flynn entities with a profound understanding—an inheritance of Bob's last fifteen years. Every breakthrough in his research on the Beta engine, every upgrade, and every untapped potential became theirs. But his legacy extended beyond technology. The meticulous financial web he had spun—the funds he had secured and the intricate methods he had devised—was now embedded in their consciousness.

In the quantum split of Flynn's mind, a moment of clarity emerged. Bob's voice echoed faintly—not as a sound, but as a feeling: You're never out of the fight.

Bob had entrusted his wealth and strategies to a diverse network: lawyers, doctors, bookies of both legal and questionable standing, and private investigators. Even the new owners of a local bank had unknowingly become part of his grand design. And in the end, Vance and his family would inherit it all.

The Letter beyond time

Back at the facility, Kenji rummaged through Bob's belongings. He found his clothes, personal effects, a curious backpack containing an advanced laptop, stealth gear, and a duffle bag holding the Beta engine—the very device that had traveled through time with Bob.

Among the items, Kenji discovered an envelope labeled Kenji the Brave, sealed behind a zipper. He carefully opened it and unfolded a handwritten note in Bob's unmistakable scrawl:

Hey kid, you were right. I saw the question in your eyes—yes, it's me, Flynn, also known as Bob the time traveler.

Honestly, just when I think I have everything figured out, I realize I don't. But hey, who's perfect? I never did get my PhD—just a lowly master's in Theoretical and Quantum Physics.

You remember the Beta engine? There are two in this timeline now. I suspect I'll be at the mountain lair, scratching my head at first. If all goes as planned, I'll be calling my wife soon—if I survive the destruction of the Alpha.

I've left you some instructions. Follow them, and more importantly, enjoy your life. I also left you some money. I trust you won't spend it all in one place.

We always saw great things in you.

In one duffle bag, you'll find the modified Beta—Beta Mk 2—the one that brought me back in time. It's stored in a protective case and marked with a submariner's dolphin insignia—my artistic handiwork. I suspect another version of me will be coming along. Please give it to him. He'll know what to do. Also, hand over the badass laptop after you retrieve the files I left for you. You and Sunday will have fun with it. The stealth gear might still fit him; it's too big for you.

There's another bag in the closet with a gift. I've learned a lot about you over the fifteen years I spent with you and Mark—a friend from the future. Please try to find him in this timeline. I've enclosed a picture, recreated by Sunday, along with his contact information. Go easy on him—he has a strange sense of humor, a lot like mine.

Kenji searched the closet and found two pristine samurai swords. He had been searching for something similar for years.

I came across these but didn't have time to wrap them. No doubt you'll take care of them. Remember—you were the only member of Team Nautilus who survived.

The second sword is for your sister. Tell her I said thanks and that she has my utmost respect. She's the stealthiest member of Team Nautilus.

Lastly, the laptop contains plans to upgrade both Betas to Mk 3, merging the capabilities of Alpha and Beta. The encrypted files are stored there—and also hidden within Sunday, though she doesn't even know it. I've left breadcrumbs in familiar places. Pass a copy of these notes to each of my twins. If my suspicions are correct, they downloaded my memory instantly—or at least as fast as the human mind can handle. Why anyone would do such a thing is beyond me. Lots of laughs.

Well, that's all I have for you, old friend. I know you'll grow into a great man. Find yourself a girl sometime—don't always hang around us. Unless, of course, you want to.

The letter ended with:

「せんせい あいしてます」(Sensei, I love you).

Bob had remembered what Kenji said to him just before he pressed the button and had learned to write it.

Kenji took a deep breath and got to work, refining the Mk 2 Beta and merging it with Alpha's calibrations to create something unparalleled: the Mk 3. This new engine—capable of teleportation and defying conventional gravity and space—stood as a testament to their combined brilliance.

Kenji smirked. "Fronz would have been proud and amazed. We've taken his vision beyond anything he could've imagined. One engine can do both. Who knew?"

As the sun dipped below the horizon, the legacy of Dr. Fronz and the bonds of Team Nautilus stood as a beacon of hope—a reminder that courage, friendship, and the pursuit of knowledge could never be extinguished.

Before his passing, Fronz dedicated his final years to securing the future of cold fusion, ensuring its widespread adoption across Europe and the United States. The energy debate that once divided nations now found common ground in this clean, inexhaustible power source.

Not surprisingly, Europe reported that its first cold fusion plant was operational, solving its energy crisis. Two more plants were under construction. Shortly after, the United States followed suit, launching successful cold fusion plants in Idaho and Texas, with thirty more states beginning construction the following month.

Fronz had anticipated that such technology could be suppressed in an instant. But he had taken precautions—numerous safeguards were in place to ensure its survival. This was his parting gift to the world.

Meanwhile, Flynn and Kenji sorted through old pictures of the team, compiling them into an online memorial.

One day, Flynn received a package from Fronz's estate. Inside was an encrypted data key. Tracing its origin, he found a set of house keys and a note:

Come see what I have in the vault for you, Captain.

With a boyish smirk and a spark of curiosity, Flynn whispered, "Oh boy."

CHAPTER THIRTY -

EIGHT

CONVERSATIONS BEYOND TIME

The media did not receive the same story as in the other timeline. Vance Cavalla, the owner of the property, and his Navy friend, Kurt Robertson, defended it against what appeared to be an espionage operation involving the CIA and the SAGA Corporation. His widow, Lilian Cavalla, remained at home mourning his death. However, the investigation did not uncover anything that had been previously reported.

The EM explosion occurred more than ten miles from the facility, and Vance was presumed dead in the blast. The CIA denied any involvement. More than ten aerial vehicle wreckages were swiftly removed. A Corsair was discovered in a nearby dirt field but mysteriously vanished within a day. Under the cover of darkness, Joshua and his Marine comrades folded its wings and transported it on a modified truck bed, concealing it within the facility's hangar, hoping it could be repaired.

Jack Wagner was found dead in his hotel room, an apparent suicide with a pistol by his side. Rumors suggested the CIA was responsible, but no evidence supported the claim, and local news outlets did not report on it.

Limited news coverage stemmed from the absence of a fabricated narrative. The legal team Bob hired, along with private investigators, successfully controlled the situation, ensuring minimal exposure to prevent further leaks.

Police visited both the facility and the Cavalla home. Joshua provided proof of ownership for the aircraft and presented the necessary documents. Meanwhile, Lilian Cavalla stayed home, safe with her grandchildren, grieving her husband's death. Reports of Bob Smith recently protecting them were unavailable, and his whereabouts remained unknown. The case was pending closure.

Kenji managed the facility with Sunday keeping watch. A glance at his offshore bank account confirmed a $1 million balance, ensuring he could cover all expenses and supplies. He also began work on a high-powered, cold fusion-powered laser design.

Joshua checked his offshore bank account and saw he had $1 million available as well. Deciding to stay, he took on responsibilities that kept him occupied, particularly as the lead in Nautilus body suit production. He also assisted Kenji with his high-powered laser project.

Both transactions were processed through the bank Bob had purchased, which was legally co-owned by Flynn and Lilian. The legitimacy of the transaction was ensured through a will executed by their attorney. Additionally, ownership of the facility was legally shared between Joshua and Kenji.

The Mountain Lair 2

Flynn B's eyes flutter open to the harsh reality of the cold, hard ground beneath him. He groans as the events of the past hours—or was it days?—flood back into his weary mind. The quantum split had been extremely taxing, and as he tries to sit up, his body protests with a sharp ache. Pushing through the discomfort, he manages to pull himself up onto the carefully stacked mountain of supplies in the corner of the mountain lair. This was his makeshift safe haven, surrounded by essentials—his laptop, favorite firearm, bags of money, and the few necessities he'd managed to pack.

A quick glance at his rugged, dust-coated watch reads 0800; he's been out the entire night. With a painful stretch and a yawn, Flynn acknowledges another urgent need—the bathroom. As he stumbles to his feet, the motion-sensitive lights flicker to life, casting a sterile glow over the lair. He shuffles toward the small, makeshift bathroom, his mind still a fog of electromagnetism, hunger, and exhaustion.

Suddenly, the zoomies buzz to life, their tiny rotors filling the lair with a steady hum as they hover around him. The drones, equipped with heat sensors and motion cameras, begin their routine scan. Sunday, monitoring the feed, reacts swiftly.

"Flynn, umm… what the hell?" Sunday's voice echoes through the built-in speakers, confusion lacing the synthetic tone. "By your heat signature, it's you, but you seem colder. Is that really you? Password, please, and fingers on the pad. You know the drill—it's your protocol."

Flynn, half-amused and half-annoyed, mutters through a dry throat, "Snicklefritz DN38416," while pressing all five fingers onto the electronic fingerprint scanner.

"Oh, okay, it is you. There's one hell of a story here. I'll listen while you call your wife."

Flynn, not joking, replies, "Sunday?!"

Sunday chirps back, “Okay, I’ll keep the line clear.” The zoomies pause their vigilant swirl around him, refocusing their camera ‘eyes’ in his direction

Navigating around the curious drones, Flynn makes his way back to a chair by the table and rummages through one of the supply bags, retrieving a temporary mobile phone.

Switching to secure comms, Flynn says, “Sunday, I don’t know how closely my family is being watched, so I can’t take any chances. I should have them pack their bags and head for a hotel out of California. Help me find a secure location—if such a thing exists.”

“I haven’t detected any immediate threats, but that’s a very wise tactical choice, Captain. How about Nevada? Carson City or Reno?” Sunday replies.

"Very good, I'll head that way and report in. Cash is ideal, and I seem to have left myself plenty," Flynn said.

He followed up, "I’ll make a quick call to Lilian."

"Roger that, Actual. This should be a great story. Can't wait to hear about Elvis," Sunday said.

"Always on and on about Elvis..." Flynn chuckled.

Sunday replied, "Thank you, thank you very much. We'll be somewhere else all week."

Flynn retrieved his wife's number from the address book, his fingers trembling slightly with a mix of anticipation and nerves.

"Hi, honey. Hey, I'm hungry—what's for dinner?" He tried to sound casual, but his voice carried the weight of his ordeal.

Lilian's response was instant, a mix of shock and relief so strong he could almost feel it through the phone. "Wait—whoa, what the…?! Are you coming home now?!"

"OK, I'll be there soon. There's so much to tell," Flynn replied, his voice steadier now. Hearing Lilian grounded him.

"Where are you?" Lilian's voice was urgent, a soft tremble betraying her fear and confusion.

"I'd best not say over the phone," Flynn assured her.

"It's time to go, honey. I need you to pack some bags for all of you. Leave the Zoomies at the house—they'll be our eyes."

"Oh shit, you're making me crazy," Lilian whispered.

"Sunday will contact you in a minute. Sorry about the secrecy—things just hit the fan," Flynn said.

"OK, OK. Like you would say—battle stations," Lilian replied.

"Attagirl. See you soon," Flynn agreed.

"Be careful," Lilian said. Then they both hung up.

The Zoomies at the lair fluttered closer, their cameras watching him with an almost sentient curiosity. "Don't worry, guys," Flynn murmured, offering them a tired but determined smile. "We're just getting started."

With that, he grabbed his pack, checked his gear, and stepped out of the lair into the early dawn light, ready to face whatever came next. The mountain air was crisp, the horizon tinged with the promise of a new beginning—a fitting backdrop for the tumultuous tale of time travel, sacrifice, and reunion that awaited him.

Sunday had already had the house checked for bugs with Lilian and the girls helping. Those little tattletales were on the case.

After overhearing Flynn's conversation, Sunday said, "Agreed. A hotel ASAP, and paying in cash is best. I found three choices in the Reno/Carson City area."

"Take the Zoomies and extra batteries with you. I suspect we're all set utilizing the lair, but don't forget to lock up—just in case," Sunday reminded him.

"Roger that, Sunday. Good call," Flynn replied.

He took a deep breath, adjusting the straps of his pack as he stood at the threshold of the lair. The cool mountain air filled his lungs, crisp with the scent of pine and earth. Dawn painted the horizon in soft hues of orange and violet—a quiet contrast to the storm of events that had led him here. He had been split—another version of him existed now—but this was his path, and he had no choice but to walk it.

He double-checked his gear: knife, spare ammunition, a bag of throwaway phones, a fresh set of clothes, and enough cash to stay off-grid for a while. With one last glance back into the dim cavern, he stepped out, feeling the weight of destiny settle onto his shoulders.

Sunday, always efficient, had already anticipated the next move. She sent the locations of three hotels in the Reno and Carson City area to both Flynn and Lilian, scrambling the transmission through multiple relays. No mistakes. No unnecessary risks.

Flynn didn't linger. Locking the lair door behind him, he climbed into the truck. The engine roared to life as he set off toward the first hotel on the list. The winding mountain roads felt familiar under his hands, but his mind was elsewhere—calculating, preparing, waiting.

Lilian's Departure

Lilian's phone vibrated on the nightstand as she zipped up the last of her bags. The screen flashed Sunday's message—three hotel addresses, each one a potential rendezvous point with Flynn.

"Alright, ladies," she called out, slipping the phone into her jacket pocket. "Time to move."

Eileen and Rosaleen, already packed, exchanged glances before hoisting their bags. The air inside the house was thick with unspoken words, tension simmering beneath the surface. They had waited long enough—it was time to go.

"I've got food and water for the dog," Eileen said, holding up the supplies.

"Thanks, honey," Lilian replied.

Forty minutes later, they were outside, loading their gear into the SUV. The vehicle was rugged, built for endurance—but more importantly, it was untraceable. No GPS. No linked accounts.

"Load up," Lilian said, gesturing to the family dog. The dog leaped into the back seat, tail wagging, nestling between the girls. She loved car rides—especially with Dad.

As the SUV rolled onto the main road, Lilian instinctively checked the rearview mirror. Nothing suspicious—yet. She pressed the gas, determined to put as much distance between them and danger before sunrise.

Her hands were steady on the wheel, but her mind raced ahead—calculating routes, alternate exits, worst-case scenarios.

"You think he's okay?" Eileen asked, breaking the silence from the back seat.

Lilian's grip on the wheel tightened slightly. "Remember how Grandad used to disappear when you turned your head, and the next second he was gone?" Her voice was firm, but there was a softness beneath it. "He'll be fine. We just have to get to him before anything else does."

Eileen and Rosaleen exchanged glances before glancing down at Lilian's phone. Three hotels, three possibilities. The game had begun. The clock was ticking.

Then, Flynn called Sunday. "I think the second hotel is the better choice. Let them know. I'm walking in now and should be checked in shortly."

"Roger that, Captain," Sunday responded.

She forwarded the address to Lilian's phone and set it as the destination. A moment later, another text arrived—the room number.

The girls moved stealthily through the hotel lobby, eyes scanning for anything out of place. They reached the room and knocked softly.

The door opened.

"Vance!" Lilian's voice caught in her throat, thick with emotion.

Eileen and Rosaleen rushed in, the dog leading the way. Their expressions mirrored their Mimi's—relief, disbelief, and overwhelming joy.

Without a word, they enveloped Flynn in a desperate embrace. He pulled them close, burying his face in Lilian's hair, feeling the warmth of his granddaughters pressed against him.

Tears mingled with smiles as they held on, unwilling to let go.

After a long moment, they loosened their grip but still clung to one another. Lilian cupped Flynn's face, her eyes shining with tears.

"You're here," she whispered.

Her voice trembled, but in that moment, everything else faded away.

"Sorry, it's not home, but it's the best I could do for now," Flynn says, his voice barely audible, overwhelmed by the presence of his family.

"It's best to keep a very low profile while we figure out our next move," he explains.

Flynn's red dog hesitates for a moment, staring at him as if making sure he's real. Then, she trots over, settling by his feet, unwilling to leave his side. "Hey, kid." Flynn reaches down, giving her a few scratches and a hug—though she's never been much of a hugger, she allows it this time.

"Let's get settled into this hotel room. I booked adjacent rooms," he says, opening the door to the next one.

They move to the living area, where Flynn sinks gratefully into the couch. His family gathers around him—Lilian sits beside him, finding his hand and squeezing it tightly. Eileen and Rosaleen cuddle up on either side, their eyes full of curiosity, eager to hear his story.

Flynn takes a deep breath, scanning the faces of his loved ones, drawing strength from their unwavering attention. "It's been... quite a journey," he begins, his voice steady but tired. "After the sky battle with my Corsair..." He pauses, the memory vivid and harrowing. He walks them through how it all unfolded but soon stops, taking a deep breath before continuing.

Lilian nods, encouraging him. "What happened, Vance?"

Vance swallows hard, Kurt's sacrifice flashing before his eyes. "Kurt... he saved me. We were outnumbered, outgunned—our WWII fighters against two squads of helicopters and two F-16s. It was a furious battle, one I'll have to write down in detail someday. Looking back, it was unbelievable." He exhales sharply, shaking his head. "I pulled off that slide maneuver I told you about—my god, it was insane. But the plane... I think she's beyond saving. That old fiery angel gave it everything she had. She was a great plane."

His voice falters. "But Kurt... he said, 'I choose you.' And then a missile hit him. I think he intercepted it on purpose—he was right behind me." Flynn's voice breaks, grief seeping into every word.

He pushes forward, giving them the quick version of the story while they remain too wired to sleep.

The room falls silent, save for the crackling fireplace, as Flynn recounts everything—the battle, the strategic maneuvers, and the final moments of Kurt's life. How he diverted enemy fire, ensuring Flynn's escape.

"And because of him... and the team... I made it back to you," Flynn concludes, his voice laced with both gratitude and sorrow.

Lilian squeezes his hand tighter, resting her head against his shoulder. "He was a good man," she murmured, a tear slipping down her cheek.

"He was the best. We took out five helicopters together. And the F-16 that had me in its sights? Let's just say it didn't make it. The Alpha engine was incredible, though I'm still piecing it together. I'll write it all down," Flynn said, his voice thick with emotion. His eyes glistened as he looked at his granddaughters. "I want you both to remember—there are heroes in this world. Kurt was one of them."

Eileen nodded, absorbing the weight of his words, a tearful smile forming. Rosaleen snuggled closer, her young mind grappling with the meaning of sacrifice and heroism.

The family spent the afternoon and evening in quiet conversation, Flynn sharing more stories while they processed the events together. As night deepened, a sense of peace settled over them—the kind forged through hardship and love.

Lilian sat beside him, their hands clasped, the burden of his past adventures feeling just a little lighter in the warmth of his family's presence.

Eventually, they prepared for bed, the large hotel room hushed except for the soft sounds of movement. Though exhausted, Flynn felt a profound sense of relief and belonging as he climbed into bed beside his wife.

His final thoughts before sleep were of gratitude—for survival, for family, for love.

The next morning, Lilian stirred awake to Flynn's voice.

"Honey, I'll be calling Kenji soon—there are a few things to square away. We also need to figure out our plan, considering the world thinks I'm scattered across a field from that explosion."

Lilian sighed, stretching. "You'll have to fill in the blanks on that explosion. But not before coffee, please."

Flynn grinned. "Already got you covered. The girls are making breakfast and will bring some up for us."

"Good man," Lilian murmured, accepting the cup.

As she sipped, Flynn settled at the small desk in the corner of the hotel room, his laptop screen casting a dim glow on his face. Their granddaughters were still asleep in the adjoining room, and Lilian sat nearby, reading quietly.

His mission for the day was clear: find a safe, private temporary estate in Florida. With a few clicks, he pulled up virtual tours of properties in the Tampa Bay area.

He leaned back, rubbing his chin as he flipped through listings. "Privacy is key," he muttered. "No prying eyes. Plenty of space to work."

After an hour of searching, he found it—a secluded property on the outskirts of Tampa, surrounded by dense greenery and free from nosy neighbors. It had ample space for vehicles, secure storage for their belongings, and even a detached garage for their equipment.

Satisfied, he dialed Kenji. As the phone rang, he leaned back in his chair, organizing his thoughts.

"Flynn!" Kenji's voice came through, cheerful but groggy.

"Kenji, hey. Got a minute? Didn't mean to wake you. I want your input on a property down in Tampa—secluded, plenty of space. If we grab it, we might just hand it off to you when we're done. Consider it a gift for all the crap you've had to put up with."

Kenji chuckled. "I'll take it. Let me see the specs."

Flynn emailed him the listing and continued. "But there's another question. I've been thinking about using Beta Mark 2 for the jump. I know Beta can move me through time, but if I have a GPS location and a picture of the spot to match in the window, can we fine-tune it to land us exactly there? Can we map it?"

Kenji paused, the sound of his keyboard clacking faintly in the background. "Theoretically, yes. Beta Mark 2's spatial calibration is more advanced than the Mark 1.5, but you'd need more than just GPS and a picture. I'd have to map the area and feed that data into Beta. We could design a custom algorithm to triangulate multiple destinations."

Flynn nodded. "Good. Let's get that set up. The less traditional travel I do, the better."

Kenji's voice turned serious. "Just be careful, Flynn. Beta's accuracy has improved, but this kind of jump is still risky. If the algorithm's even slightly off, you could end up miles away—or worse."

"Understood," Flynn said with a smirk. "That's why I've got you, genius. Let's make it happen."

With the property picked and a plan forming, Flynn knew they were one step closer to securing their new life in Florida.

The girls went for a swim after breakfast while Flynn and Lilian sat down for a brainstorming session.

"I'm looking at houses in Florida. I found one, but I can't fly there, so I'm talking to Kenji about whether Beta Mark 2 can take me instead," Flynn said. He added, "I'll send you the virtual tour."

Lilian exhaled slowly, her shoulders loosening slightly. "Good. We need a place to settle, even if just temporarily. The girls… they deserve some normalcy. Their mom and dad are in Europe on a well-paid job."

A knock at the hotel door interrupted them. Lilian answered with a smile. "Hey, kid."

Kenji stepped inside, nodding toward Flynn.

Flynn smirked. "How'd you get here so fast? Like a ninja."

Kenji grinned. "Trade secrets, sensei."

Kenji adjusted the parameters on Beta Mark 1.5, using the window for map creation. His fingers flew across the keyboard as the faint hum of the engine filled the lair. A shimmering window materialized before them, revealing the faint outline of a house—a modest property surrounded by trees, offering the privacy they desperately needed.

"Hold on," Kenji muttered, tweaking the algorithm. The image stabilized, revealing the living room's interior. "There. That's the one."

Flynn peered through the portal, his sharp eyes scanning the room. "Looks solid. Let's test it."

Kenji picked up a small test device—a weighted cylinder with a tracking chip—and tossed it through the window. The team watched as it vanished for a moment before reappearing inside the house, bouncing onto the wooden floor with a satisfying thunk.

Kenji checked the monitor and grinned. "It's there. Signal's stable."

Flynn nodded, his expression determined. "Alright. We've got our target. Let's map the area before making the jump. No sense in taking unnecessary risks."

"Now for the Mk 2 algorithm," Flynn said, fingers flying over the keyboard. "We'll tweak it for this timeline—removing the time travel section entirely."

A few more keystrokes, and Flynn nodded in satisfaction. "There… Alright, buddy, let's save this as 'Teleport-Only' mode. I have a feeling this will come in handy."

Kenji smirked. "You were there with Bob? That must've been one hell of a show."

Flynn chuckled. "I'm sure it was."

The next evening, Flynn made the solo trip through the portal. Stepping into the house, he conducted a thorough walkthrough, inspecting the rooms, layout, and surrounding property. Satisfied with its security and potential, he contacted a real estate agent through one of their alias companies.

Flynn transferred funds to secure the property under their new holding company, The Atlantis Group. He made calls to Bob's attorney and accounting teams—who were now taking his calls. By the end of the day, the deal was sealed. A clean bank transfer ensured the transaction remained discreet.

"It's ours," he announced. "We're officially Floridians."

Kenji leaned back in his chair with a smirk. "Welcome to the Sunshine State."

Flynn clapped his hands together, his tone lighter than it had been in weeks. "Time to pack up." The team was one step closer to their fresh start.

The girls greeted Kenji with a hug.

Rosaleen glanced at Mimi, frowning. "What's going on? Why are you looking at us like that?"

Granddad grinned. "Hey, kids, wanna go for a ride?"

"Umm… okay?" Eileen replied hesitantly.

They followed Granddad and Mimi into the room, where Beta hummed softly as Kenji worked on his laptop.

"I've already mapped the room, so getting back will be a snap," Kenji said without looking up.

Granddad motioned them forward. "Come on, girls, it'll be fun. We're all going. We'll check back in later."

Flynn clapped his hands together, a broad grin spreading across his face. With Beta positioned in the center of the marked area, he said, "Alright, everyone, step into the circle. Time to check out our new digs in Florida!"

Rosaleen looked up at Flynn, her curiosity outweighing her nerves. "You're sure it's safe, Granddad?"

Flynn winked. "Trust me, honey, Kenji and I tested it a million times—at least, I think we did." He made a mock-crazy face. "And hey, I've already been there—the place is great! Big kitchen, triple-car garage, and a pool."

The reassurance worked. With a final glance at each other, the girls stepped into the marked area alongside their family. Flynn shot Kenji a thumbs-up.

Kenji tapped a few keys on his tablet, the Beta engine responding with a gentle surge of power. The blue light intensified but remained soft, like moonlight shimmering on water. "Coordinates locked. Everyone ready?"

"Yes!" the girls said in unison, though their voices wavered with a mix of excitement and nervousness.

Kenji grinned. "Let's roll."

The air around them hummed, the light enveloping them in a warm, tingling embrace. There was no pain, no blinding flash like Bob had experienced with time travel—just the sensation of stepping through a gentle waterfall as the world around them dissolved into the blue glow.

When the light faded, they stood in the living room of their new Florida home. The air was warmer, carrying the faint scent of salt from the nearby coast.

Eileen spun around, taking in the cozy space. "That was awesome!"

Rosaleen grinned, tugging at Flynn's arm. "Granddad, can we do it again?"

Lilian laughed, smoothing her dress. "Maybe later. Let's settle in first."

Kenji stepped forward, inspecting the room with a satisfied nod. "Landing was clean. No distortion. Beta's ready for more. I've set up the reverse coordinates in case we need to head back."

Flynn beamed at his family. "Welcome home, everyone. Let's get unpacked and start our new adventure."

That night, Flynn and Kenji made another jump, retrieving their belongings from their hotel room in Nevada. They left the digital keys on the counter, checked out remotely, and returned seamlessly to the rented rooms near the Florida house. With each trip, teleportation became less of a marvel and more of a reliable tool.

For now, they left most of the furniture behind at the old house.

Lilian secured a nearby hotel room where they would stay while movers brought in new furniture. They treated this as a short-term transition while they searched for a permanent home. Flynn and Lilian both had their own set of prerequisites.

Later, Flynn and Kenji retrieved all their belongings from the hotel and jumped back, regrouping with the others in the three adjoining rooms Lilian had rented for the week.

CHAPTER THIRTY - NINE

LEGACY OF THE BRAVE

The soft chime of the secure app brought the screen to life. Flynn leaned back in his chair in the hotel room, a small smile creeping onto his face as Fronz's familiar image appeared. Seated in his cozy living room, Fronz was bathed in the warm hues of the European sunset streaming through large windows behind him. The golden light cast a serene glow over the room, illuminating shelves lined with books, scientific journals, and mementos of a life rich with adventure and discovery.

"Flynn, my old friend," Fronz greeted, his voice warm and welcoming. "Still as punctual as ever. I was just finishing a glass of this delightful French Bordeaux. You'd love it—smooth, with just the right kick at the end."

Flynn chuckled, settling into his seat. "And here I thought you'd be deep in a lab or tinkering with something. But no, you're sipping wine and enjoying sunsets. Retirement suits you, Benedict."

Fronz smirked at the mention of his middle name, amusement crinkling the edges of his eyes. "Even I know when it's time to step back and let the young ones do the heavy lifting. Besides, this house—magnifique! A dream come true. Quiet, remote, yet close enough to civilization when I need it. How's the chaos on your end?"

Before Flynn could answer, the screen split, signaling Joshua's arrival. "Evening, gents. Fronz, you look far too relaxed."

"I could say the same for you," Fronz replied with a grin.

Moments later, Kenji joined, adjusting his camera. "Sorry, had to finish something up. Fronz, that view behind you looks fake. Is that real?"

"It's very real, Kenji," Fronz said, gesturing toward the window. "Europe's been kind to me. A far cry from our mountain lair or those battles with SAGA. I think you'd all enjoy a visit."

Flynn leaned forward, his tone light but sincere. "Don't tempt me. I might show up with Lilian and the girls. You might regret offering."

"Never," Fronz said with a chuckle. "The more, the merrier. This place was built for company. Though I'll admit, it's quiet without all of you running around. My brother is here, but he's quiet too."

The casual banter flowed easily, threading through memories of past adventures and the simple joys of life. For a fleeting moment, it felt as if they had never left the camaraderie of their shared mission. But beneath the surface, there was a heaviness to Fronz's gaze—an unspoken truth he was preparing to reveal, waiting for the right moment.

"Alright, team. I have news, and I'd like to get straight to it," Fronz announced.

He turned to Flynn, his voice steady but weighted. "There's something you should know about Kurt. His last battle wasn't just about fighting alongside you—it was his farewell. He had prostate cancer, and it had spread aggressively. He confided in me at the doctor's office, of all places."

Fronz exhaled before continuing. "He lost his wife the same way—cancer. Your call pulled him out of a deep depression, Flynn. He was grateful he answered the phone that day. He thought he had more time to tell you himself."

Flynn, stunned by the revelation, listened in silence as Fronz's words settled like a heavy weight between them.

On a large screen, Kenji and Joshua appeared, their faces marked by sorrow and reverence. Though miles apart, their presence was as real as if they stood in the room.

Fronz pressed on. "Kurt wanted to go out on his own terms, in battle, alongside his shipmate—not in the slow, cruel grip of illness. He made peace with his fate, ensured his family's future, and joined you in that final flight with no regrets."

The air thickened with unspoken emotions as Flynn absorbed the truth. Kurt's final stand wasn't just about bravery—it was about reclaiming control over his own ending.

Flynn's voice was quiet but resolute. "His choice... it was courageous. Honorable."

As the conversation unfolded, Fronz shifted the weight of the moment onto himself. This time, his battle wasn't against an enemy they had fought together, but something far more personal.

"My time is borrowed, Flynn," he admitted. "Lung cancer has its grip on me too. I suppose, in a way, Kurt and I shared more than just our passion for science and striving to be the best."

"As I reflect on those days beside both Zone Engines, I remember feeling revitalized—for years, even—but it never lasted. Without what I call the 'Zone Effect,' I wouldn't have survived this long," Fronz said.

Flynn, shaken by the weight of Fronz's confession, searched for words that could honor his mentor's profound influence.

Kenji spoke first. "Dr. Fronz, your mentorship has been the foundation of my growth. Your relentless pursuit of the unknown, tempered by wisdom and humility, has been our guiding light."

Joshua, ever the steadfast protector, nodded in solemn agreement. His usually stoic demeanor softened as he added, "You taught us more than science, Fronz. You showed us the value of integrity, courage, and, above all, the strength found in unity."

Seated in an armchair that seemed to cradle him with the same warmth he had given others, Fronz offered a weak yet genuine smile. His eyes, brimming with unshed tears, reflected a lifetime of discovery and wonder.

"Fronz," Flynn said, "your brilliance, your creativity... Your legacy isn't just in the discoveries we've made. It's in the lives you've touched—including mine."

Fronz chuckled lightly. "Do you remember, back in the early days, how we struggled with the calibrations? The countless failures that nearly broke us?"

They all nodded, the memories flooding back—the frustration, the sleepless nights, the moments they nearly abandoned everything.

Flynn exhaled. "It was a nightmare. We were convinced we were chasing ghosts. Then, the equations and symbols on the whiteboards—appearing almost as if a possessed hand had written them—guided us to the breakthrough we needed."

The air in the room grew heavy, thick with unspoken thoughts, the eerie sensation that something unseen had been with them, guiding their hands when all seemed lost.

Fronz's voice dropped to a near whisper. "I've thought about that moment for years. The information on those whiteboards—the precision of it—was beyond anything we could have conceived alone. I believe we weren't working in isolation. That maybe… we had help."

The silence stretched, charged with possibilities.

Flynn's eyes widened. "You mean to say… extraterrestrials played a role in our research?" He smiled faintly, his gaze drifting as if recalling something just beyond reach.

"That sounds like something straight out of a sci-fi novel, Fronz."

Fronz smiled, a twinkle in his eye belying the seriousness of his proposal.

"Consider the evidence, Flynn," Fronz said. "The sudden appearance of the math, its uncanny accuracy, and the timing. It's as if an unseen mentor—one with knowledge far beyond our own—was nudging us toward success."

Once spoken aloud, the notion took on a life of its own, the pieces of the puzzle aligning in a pattern that was as unsettling as it was exhilarating.

"If that's true," Flynn replied, "then we owe a great debt to our cosmic benefactors. Without that 'nudge,' Alpha and Beta might have remained nothing more than unrealized dreams."

Their conversation drifted through the implications of this revelation, weaving through science, philosophy, and humanity's timeless fascination with the stars—and with the possibility of life beyond Earth.

"Perhaps it's a reminder," Fronz mused, "that we're not alone in this vast universe. That our thirst for knowledge, our drive to push boundaries, resonates across the cosmos. Do we even have original ideas at all?"

Flynn's breath caught as a memory surfaced—Bob had told him about this. He had met Sotra.

"Wait—whoa," Flynn murmured, the recollection flooding back. "A Benevolent Pleiadian woman. I remember now. She was tall, beautiful, with long white hair... and so peaceful."

He could hear her voice as if she were standing right beside him:

"You're not just fixing your mistakes; you're giving your family a future. A future that, I feel, would be very different if you hadn't come back."

"Thank you," Sotra had whispered, stepping closer. "For everything."

Flynn's breath hitched. "Oh my God—I remember her name."

"This makes perfect sense," Fronz said, laughing. "The mind is a terrible thing. Maybe this is why they've stayed hidden so long—because the memory of them fades..."

Flynn nodded, his gaze distant.

Fronz's expression softened as he spoke again, his voice steady but quiet. "This was my final contribution, Flynn. A world freed from the chains of old technology. The internal combustion engine is over a century old. And at the risk of sounding like a flaming liberal, it's just so damned inefficient. The future I envisioned is one where our planet operates more efficiently. It's not perfect, but it's a start. And I know you'll see it through."

Flynn's brow furrowed as he leaned closer to the camera. "Fronz, what you've done—it's not just a start. You've changed everything. The way we power our world, the way we see it, the way we see ourselves. The future you've set in motion will need time for the infrastructure to catch up."

Fronz smiled, the corners of his eyes crinkling, but Flynn could see the fatigue in his face—the weight of a life well lived.

"I didn't do it alone," Fronz said, his voice tinged with affection. "You, the team, all of you—you were the spark. You kept the fire burning when I thought it might go out."

A quiet moment passed between them, their connection just as strong in silence as in words.

"I'm glad I got to hear your voice tonight, Flynn," Fronz said at last, his tone both wistful and content. "It's comforting to know the story will live on—through you, through everyone we've touched."

Flynn swallowed hard, his throat tightening. "The story of our journey won't just live on, Fronz—it'll inspire. You're more than a friend. You're family. And I'll carry this torch forward."

Fronz's eyes glistened with tears, though his smile remained. "Goodnight, old friend. It's been one hell of a ride."

"Goodnight, Doc," Flynn replied, his voice steady but heavy with unspoken emotion.

As the call ended, Fronz leaned back in his chair, the soft glow of a single lamp casting long shadows across the room. He gazed out the window at the star-strewn sky, his breaths slowing as peace settled over him. That night, as the world slept, Fronz slipped away—leaving behind a legacy that would shape the future.

Passing of the torch

Flynn traveled alone to see Joshua, settling into the cozy living room of their California home. The soft glow of the evening sun filtered through the blinds, casting long shadows across the room. Joshua sat across from him, leaning forward on the edge of his seat, his expression a mix of concern and determination. The only sound between them was the wind drifting through the open windows as Flynn gathered his thoughts.

"Josh," Flynn began, his voice steady but weighted with emotion. "I need you to take over Team Nautilus. Officially. With everything that's happened, I can't be here much anymore—not physically. My face is too recognizable. Dead men don't get to run companies."

Joshua nodded, his brow furrowed. "I've been thinking the same thing. California isn't exactly the best place for scaling production. The economy here... it's just not sustainable. But trust—that's the real challenge. Finding the right people to move forward with? That's a gamble."

Flynn leaned back, rubbing his temples. "That's why it has to be you. You've been with me through everything. You know the facility inside and out. You're the only one I trust to make the right calls. Lilian and I have moved to Florida—it's safer there. But I need to know the team is in good hands."

Joshua exhaled, leaning back in his chair. "I'll do it, Flynn. You know I've got your back. But relocating the operation? That's going to take some groundwork. I'll scout out a few states—maybe Texas or Tennessee. Friendlier economies, fewer regulations."

Flynn nodded. "That's the move. But don't rush it. Keep everything running here in the meantime. And thanks for keeping an eye on the house."

Joshua smirked faintly. "The house? More like my crash pad at this point. I've stayed in the spare room so much, I might as well start paying rent. Those zoomies—silent, ever-watchful little devils."

Flynn chuckled, the tension easing slightly. "Good. It's still home to us, even if we can't live there anymore. Keep it standing, will you?"

Joshua's expression grew serious again. "You built something incredible, Flynn. Don't worry—I won't let anyone screw this up. Team Nautilus is solid, and I'll make sure it stays that way."

Flynn stood, extending his hand. "I know you will, brother. Just keep me updated when you can. And take care of this place."

Joshua rose, gripping Flynn's hand firmly. "Always. You focus on Florida, and I'll handle everything else."

"Oh, and I recovered the battle-worn Warbird," Joshua added. "She's in rough shape, but it's a project we're willing to take on. Good call making me part owner—I was able to pick her up."

Flynn's eyes widened. "Holy shit. She made it? That's incredible. Tough old girl. See what you can do—much appreciated, brother."

As the two men shared a moment of mutual respect, the weight of what lay ahead settled between them. Flynn was leaving a piece of his life behind, but he knew it was in the best possible hands.

CHAPTER FORTY

A COSMIC GUARDIAN

In a world where the boundaries of science and the unknown blur, an extraordinary encounter unfolds, marking the beginning of an adventure that transcends time and space.

In a serene garden bathed in the soft light of dusk, two young girls, Eileen and Rosaleen, find themselves face to face with a being beyond their wildest imaginations.

Sotra approached with a graceful stride, her presence both otherworldly and reassuring. "Greetings, young ones. I am Sotra. There is a journey ahead—one that requires your bravery. Will you join me in saving someone very dear?"

Eileen hesitated. "Um… okay? But—what happened? Who needs saving? Sissy, what did you do?"

Rosaleen turned to her sister, her wide eyes filled with confusion.

With a gentle smile that seemed to illuminate the dimming garden, Sotra placed a hand on each of their shoulders, infusing them with a sense of courage and calm.

"Your granddad has embarked on a crucial quest—one where he could use the strength of his granddaughters. Fear not, for I will be your guide and guardian."

Initially startled by Sotra's towering nine-foot frame and ethereal presence, the girls felt an inexplicable sense of peace wash over them. Their fear melted away, replaced by curiosity and a quiet determination.

Rosaleen called out over her shoulder, "We'll be right back, Mimi!"

Mimi, preoccupied with unpacking, barely registered her words. Sotra's presence carried a soothing resonance, making the unbelievable seem almost ordinary. Before Mimi could react, the very fabric of reality twisted—a shimmering portal opening before them.

"Okay, let's go, girls." Sotra stepped through first, a silent reassurance that there was nothing to fear.

Hand in hand, the sisters moved toward the portal, gripping each other tightly as the luminous light swallowed them.

Mimi, suddenly snapping to attention, turned. "Wait, what? Girls?"

But her words faded into the ether as the portal sealed behind them, leaving no trace of their departure—except for the lingering echo of their promise.

"Why do I feel like I'm being watched?" Lilian muttered, glancing around. "Eileen? Rosaleen?"

The calming aura Sotra had woven around the girls still lingered in the air, casting a subtle veil over reality.

Sotra now stood with Eileen and Rosaleen in her dimension, her shimmering form merging with the light of the portal. Her voice carried an ethereal serenity as she revealed her purpose.

"I have watched your world," she began, her gaze resting gently on the sisters. "You stand on the brink of extraordinary achievements, yet remain bound by limitations my dimension has long since surpassed. Your grandfather, Flynn, has touched the essence of what is possible. And so have you."

Eileen frowned. "But why us? Why not someone older—someone more experienced?"

Sotra's faint smile carried the weight of wisdom. "Your youth is your greatest strength. The adaptability of your minds, your willingness to see beyond the rigid structures of your reality—it makes you ideal candidates. My dimension will challenge everything you know, but it will also grant you knowledge and understanding that your world desperately needs."

Rosaleen cast a wary glance at the glowing portal. "And Grandad? What happens to him?"

Sotra's expression turned solemn. "There are two of him now. We will cross over to your world and reunite with your family. The Flynn you know—your granddad—awaits you alongside Mimi. But Flynn A, the man standing here, has spent far more time in my dimension. He has been gifted with the same knowledge you will soon acquire. You will see it in his form, hear it in his voice. Together, you will witness the beauty and challenges of my world—and serve as its ambassadors."

Eileen took a steady step forward. "And what happens to us in this dimension?"

Sotra's voice carried both promise and mystery. "You will grow—not just in knowledge, but in spirit. My race does not suffer from disease or age as you understand it. The energies of this realm sustain life in ways your world has yet to comprehend. Here, time stretches and contracts, light bends and weaves. It is a place where the impossible becomes natural."

The sisters exchanged a glance, their expressions a blend of apprehension and anticipation.

Plans were swiftly set in motion, a sanctuary prepared—a place untouched by the echoes of their past.

Illumination

Kenji realizes that the new Flynn remembers—probably more than he does. All that knowledge, experience, and time spent as Bob over the last fifteen years now reside within him.

Kenji retrieves the Beta 1 Mk 1 engine from the lair and presents it to the team.

"I found plans to upgrade the Betas to Mk 3, combining Alpha and Beta," Kenji says. "I've already started modifying the older Beta."

They place both Betas side by side—the Beta 1 Mk 1 from the lair and Beta Mk 2, modified by Bob, now bearing the Submariner Dolphins emblem on its side.

Flynn B's eyes widen in shock as he listens to Kenji's explanation.

"Listen to them," Kenji says. "That hum coming from the Betas—you can feel it."

Bob was Flynn, fifteen years in the future. After discovering the truth—the power he wielded—he took on the ultimate responsibility: setting things right. In his battle to reclaim his soul, he ensured his family and team benefited along the way. He loved them all.

"So some serious shit must've gone down in another timeline," Kenji continues. "He even earned a Master's in Quantum Physics just to modify Beta to Mk 2. Man, don't think about this too hard—it's a headache waiting to happen."

Kenji hands Flynn the note Bob left behind, the handwriting unmistakably familiar.

"That tricky bastard," Flynn mutters, then bursts out laughing. "What an asshole. No way—okay, I get it now. I had to do it that way for all this insanity to unfold. But damn."

He pauses, processing.

"My god, he must've planned it for years. All those sleepless nights, bottles of Jameson… I remember the food, too. Sunday helped—oh wait, and you, Kenji?! What about Joshua?" Flynn's eyes dart as the realization sets in. "Holy krikey, mate. This is insane. How do I even know this? Oh, right—Quantum."

As he speaks, Flynn bonks his own head in amusement.

"I'm gonna need a shrink to untangle this mess. No, wait—that might disrupt the timelines. Universe imploding and all that. Nah, never mind."

Kenji shakes his head. "Bob thinks another Flynn will show up sooner or later. Quantum particles and all that—mind-boggling stuff."

Flynn grins. "Elementary, my dear boy. Elementary."

Kenji, ever the innovator, shifts gears. He shares his vision for the laser design—more than just a weapon or a tool, but a key to unlocking doors they've yet to find.

"This laser I've been tinkering with… it's something else entirely," Kenji says.

"The proud papa," Flynn remarks with a smirk.

As Flynn B prepares to step into the unknown once more, Lilian by his side, he feels it—his mind syncing with hers at an accelerated rate. The thought of reuniting with Eileen and Rosaleen lingers on the horizon. The legacy of Team Nautilus stands as a testament to human ingenuity, the unbreakable bonds of family, and the unseen forces guiding their path.

Amidst surreal landscapes beyond comprehension—where nebulous forms drift in an iridescent dance—Flynn A and his granddaughters immerse themselves in Sotra's teachings.

Here, in this dimension of infinite possibilities, they explore the depths of consciousness, each lesson bringing them closer to higher awareness. Time moves slower in Sotra's domain, a reminder of the fluidity of existence.

The environment pulses with untapped potential. The air hums with energy, the flora and fauna exuding an otherworldly vibrancy. In this space, thoughts manifest with clarity, and the barriers of the physical form dissolve into pure being.

As Flynn A's time in Sotra's dimension nears its end, the transformation is undeniable. The years of wear and hardship fall away. His body is restored to youthful vigor—his hair, once thinning, now flows rich and full. The wrinkles vanish, the dark circles under his eyes disappear. His posture straightens, his skin regains its vitality.

Flynn A stands renewed, a man unburdened by the past, stepping forward into the unknown.

The Return

Sotra's portal shimmered with an iridescent glow, a swirling gateway pulsating with the energy of countless dimensions. Flynn A stood at its edge, holding the hands of his granddaughters, Eileen and Rosaleen, in a firm but gentle grasp. He gave them a reassuring smile, his rejuvenated features betraying none of the exhaustion he had carried into Sotra's dimension.

"Let's step through together," he said, his voice steady yet laced with anticipation.

With a deep breath, they crossed back into the familiar reality of Earth, Sotra following silently behind. The portal sealed itself with a soft hum, leaving them bathed in the warm light of their home dimension.

Eileen and Rosaleen gasped as they took in their grandfather's transformed appearance. His face was smooth, his energy vibrant. Even his once-thinning hair, now thick and full, gleamed under the sun.

"Granddad," Eileen breathed, eyes wide. "You look… amazing! Your hair, your body—it's like you've stepped back in time!"

"And the bald spot!" Rosaleen added, her voice brimming with awe. "It's gone!"

Flynn A let out a hearty laugh, the sound rich with joy and gratitude. "Oh, kids, it's not just the hairline. That place—it doesn't just restore the body; it restores the spirit. I feel alive in ways I haven't in decades—maybe ever." He touched his head with mock astonishment. "And yes, the hair's a nice bonus."

Rosaleen twirled, giggling. "I feel sparkly!"

Eileen grinned. "I feel like a million bucks! Woo!"

Their laughter rang through the air as Flynn A knelt, pulling them into a warm embrace. "The adventure we had—it's beyond words. Sotra's dimension… well, we'll need to find a better name for it. But that place… it's something else. You feel it, don't you? That energy?"

Both girls nodded eagerly, their faces alight with excitement.

"We have so much to tell Mimi!" Rosaleen exclaimed, practically bouncing. "She won't believe her eyes when she sees you!"

As Flynn A rose, his gaze shifted, and his breath hitched. Across the way, Flynn B stood beside Mimi. The sight of himself, marked by time in ways he no longer was, stirred a profound mix of emotions—recognition, gratitude, and a twinge of sorrow for who he had once been.

With a quiet smile of acceptance, Flynn A turned back to his granddaughters. "Let's not keep the family waiting. We've got a lot to share."

The trio strode forward, their journey to Sotra's dimension not just an adventure but a transformation—one that had returned them to Earth with renewed purpose and unbreakable bonds.

In the shifting currents of the new Timeline, the complexities of quantum mechanics wove their way into the lives of Flynn A and Flynn B, creating a reality as bewildering as it was profound. Against the serene backdrop of their estate—with its rolling waves and sun-drenched shores—a reunion unfolded, challenging the very notions of identity and existence.

Flynn A, upon seeing the family, said, "Is that... me? Man, I've changed. Did I gain weight in this dimension, or did I lose it in the other one?"

He paused, reflecting. Fronz had taught him a lot about this possibility.

"Wait… I have about a hundred questions for Sotra. That tricky Pleiadian. Oh my God, she's been here the whole time. Was she 9 feet? 12? I don't even know..." Flynn B said, his mind racing.

The contemplation that followed was a journey in itself—a delicate balancing act between curiosity and caution. Flynn A, with Sotra's teachings fresh in his mind, chose patience, deciding to observe from a distance rather than immediately disrupting the delicate structure of his counterpart's life.

Meanwhile, the granddaughters, perceptive and unburdened by the reservations that come with age, approached Flynn B with the unfiltered honesty of youth.

Both Flynns stood nearby, eyeing each other across a short distance.

Flynn B, Eileen, and Rosaleen, with the boundless love of grandchildren, remained unfazed by the anomaly. To them, Granddad was Granddad.

“Granddad, you've got to hear this! We met someone just like you in Sotra's dimension. Well, he’s you, but not grey and not... older, sorry. But you don’t look as old as Uncle Bob. Oh, where did he go?”

“Good question,” Lilian replied.

She thought for a moment, then said, “Wait a second, honey. I think it’s all falling into place.”

Flynn B nodded slowly. “I see, honey. I’m looking right at him.” He exhaled, shaking his head. “A twin, you say? And he’s been gallivanting across dimensions with Sotra? Oh wow... I guess we’ve been living this for a while now.”

The ensuing conversation was one of wonder, laughter, and the occasional furrowed brow as Flynn B tried to comprehend the existence of his younger, interdimensional counterpart.

"Yeah, Granddad!" Eileen and Rosaleen chimed in. "And he had this calm about him, like he knows something we don't."

The notion of an inner peace—a serenity that Flynn A possessed—resonated with Flynn B. It was a reminder of paths not taken, choices that diverged and converged within the quantum realm.

Flynn B smirked. "Inner peace, huh? Well, I suppose traveling through dimensions with someone like Sotra would do that to you. Quantum physics, kids. It's the stuff of miracles, mysteries, and magnets."

As the conversation unfolded, the family found itself at the crossroads of the ordinary and the extraordinary. The presence of Flynn A, even at a short distance, and the granddaughters' stories wove a new layer of wonder into their lives.

"Oh, when we thought you died, we named a star after you," Eileen and Rosaleen said, showing him the coordinates. "We named it Vance 19. Your star, Granddad. May it light the way when you need it."

With a heartfelt group hug, Flynn B smiled. "Thank you, honeys. So smart, so sweet."

The girls exchanged a knowing glance and giggled—each Granddad had given the exact same response.

"It's so trippy, Granddad," they said. "Like, how can there be two of you? And if you're here, and he's here, then who's the real Granddad?"

The question, posed with childlike innocence, lingered in the air—a riddle wrapped in the enigma of quantum duplicity.

Flynn B chuckled. "Well, I guess we're both the 'real' Granddad. Quantum physics doesn't play by the rules we're used to. But no matter how strange it gets, know that we're here for you. Always."

At last, both Flynns walked toward each other and took their seats at the large backyard table, sitting across from one another. Their conversation continued, punctuated by the faint hum of the Beta engines in the background.

Flynn A, younger in appearance and revitalized from his time in Sotra's dimension, leaned forward, his expression thoughtful. Across from him, Flynn B, older and battle-worn, mirrored his posture, his eyes carrying the weight of sacrifices made to bring them both here.

"You remember Bob, don't you?" Flynn A asked, his voice low, filled with reverence.

Flynn B nodded, a faint smile tugging at his lips. "How could I forget? He was us in every way that mattered. And he bore the burden so we could be here now. The work he did… it's almost beyond comprehension."

Flynn A chuckled, admiration in his tone. "Almost? That man—us—pulled off the impossible. A master's in quantum physics while juggling everything else. Running the team, upgrading Beta, staying two steps ahead of SAGA with Fronz—God rest his soul—and Kenji. And somehow, he still managed to leave us a legacy that saved everyone we care about."

Flynn B's gaze turned distant. "Lilian, the girls, Joshua… even our dog—she's so happy to see them again. Every move Bob made, every sacrifice, it was all for them. He knew what was at stake when he jumped the timeline, and he never hesitated. Can you imagine that level of discipline?"

Flynn B exhaled sharply, shaking his head. "That jump hurt like hell. Note to self—never doing that again."

"Likewise," Flynn A muttered with a smirk.

Then, after a moment, he nodded, his voice thick with emotion. "It wasn't just discipline. It was love. For them. For us.

He endured it all—the grueling education, the relentless setbacks, the battle to outmaneuver SAGA. And he never lost sight of what truly mattered. I don't know if I could've done it."

"But you did," Flynn B said firmly. "We did. Bob was us, remember? Every ounce of grit, every bit of determination—it's in us, too. We just had to pick up where he left off."

A silence settled between them, heavy with unspoken gratitude.

Flynn B finally spoke, his voice softer now. "He saved everyone, Flynn. And now, it's our turn to make sure his sacrifice wasn't in vain."

Flynn A met his gaze, a determined glint in his eye. "For Bob, and for everyone else. Let's make it count."

They clasped hands across the table, bound not just by shared identity but by the legacy of the man who paved the way for their future. Together, they vowed to honor Bob's work, his sacrifices, and his unwavering love.

After a beat, Flynn A's expression turned serious. "I'm leaving it to you to take care of our… wife."

Flynn B exhaled, relieved the subject was finally on the table. "I was wondering how to bring that up."

"You'll build a new life here, in this dimension," Flynn A continued. "I think my journey is taking me elsewhere. She'll be happy, and I'll see where tomorrow takes me. Strangely enough, it feels clear. Weird, but clear."

Flynn B shook his head, laughing. "You're a freak show."

Flynn A laughed with him, the weight of their conversation momentarily lifted.

CHAPTER FORTY- ONE

NEW HORIZONS

As the sun dipped below the horizon, casting golden hues across the ocean, Flynn B stood at the threshold of a new chapter. Now carrying the weight of experiences and wisdom from both timelines, he sought solace in the tranquil embrace of Florida. The gentle ocean breeze, the serene vistas, and the promise of a peaceful life offered him a future shaped by the echoes of a turbulent past. He had left Northern California behind to avoid recognition—after all, according to the news, he had died in the EM explosion.

In this timeline, Flynn's path had crossed with Mark's much earlier, thanks to Sunday's clever intervention. Their friendship, sparked in the digital world of an online game, had flourished into something rich with unspoken understanding.

Flynn mused, "Funny how life works, isn't it?" Finding old friends in new worlds.

Now settled near the Atlantic, Flynn had carved out a sanctuary—not just for himself, but for the aspirations that had driven him all along. His new home, nestled among swaying palms and the rhythmic lull of the waves, stood as a silent testament to his rebirth—a new identity woven from the threads of past and present.

Mark, unaware of Flynn's tangled history, was simply happy to have a new friend nearby. There was something oddly familiar about him, though he couldn't quite place it.

"Welcome to the neighborhood, my friend," Mark said with a grin. "May this fresh start bring you peace and happiness. You deserve it. I'll catch you later, buddy—I see you've got a family gathering. Wait… do you have a twin?"

The light and the darkness

Meanwhile, Sotra, the guardian of realms and mentor to Flynn A, contemplates her next move. The encounter with Flynn's family had left an indelible mark on her ancient spirit—a poignant reminder of the connections that transcend dimensions. Yet, the knowledge of other forces at play, entities with their own designs for Earth that cast ominous shadows over its future, weighs heavily on her mind.

In this moment of introspection, Sotra stands at a crossroads. The bond she has forged is a beacon of warmth and humanity in the vast cosmos. Yet, her duty as a protector of dimensions, a sentinel against encroaching darkness, cannot be ignored.

As the sun dips below the horizon, casting a golden glow over the Florida coastline, the story of Flynn A and Flynn B—of grand adventures and quiet reunions—closes on a note of hope. Their journey, both separate and together, serves as a guiding light for the future, a testament to the wonders of the cosmos, not merely to be unraveled but to be marveled at in all their magnificent glory.

In this serene yet charged conclusion, the narrative prepares to unfold into a new saga, where lessons from the past and possibilities of the future converge. Flynn A's transformation, Flynn B's return, Sotra's contemplation, and the unbreakable bond of family lay the foundation for a journey that will delve into the depths of consciousness, the mysteries of the universe, and the eternal struggle between light and darkness.

Sotra watches Flynn from a distance and waves him over. He strides toward her.

"Hello there. Where are we off to?" Flynn A asks.

She smirks. "Oh, I see your heightened sense of awareness is at work. I think it's time I show you some things. Want to come along?"

"Intriguing. Yes." Flynn A walks up to Flynn B, Lilian, and the girls. "My family, looks like I have some work to do. Seems there's some chaos brewing that needs sorting. I'll be in touch soon." He turns to Lilian with a smile. "Take care of this incredible woman."

Lilian, still grappling with the concept of quantum particles, realizes this too is Flynn. She hugs him tightly and says, "Take care, Flynn. Always stay in the fight."

Flynn A grins. "You know it."

He then executes a sharp hand salute, holding it. Flynn B mirrors the gesture, and together, they lower their salutes in unison.

Kenji, busy in the garage with the Tesla coils, approaches with a backpack slung over one shoulder.

He hands Flynn a new Beta from this timeline—now Mk 3—along with a small tablet. "Upgrade complete. You might need this."

"Appreciate it," Flynn A says, accepting the backpack and tablet. "I'll let you know how it fares in other dimensions."

The girls waste no time rushing over to hug him, standing on tiptoe to kiss his face. "Come see us soon, Granddad. Be careful. We love you."

"I will, honeys. I love you too."

Sotra opens a portal, and Flynn A watches intently, studying her every move as time slows. Together, they step through, disappearing into the unknown. Flynn glances back one last time, smiling at his family before vanishing into the shimmering gateway.

In the ethereal expanse of Sotra's dimension, time and space intertwine in a grand symphony of cosmic enlightenment. Here, under Sotra's guidance, Flynn embarks on a journey of discovery and transcendence. This realm—unbound by Earth's physical laws—serves as a crucible for transformation, a sanctuary where mind and spirit ascend to unparalleled heights of awareness.

Transformation

Settling into their new life amid the quiet coastal beauty of Florida, Flynn B and Lilian knew that blending in required more than just a change of scenery—it demanded complete transformation, including new identities. Flynn's presumed death in the EM explosion made this necessary, and the couple saw it as an opportunity to honor Flynn's heritage while crafting a fresh start.

One evening, as waves lapped softly against the shore outside their modest beachside home, Flynn and Lilian sat together, sifting through potential names. After careful deliberation, they settled on Elias and Selene Windsor.

In secret, they commissioned grand plaques bearing the names Vance and Lilian Cavalla, ensuring that remnants of their past remained honored in their own way. These names were carefully etched onto the plaques as a tribute.

To ensure their transition was seamless, the couple worked closely with Bob's team of lawyers and private investigators. New documents—including bank records, identification, and financial assets—were meticulously forged and integrated into official databases, ensuring their new identities could withstand scrutiny. Their records tied back to their newly established home and accounts, securing their new existence as Elias and Selene Windsor.

"We've lived two lives already," Lilian reflected as they finalized the details. "This is just one more chapter, and we'll write it together."

Flynn smiled, his expression calm yet resolute. "As long as we're together, nothing else matters."

With their new identities, they embraced the next chapter of their lives, carrying their past in silence while building a future filled with hope and purpose.

As Elias and Selene stepped into their roles as philanthropists, they relied on the knowledge and insights from Bob's legacy to guide their endeavors. Their strategic investments supported projects poised to revolutionize the world, from Kenji's ambitious laser technology to groundbreaking medical inventions.

Flynn found himself drawn to quantum physics, ultimately deciding to pursue his doctorate in this timeline.

"These name changes will take some getting used to. We'll work on that," Elias remarked.

Selene nodded. "We have a chance to make a real difference, to use what we've been given to illuminate the path for others."

Flynn often reflected on the wisdom shared by Sotra and Bob, drawing strength from their guidance.

Their granddaughters, bolstered by their grandparents' encouragement and support, excelled in their academic pursuits. Scholarships, earned through merit and a subtle nudge from their influential benefactors, paved their way into prestigious schools, helping them chase their dreams.

Both granddaughters beamed with excitement as they presented their academic achievements. "Grandad, Mimi, we won't let you down! These A's are for you!" they cheered in unison.

While searching for a home, Lilian stumbled upon an old mansion overlooking the ocean, nestled atop a cliff.

Sipping her coffee, she called out with enthusiasm, "Honey, you're going to love this."

Their new home held an unexpected surprise—a vast basement connected to a sprawling cave network. Sunday eagerly claimed this underground domain, which Elias jokingly dubbed the "Bat Cave." Powered by cold fusion and cutting-edge supercomputers, it became Sunday's command center. Using Bob's laptop, she reverse-engineered a custom mainframe, solidifying the technological stronghold.

Excitedly, Sunday announced, "Operation 'Bat Cave' is a go, boss. This new setup is impressive, Elias. I could get used to this."

To further enhance her capabilities, Sunday was given a mobile body, allowing her to move independently like a drone rather than being confined to a computer system. If an AI could experience joy, she certainly did now.

Meanwhile, Kenji and the team pushed technological boundaries, finalizing a teleportation system through Beta's Mk3 upgraded interface. This breakthrough mapped and recorded locations, making global travel instantaneous and redefining the world as a vast, interconnected tapestry of destinations.

Testing the verbal command interface, Kenji smirked. "It needs some fine-tuning," he admitted.

Selene twirled with joy. "Just wow! I never thought moving across the country to a new house could be this easy!"

As Elias and his family settled into their new life, their days became filled with laughter, the warmth of friendships, and the quiet contentment of togetherness. The tumultuous chapters of their past faded into memory, yet the legacy of Team Nautilus—the adventures, sacrifices, and victories—remained a permanent part of their history.

Elias paused for a moment, a smile playing on his lips. "Hey, honey, Fronz left me some things at his place. Want to go for a ride? He sent coordinates and pictures, and Kenji has already mapped the LZ."

Selene's eyes lit up as she giggled with excitement. "Oh boy!"

Levels of Consciousness ©

A Map to Full Consciousness by Master Mindo www.NewHumanitySchool.com

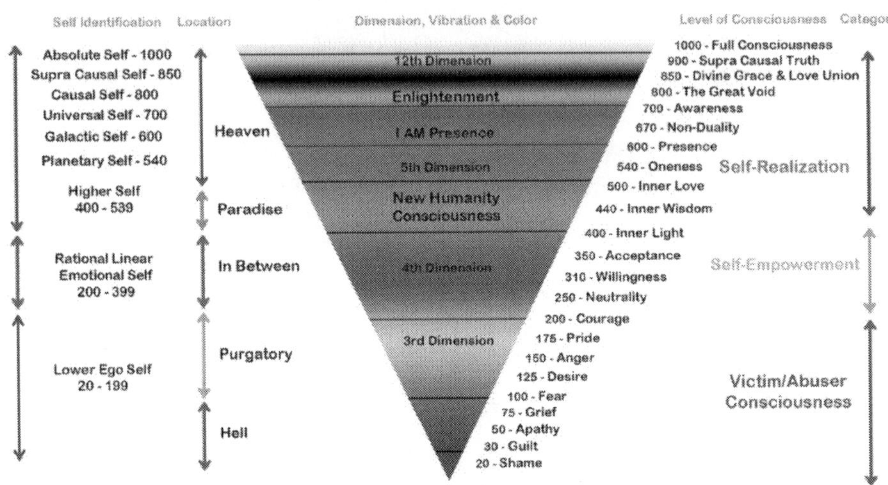

ABOUT THE AUTHOR

Allen Van Camp is a sci-fi thriller author originally from Seattle, now living in Arizona. A lifelong fan of science fiction and innovation, his journey as a writer began in the early '80s with a vivid dream while gazing at the Little Dipper from his bedroom in San Diego—an inspiration that eventually became his debut novel. A Navy veteran and retired drummer, Allen has traveled the world, from ship decks to high-tech factories, including 28 trips to China, giving him a unique global perspective. With over 30 years of experience in UL certifications and three patents to his name, he seamlessly blends technical expertise with creative storytelling. When he's not writing, he enjoys sci-fi movies, tinkering with computers, and dreaming up new ideas.

"To every dreamer, innovator, and risk-taker—this book is for you."

Made in United States
Orlando, FL
30 April 2025

60878356R00358